A LIFE-CHANGING LETTER

Several years ago I received a letter that changed my life. Sadly, I don't remember who wrote it, only what she said. In essence, this was her plea:

> Dr. Wheeler,
>
> I have a big favor to ask you. First of all, though, I want you to know how much I enjoy your story collections; they have greatly enriched my life. Now for the favor: I was wondering if you have any interest in doing with books what you are doing with stories.
>
> You see, while I love to read, I haven't the slightest idea of where to start. There are millions of books out there, and most of them—authors too—are just one big blur to me. I want to use my time wisely, to choose books which will not only take me somewhere but also make me a better and kinder person.
>
> I envy you because you know which books are worth reading and which are not. Do you possibly have a list of worthy books that you wouldn't mind sending to me?

I responded to this letter but most inadequately, for at that time I had no such list. I tried to put the plea behind me, but it dug in its heels and kept me awake at night. Eventually, I concluded that a Higher Power was at work here and that I needed to do something about it. I put together a proposal for a broad reading plan based on books I knew and loved—books that had powerfully affected me, that had opened other worlds and cultures to me, and that had made me a kinder, more empathetic person.

But that letter writer had asked for more than just a list of titles. She wanted me to introduce her to the authors of these books, to their lives and their times. To that end, I've included in the introduction to each story in this series a biographical sketch of the author to help the reader appreciate the historical, geographical, and cultural contexts in which a story was written. Also, as a long-time teacher, I've always found study-guide questions to be indispensable in helping readers to understand more fully the material they're reading; hence my decision to incorporate discussion questions for each chapter in an afterword at the end of the book. Finally, since I love turn-of-the-century woodcut illustrations, I've tried to incorporate as many of these into the text as possible.

There is another reason for this series—perhaps the most important. Our hope is that it will encourage thousands of people to fall in love with reading, as well as help them to discover that a life devoid of emotional, spiritual, and intellectual growth is not worth living.

Welcome to our expanding family of wordsmiths, of people of all ages who wish to grow daily, to develop to the fullest the talents God lends to each of us—people who believe as does Robert Browning's persona in *Andrea del Sarto:*

> Ah, but a man's reach should exceed his grasp,
> Or what's a heaven for?

Joe Wheeler

Note: The books in this series have been selected because they are among the finest literary works in history. However, you should be aware that some content might not be suitable for all ages, so we recommend you review the material before sharing it with your family.

"There's something so stylish about you, Anne," said Diana.

FOCUS ON THE FAMILY®
Great Stories

Anne of Green Gables

by
L.M. Montgomery

Introduction and Afterword by
Joe Wheeler, Ph.D.

TYNDALE

Tyndale House Publishers, Wheaton, Illinois

ANNE OF GREEN GABLES

Copyright © 1999 by Joseph L. Wheeler and Focus on the Family

Library of Congress Cataloging-in-Publication Data
Montgomery, L. M. (Lucy Maud), 1874–1942.
    Anne of Green Gables / by Lucy Maud Montgomery, with an introduction and afterword by Joe L. Wheeler.
        p.   cm. — (Focus on the Family great stories)
    Summary: Anne, an eleven-year-old orphan, is sent by mistake to live with a lonely, middle-aged brother and sister on a Prince Edward Island farm and proceeds to make an indelible impression on everyone around her.
        ISBN 1-56179-625-5
        [1. Orphans—Fiction. 2. Friendship—Fiction. 3. Country life—Prince Edward Island—Fiction. 4. Prince Edward Island—Fiction.] I. Title. II. Series: Great stories series (Colorado Springs, Colo.).
PZ7.M768An   1999
[Fic]—dc21   97-51658
                                                                                                          CIP
                                                                                                           AC

A Focus on the Family book published by Tyndale House Publishers, Wheaton, Illinois.

Quotations from *The Selected Journals of L. M. Montgomery,* Volumes I, II, and III © 1985, 1987, 1992 University of Guelph, edited by Mary Rubio and Elizabeth Waterston and published by Oxford University Press, Canada, are reproduced with the permission of Mary Rubio, Elizabeth Waterston, and the University of Guelph, courtesy of the L. M. Montgomery Collection Archives and Special Collections, University of Guelph Library. Excerpts from *The Alpine Path* by L. M. Montgomery are reproduced here with the permission of David Macdonald, trustee, and Ruth Macdonald. *The Alpine Path: The Story of My Career,* originally published in *Everywoman's World* in installments, is published as a book by Fitzhenry & Whiteside, reprinted in 1997.

Halftone illustrations by M. A. and W.A.J. Claus are the original illustrations from the first edition of L. M. Montgomery, *Anne of Green Gables* (Boston: L. C. Page, 1908); plates used for the impressions are from the Seventh Impression, December 1908. All illustrations are from the library of Joe Wheeler.

Joe Wheeler is represented by the literary agency of Alive Communications, 1465 Kelly Johnson Blvd., Suite 320, Colorado Springs, CO 80920.

Cover Design: Charles Hubbard

Cover photo of girl by Tim O'Hara Photography, Inc.

Printed in the United States of America

99 00 01 02 03 04 05/10 9 8 7 6 5 4 3 2 1

TO THE MEMORY OF
My Father and Mother

TABLE OF CONTENTS

LIST OF ILLUSTRATIONS

Introduction

LUCY MAUD MONTGOMERY AND *ANNE OF GREEN GABLES*

Anne of Green Gables is "the dearest and most lovable child in fiction since the immortal Alice" of *Alice's Adventures in Wonderland*. So observed Mark Twain of Montgomery's unforgettable character (Harry Bruce, *Maud: The Life of L. M. Montgomery* [New York: Bantam Books, 1994], 153). Today hundreds of Anne devotees make their pilgrimages every year to Prince Edward Island to visit the sacred Avonlea sites mentioned in Montgomery's book. The Islanders themselves are ambivalent about Anne: On the one hand, they love and cherish her; on the other, they tire of the commercial overkill, for, on the island, Anne-ism is omnipresent and inescapable. The locals often shake their heads in disbelief that so many people from so many nations take Canada's most famous heroine so literally. The legend has become more real than the reality.

Prince Edward Island (or P.E.I., as the locals call it) is a small island, only 145 miles from cape to cape, lighthouse to lighthouse. Dazzling white churches crown every rise—or so it seems—and quaint, colorful houses, little changed since Anne's day, dot the countryside. Flowers of many colors ravish the senses, and everywhere the blue of the sea is offset by the green of the land. The longest continuous marine bridge in the world, the Confederation Bridge, spans the sea between the island and the continent. When it opened recently, it ended thousands of years of relative isolation (accessibility was possible only by ferry boats). The capital city of Charlottetown, once the only city, now shares honors with that coastal upstart, Summerside.

When my wife, Connie, and I arrived on Prince Edward Island in late June 1997 to do research for this book, the skies were overcast and drizzly. The next morning, however, the clouds had lifted and a gentle breeze blew. Bathed in bright sunlight, the greens, blues, and whites of the landscape blinded us, for they were more intense than one would believe possible. Islanders admitted it had been many a week since they had experienced such an Edenic day. It was on just such a breathtaking day in June that an eleven-year-old, pigtailed orphan girl named Anne—with an "e"—climbed into a buggy with a man named Matthew, who didn't have the heart to tell her a terrible mistake had been made. And so their journey began. Now—more than ninety years after *Anne of Green Gables* first appeared—their journey has become *our* journey.

About the Introduction

For decades, one of the few absolutes in my literature classes has been this: *Never read the introduction before reading the book!* Those who ignored my thundering admonition lived to regret their disobedience. Downcast, they would come to me and say, "Dr. Wheeler, I confess that I read the introduction first, and it wrecked the book for me. I couldn't enjoy the story, because all the way through, I saw it through someone *else's* eyes. I don't agree with the editor on certain points, but those conclusions are in my head, and now I don't know *what* I think!"

Given that God never created a human clone, no two of us will ever perceive reality in exactly the same way—and no two of us ever should! Therefore, no matter how educated, polished, brilliant, insightful, or eloquent the teacher might be, don't ever permit that person to tell you how to think or respond, for that is a violation of the most sacred thing God gives us—our individuality.

My solution to the introduction problem was to split it in two: an introduction/biography, to whet the appetite for, and enrich the reading of, the book; and an afterword, to generate discussion and debate *after* the reader has arrived at his or her own conclusions about the book and is ready to challenge my (the teacher's) perceptions.

About the Illustrations

Unlike most books of the time, Montgomery's works apparently were underillustrated in the early years. Some people said that her first and greatest book, *Anne of Green Gables,* had been illustrated; others said it had not. Early copies of the book are rare, and first editions command a fortune. Finding no copies in the United States, my wife and I crisscrossed Prince Edward Island in June 1997, hoping to find an edition with illustrations. Joy of joys, in an antique shop on a pothole-ridden side road, we found a copy printed six months after the first edition, and it contained all eight of the original plates. Thanks to that antique dealer in Canada, you now have in your hands the original *Anne of Green Gables* illustrations by M. A. and W.A.J. Claus.

Movie History
Two movies have been made of *Anne of Green Gables:*

Year: 1934, RKO, 79 min., Black and White
Cast: Anne Shirley (stage name of actress Dawn O'Day), Tom Brown, O. P. Heggie, Helen Westley, Sara Haden, Murray Kinnell
Director: George Nichols, Jr.
Producer: Kenneth Macgowan

Year: 1985; Collaboration: Canadian Broadcasting System, Walt Disney Studios, and PBS; 197 min.; Color
Cast: Megan Follows, Colleen Dewhurst, Richard Farnsworth, Patricia Hamilton, Schuyler Grant, Jonathan Crombie, Marilyn Lightstone, Charmion King, Rosemary Radcliffe, Jackie Burroughs
Director: Kevin Sullivan

About the Author
Lucy Maud Montgomery
1874–1942
In the process of researching this biography, I have read the following books: Mollie Gillen, *Lucy Maud Montgomery: The Wheel of Things* (Halifax, Nova Scotia: Formac Publishing Co., Ltd., 1975, 1983); Catherine M. Andronik, *Kindred Spirit* (New York: Atheneum Books, 1993); Harry Bruce, *Maud: The Life of L. M. Montgomery* (New York: Bantam Books, 1994); Francis W. P. Bolger, *The Years Before Anne* (Halifax, Nova Scotia: Nimbus Publishing, 1991); John H. Willoughby, *Ellen* (Charlottetown, Prince Edward Island: Privately published, 1995); Nancy Rootland, *The Sacred Sites of L. M. Montgomery* (Halifax, Nova Scotia: Nimbus Publishing, 1996); Francis W. P. Bolger, Wayne Barrett, and Anne MacKay, *Spirit of Place* (Toronto: Oxford University Press, 1982); *Prince Edward Island Visitors Guide* (Charlottetown, Prince Edward Island: Privately published, 1997); *The Selected Journals of L. M. Montgomery*, vols. 1–4, edited by Mary Rubio and Elizabeth Waterston (Toronto: Oxford University Press, 1985, 1992, 1995); Mary Rubio and Elizabeth Waterston, *Writing a Life: L. M. Montgomery* (Toronto: ECW

Press, 1995); *The Annotated Anne of Green Gables*, edited by Wendy E. Barry, Margaret Ann Doody, and Mary E. Doody Jones (New York, Oxford: Oxford University Press, 1997); and Lucy Maud Montgomery, *The Alpine Path* (Don Mills, Ontario: Fitzhenry & Whiteside Ltd., 1975), originally published in the June, July, August, September, October, and November issues of *Everywoman's World*, Toronto, 1917.

I encourage all those interested in reading further into the life and times of Lucy Maud Montgomery to consider these books as an avenue to such knowledge. Unquestionably, the place to start is Rubio and Waterston's concise *Writing a Life* and their monumental *The Selected Journals of L. M. Montgomery*, vols. 1–4 (Volume 5 will be completed and published some time after the appearance of Rubio's definitive biography of L. M. Montgomery). Second only to the insights gained from Rubio and Waterston are the ones given in the treasury of Anne-ism, *The Annotated Anne of Green Gables*. I also found the books by Gillen, Andronik, and Bolger to be helpful. Bruce's book is significant because of his sociological data and insights; and Montgomery's own *The Alpine Path* is an appropriate base to build on (most L. M. Montgomery biographers have done just that.)

If this modest life sketch is accurate and true to life, it will be because Dr. Mary Rubio was there for me, every step of the way, as I wrestled my way though the mountains of biographical data (some accurate, some not). In appreciation, I can only say, *"Bless thee!"*

- - -

The Fluttering Veil

But life never held for me a dull moment. I had, in my vivid imagination, a passport to the geography of Fairyland. In a twinkling I could—and did—whisk myself into regions of wonderful adventures, unhampered by any restrictions of time or place.

Everything was invested with a kind of fairy grace and charm, emanating from my own fancy, the trees that whispered nightly around the old house where I slept, the woodsy nooks I explored, the homestead fields, each individualized by some oddity of fence or shape, the sea whose murmur was never out of my ears—all were radiant with "the glory and the dream."

I had always a deep love of nature. A little fern growing

in the woods, a shallow sheet of June-bells under the firs, moonlight falling on the ivory column of a tall birch, an evening star over the old tamarack on the dyke, shadow-waves rolling over a field of ripe wheat—all gave me "thoughts that lay too deep for tears" and feelings which I had then no vocabulary to express.

It has always seemed to me, ever since early childhood, that, amid all the commonplaces of life, I was very near to a kingdom of ideal beauty. Between it and me hung only a thin veil. I could never draw it quite aside, but sometimes a wind fluttered it and I caught a glimpse of the enchanting realm beyond—only a glimpse—but those glimpses have always made life worth while.
—L. M. Montgomery, *The Alpine Path*, 47–48

Anchored nine miles offshore of New Brunswick, in the deep blue waters of the Gulf of St. Lawrence, protected from the full force of Atlantic breakers by Nova Scotia and Newfoundland, lies Canada's smallest province, Prince Edward Island. The Island has always been a quiet place—a small Eden tucked away in Canada's Maritime Provinces. It would be a serene place in which to be born even today; but it was much more so on that early winter day, November 30, in the year of our Lord 1874, when the first and only child of Hugh John Montgomery and Clara Woolner Macneill cried her way into the world. Her name was Lucy Maud Montgomery—Lucy in honor of her maternal grandmother, and Maud after one of Queen Victoria's daughters, the Princess of Hesse. To those who knew and loved her, she would always be known as Maud.

Politically, Maud's world was the sprawling British Empire, encompassing almost a third of the land surface of the globe, as well as almost a third of the world's population. Protecting all this was the greatest navy the world had ever known, and servicing it was the greatest merchant marine fleet in history. Its very core, London, was the undisputed center of world trade and banking. Lucy Maud Montgomery, during her sixty-seven years of life, would never have to face the disintegration of that vast empire, but she would witness three significant conflicts: the Boer War, World War I, and the beginning of World War II. During those three conflagrations, the best, the bravest, and the brightest of three generations of British and Commonwealth men would be mowed down in the springtime of their lives. By 1945, the three wars had so hemorrhaged the British Empire that the path was cleared for a new colossus to take its place: the United States of America. But Pax Americana would prove very different from Pax Britannica.

Baby Maud was born into a clannish aristocracy, in which both her ancestors and her living family played leading roles. Maud's maternal great-grandfather, William Macneill, was a member of the P.E.I. House of Assembly for twenty years; he sat as speaker for sixteen of those years, hence earning the title he was ever afterward known by: Speaker Macneill. Her paternal great-grandfather, Donald Montgomery, was a member of the House of Assembly for thirty-five years. His son (Big Donald), and Maud's grandfather, served as a member of the House of Assembly from 1838 to 1862, four of those years as speaker; when the Legislative Council became elective, he served as its president until he became one of the Island's four senators in the Canadian Parliament (1874–1893). In his fifty-eight years in government, Big Donald Montgomery never missed a single session, "a record perhaps unrivalled in the annals of Canadian political life" (Bolger, 8).

Maud's earliest memory was of her mother's funeral when Maud was barely out of babyhood. It was a day that stood out above all others as the good-bye to Shangri-la with her beautiful mother and handsome father and hello to thirty-five lonely years with her maternal grandmother, Lucy Woolner Macneill. In those days, life expectancy was short: Many women and babies died in childbirth or shortly after (often due to the failure of doctors and midwives to wash their hands or sterilize instruments between patients). Those who were lucky enough to survive the birth process faced any number of deadly diseases—measles, mumps, whooping cough, diphtheria, typhoid, cholera, tuberculosis, smallpox, influenza—that too often resulted in another grave in the town cemetery. In lovely Clara's case, the enemy was galloping consumption (a fast-acting form of tuberculosis), and once she contracted it—as was true so often in those preantibiotics days—she was doomed.

> When I was twenty-one months old my mother died, in the old home at Cavendish, after a lingering illness. I distinctly remember seeing her in her coffin—it is my earliest memory. My father was standing by the casket holding me in his arms. I wore a little white dress of embroidered muslin, and Father was crying. Women were seated around the room, and I recall two in front of me on the sofa who were whispering to each other and looking pityingly at Father and me. Behind them the window was open, and green vines were trailing

across it, while their shadows danced over the floor in a
square of sunshine.

I looked down at Mother's dead face. It was a sweet
face, albeit worn and wasted by months of suffering.
My mother had been beautiful, and Death, so cruel in
all else, had spared the delicate outline of feature, the
long silken lashes brushing the hollow cheek, and the
smooth masses of golden-brown hair.

I did not feel any sorrow, for I knew nothing of what
it all meant. I was only vaguely troubled. Why was
Mother so still? And why was Father crying? I reached
down and laid my baby hand against Mother's cheek.
Even yet I can feel the coldness of that touch.
Somebody in the room sobbed and said, "Poor child."
The chill of Mother's face had frightened me; I turned
and put my arms appealingly about Father's neck and
he kissed me. Comforted, I looked down at the sweet,
placid face as he carried me away. That one precious
memory is all I have of the girlish mother who sleeps in
the old burying-ground at Cavendish, lulled forever by
the murmur of the sea. (*The Alpine Path*, 16–17)

Hugh was devastated by his wife's long illness and untimely death—so
much so that, his business having recently failed due to his partner's
mismanagement, it was decided that the baby Maud would remain
where she was, in her grandparents' home. Early on in her illness, Clara
had come with her child to her parents' home to see if their nursing
could reverse her steady decline; eventually, she had died in her room
there.

Always restless, Hugh flitted here and there. When he was in the vicinity, he saw his daughter often; but gradually the Island saw him less and
less as he felt the call of the west. By the time Maud was seven, her father
had moved to Prince Albert, Saskatchewan, in the Northwest Territory;
thereafter, she would see him but rarely.

Grandmother Macneill had already raised a large family and was fifty-
two when she agreed to keep her homeless granddaughter; her husband,
Alexander, was fifty-six. Needless to say, there was a tremendous generation gap. By the time Maud was in her late teens, her grandparents were
in their late sixties.

In retrospect, it isn't easy to accurately portray Maud's relationship with
her grandparents—especially her grandmother. On the basis of the many

references to her in Maud's first three journals and the biographical material currently available, Grandmother Macneill appears to have been stern, rigid, and narrow-minded, a person Maud found difficult to relate to in a positive way. In a letter to me, Rubio notes that Maud's grandmother, for all her shortcomings, spent her own money to help Maud get an education. So, even though Maud found it difficult at times to communicate with the older woman, she knew that her grandmother loved her deeply and unconditionally. Maud's grandfather was a different story. Crusty, unsympathetic, and unempathetic where his granddaughter was concerned, Grandfather Macneill humiliated Maud often, both privately and in front of the extended family. So why did they take her in? Evidently, because they felt it was their family obligation and Christian duty to raise their dead daughter's child.

Thus it was that Maud had to create her own world. Deprived by death of her mother just when she needed her most; deserted by her wandering father; treated as an imposition by her crusty grandfather; raised by a grandmother who was fifty years older than she; and treated as somewhere between a poor relative and a servant by the extended family, there was nowhere to go but inside her own mind. Not that she was physically lonely: Grandfather Macneill had been one of seventeen children, and Grandmother Macneill one of eleven; Uncle John's children, in fact, lived next door. According to Rubio, "the Alexander Macneill house was the center of the community because they held the post office in their *Kitchen*. The school was down the lane. The church was on the edge of their property. . . . [Maud's] grandmother even brought in . . . two little . . . boys as boarders so [Maud] would have playmates when she was young" (Rubio to Wheeler, August 27, 1997, 3). It wasn't until Maud was a teenager that her grandparents became overly strict. No, the loneliness Maud experienced was one born of a half-century generation gap with her surrogate parents.

Maud grew up with both an aching mother-hunger and a yearning for her absentee father. Her father's failure to contribute financially to her childhood expenses was made much of by her grandfather, who, from time to time, would lash her with this terrible whip of parental nonsupport. Little surprise that most of Maud's fictional protagonists, in years to come, would be orphaned or abandoned girls.

Speaking of "orphans," extensive research was done on this subject by the editors of the *Annotated Anne of Green Gables*. They note that Maud herself grew up reading stories about orphans, a genre popular at that time. Examples include Charlotte Brontë's *Jane Eyre,* Kate Douglas

Wiggin's *Rebecca of Sunnybrook Farm*, Mark Twain's *Tom Sawyer*, Frances Hodgson Burnett's *The Little Princess*, Johanna Spyri's *Heidi*, Charles Dickens's *David Copperfield*, and Eleanor Porter's *Pollyanna*.

Since life expectancy at that time was short, the chances of a child becoming an orphan were high. Within Canada and the British Empire, male deaths from war and work-related accidents were all too frequent; and in the Maritime Provinces, drowning was the common fate of fishermen caught in sudden storms. When one adds to these deaths those from the many then-incurable diseases, the odds against living a long time were sobering. We have already noted reasons why so many women died young.

Willoughby postulates that in England many "orphans" were not literal orphans. Most of these children had at least one living parent. Perhaps the father had deserted the family or been incarcerated, leaving the mother incapable of taking care of the large family of children, which in pre-birth-control days was the norm. Quite often these children would be released onto city streets to survive if they could. Since the colonies were continually short on cheap labor, orphans in Britain would be collected, fed, clothed, and then sent overseas. Upon their arrival, brothers and sisters would be separated and sent to different employers, never to see each other again.

The best-known orphan emigration society in England was administered by a Dr. Thomas Barnado. His charges were known as "Barnado boys" or "Barnado girls." Evidently, Dr. Barnado himself was the one who first referred to these waifs as "street Arabs" (Willoughby, 26–36, 45–46). Barry, Doody, and Jones note that in 1876, Dr. Barnado reported that "some 30,000 children under sixteen years of age slept out in the streets, under the arches . . . in empty barrels . . . anywhere. . . . The objective of the Barnado homes was to rescue homeless children from a life of crime" (*Annotated Anne of Green Gables*, 46).

In the eighteenth century, homeless orphans had almost no one to speak up for them, but by the nineteenth, powerful defenders such as Charles Dickens were arousing the consciences of men and women everywhere to their plight. In the Maritime Provinces, caring orphanage leaders made periodic inspection trips to check up on their charges' welfare. Surprisingly, the Maritime Society for the Prevention of Cruelty to Animals added children to its agenda, for cruelty to one group was considered not much different from cruelty to the other.

Since P.E.I. had no orphanage until 1907, and since farm workers were perpetually in demand, the Islanders were dependent on orphanages elsewhere. Thus in spite of protests in London, boatloads of children kept arriving in Canada until 1939. In the first chapter of *Anne of Green Gables*, Marilla Cuthbert explains to her neighbor Rachel Lynde why she and her brother, Matthew, decided to adopt an orphan.

> ". . . you know how desperate hard it's got to be to get hired help. There's never anybody to be had but those stupid, half-grown little French boys; and as soon as you do get one broke into your ways and taught something, he's up and off to the lobster canneries or the States. At first Matthew suggested getting a Barnado boy. But I said 'no' flat to that. They may be all right—I'm not saying they're not—but 'no London street Arabs for me,' I said. 'Give me a native born at least.'"

The French boys referred to above are the remnants of the ill-fated Acadians who were expelled from the Maritimes by the British (1763–1768); most of them ended up in Louisiana (today's Cajuns). These French descendants on P.E.I. were looked upon as little better than orphans. The lowest of the low, however, were the Barnado boys and girls and the children of unmarried mothers; they were viewed as undeserving of any rights and suited for lifelong servitude. Anne, as a child born to married schoolteachers, clearly did not belong in this group and would have been placed at the top of P.E.I. adoptive lists. Her rise to professional success was also completely out of the norm, for traditionally Maritime orphans, since they were considered inferior to the other Islanders, were granted only a minimum of educational opportunities.

Only with this background can we truly appreciate the plight of such an orphan as Anne in this book and the powerlessness of these children to do anything but obey orders, oftentimes given by sadistic guardians of their welfare. And only within this frame of reference can we understand Anne's joy at her deliverance from such taskmistresses.

Maud herself was not literally an orphan, but she *felt* herself to be one. Not that she was not loved by her father—she never doubted his love for her; nor that she was not loved by her Macneill grandparents—in their own undemonstrative way, she knew they cared for her, otherwise they would never have taken her in. It was just that her heart cried out for so much more.

This awareness would come to Maud gradually during her growing-up years. In fact, other than that one scene at her mother's funeral, Maud remembered nothing of those first few years with her grandparents. She just accepted her life as being all that she could expect, and she made the most of her limited options.

Maud of Cavendish

Maud—or "Maud without the 'e,' " as she called herself—was born precocious, with a prodigious memory. She never could pin down exactly when she had learned to read. It seemed to her that she had always known how.

The world of her childhood was a tiny one indeed. The heart of it was the old Macneill homestead in Cavendish on the north shore of Prince Edward Island. Eleven miles away was the door to that greater world she rarely saw—Hunter River, the nearest railroad depot. Thirteen and a half miles from there was Charlottetown, the only city she knew. Thirteen miles west was Park Corner, her other home, where lived her dear Grandfather Montgomery—the Senator—and Grandfather's second wife (never very close to Maud); across the road lived Uncle John and Aunt Annie Campbell, two of the dearest, kindest, and most loving people Maud ever knew. Their house was always *home* to her.

The smallness of this world of hers is perhaps best portrayed in the life story she wrote for *Everywoman's World:*

> Away to the westward, six or seven miles the view was bounded by New London Cape, a long, sharp point, running far out to sea. In my childhood I never wearied of speculating what was on the other side of that point, *a very realm of enchantment, surely*, I thought. Even when I gradually grew into the understanding that beyond it was merely another reach of shore like my own it still held a mystery and fascination for me. I longed to stand out on that lonely, remote, purple point, beyond which was the land of lost sunsets.
>
> I have seen few more beautiful sights than sea-sunset off that point. In later years a new charm was added, a revolving light that flashed like a magnificent star through the dusk of summer nights, like a beacon on an outpost of fairyland.
>
> I did not often fare far afield. An occasional trip to town—Charlottetown—and another to Uncle John Campbell's at Park Corner, were my only excursions beyond my horizon line, and both were looked on as great

> pleasures. A trip to Park Corner was of comparatively frequent occurrence, once a year at least, and perhaps twice. A trip to town was a very rare treat, once in three years, and loomed up in about the same proportions of novelty, excitement, and delight as a trip to Europe would now. . . . It meant a brief sojourn in a wonderful and fascinating place, where every one was dressed up and could have all the nuts, candies, and oranges they wanted, to say nothing of the exquisite pleasure of looking at all the beautiful things in the shop windows. (*The Alpine Path*, 41–42)

Maud—like her alter-ego Anne—knew every inch of the Cavendish homestead. And not abstractly either; rarely did she know anything abstractly. She personified *everything*. In her journal entry for April 15, 1914, she rhapsodized about her favorite things, among them, trees.

> In a corner of the front orchard grew a beautiful young birch tree. I named it "The White Lady" and had a fancy about it to the effect that it was the beloved of all the dark spruces near, and that they were rivals for her love. It was the whitest, straightest thing ever seen, young and fair and maiden-like.
>
> On the southern edge of the Haunted Wood grew a most magnificent old birch. This was the tree of trees to me . . . and [I] called it "The Monarch of the Forest". . . .
>
> Dear old trees! I hope they all have souls and will grow again for me on the hills of Heaven. I want, in some future life, to meet the old "Monarch" and the "White Lady." (*The Alpine Path*, 33–35)

Flowers, too, she personalized: case in point, Bonnie the geranium. Maud was twelve when she was given the plant as a present. Bonnie lived a long time and was her inseparable companion. Maud hoped that in heaven she would be able to rejoin Bonnie and the other plants she knew and loved during her life on earth. In a May 1905 letter to a friend, she wrote, "Today I read that Henry Ward Beecher said once: 'Flowers are the sweetest thing God ever made and forgot to put souls into.' But I don't believe He forgot. I believe they *have* souls. I've known roses that I expect to meet in Heaven" (Bolger, 4). Maud never put more than two kinds of flowers together in a vase because, she'd say with a chuckle, she didn't want them to fight.

But above all Maud adored cats. She was nine when one of them brought her a life-changing experience.

> I had two pet kittens, Catkin and Pussy-willow. Catkin was a little too meek and pink-nosed to suit me, but Pussy-willow was the prettiest, "cutest," little scrap of gray-striped fur ever seen and I loved her passionately.
>
> One morning I found her dying of poison. I shall never forget my agony of grief as I watched my little pet's bright eyes glazing, and her tiny paws growing stiff and cold. And I have never laughed with grown-up wisdom at my passionate sorrow over the little death. It was too real, too symbolical! It was the first time I *realized* death, the first time, since I had become conscious of loving, that anything I had loved had left me forever. At that moment the curse of the race came upon me, "death entered into my world," and I turned my back on the Eden of childhood where everything had seemed everlasting. I was barred out of it forevermore by that fiery sword of that keen and unforgettable pain. (*The Alpine Path*, 45–46)

All her life, Maud felt things more intensely than any of her friends or family. It was this very intensity that gave her the capacity to so vividly recapture rapture and agony on paper. In her joy, she soared singing into the heavens; in her sorrow, she was hurled into the abyss. These extreme mood swings did not make her the easiest person to live with.

Her grandparents neither welcomed her teenage friends in her early years nor her adult friends later on. Consequently, at a very young age, she was already *imagining* friends. Today visitors to the Anne of Green Gables Museum at Silver Bush revel in peering into "Anne's Enchanted Bookcase," the real-life prototype for the fictional one in *Anne of Green Gables:*

> In our sitting room there had always stood a big bookcase used as a china cabinet. In each door was a large oval glass, dimly reflecting the room. When I was very small each of my reflections in these glasses were "real folk" to my imagination! The one in the left-hand door was Katie Maurice, the one in the right, Lucy Gray. Why I named them thus I cannot say. . . . Katie Maurice and Lucy Gray

lived in the fairy room behind the bookcase. Katie Maurice was a little girl like myself, and I loved her dearly. I would stand before that door and prattle to Katie for hours, giving and receiving confidences. . . .

Lucy Gray was grown-up and a widow! I did not like her as well as Katie. She was always sad, and always had dismal stories of her troubles to relate to me; nevertheless, I visited her scrupulously in turn, lest her feelings should be hurt, because she was jealous of Katie, who also disliked her. . . . I never passed through the room without a wave of my hand to Katie in the glass door at the other end. (*The Alpine Path*, 74)

Not an Easy World

For Maud, there would be home with Grandmother and Grandfather Macneill at Cavendish; home with the Campbells—Uncle John, Aunt Annie (her mother's sister), and her cousins—at Park Corner; and across the road, home with Grandfather and Grandmother Montgomery. From each of these households, Maud learned a different kind of love. From her Grandmother Macneill, she experienced unconditional, life-long but rather nondemonstrative love and affection; from Grandfather Montgomery, she received an empathizing love her Grandfather Macneill was unwilling to give her; and from Uncle John and Aunt Annie, she learned what family life was all about.

Maud loved to visit Park Corner because it was always a joyful adventure. When she arrived, her three "merry cousins [would] rush out and drag me in with greeting and laughter. The very walls of that house must have been permeated by the essence of good times. And there was a famous old pantry, always stored with goodies, into which it was our habit to crowd at bedtime and devour unholy snacks with sounds of riot and mirth" (*The Alpine Road*, 43).

As for Maud's relationship with Grandfather Montgomery, whenever she came to Park Corner for a visit, she spent as much time with him and his family as possible. Bolger notes that many of Maud's happiest childhood memories are associated with her visits to Grandfather Montgomery's farm. She later wrote that she loved her grandfather very much because he was always kind and gentle to her.

Then there was her dear great-aunt Mary Macneill Lawson, to whom Maud would dedicate her sixth book, *The Golden Road*. Aunt Mary was the family historian, biographer, humorist, folklorist, elocutionist, raconteur, and source for many of the little girl's memories. Maud later wrote that she and her aunt Mary were " 'chums' . . . when she was in the seventies and I was in my teens. I cannot, in any words at my command, pay the debt I owe to Aunt Mary Lawson" (*The Alpine Path*, 15–16).

Rubio feels, however, that here Maud shortchanged her maternal grandfather, noting that he was "an excellent historian, humorist, folklorist, raconteur, etc. LMM prefers to give the credit to Aunt Mary, who almost never visited in their home. She did get to see quite a lot of Aunt Mary when she was teaching in Belmont. But it was her grandfather who had the most influence on her" (Rubio to Wheeler, 3).

Maud was never far from the ocean during her growing-up years. In the summer months, Grandfather Macneill, with several French Canadian helpers, fished for mackerel. The men would get up around 4:00 A.M.; by 8:00 A.M., Maud would have gotten up and taken their breakfast down to the beach and, depending on how long the fish stayed in the vicinity, she would deliver dinner and supper, too. She spent her days watching the boats at sea, paddling in the waves (she never learned to swim), and exploring every cove and headland on the shore, collecting shells, pebbles, and mussels. Those were wonderful times for her.

Life on the Island was not easy. Almost everyone did some farming, so most Islanders rose before dawn, often working sixteen hours a day, seven days a week. Maud's grandfather was not only a farmer but also the postmaster of the little town, the kitchen serving as the post office. There was neither plumbing nor electricity, thus outdoor privies and candles and kerosene lamps were the norm. Without air conditioning, cooking made the kitchen and house unbearably hot during the summer. The Islanders had little variety in their diet. In fact, since stores were few, they relied mainly on their own home-grown vegetables and fruit orchards; peddlers provided for some of their other dietary needs.

When it came to chores, there was more than enough to do. Maud quickly discovered that the sewing was never done. For changes of pace, she would wash dishes, clean the house, or do some gardening. Canning for the long winters was done during the summer months. Laundry itself was an all-day job—and when there was company, it was endless.

The winters were long, and sometimes the snow was so deep that communication with the outside world was completely cut off. Since there was no indoor heating, it was a major task to keep fires going in the fireplaces so people didn't freeze to death. The upstairs bedrooms stayed so cold that it was like sleeping in iceboxes. Washing clothes in the winter was, of course, a herculean job.

At the very center of family life was the Presbyterian Church, the largest church on the island, since Islanders of Scottish descent outnumbered all others. There were also many Baptists, some Methodists, and some Roman Catholics. But while the Presbyterians intermingled with other denominations in town hall meetings, listened to well-known preachers of other faiths, and attended other churches' socials, Maud's grandparents warned her that on no condition should she ever marry a non-Presbyterian. Since the church was both the spiritual and social center of life, failure to attend either Sunday or midweek prayer meeting services was unthinkable. For the youth, prayer meetings represented their only social outlet—they were actually viewed as happy times, and many a courtship started there with a bashful "May I see you home?" At church pie socials, the bidding was intense for pies baked by town belles.

Religion at home with her grandmother was for Maud, more often than not, rather rigid. Gillen feels that there was more than a little of Maud's grandmother in both *Anne*'s Marilla Cuthbert and *Emily*'s Aunt Elizabeth Murray: "strong women endowed with human character weaknesses they may recognize and deplore but be powerless to change; women stern but just, governed by a sense of duty, slightly tyrannical, not dour but not outgoing, capable of more affection than they can allow themselves to show, seldom uncertain of the principles by which they lived" (Gillen, 14).

Never, as long as she lived, could Maud forget one incident that angered, humiliated, and disgusted her. She had done something rather minor that her grandmother considered naughty, and the little girl was forced to kneel on the floor and ask God to forgive her for being so bad. That forced prayer for forgiveness seared Maud's heart, for she felt her conscience and will had been violated. After that, both prayer and religion were cheapened in Maud's eyes, coloring all future spiritual activities: "Something inside me was outraged. . . . To force a human soul to utter words of prayer and contrition when not in a fit state to do so— when stormy rebellion and bitterness filled it!" (Gillen, 14–15).

So it was that her strict Presbyterian upbringing left Maud with a keen sense of right and wrong, an undeviating sense of duty, as well as a murky sense that an awful lot of life's questions remained completely or partially unanswered.

Maud was six when she was first escorted by one of her aunts to Cavendish's whitewashed one-room schoolhouse, just a few feet on the other side of the Macneill property line. But the building itself took second place to the setting: "That old spruce grove, with its sprinkling of maple, was a fairy realm of beauty and romance to my childish imagination. I shall always be thankful that my school was near a grove—a place with winding paths and a treasure-trove of ferns and mosses and wood-flowers. It was a stronger and better educational influence in my life than the lessons learned at the desk in the school-house" (*The Alpine Path*, 25).

Like most children, nothing was more important to Maud than to "fit in." Because she had to wear buttoned boots while all the others came barefoot, and because she had to go home for dinner while the others got to eat their lunches together outdoors, she felt doubly blighted. But she soon moved beyond these differences to establish some of the strongest friendships of her life.

A voracious reader, Maud devoured every book in the house—from Hans Christian Andersen's *Tales* to a two-volume history of the world, from Sir Walter Scott's *Rob Roy* to Charles Dickens's *Pickwick Papers*, from Paul Bunyan's *Pilgrim's Progress* to Lord Bulwer-Lytton's *Zanoni*, as well as poetry by Tennyson, Whittier, Longfellow, Scott, Byron, Milton, and Burns. On Sunday, her reading was restricted to "uplifting" reading; fortunately, her beloved *Pilgrim's Progress* qualified, as did her all-time-favorite *The Memoirs of Anzonetta Peters*, a deeply spiritual "autobiography" of a saintly little girl who spoke King James rather than current English, and who maintained her halo untarnished through five long years of a weakening illness—until her suffocatingly good little heart finally stopped and she fluttered off to join the angels. It was the kind of sentimental overkill Victorians never seemed to tire of—and since so many children *did* die young, it was accepted as realism. Maud wished she could be as holy as Anzonetta and the subject of such a sniffly book.

At nine, inspired by James Thomson's famous book, *The Seasons*, Maud began to write poetry of her own, morning, noon, and night. Writing paper was incredibly rare to her generation, thus people tended to write on anything they could find. Fortunately for Maud, as postmaster her grandfather received, three times a week, long, red "letter-bills" with writing on only one side; these she filled with feverishly written poetry. She couldn't even stop writing in school but wrote painfully candid verses about teachers. Not long after this, her current teacher, a bit dubious about her diligent slate writing, seized that unlucky instrument to her horror and mortification (the incident would later be immortalized in *Emily of New Moon*). Two years later, the recently formed Cavendish Literary Society set up a small library. Thanks to that little library and the Society, which she later joined, Maud's literary horizons widened dramatically.

At twelve, she began submitting her poetry to publishers—but everything she sent out faithfully returned. Her poems were most melodramatic—full of tragedy and death. One, for instance, she titled "My Graves"; it portrayed the wife of an itinerant Methodist minister who left behind dead babies all across Canada: "The oldest was buried in Newfoundland, the last in Vancouver, and all Canada between was dotted with those graves. I wrote the story in first person, described the children, pictured out their death beds, and detailed their tombstones and epitaphs" (*The Alpine Path*, 57).

In the same tragic vein, she and two other sister-scribblers, after organizing the Story Club, wrote take-offs from the same plot, in which all the heroines dutifully drowned and washed up on the Cavendish seashore. *That*, she later incorporated into *The Story Girl.*

Prince Albert

In 1887, Hugh Montgomery, at forty-six, married Mary Ann McRae, a well-connected woman of only twenty-four, and the two of them settled down in the Northwest Territory boomtown of Prince Albert. *A mother at last!* thought Maud, and she wrote her stepmother a number of letters, pouring out her heart and her dreams. Now that he finally had a home again, Hugh asked if his daughter would like to join them. She said she would. Three years later, on August 11, 1890, Grandfather Montgomery took his fifteen-year-old granddaughter on a trip she would never forget. She was finally going home to her father! And she who had never traveled more than twenty-four miles from her house was now to travel 2,500 miles on transcontinental trains—it might as well have been a rocket trip to the moon!

It didn't take long for Maud to realize that her grandfather was a very important man. They had just reached the Kensington train station when word came that Sir John Macdonald, prime minister of Canada and a great crony of the Senator's, was touring the Island. When the special train drew into the station, Maud and her grandfather boarded it and rode with the prime minister and his wife to Summerside. This was the first time in her life that Maud had ever been on a train.

The next day they took a boat across to Pointe du Chene, where they boarded another train and soon were racing west. Along the way, a new world opened up to Maud. She had, for instance, never seen indoor plumbing before, or electricity in any form, or streetcars; at Montreal she saw them *all*. In fact, her grandfather took her for a five-mile ride on a streetcar. Of course, some things remained the same as at home—for instance, at train stations along the way, passengers would disembark and pick blueberries along the tracks.

The train rumbled into Regina on a cold and foggy August 18. Getting off the train, Senator Montgomery and his granddaughter secured passage to the Windsor Hotel, where they would wait until they could find transportation to Prince Albert on the following day. After they had settled in, Maud's grandfather left her to see if any letters from her father had arrived. A short time later, there was a knock at the door. When Maud opened it, there standing beside her grandfather was her father. Maud was overjoyed; it had been five years since she had last seen him.

The trio finished their journey to Prince Albert by buckboard, through prairies alive with flowers. They reached Prince Albert, "rather straggly" along a riverbank, about 4:00 in the afternoon. Maud pronounced her father's house on Church Street and her new mother "nice," and her two-year-old half sister, Kate, "very pretty."

But three days later, reality struck: a gut-wrenching disappointment almost too much to bear. For over thirteen years, Maud's greatest longing had been to be with her father and to have a loving mother of her own; thus her trip to Prince Albert had seemed like a dream come true. But already she sensed that in this Eden there was a serpent—and that serpent was her new mother. In her journal, Maud wrote, between tears:

> It is lovely to be with father again. . . . He is *such* a darling. His eyes just *shine* with love when he looks at me. I never saw anyone look at me with such eyes before.
>
> But, to speak plainly, I am afraid I am *not* going to like his wife. I came here prepared to love her warmly and look upon her as a real mother, but I fear it will prove impossible. (*Selected Journals I*, 28–29)

Never had she known anyone as mean, sarcastic, demeaning, or cutting as her new mother, not only to her but also to her father. Mrs. Montgomery appeared to be deeply jealous of the loving bond between her husband and her stepdaughter—even of his calling her by the pet name he had always used, "Maudie." When she'd leave the house, Mrs. Montgomery always locked the pantry to keep Maud and Edith, a boarding girl Maud's age, from getting a bite to eat while she was gone.

Maud also discovered that her role in the home was going to be more that of a servant than of a daughter. And whenever anything or anyone displeased her stepmother, the entire household would get the silent treatment for days. Finally, Edith couldn't take any more and left, leaving poor Maud more forlorn than ever, especially when her father wasn't home.

School started on September 1—but it was not at all what Maud was used to: the white schoolhouse in a spruce grove, with a sparkling creek nearby. This one was in a bleak building that also housed the jail, and the schoolroom was unbelievably filthy. There were only nine pupils (six boys and three girls); and Maud soon discovered that the teacher, Mr. Mustard, hadn't the faintest idea of how to teach. Also, she recoiled in disgust whenever Mr. Mustard took out his "murderous-looking rawhide whip as long as himself" (*Selected Journals I,* 32) and lashed one of her classmates into submission.

When her grandfather left on his western tour of Canada's railroads, Maud felt lonelier than ever. But as time passed, she found much that was beautiful in the Prince Albert area. Also, her elocution skills and ability to captivate an audience quickly made her into a local celebrity, both at church and in secular gatherings. At school, she made two new friends: Willie and Laura Pritchard. Both sister and red-haired, green-eyed, and crooked-mouthed brother were kindred spirits and joys to be around.

But the cold! Maud had never before experienced such marrow-numbing temperatures: forty to sixty degrees below zero! Her father gave her a buffalo coat that left unprotected only her pert little nose and part of her legs. However, there was a compensation to the dismal weather: tobogganing!

Maud soon realized that her teacher, Mr. Mustard, had a crush on her. He began calling on her three times a week, and when he arrived, "Mrs. Montgomery"—Maud could not call her "Mother"—would always leave, so Maud would have to entertain this unwelcome beau by herself. Not only did Maud dislike him, but he bored her. Meanwhile at school, Willie's friendship was rapidly becoming something deeper and more intense.

Always, it seemed, someone—usually a number of someones—was in love with Maud. What was there about her that so attracted suitors? According to contemporary accounts and photographs, she was extremely slim and had a perfect figure. Gillen notes that Maud at fifteen was "small, intense . . . , delicate of feature, and graceful in person . . . , eyes shining with excitement; with the determination to excel that informed her every act; proud of achievement; her secret heart impatient for the future in which she intended to succeed" (Gillen, 23).

Even at fifteen, Maud was determined to be a writer. Gillen points out that Maud's refuge from the harsh realities of the world was always to retreat inward, "catching that elusive thought, or scene, or experience, in a net of words. In *Emily's Quest* she spoke of herself through her heroine: "'A thing—an idea—whether of beauty or ugliness, tortured her until it was *written out.'* . . . The comedy and tragedy of life enthralled her and demanded expression through her pen" (Gillen, 33). Then, a week after her sixteenth birthday, Maud experienced the proudest day of her life. One of her poems was published in the Charlottetown *Patriot*. Her father was very pleased, but her stepmother displayed a different reaction. That night Maud wrote in her journal: "Mrs. Montgomery looks as if she considered the whole thing a personal insult to *her* and has never mentioned the poem at all" (*Selected Journals I*, 36).

The new year was jammed with new experiences for Maud: declaiming in public, Sunday school teaching of children, sleigh riding and tobogganing with Laura and Will, running the house and taking care of Kate and the new baby, Bruce (leaving Mrs. Montgomery free to flit around town), and living for those rare meals when she would be alone with her father. She also enjoyed tormenting Mr. Mustard on his three-times-a-week calls—even torrential rains didn't stop him. On July 1, Maud gleefully wrote in her journal: "Mustard actually *mustered*—oh, forgive the pun. It just *made itself up*—enough [courage] to put his fate to the test this evening. He did it about as awkwardly as possible but he did it. . . . I wanted to laugh all the time" (*Selected Journals I*, 55). Maud tried to turn him down kindly but firmly enough so he wouldn't shadow her for the rest of her days.

After eight months of slavelike labor in her stepmother's house, Maud was exhausted. The Pritchards invited her to spend some time at their Laurel Hill Farm, where Maud was finally able to relax and have fun. Her visit was a blessed, even though temporary, relief from the "espionage of a hostile and malevolent eye, ever on the alert for anything that can be twisted and interpreted to my disadvantage" (*Selected Journals I*, 57). The three friends knew that a parting was imminent: Maud's father, aware that his wife would never be a mother to his oldest child, had regretfully agreed to let Maud return to Prince Edward Island. Will asked to keep one of Maud's rings, as well as requesting a lock of her long, luxurious hair. The trio exchanged "ten-year" letters (the latest rage), which were not to be opened until ten years had passed.

On Maud's last evening in Prince Albert, Will came by and stammered an emotional good-bye. He and Maud shook hands, and he handed her a letter. Then he was gone. Though Maud liked Will better than any other boy she'd known, she didn't love him. Later she wrote, "I felt so badly I couldn't cry—I just felt stupid. I went up to my room and read his letter. He said in it that he loved me and always would. I curled up on my bed after I had read it and had a good cry. I felt so lonesome and horrid. If I hadn't known that Will had left town, I believe I'd have run out after him" (*Selected Journals I*, 62).

In those days, an engagement was almost as binding as marriage itself. Had Maud made such a commitment to Will, she most likely would have kept it, even if she had returned to Prince Edward Island. But had she yielded, it is most unlikely that we would ever have heard of *Anne of Green Gables*. Many a time Maud would relive that last moment with Will and wonder, *What if . . . ?*

But Will had gone, and she did not call him back.

The next morning, everyone rose early. After hearing the lonesome train whistle, Maud went upstairs for the last time, put on her cloak and hat, and left for the depot. Mrs. Montgomery did not go to the station with her. Both women knew why Maud was leaving.

At the station, there was quite a crowd to see Maud off. Never would she be able to erase from memory those last good-byes and Laura's tear-stained face receding down the tracks. Maud returned to her seat and cried. The great experiment—going home to her father at last—was over. Though it had been a failure, the memory of that year would remain with her always. The young woman who returned alone to Prince Edward Island, traveling over 2,500 miles, was a far different person than the girl who had been escorted west by a devoted grandfather twelve months before.

The Alpine Path

Many years ago, when I was still a child, I clipped from a current magazine a bit of verse, entitled "To the Fringed Gentian" [*not* William Cullen Bryant's poem], and pasted it on the corner of the little portfolio on which I wrote my letters and school essays. Every time I opened the portfolio I read one of those verses over; it was the key-note of my every aim and ambition:

> Then whisper, blossom, in thy sleep
>   How I may upward climb
> The Alpine path, so hard, so steep,

That leads to heights sublime;
How I may reach that far-off goal
Of true and honoured fame,
And write upon its shining scroll
A woman's humble name.

—L. M. Montgomery,
The Alpine Path, 10

Maud reached her beloved Island on September 5, 1891. At Kensington, she hired a team to take her to Park Corner: "How I did enjoy that drive! It was all so lovely—the beautiful sunset, the rich harvest scenery, and the aroma of firs along the road. I just gazed my eyes out. And when we came in sight of the sea I could not speak for emotion. I listened to its hollow roar in unspeakable delight" (*Selected Journals I*, 66). After a joyous reunion at both houses, it was on to Cavendish and another reunion.

Now that her original Prince Albert dream was dead, now that she was back home on her beloved Island, it was time for Maud to take stock of her future. Just what was she to do with her life? That wasn't an easy question for a pretty P.E.I. girl of sixteen to answer in 1891, for a young woman at that time had few options. She was expected to marry, settle down, have children, support her husband in whatever he did, and sublimate all her dreams and goals to his—even turn over to him any personal money or property she owned or inherited. The drudgery of this narrow world made women old before their time.

Maud knew that to achieve her lifelong dream of becoming a professional writer, she would have to obtain a university degree. The additional education would not only help her to become self-sufficient, but it would also give her credibility. Most of the universities in Canada were founded by Scots, who considered education very important, even for women. As a matter of fact, on Scots-dominated Prince Edward Island, nearly half of the students who attended local Prince of Wales College were women; furthermore, the daughters of wealthy P.E.I. farmers often went to Nova Scotia to continue their education. Thus Maud was not unusual in wanting to get a university degree. The problem was her grandfather. According to Rubio, "he didn't want to waste a penny on her. So her grandmother interceded and saw that Maud got to go on. Her grandmother was the one who always helped Maud come up with money to do things . . . when her heart was set on something, and that made old Alex madder" (Rubio to Wheeler, 4).

After spending the winter with the Park Corner clan, Maud returned to Cavendish and began to prepare for the entrance examinations required of any who wished to attend college. The British system of education was a singularly unforgiving one. It can be likened to a road with many forks in it, each fork a battery of tough exams. Grades meant little: Either you passed on to the next level or you didn't. If you didn't pass, not only were you frozen careerwise, with no hope of advancement, but you also carried the stigma of your failure for the rest of your life—even if you retook and passed the exams later. This year of preparation was a busy one for Maud. At the end, she placed fifth in the entire Province, out of 264 who took the exams.

Barely two weeks afterward, on August 3, 1893, the news flashed across the Island, and then across Canada, that Senator Montgomery was dead. Grandfather Macneill took Maud to the funeral. As she sat among the hundreds of other mourners, she remembered the Senator's kindness to her and how he had escorted her across Canada to the Northwest Territory. Oh, how she would miss him!

A month later, Grandmother Macneill drove Maud to Charlottetown. In the end, Lucy Macneill had won over her husband, and he had agreed to supplement the money Maud's father had sent her, thus making possible the year at Prince of Wales College. The pressure would be intense because Maud was attempting to complete two years' work in one. She had only enough money for one year, so she had no other option. Despite poor food, cold weather, and a heavy workload, that year was one of the happiest and most carefree that Maud would ever experience.

Two sets of grueling exams came at the end. One set was needed to pass the course, and one was needed for teacher certification. This was an incredible ordeal for Maud, considering that the exams covered two years' worth of material in one. Even so, she earned the highest score in English drama, English literature, agriculture, and school management. Each year, the best English essay was presented at graduation. Maud's essay on Shakespeare's "Portia" was chosen that year, and she read it to the commencement crowd.

After graduation, Maud returned home to Cavendish to look for a teaching position. That proved harder than she had anticipated because her grandfather not only refused to drive her to interviews, but he also refused to let her use his horse and buggy so she could drive herself. Since almost no school hired without a personal interview, no position was offered.

Barry, Doody, and Jones point out that most P.E.I. teachers tended to be young (seventeen to twenty-three years old) because once a woman married, she was expected to quit teaching. Those who failed to marry and continued to teach until they were middle-aged were considered failures. Male teachers who failed to move up to key leadership roles later on were also viewed as failures.

Finally, one school—Bideford, about fifty miles south of Cavendish—hired Maud without meeting her first. Because women were paid less than men, there were usually school trustees so eager to save money that they'd hire the cheaper applicant. The schoolhouse, to put it mildly, did not impress the new schoolmistress; nor did its rather bleak setting, devoid of trees. But at least Maud had a nice place to stay: the Methodist manse with Reverend Estey and his wife and daughter. Though initially homesick and discouraged, Maud soon regained her equilibrium and set out to make the most of things. She started with only twenty students, but more arrived almost every day. Soon forty-nine children crowded into the little one-room building. Maud ended the year with sixty.

As always, Maud had no shortage of beaus. That winter, she turned down two proposals, one of them from a Methodist minister named Lewis Dystant. Meanwhile, she kept writing, often in the bitter cold of the morning. She submitted her work to magazines in both Canada and the United States, but all she met with was rejection.

> I often wonder that I did not give up in utter discour-
> agement. At first I used to feel dreadfully hurt when a
> story or poem over which I had laboured and agonized
> came back, with one of those icy rejection slips. Tears of
> disappointment *would* come in spite of myself, as I
> crept away to hide the poor, crimpled manuscript in the
> depths of my trunk. But after a while I got hardened to
> it and did not mind. I only set my teeth and said, "I
> will succeed." I believed in myself and I struggled on
> alone, in secrecy and silence. I never told my ambitions
> and efforts and failures to any one. Down, deep down,
> under all discouragement and rebuff, I knew I would
> "arrive" someday. (*The Alpine Path,* 60)

Maud did not sign her teacher's contract for the coming year, not because it had not been a good year—it turned out to be the best teaching year she would ever have—but because she had decided to go back to school. This time she would attend Dalhousie College in Halifax, Nova Scotia. She had been able to save $100 from her meager teacher's salary ($179.58 for the entire year), and surprisingly, her grandmother agreed to help simply because Maud was so anxious to go—in spite of her grandfather's scorn at the request. The September evening before she left for Halifax, Maud wrote in her journal: "If I had just *one* friend, whose opinion I valued—to say to me 'You are right. You have it in you to achieve something if you get the proper intellectual training. Go ahead!' what a comfort it could be!" (*Selected Journals I*, 143).

Maud's objective during this year was to study English literature at the feet of the legendary Archibald MacMechan. She loved her classes, and, oh, how she wished she could study four years for a bachelor's degree; but financially that was out of the question. That Christmas was a gloomy one, for her grandparents told her to stay at school as she might run into bad roads on the way home. Since almost all of her classmates were going home, bad roads or not, she knew there was another, darker reason for her grandparents' request—*they didn't really want her.*

Maud continued to get good grades. On January 8, 1896, papers were passed back, and she got Firsts in history, Latin, and English, and a Second in French.

Mid-February brought the biggest week of Maud's life: First, she won a $5 award from the Halifax *Evening Mail* for the best letter on the question "Which has the most patience under the ordinary cares and trials of life—man or woman?" Then she received another $5 from a Philadelphia magazine, *Golden Days,* for a story titled "Our Charivari." Finally, joy of joys, she received $12 from the prestigious *Youth's Companion* for her poem "Fisher Lassies." Eighteen dollars in one week! It was a lot of money when you consider that most Canadians at that time earned less than $300 a year. When the first $5 came, Maud splurged and bought five precious volumes of poetry: Tennyson, Byron, Milton, Longfellow, and Whittier. "I wanted something I could keep for ever in memory of having 'arrived'" (*The Alpine Path*, 60–61).

Upon her return to Cavendish that summer, Maud encountered the same story: No school would hire her because her grandfather wouldn't take her to be interviewed or let her use his horse and buggy. Finally, just when she had almost given up, her cousins Alf and Edwin Simpson came by. Ed offered her the Belmont school, at which he had been slated to teach before he had decided to go to college instead.

It was a busy year for Maud at Belmont. Not surprisingly, she had more than enough escorts for church services and prayer meetings. The Simpson brothers, in fact, fought over her. It was not a happy year for her, however, because she was cold most of the time and her accommodations were not conducive to writing or comfort. Ed Simpson proposed, and she told him no, that she was not in love with him. At the end of the year, she did not sign a contract to return.

In April 1897 Maud received a letter from Laura Pritchard explaining why Will hadn't answered her last letter. He had come down with influenza and, as was sadly true of others in those days, had not been able to fight it off. After terrific suffering and valiant attempts to hold off death, he had died on April 2. Laura and her parents were heartbroken. Maud too was grief-stricken, remembering how full of life and fun Will had always been. After she had had her cry, she went upstairs to her trunk and took out the ten-year letter Will had given her six years before. After opening it and reading it, she wrote in her journal:

> The letter seemed like a message from the dead. . . .
> It was a letter of love, speaking more plainly than he
> had ever ventured to do in ordinary letters, and oh, how
> it hurt poor lonely me to read it!
> Willie dead! And buried in his grave on that faraway
> prairie! It *can't* be! Wasn't it only yesterday that we sat in
> the old High School and wrote our notes and laughed
> over mutual jokes and walked home from school
> together in the winter evenings? Wasn't it only yesterday
> that we sauntered by the river in the purple June
> twilights or roamed over the prairies gemmed with
> bluebells? And wasn't it only yesterday we spent at the
> Maiden Lake picnic and cut our names together on the
> old poplar by the lake?
> Alas, no, it is six long years ago! And Will is *dead!*
> (*Selected Journals I*, 184–85)

Perhaps it was Will's untimely death, for no suitor had ever meant more to her or been a closer friend than he. Perhaps she was just lonely and tired of saying no to all her proposals. Whatever the reason, when importuned one romantic evening by Ed Simpson, she agreed to marry him. But in the clear light of day, as she listened to him and appraised him objectively, she realized to her horror that she had made a terrible mistake. She now saw how incredibly self-centered Edwin was, how insensitive to the feelings of others, and she was filled with loathing. Fortunately, he had the Simpson malady of talking nonstop, never bothering to see whether or not others were listening—so he didn't notice her changed attitude and nonresponsiveness.

It was to be a long engagement, and it was to be kept secret. These were Maud's two life rafts. She knew what her grandparents would say: "Edwin is a Baptist; worse yet, he is a relative—the Island families are too inbred already." On June 30, 1897, she poured out her anguish, hour after hour, into her journal. What a terrible, terrible mess she had made of her life! The suffering would continue because she didn't know how to tell the truth to Edwin without destroying him.

As people often do when they experience intense suffering, Maud grew from it, maturing from a girl to a woman. Laura Pritchard sent her a tiny packet, returning the ring she had given Will and which he had faithfully worn to the day of his death. Maud slipped it back on her finger once more and thought of all that had happened since the day she gave it to him. "It seems like a golden link between me and my lost self, between the present and the past. Poor little ring! I shall always wear it in remembrance of those dear old days. Its circle is the symbol of eternity and eternal friendship. Surely, surely, those who knew each other so well and dearly here will meet again in some fair Hereafter" (*Selected Journals I*, 195–96).

That fall Maud took another school, this one in Lower Bedeque, about thirty-five miles south of Cavendish. The situation with regard to Edwin remained unresolved. Although she despised herself for her cowardice, she could not overcome it and ask Edwin to release her. But now something even worse happened: She fell in love—passionately in love—for the first time in her life. But even that was not the worst of it. She knew this new love was wrong for her and wrong for all her plans for the future.

At Lower Bedeque, Maud boarded with the Cornelius Leard family. Their son Al's desire for a leave of absence had opened up the teaching position for her. Herman was the oldest son, at twenty-eight. Maud had not been impressed with him at first, but as time passed, his magnetic blue eyes and tender strength paralyzed her will. When she was with him, words were superfluous; no other boy or man had ever stirred her as he did.

But she was still engaged to Edwin. In fact, Edwin came for a visit, and Maud's inner torment burned even hotter. Still she found herself unable to tell Edwin the truth. As for Herman, it was not that he was not a Christian—he was. It was not that he did not have the personal traits she most admired—he did. No more likable man, and more beloved by the community, had she ever dated. The problem was, first, a matter of caste:

She felt herself above him socially. Second, he was not at all interested in the world of the mind and had not bothered to get much education. Furthermore, he was jealous of the time she devoted to writing. Maud knew that if she married Herman, she would regret it for the rest of her life. Yet her passion for him showed no sign of diminishing.

She was saved by the sudden death of Grandfather Macneill on March 6, 1898. In shock, she returned home for the funeral. She had received little outward love from him; in fact, she had even been afraid of him. But now that he was gone, she remembered the good times—the fact that he had been willing to take her in as a baby and raise her, his marvelous vitality and ability to hold an audience, and the inexhaustible mother lode of Island stories from which he drew. When she walked into the parlor, the same room where she had last seen her mother, there lay her grandfather, his face more gentle, more kind, than she had ever seen it before.

After the funeral, Maud left her sorrowing grandmother and returned to her school. She had intended to wait until the term was over before leveling with Edwin, but she now felt that it must be dealt with immediately. So she wrote him, telling him she did not love him and abjectly asking for forgiveness and for release. As for Herman, she knew her only defense was to never be alone with him again.

At the end of March, Maud decided to return to her grandmother.

That October, as the leaves began to fall—always the most reflective time of the year—Maud again thought back to her last visit to Lower Bedeque, and her conviction that she would never return: "I feel that no love can ever again be to me what mine for [Herman] was—that never again will I meet any man who will have the power to stir my heart and soul to their profoundest depths as did Herman Leard." Most provocative are her conclusions, reminiscent of Brontë's in portraying Heathcliffian fireworks over brooding *Wuthering Heights:* "And, all in all, I think it is best so, for I believe that such love is hardly ever the forerunner of happiness—it is a 'challenge to fate' and she punishes it surely and severely."

Maud went even further in that remarkable October 8, 1898, entry (one of those rare marathon all-nighters), for she arrived at a conclusion reached by so many other writers and psychologists:

> I am not unhappy now—at least not with a *positive* unhappiness. There is a certain *negative* unhappiness in my life—the unhappiness not of present pain but of absent joy. But I think there are very few *really* happy

people in the world—I can count on my ten fingers all
I know who I believe are really perfectly happy—and I
cannot expect to be more favored than the majority.
(*Selected Journals I*, 227)

Duty and Responsibility

"Duty" is an old-fashioned word today, but it wasn't 100 years ago. The
government did not take care of you then—*families* took care of their
own. "Responsibility" is another old-fashioned word today, but in the
nineteenth century it was coupled with "duty"—together they added up
to a way of life.

Maud had done much thinking and struggling during the long nights
after her grandfather's funeral and her return to Lower Bedeque. Her
passion for Herman had torn at her heart, and often it seemed that she
would never again find peace. But finally her feelings for him subsided,
and she could again hear the voice of her rational self. For months afterward, Maud shuddered every time she realized how close to the abyss she
had come in her infatuation with Herman.

But now that she was free of that passion, what should she do? She
analyzed the situation from every angle, then arrived at conclusions. First
and foremost there was Grandmother and her health and happiness.
Second, there was Grandfather's foolish will, leaving everything to his son
John and protecting his wife not at all—nor her, his granddaughter.
Women, old or young, did not live alone in those days, so one thing was
certain: Grandmother could not stay in the big house without her. But
if she *should* accept the responsibility of caring for her grandmother, it
would have to be for as long as her grandmother lived, and she might
very well live for another ten, fifteen, even twenty years. By that time,
Maud would be middle-aged herself, a spinster. Who would want her
then? And what about her career? Could she wait that long before she
started on it? As for writing—how could she fit it in?

In the end, duty won out. Maud realized that when she had needed
help most, her grandparents had come to her aid. Regardless of how she
felt about their lack of empathy and lack of support over the years, she
had to balance that against all they *had* given her since she had been a
baby. And they had taken her on in their old age—never an easy thing to
do. So, she informed Grandmother and the family that she was committing her life to her grandmother's welfare. In effect, Maud put her own
life on hold for the indefinite future . . . just as would her alter-ego Anne
some years down the line.

It was with both a sigh and a leap of the spirit that Maud had moved back into her beloved old home. If only Grandfather had willed the place—at least the *house*—to her! She would never want to leave it; in fact, she wondered if leaving it wouldn't do something awful to her soul. But the law of British primogeniture gave scant thought to female heirs, even widows. Many sons tossed their mothers out into the streets on inheriting an estate. Well Maud knew that she must be prepared, on a heartbeat's notice, to be evicted herself. And she and Uncle John Macneill had never been close, so there wasn't anything to build on there.

Maud found life with her grandmother constricting after having been on her own. Maud would have few visitor friends, for Grandmother would not welcome them. And she would not be free to travel, except on rare occasions, even for short distances such as to town. Just as bad, she would not even be treated as an adult, with adult privileges, but must go to bed early in the evening, the minute Grandmother went. It would be anything but an easy road.

Maud decided to focus on her writing. In her last journal entry for 1898, she made several resolutions, one of which had to do with the role of writing in her life: "How I love my work. I seem to grow more and more wrapped up in it as the days pass and other hopes and interests fail me. Nearly everything I think or do or say is subordinated to a desire to improve in my work. I study people and events for that, I think and speculate and read for that" (*Selected Journals I*, 228).

One of the means she used to season her style was to read all the books worth reading. Her journals reflect this multilevel reading pattern: She stayed on the cutting edge of current best-sellers, read heavy book series such as Gibbon's *Decline and Fall of the Roman Empire,* and reread the classics she had always loved. The result was that her writing continued to improve, not only in craft but also in understanding, wisdom, and insight.

Less than seven months into the new year, a jolting entry appeared in Maud's journal: "I have something else to write here yet before I conclude—no less than the 'finish' to the most tragic chapter of my life. It is ended forever and the page is turned. Herman Leard—is *dead!*" (*Selected Journals I*, 240). When first told the news that Herman had died from a respiratory illness, Maud could only stare stupidly in utter denial. She did not shed many tears—she had shed all those long before. But how awful to think she would never again see his magnetic blue eyes turn tender as he looked at her—never again this side of heaven.

In early January of the following year, 1900, Maud was awakened one morning by a knocking on the front door. Sleepily, she opened it, and there was the telegram deliveryman. Her heart stopped beating: What could have happened now? She opened the telegram with shaking hands. The words swam on the yellowish sheet of paper: "Hugh J. Montgomery died to-day. Pneumonia. Peacefully happy and painless death" (*Selected Journals I*, 248).

Only a short time back, her father's last cheerful letter had given no indication he was sick. Then—like a stroke of lightning out of a clear sky—that "brutal telegram" had arrived.

> Oh, [he] meant so much to me! Others, losing a father, have still a mother or brothers or sisters left. I have nobody except poor old grandmother. And father and I have always been so much to each other. He was so good and kind and tender. Long, long ago, before he went west, when I was a tiny girl, we were much together, and how we loved each other! Even when he went so far away and for so many years we never grew apart, as some might have done. We always remained near and dear in spirit. Oh father, can it really be true that you are dead? Have you left your "little Maudie" all alone? (*Selected Journals I*, 249)

Later, looking back, she recounted what a "long, dreary, dismal" winter it had been. She had tried so hard to be "brave and courageous" in spite of all that had happened to her. Each evening, at eventide, it had long been her practice to think of her father and to yearn to see him soon. Henceforth she could only think of him as he had once been.

She thought back to those terrible weeks after receiving the telegram about his death. For a long time she could not write at all. Why should she! "What good was it when there was nobody to care whether I succeeded or not? Father was always so proud of me and my little talent—and now he could never know or care." But eventually she came to realize what a blessing work was.

> Oh, as long as we can work we can make life beautiful! And life *is* beautiful in spite of all its sorrow and care. . . . There is so much in the world for us all, if we only have the eyes to see it and the heart to love it and the hand to gather it to ourselves. . . .
>
> Well, I must henceforth face the world alone. Let me see what my equipment for such a struggle is. I am young; I have a scanty and superficial education, . . . I

have three hundred dollars—father left me two hundred in his will and I saved another hundred these last two years. I have no training for anything save teaching, which I cannot at present do; I have no influence of any kind in any quarter. Is that all? It seems a meagre list. Yes, there is something else—my knack of scribbling. Is it a feather's weight—or is it a talent of gold that will eventually weigh down the balance in my favor? Last year I made exactly ninety-six dollars and eighty-eight cents by my pen! That does not promise extravagantly. But we shall see. I have forgotten to mention another asset and a very valuable one—a belief in my power to succeed. As long as I possess that I shall face the future with an unquailing heart. (*Selected Journals I*, 248–49)

In 1901 Maud took her only "vacation" from Cavendish when she went to Halifax for six months to work as a copy editor for the *Daily Echo*. It was exciting to be able to more than hold her own in the male-dominated newspaper profession. One of the highlights of her Nova Scotia sojourn was when half of a serializing story was lost and the editor, in a panic, asked her to finish it. The paper then ran her copy, and the readers were none the wiser. And then came the serializing story that was going nowhere. She was asked to put it out of its misery as quickly and efficiently as possible. About a month after this textual surgery had taken place, Maud was convulsed by a comment made to her by an associate not in the know: " 'That story *Under the Shadow* is the strangest story I ever read. It wandered on, chapter after chapter, for weeks, and never seemed to get anywhere; and then it just finished up in eight chapters, *lickety-split*. I can't understand it!' " (*Selected Journals I*, 281).

Mary Rubio and Elizabeth Waterston, the definitive biographers of Montgomery, point out a fascinating aspect about Maud's life and writing. Rubio notes that Maud was really two women: one that the world knows and loves—bubbly, lighthearted, cheerful, and upbeat; the other a writer who poured out all her frustrations and heartbreak onto her journal pages. She was in essence neither as cheerful as her novels imply nor as depressed as her journals make her appear. One needs *both of them* to gain a true perspective of who Maud Montgomery really was (Rubio to Wheeler, 4).

In June 1902, Maud returned to Cavendish and resumed her responsibilities with her grandmother. Four friends came into her life around this time—each would have a significant impact on her. Two were on the Island: Nora Lefurgey, the new schoolteacher at Cavendish—she and Maud took to each other at once; and Frederica (Frede) Campbell, her youngest Park Corner cousin—Maud had known her, of course, as a child; but now, grown up, she gradually became friend, confidante, and sister, the closest and dearest human being Maud would ever know. The other two were pen pals brought to her by Miriam Zieber, a correspondent in Philadelphia who believed that authors could profit by being put in contact with other compatible writers. Maud she matched with Ephraim Weber, a thirty-one-year-old Mennonite farmer from Alberta. Once this correspondence developed momentum, Zieber struck again; this time stirring in George Boyd MacMillan of Alloa, Scotland. Weber's letters could be counted on to be intellectually stimulating, MacMillan's to be humorous and unpredictable. This correspondence would last throughout the rest of Maud's life, and she would say things to these two men that she would never share with anyone else—except Frede, to whom she told almost everything. Neither pen pal ever evolved into a romantic interest; rather, each remained a pillar of support and empathy through the years.

Meanwhile, Maud continued to write. In 1902, thirty of her submissions were accepted; in 1904, she earned almost $600; and in 1906, $700—a lot of money for those days. Maud had developed her own system: When one editor turned something down, she would merely repackage it and send it to another—and another—until she found a match. It paid off. Soon, editors of prestigious magazines in Canada and the United States began asking her for articles, stories, and poems.

Like many writers, Maud always kept a notebook into which she put "ideas for plots, incidents, characters, and descriptions" that came to her. In the spring of 1904, she was looking through the notebook and came across an entry written in 1895: " 'Elderly couple apply to orphan asylum for a boy. By mistake a girl is sent them' " (*Selected Journals I,* 330). From this, Maud began to

> block out the chapter, devise and select incidents and
> "brood up" my heroine—Anne. She was not so named
> of malice aforethought, but flashed into my fancy
> already christened, even to the all important "e"—she
> began to expand in such a fashion that she soon seemed
> very real to me and took possession of me to an unusual
> extent. She appealed to me, and I thought it rather a
> shame to waste her on an ephemeral little serial. Then

the thought came, *Write a book. You have the central idea. All you need to do is to spread it out over enough chapters to amount to a book.*

The result was *Anne of Green Gables.* I wrote it in the evenings after my regular work was done, wrote most of it at the window of the little gable room which had been mine for many years. I began it . . . in the spring of 1904. I finished it in October of 1905. (*Selected Journal I*, 330–31; Bolger, 189–92)

After the book came out, many people asserted that either they *were* or they *knew* the original characters. Maud categorically denied that, saying that to put a *real* character in a book could not but injure it. "*Study* from life [the writer] must, copying suitable heads or arms, appropriating bits of character, personal or mental idiosyncrasies, making use of the real to perfect the ideal. But the ideal, his ideal, must be behind and beyond it all. The writer must *create* his characters, or they will not be life-like" (*The Alpine Path,* 71).

Once she finished the book, the next question was who should publish it—or, perhaps more candidly stated: who *would* publish it. She sent it off to Bobbs-Merrill of Indianapolis. Since it was a new firm and had published a number of best-sellers already, she felt it might be a good choice. Bobbs-Merrill promptly sent it back without any comments— only a printed rejection slip. After a few tears, she bravely repackaged it and sent it off to Macmillan in New York, an old established firm. They sent it back, too, complete with a printed rejection slip. Repackaged, off it went to Lothrop, Lee and Shepard of Boston. Again it and the odious printed rejection returned all too quickly. So off it went again; this time to Henry Holt of New York. But they, along with the returned manuscript, sent "a typewritten screed" stating that their readers had found "some merit" in the story but "not enough to warrant its acceptance" (*Selected Journals I*, 331). That did it! The "damning with faint praise" was the last straw—Maud heaved the manuscript into an old hatbox, stashed it in her closet, and forgot about it.

Living alone with her grandmother, Maud sometimes wondered if marriage would ever come to her. If it did, what would she like the ceremony to be like? On Christmas Eve, the day before her cousin Bertha's wedding, she wrote down her dream-wedding scenario:

In the morning—a June morning when a glorious sunrise should be blossoming over the silvery east and the roses in gardens and wilding lanes should be as sweet as roses could be—I would rise early and dress—dress for the one man in all the world and for the eyes of no other and make me as fair as might be for his delight; and then in the expectant hush of dawn I would go down to meet him, unknown of any others and together we would go to the heart of some great wood where the arches were as some vast cathedral aisle and the wind of the morning itself sang our bridal hymn; and there we should pledge to each other a love that should last for all time and all eternity. Then we would turn, hand in hand, back to the busy world that would forevermore be glorified because of our life together!

Well, that's my *ideal*. But the *Real* is quite another thing! (*Selected Journals I*, 312–13)

In September 1903, a new Presbyterian minister, Ewan Macdonald, came to Cavendish. He was of medium height, "erect and dignified. . . . He has thick black hair, black roguish eyes, a clean rosy wholesome face, a fine profile and a very pleasant smile which brings out engaging dimples in his cheeks—altogether a very personable young man of about 34" (*Selected Journals I, 320*).

Ewan had early on been taken by his fair parishioner Miss Montgomery, and he spent so much time in or near the post office, waiting on a bench outside the house to talk with the associate postmistress—Grandmother Macneill had inherited her husband's position as postmaster—that it was the talk of the town.

Maud, on the other hand, was not overly impressed. She did enjoy their discussions, however, usually either philosophical or theological. As the days, weeks, and months—even years—went by and he continued to call, Maud's sixth sense warned her it was leading to a proposal. If he did, and she accepted, she did not delude herself that it would be a Hermanesque love match, or even a deep Willesque friendship. What it *would* be, she sighed, was a respectable marriage to someone her social equal, someone she liked more and more, someone with good values who would be a good father to their children—*children*, whom she had longed for, for so many years now. And he would be a far preferable alternative to a cheap boardinghouse.

Friday afternoon, October 12, 1906, Ewan came to say good-bye; he was leaving for advanced study in Scotland. Maud's heart sank, for his going would leave her lonelier than she would have believed. Herman was dead. Will was dead. And she would be thirty-two next month. What other comparable marital option would she ever have? *And*—if he asked and she accepted, it would have to be on the provision that he would wait until her grandmother's death released her from her promise. How many men would agree to such terms?

Ewan both proposed and agreed to the terms she specified—then left for Scotland. Maud was engaged again. She no longer dreamed of rapture; at this point she would be content with "workaday, bread-and-butter happiness—to be *reasonably* happy" (*Selected Journals I*, 323).

Six weeks later, during the first real snowstorm of the season, she pulled out her old journal and reread the Herman sections, comparing her feelings then with the placidity of her relationship with Ewan. Did she have regrets?

> What a mad infatuation it was! And yet it taught me some lessons it was well to know. I am not sorry I felt it—nay, I'm glad. Every experience enriches our life and the deeper such an experience the greater the richness it brings. I am a deeper-natured, broader-minded woman than I would or could have been if it had not been for that old love, that old temptation, that old anguish. It stirred my soul to depths that I would never otherwise have sounded or been conscious of. I am glad I knew it. It would have been a sorry thing to go through life and never have known love, even though it was an unhappy and unsatisfied love. I shall never know the *fullness* of life—to love absolutely and give myself to the man I so loved, knowing he loved me as well. But I have not been cheated out of everything. (*Selected Journals I*, 325)

Anne

The year 1907 did not start out well. Ewan's letters were not at all what Maud expected them to be: They were depressing, partially as the result of Ewan's experiencing headaches and insomnia. Maud strongly suspected there was something ominous here, a secret he had never shared with her, something that could very well destroy whatever happiness there might be for them down the line.

One winter day, as fate would have it, Maud was rummaging around her closet, looking for ideas and projects, when she stumbled on the hatbox containing the *Anne of Green Gables* manuscript. She pulled off the lid, took out the manuscript, and started scanning it, intending to perhaps do a hatchet job on it; maybe by heaving it onto a Procrustean bed and lopping off a few appendages, she could salvage *something* out of it. As she reread it, it didn't seem so bad. It would really be a pity to dismember it. She decided to give it one more try and sent it to L. C. Page of Boston. Years later she heard the story behind the manuscript's acceptance. It was all ready to be returned, complete with one of those "wonderful" rejection slips, when an employee, a native of Prince Edward Island, urged them to reconsider it; in fact, she made such a nuisance of herself that they, just to get her off their backs, so to speak, gave it a serious read. And that did it.

On Friday, April 15, 1907, Maud received a letter from L. C. Page accepting the manuscript and offering a ten percent royalty on the wholesale price earnings; also, all future manuscripts during the following five years would be locked in at the same percentage.

A book of her own to be published at last! After calming down a bit, Maud wrote: "The book may or may not succeed. I wrote it for love, not money, but very often such books are the most successful, just as everything in the world that is born of true love has life in it, as nothing constructed for mercenary ends can ever have" (*The Alpine Path*, 76).

On June 20, 1908, Maud received her copy of the bound book. Smiling through proud tears, she wrote: "Today has been, as Anne herself would say, 'an epoch in my life.' My book came today, 'spleet-new' from the publishers. I candidly confess that it was to me a proud and wonderful and thrilling moment. There, in my hand, lay the material realization of all the dreams and hopes and ambitions and struggles of my whole conscious existence—my first book. Not a great book, but mine, mine, mine, something which I had created" (*The Alpine Path*, 77).

But would the book sell? Maud didn't have to wait long to find out the answer: *Anne of Green Gables* was one of those rarities—an instantaneous best-seller. So much so that Page had trouble keeping up with the demand, as printing after printing rolled through the presses. Maud was asked to write a sequel, which she began on October 9, after spending all summer collecting material, "blocking out chapters, devising incidents and fitting them into each other, and 'brooding up' the characters. This is the disagreeable part of the work but it is done now and the rest is pure joy. To breathe the breath of life into those dry bones and make them *live* imparts the joy of creation. Anne is as real to me as if I had given her birth—as real and as dear" (*Selected Journals I*, 332).

The reviews for *Anne of Green Gables* were generally very positive, and the mail from enamored readers began its never-slowing flow. "One of the reviewers says 'the book radiates happiness and optimism.' When I think of the conditions of worry and gloom and care under which it was written I wonder at this. Thank God, I can keep the shadows of my life out of my work. I would not wish to darken any other life—I want instead to be a messenger of optimism and sunshine" (*Selected Journals I,* 339). In 1909, *Anne* was translated into Swedish, followed by Dutch in 1910, Polish in 1912, Norwegian in 1918, Finnish in 1920, French in 1925, Icelandic in 1933, and six other languages after Maud's death.

When the sequel to *Anne of Green Gables,* titled *Anne of Avonlea,* arrived on September 1, 1909, Maud ruefully noted how quickly success palled. "When my first book came to me I was much excited and half intoxicated with joy. But the new book only interested me mildly" (*Selected Journals I,* 358). On Saturday, February 19, 1910, she received a royalty check of $7,000. If she'd only had a tiny part of that money when she had needed it for her education!

The reality of her burgeoning fame came home to her in mid-September 1910 when she was told that Lord Earl Grey, governor-general of Canada, wished to meet her while he was in the Maritimes. During their long chat together, he told her how much *Anne* meant to him and his family. This was only the first of a number of such experiences for Maud as the years passed.

Maud had begun her next book, *The Story Girl,* on June 1, 1909. When she finished it in late 1910, she laid down her pen and bid adieu to her characters—with extreme reluctance. "I consider *The Story Girl* the best piece of work I have yet done. It may not be as popular as *Anne.* . . . But from a literary point of view it is far ahead of it. It is an idyl of childhood on an old P.E. Island farm during one summer. I have written it from sheer love of it and revised it painstakingly—up there by the window of my dear white room. It may be the last book I shall ever write there" (*Selected Journals II,* 20).

Then occurred one of the pivotal fortnights of her lifetime: her two-week tour of Boston as the guest of her publishers, George and Lewis Page. In those magic fourteen days, she would "live" more than she had in the last twelve years, and by the end, she would be "rebathed in youth." Maud had felt put down and demeaned by the publishing world for so long that she could not believe the adulation she received in Boston: flowers, city tours, teas, gifts, dinners, parties, celebrations, receptions, interviews—all for her! She even met such literary luminaries as Basil King, Thomas Wentworth Higginson, Abbie Farwell Brown, J. L. Harbour, and Ellen Douglas Deland.

But Maud wasn't completely happy with the Page brothers. Her woman's instinct warned her not to trust them, particularly Lewis, and she soon had evidence to back this premonition. She had told Lewis by letter that she would not sign another contract with a binding clause in it. That clause, locking her in at ten percent of wholesale, was sneaked into the contracts of the two previous books she'd done for them, and she, a babe in the woods without legal counsel or an agent, had ended up signing. She thought she had made her point and thus wondered when Lewis, on the last day of her dreamlike stay in Boston, asked her to take to her room the next contract, sign it, and get it back to him that evening. When she got back to her room, she studied the contract and saw, to her disgust, that the binding clause had been included.

Should she refuse to sign it? Or should she avoid making a scene in what had been the most idyllic two weeks of her life? She strongly suspected that Lewis had deliberately banked on her following the latter line of reasoning. If so, he was justified in his Machiavellianism, for she signed the contract, locking herself in to five more years at only ten percent, and that of wholesale rather than retail. But Maud vowed that she'd never do it again. From then on, she felt convinced that she was dealing with a man who was not only unprincipled but, while willing to make a fortune from her writings, was not willing to be equitable with her. It was one of the most disillusioning moments of her lifetime.

As 1911 dawned, Maud had no way of knowing that it would bring seismic changes in her life. Ewan had returned after one year in Scotland, and he seemed happier. He had accepted a pastorate in Leaskdale, Ontario, so she didn't see him very often. On February 24, Maud noted in her journal that her grandmother was looking particularly frail and old, and there was a look on her face that "sent a chill" through Maud's heart. On March 4, her journal entry revealed that both she and her grandmother had caught the grippe, which was then making the rounds. The night of March 4 was the last night Maud would spend in her dear old room, for by the next evening her grandmother had begun to cough almost continuously, and Maud spent the night with her by the kitchen stove so she would stay warm. A doctor was called, and his verdict was a sentence of death: *pneumonia*. For the first time in five years, Lucy Macneill's son and heir, John, came over from next door to see her. In spite of the doctor's predictions, the old woman lived almost a week after that first night of coughing. During those last days, the only living creature Grandmother Macneill expressed interest in was her constant companion, Daffy, the cat. When he was brought in, she feebly stroked his gray fur, saying, "Poor little Daffy! Poor little Daffy!" Those were close to the last words she ever said. She died on March 10.

It seemed impossible to Maud that she would never see her grandmother again, for she had always been there. That night, Maud looked out of a manse window toward the now-deserted house: "For the first night perhaps since it was built, certainly for the first time in my recollection, no light shone out from its windows through the old trees. The soul of the home was gone. It was henceforth to be but an empty shell, the mockery of wind and storm. . . . Never again would I enter it" (*Selected Journals II*, 52–61). Not being able to bear the sight any longer, she moved her belongings over to Park Corner. There, night after night, she cried herself to sleep. She had only one link that came with her—Daffy, who was soon adopted by the entire household.

Now there was no reason to postpone her long-delayed marriage to Ewan, which was set for July. Maud's soul mate, Frede, came home from Macdonald College on June 17 to help her get ready for the wedding. Her wedding dress (which can be seen today at Maud's birthplace in Clifton) "was of white silk crepe de soie with a tunic of chiffon and pearl bead trimming—and of course the tulle veil and orange blossom wreath" (*Selected Journals II, 66*).

The night before she was to be married, Maud cried. In her journal, she admitted that it was not because she was unhappy, but because "I wept a lost dream—a dream that could never be fulfilled—a girl's dream of the lover who should be her perfect mate, to whom she might splendidly give herself without reservations. We all dream that dream. And when we surrender it unfulfilled we feel that something wild and sweet and unutterable has gone out of life!" (*Selected Journals II*, 66).

Mrs. Macdonald

Maud hated to give up her old name—her father's name, her literary name; but, in those days, keeping one's maiden name just wasn't done. The wedding was small, since her grandmother had died only a few months before. Twice during the ceremony, Maud was wrenched with a terrible feeling of being a prisoner. She felt wild and untamed, and she knew that Ewan would never have husbandly power over her. After the ceremony, she never experienced the feeling again.

The honeymoon was a long one, paid for by Maud's royalties. The newlyweds boarded *The Megantic* at Montreal, crossed the Atlantic to Scotland (arriving there in mid-July), then toured all their favorite spots in the British Isles. By late September, they were heading home—a home Maud had never seen: Leaskdale, Ontario. Depressingly, they arrived, over muddy roads, late one damp and murky night. The next day, however, the situation didn't seem quite so hopeless, even though the rain continued to fall. Ewan pastored two small churches, in Leaskdale and Zephyr: Leaskdale itself was so small that it consisted of only ten or twelve houses—it reminded Maud of Cavendish.

The manse, filled with boxes of their goods and in a terrible mess, was yet home to Maud, the first home of her own she had ever had. Not long afterward, a railway express man delivered a slatted box, which had been three days en route to the manse. When Maud opened it, Daffy climbed leisurely out and stretched himself. "He was not at all hungry . . . but he was extremely thirsty and drank three saucers of milk and one of water without stopping. Then he climbed into my lap and kissed me as gravely and humanly as possible" (Gillen, 99). With Daffy there, a living link to her past, Maud breathed a sigh of happiness. She—and Daffy—were *home*.

And so began Maud's life as a Presbyterian minister's wife. Her acceptance of her role, and her proceeding to make the most of it—even in the dark and tragic days ahead when she felt herself to be utterly alone—is an incredible story. She had made a commitment, and she would honor it for the rest of her life.

Although she was now a world-famous author, no one would have known it in Leaskdale. For fifteen years, she remained in the bathroom-less manse and fulfilled her chosen role: making regular pastoral visits; attending quilting parties and pie socials; leading the Women's Missionary Society and the Young People's Guild meetings and directing church-run dramatic productions; attending wedding receptions; and giving comfort at funerals or assistance in times of illness. It was a lonely life, because as a minister's wife, Maud could not safely unburden herself of her own frustrations and doubts.

Early in November 1911, she realized she was pregnant. With a heart overflowing with joy, she wrote,

> I am to be a mother. I cannot realize it. It seems to me so incredible—so wonderful—so utterly impossible as happening to *me!*
>
> But I am glad—so glad. It has always seemed to me that a childless marriage is a tragedy—especially in such a marriage as mine. I realize that maternity is a serious

thing and all the more serious to a woman of my age [she was 37]. But not for that would I wish to avoid it. I want to have a child—something to link me with the future of my race. I want to give a human soul a chance to live this wonderful life of ours. I want something of my very own—bone of my bone, flesh of my flesh, to love and cherish. . . . The thought that within me I carry *life*—a *soul*—a human being who will live and love and suffer and enjoy and struggle—is so amazing that I am lost before the marvel of it. (*Selected Journals II*, 90–91)

Frede Campbell joined them for Christmas. Oh, how Maud needed that relief—*especially* Frede's companionship, for Frede was not only a soul sister, she was also a safety valve. With her, Maud felt free to be herself, to laugh until her sides ached, to be foolish, to be young.

In July 1912, a heat wave struck Ontario right before Maud's delivery date, and there was no relief day or night. Frede was there, along with a nurse, to help bring little Chester into the world. Maud had worried that maybe she wouldn't be able to love as a mother should, but then the nurse laid the baby in her arms: "It seemed to me that my whole being was engulfed in a wave of love for that little blinking mite of humanity that lay cuddled to my breast. Love—such love! I never dreamed there could be such love. It seems blent and twined with the inmost fibres of my being—as if it could not be wrenched away without wrenching soul and body apart also" (*Selected Journals II*, 101). How she wished her father were alive to see his first grandchild!

With the money from her books, Maud was able to hire a maid so she'd have time in which to write. On May 21, 1913, she finished *The Golden Road*, the second Story Girl book. With all the interruptions, it had been a difficult book to complete. By July, she so yearned for Cavendish that she took the train east. When they neared the north coast of the Island, a flood of emotion swept over her: "I was stirred to the very depths of my being. Tears poured into my eyes—I trembled! For a moment it seemed passionately to me that I could *never* leave it again. I *belonged* here" (*Selected Journals II,* 127). At Park Corner, she was grieved to see how frail Uncle John Montgomery had become.

Before leaving the Island, she made a pilgrimage to Cavendish. It was evening when she arrived there. As she walked up the lane toward the house, she pretended it was four years earlier, and memories flooded in upon her. She would see the kitchen light shining through the trees. I would pass under the birches and then under the cherry trees and then around the curve. The old house would be before me; Daffy would come frisking across the yard and bound before me to the old red door. I would lift the latch and walk in, a little tired, and glad to be home again. Grandmother would be sitting in her old arm-chair by the table, reading with her gray shawl about her shoulders. (*Selected Journals II*, 127)

In Flanders Fields

In Flanders Fields
    the poppies blow
Between the Crosses,
    row on row,
That mark our place;
    and in the sky
The larks still bravely
    singing fly.
Scarce heard amidst
    the guns below.
We are the dead,
Short days ago we lived,
    felt dawn,
    saw sunset glow
Loved and were loved
    and now we lie
    In Flanders Fields.

Take up our quarrel
    with the foe
To you from falling hands
    we throw the Torch—
    be yours to hold it high;
    if ye break faith
    with us who die,
We shall not sleep
    though poppies grow
In Flanders Fields.

—Lt. Col. Dr. John McRae,
Guelph, Canada

On August 5, 1914, Maud acknowledged in her journal that the world was at war. It was frightening to her and her countrymen, for if Great Britain fell, so would Canada—and it would become a German colony! Always intense in her feelings, Maud would feel every battle, every casualty, as if the wounds, the deaths, were her own; thus her journal entries provide a deeply moving day-by-day story of the war from the home front, as the following excerpts reveal:

> *February 4 [1916]:* Verdun, where the snow is no longer white . . .
> *March 21:* The French line is still holding. . . . The German attack on Verdun still rages. At "Dead Man's Hill" the carnage is dreadful, but the French watchword is "They shall not pass." . . . Horrible statement in the paper the other day. It haunts me. When I cannot sleep at night it tears at my soul. "No child under eight years of age is left alive in Poland. They have all perished from starvation or exposure." And this is the year 1916 of the Christian era. . . .
> *January 5 [1917]:* The third year since hell broke loose upon the earth.
> *January 20:* Is there a heart in the world that does not ache today? [Of the twenty-one young men from Ewan's churches who went to war, only fifteen would return.]
> *December 11:* A storm cloud is gathering on the Western Front. All the prophets predict a supreme effort by Germany as its troops move west from the collapsed Russian front. . . .
> *June 1 [1918]:* The Germans have reached the Marne again—the *Marne!* Have captured Chateau Thierry, an outpost of Paris itself!
> *June 8:* I wonder if there will ever again come a time when life will be free from *fear.* For nearly four years now we have lain down with fear and risen up with it. It has been the "unwelcome sharer in every meal, the unbidden guest at every gathering."

But what were the costs? It is estimated that there were more than 10 million (direct casualties) dead. There were over 21,500,000 wounded or incapacitated for life—many from poison gas. Some 7,500,000 more had suffered terrible privations in prison camps—many never came back. Of the 15 million tons of shipping lost, 9 million of them were British. Sixty-three million men had been mobilized. Virtually an entire generation of young men were left dead, wounded, incapacitated, or otherwise old before their time. Genocide took millions more—the Turks alone slaughtered over 1 million Armenians.

The Great War was indeed the most terrible, destructive, and all-inclusive war mankind had ever known. No wonder Maud called it "Armageddon"!

One reason that the Great War resulted in so much disillusionment is that the entire Western world—including many of the clergy, surprisingly—had bought into the new religion of Darwinian-Spencerianism, based on the concept of evolution and preaching the "wonderful" news that the human race did not need God after all. God was obsolete—merely a myth. What mattered was that human beings, divorced from a Higher Power, had a certain divinity of their own and were gradually evolving toward perfection. Hence the Darwinian spokesman of the early twentieth century, Emile Coeú, sold his mantra to millions: *Every day in every way, I'm getting better and better.*

Now, in the holocaust of the Great War, the human race sank back into barbarism on a scale unimagined in early 1914. As Maud repeatedly labeled it, it was a *hell* so diabolical, so cruel, so devoid of compassion in any form, that it seemed to millions that the Spirit of God had departed from the world. Only as one understands the colossal magnitude of this Western disillusionment can one realize why the young people who experienced the cataclysm firsthand came to be known as the Lost Generation. If God was a myth, and if Darwinian-Spencerianism was likewise a myth—what was left? What solid guidelines remained to live by? And since so many professed Christians had themselves slipped into only a nominal relationship with God, spiritual bedrock was in rather short supply. Complicating the picture no end was an aspect Maud pointed out in one of her journal entries: This fiendish carnage was orchestrated by so-called Christian nations, each side claiming to represent God's will!

[This section dealing with World War I is referenced by the following: *Chronicles of the 20th Century* (Mount Kisco, N.Y.: Chronicle Publications, 1987), 182–247; Bernard Grun's *The Timetables of History* (New York: Simon & Schuster, 1982), 466–73; and Montgomery's *Selected Journals II*, 150–273.]

Only eight days after World War I began, Maud's second child, Hugh, was born—dead. The cause was a knot in the umbilical cord. Never would Maud forget the misery of that October afternoon: "And he was such a lovely baby—so plump and sweet and dimpled. His dear eyes, that would never lighten with intelligence, were large and blue as violets, and so bright. His dear little feet that would never toddle to me—his dear little hands that would never reach out to cling to mine. Oh, it was cruel" (*Selected Journals II,* 151–52).

As if the war hadn't decimated the world's population enough, in June 1918 the Spanish flu swept across Europe, then across the world; in the trenches, it claimed as many victims as the military battles themselves. According to M.A.J. McKenna, of the Cox News Service, in his article "Scientists May Solve 1918 Mystery"(*Denver Post,* October 31, 1997, 25A, 27A), the deadly virus killed some 40 million people. There has never been another like it. Even the Black Plague, which killed as many as one out of every three Europeans, took over a century and a half to do it. Not so the Spanish flu: In only eleven months (March 1918 to February 1919), "it sickened and killed families, cities, regiments on the battlefield: 675,000 Americans, 90,000 people in the Philippines, possibly 20 million in India. . . . The toll was so great that it reduced average U.S. life expectancy by 13 years. . . . It killed more Americans than World War I, World War II, the Korean War, and the Vietnam War combined."

Paranoia reigned supreme around the globe: People were afraid to get near family members; servants and employees were let go. The rich fled to the remotest places they could find. Even mail was suspect—some handled it only with surgical gloves. McKenna notes that the "San Francisco City Council required the entire population to wear surgical masks." In many places, all public gatherings ceased.

And it struck with incredible speed: "The Spanish flu killed in days; its preferred victims were not the young and old, the usual targets of infectious diseases, but those in their twenties. And it killed horribly, triggering a massive immune system reaction that saturated the lungs with blood and fluid, so they drowned from within." The flesh of some of the dying turned from white to black in only two hours!

McKenna wonders why historians have been so silent on the pandemic's horrific impact. In literature, only one writer, Katherine Anne Porter, chronicled it, in her *Pale Horse, Pale Rider.*

Dark Shadows

Frede

As the war drew to an end, Maud was stricken by the Spanish flu and was deathly ill for some time. No one, it seemed, knew what caused it or how to stop it. Drugstores were mobbed by people desperately searching for any remedy that might work. Some doctors found ways to cope with it. In Maud's case, fortunately she found competent medical help in time.

Just a week after she was well enough to come downstairs, a telegram was delivered to her. Aunt Annie's only son, George, was dead of the flu. His poor wife, Ella, was left with six children under eleven. Then there were five—little George died of the flu, too. Maud took the night train and joined Frede in taking care of the family. On Armistice Day evening, November 11, 1918, Maud and Frede went out to their beloved bridge over the "Lake of Shining Waters" and talked about this world that was now upside down. It did not even seem to be the same world of four years before.

On Friday, November 15, Maud had to leave for home. Of all the family she left behind, she was most worried about Frede, who had never regained her strength after a terrible bout with typhoid a few years before—what if *she* should get the flu? On December 17, the Leaskdale Christmas concert was called off due to another outbreak of the flu. On the day before Christmas, Maud finished her ninth book, *Rainbow Valley*.

On January 21, 1919, Maud received a call: "Come at once—Frede seriously ill." *The deadly flu had got her.* When Maud arrived at Macdonald College, where Frede taught, she was taken into Frede's room in the infirmary. One look at her dear cousin told her all: "This was a grislier foe" than typhoid. "Once more those brave, kindly, clever eyes lighted up with welcome as they met mine—as they had done hundreds of times in the past—as they would never do again." On January 25, Frede's breath grew shallower and shallower. Then it ceased. She *died* . . . and now she sleeps.

> But *I* wake and must face the dreary years without her. I *must* live as long as I can for my children's sake [the couple's third son, Stuart, had been born, alive and healthy, in October 1915]. I must live—without that blithe comradeship; that intellectual companionship, that faithful, earnest friendship—live, knowing that Frede will never come again under my roof—that never again will come to me a letter addressed in her old familiar hand—that I will never hear her laugh—never save up a joke to tell her—never walk with her again under the Park Corner birches or over the old bridge in

the summer twilight! How *can* I go on living when half
of my life has been wrenched away, leaving me torn and
bleeding in heart and soul and mind. I had *one*
friend—only one—in whom I could absolutely trust—
before whom I could in Emerson's splendid definition
"think aloud"—and she has been taken from me. Truly,
as has been said, in such an instance as this "it is the
survivor who dies." (*Selected Journals II*, 288–95)

It is no hyperbole to say that half of Maud died that day with Frede.
C. S. Lewis points out in his book *The Four Loves* that each person we
love, at death, takes part of us as well. That is the tragedy of aging. With
Frede's death, a giant door to the happiest side of Maud's psyche was
slammed shut forever.

Page

The story of Maud's dealings with the Page brothers is another sad
chapter in her life's story. And it was all so needless. Lewis Page had in
Maud a gold mine—all he had to do was to treat her fairly, kindly, equi-
tably, and with respect, and she never would have left him. But from first
to last, he seemed determined to deprive her of every penny he could pry
out of her.

On August 6, 1907, the Page brothers had accepted *Anne of Green
Gables*. Maud was grateful and jubilant but clearly apprehensive and
suspicious as she studied the contract: Why wasn't there an escalation
clause for her royalty if her books did well? Why were the royalty rates
based on wholesale rather than retail? Why were those low rates locked
in for five years?

As we have noted, not only did Lewis Page trade on Maud's publishing innocence and failure to realize she needed an agent, but he also
continually found ways to sneak in extensions to that infamous five-year
freeze. Thus, no small thanks to the trick he pulled on her during her
1910 visit to Boston, Maud's entry-level servitude lasted *eight* years
instead of the original five. On March 6, 1916, thinking herself free from
the Page contract, Maud arranged to publish with Frederick Stokes of
New York. In June, Lewis Page threatened to sue Maud if she awarded
her books to anyone but him. Maud countersued. For nine long years, a
legal battle raged between them. Finally, on October 22, 1928, the court
decided in Maud's favor. The nightmare was over. Lewis Page was
ordered to pay Maud a total of $18,300. In the end, after paying court

expenses, Maud was left with about $4,000, plus the moral victory. In her journal entry for October 22, she concluded with these words: "It is over! Over!! Over!! And—I—am—free!" (*Selected Journals III*, 380).

Ewan

During the fall of 1919 Maud finally found out what her husband's dark secret was. Ever since she first knew him, Ewan had been plagued with periodic headaches, insomnia, and deep depression. Though she dreaded these episodes, Maud merely assumed they'd sooner or later go away; they always had. But starting early in June 1919, Ewan's condition became worse. He was dull and unresponsive, even with company, which was not like him. He would alternate between periods of extreme apathy and periods of restless walking, sometimes in the middle of the night. Finally, Maud insisted that he see a doctor. The doctor told Ewan he was experiencing a nervous breakdown and must take a leave of absence from his church.

But Maud felt there was more to it than that. Ewan was not one to work too hard; he always took things easy and didn't get worked up about anything. He certainly hadn't been working hard lately. When they got home, she questioned him until he gave in and told her the truth. He was experiencing these bouts because he felt certain he was *predestined to go to hell!* It had all started when he was about sixteen and had heard a number of sermons on hellfire and damnation. Ewan had taken the positive Presbyterian position of being predestined for eternal salvation and reversed it: *He was doomed to eternal damnation.* Convinced he had no hope of an afterlife, Ewan lived in dread night and day.

Maud's response was one of despair. What hope was there for him—for them—with this conviction? What would happen if someone in one of the churches found out that their minister was convinced he was going to hell? Maud was familiar with the condition of religious melancholia, but this was too close to home: "Unutterable horror seemed literally to engulf me. Was my husband going out of his mind? He had every symptom given in the encyclopedia on that type of insanity" (*Selected Journals III*, 321–32).

Maud also discovered that Ewan had experienced his first serious attack when he was eighteen, the second when he was in college six or seven years later, the third the winter he was in Glasgow after they became engaged, and now again, and this one was the worst yet.

When experiencing an attack, Ewan would refuse to do anything; he would just lie in the hammock and stare at the ceiling, his mind totally possessed by the horrible concept of eternal damnation. He would not even acknowledge his two sons. Maud felt completely alone; she had no one to turn to! Finally, she decided to send Ewan to East Braintree, near Boston, to see a specialist.

Ten days later, she received a telegram: "Ewan is no better. Can you come at once?" She caught the next train. She kept asking herself the question, *If Ewan has lost his mind, what am I to do?* When she got there, Ewan came down the stairs—*smiling.* He was better. That evening in bed, he told her that he had had a vision of both himself and the children in hell. The next day he was fine until the afternoon; then the black mood descended again. She discovered that those moods paralyzed his will: He could make no effort to do *anything.*

Maud finally got him to Dr. Garrick, the specialist. The doctor told her neither to argue with Ewan when he was in that condition *nor to let him out of her sight.* He suggested that they find out if there was kidney blockage that was causing him to retain poisons. She was to keep him drinking water heavily. As for herself, she had to take veronal to get any sleep at all.

Gradually, Ewan got better. Then, on July 10, Maud found him with a handkerchief tied around his head—a sight that always filled her with dread, for almost invariably that signaled another of his attacks. About a week afterward, she wrote: "I know just how a wretched mouse feels when it has crept a little bit away from the clutches of the cat and is pounced on again" (*Selected Journals I,* 336).

By late July, Ewan had come out of this latest siege of darkness, and they went home. Then in mid-August, there came the telltale handkerchief around his head again: "I am still the mouse in the claws of the cat." Week after week, these attacks came and went. By September 21, Ewan was well again.

Between Frede's death on January 25, 1919, and the horror of Ewan's confession four months later, Maud's relative peace and contentment left her, never to return. They couldn't, for she could never know from day to day when she would find Ewan with a handkerchief on his head again and realize with a chilling certainty that hell was back in session.

Today, we have drugs for such illnesses, and with proper medication, Ewan might have lived a fairly normal life. Yet successful treatment for such a condition, even today, is anything but a sure thing. For sixteen years, Maud fronted for her husband, either providing plausible reasons for why Ewan couldn't meet his pastoral responsibilities or doing damage control after his disastrous public appearances when he preached anyway.

As time went by, the attacks became more severe, and Ewan teetered on the edge of insanity. Maud provided a description in her journal entry for March 16, 1924:

> The suddenness of these attacks is so uncanny. Two weeks ago Ewan was well, jolly, and care free—a fine looking man with a pleasant open face and friendly, twinkling eyes. Yesterday he sat or lay all day—unshorn, collarless, hair on end, eyes wild and hunted, with a hideous imbecile expression on his face. I cannot describe how repulsive he appears—I can hardly bear to stay in the same room with him. . . . I am tempted to believe in that old theory of devil possession. There is an alien personality in Ewan during these attacks. He is an utterly different creature from the man I married. The thought of his hand on me seems like the profanation of a stranger. (*Selected Journals III*, 170)

Eventually, these attacks took Ewan out of the ministry.

But Maud could have borne his black moods if Ewan had been the man she hoped he would be: someone she could really commune with, someone who would share her obsession with beauty, someone who would share her excitement with all that the world had to offer, someone widely read who could discuss ideas and concepts on the many subjects she was interested in, someone who would appreciate her, love her, nurture her. Instead, she belatedly sensed that he was inwardly jealous of her, that he did not like to see her get public recognition and apparently did not even appreciate the years of faithful service on his behalf, when she carried him through his dark periods by taking up the slack for him and working twice as hard. He even left the children's upbringing to her. She had hoped they would raise them as a team.

Had Maud known Ewan's dark secret, she probably wouldn't have married him. Yet she could not bring herself to castigate him. After all, she had gone into the marriage with her eyes open, and he had given her the children. But . . . *oh,* how lonely she was!

Leaskdale

Now that we have dealt with the war, with Frede's untimely death, with the Page trial, and with Ewan's dark secret, it is time to go back and pick up the thread of Maud's personal and literary life where we left off: with the outbreak of the war in August 1914.

Only three months later, on November 20, Maud completed her third Anne book—originally titled *Anne of Redmond* but changed by Page editors to *Anne of the Island*; the book featured Anne's college years. Never had Maud written a book under greater stress than this one: pregnancy, the death of little Hugh, and now the death of her world in war.

By March 1915, she was pregnant again. When August 13 came around again, Maud was troubled. A year ago, she had lost Hugh. Would it happen again? And what about her? She was almost forty-one, too old to be tempting fate this way. But on October 7, Ewan Stuart was born, and his lusty wails brought a smile to Maud's face—*This one would live!*

The fifteen years at the Leaskdale manse were the most productive of Maud's life. Here her three children were born, two surviving. Chester and Stuart would spend their childhood and adolescence here. It was also the most successful and long-lasting of Ewan's pastorates; and Maud brought so much to her role as minister's wife that, had it not been for the Canadian Presbyterian Church schism, quite possibly they might have remained in Leaskdale for the rest of their lives—or at least until Ewan's psychiatric problems made it imperative that he take early retirement.

In December 1917, Maud received the sad news that her dear uncle John of Park Corner, one of the mainstays of her life—the uncle she had always loved best—was dead. Never could she remember, even once, hearing him speak a harsh word. But it wasn't just Uncle John's death that left her world a colder, lonelier place in which to live. Three years later, in the spring of 1920, Pensie, one of the closest and dearest of all her Macneill cousins, who had married two years after her, died of tuberculosis, at least partly the result of overwork. This was followed by a loss closer to home: Daffy, at fourteen years of age, was shot by a local hunter. His death caused intense anguish for Maud, because Daffy represented the last living link to her old world. Furthermore, "Daffy was not a cat—he was a *person*, and had more individuality than seven out of ten human beings" (*Selected Journals II*, 388). His death hurt all the more because Frede had so adored Daffy, so his leaving took an additional part of her with him.

These deaths reminded Maud of just how fragile life was, and not wanting to leave her final resting place to chance, she decided during her summer visit to Cavendish in 1923 to pick just the right spot in the cemetery. When she found it, she felt it had all been predestined. While there, she stumbled on one of the most beautiful gray kittens she had ever seen. Feeling she could do with an extra supply of that commodity, she named him "Good Luck"—"Luck" for short. Luck turned out to be the most lovable and personality-plus cat she had ever known, bringing into her life renewed joy, laughter, and love.

Another year brought yet another sorrow: the death of Aunt Annie. Aunt Annie's passing was one of the bitterest sorrows Maud experienced in her life. She was the only aunt who had been there for her, *at all times,* as far back as she could remember. Her visits to Park Corner would never be the same without Aunt Annie rushing out of the house to meet her.

Meanwhile, technologically the world continued to change at a dizzying rate. The Macdonalds bought their first nonhorse transportation, "Dodgie" (Maud *had* to name everything), and Dodgie had many successors. On August 15, 1917, the family motored to Lake Simcoe to see an airplane. Maud wrote about the experience in her journal: "It is all very wonderful. But will humanity be any the *happier* because of aeroplanes? It seems to me that the *sum* of human happiness remains much the same from age to age, however it may vary in distribution, and that all the 'many inventions' neither lessen nor increase it. After all, 'the kingdom of heaven is within you' " (*Selected Journals II,* 223).

By the mid-twenties, radio was the rage. Although she labeled it "wonderful," Maud sighed for the "slower days of old." In a generation or two, she prophesied, letters would probably be extinct. After all, none of these many inventions would actually *save* time—"only fill it more breathlessly full" (*Selected Journals III,* 105).

In June 1916, Maud began writing *Anne's House of Dreams,* her fourth Anne book. It was good, at least for several hours a day, for her to enter a quieter world. But Chester begrudged her even this time as she wrote in the parlor, the only door he couldn't open: "There are moving stories about little hands pushing flowers under the closed dining-room door to get the attention of [his] busy mother" (*Writing a Life,* 62). Her pattern was to write steadily for two hours every morning, then dedicate the rest of the day to her family, church work, and war efforts. This new book was more complex than any before it and incorporated quite a bit of the trauma she was experiencing. She finished it in record time—on October 5; it was the first book her new publisher, Stokes, would handle.

Maud began her fifth Anne book, *Rainbow Valley,* in August of the following year, 1917, finishing it on December 18. The wartime minister's family in it mirrored her own, both in light and shadow. By now she was getting tired of sequels!

The year 1919 was a difficult one for Maud. Her beloved Frede had died on January 25, and a few months later, Ewan had had his breakdown and confessed his terrible secret. But life must go on. Terribly lonely for Frede that spring, Maud began her sixth Anne book, *Rilla of Ingleside*, finishing it on August 4. There are similarities to Frede in the portrayal of Rilla, Anne's daughter. Maud poured all the anguish and heroism of the war into the story. John McRae's famous poem "In Flanders Fields" undergirds this deeply moving book, one of the most powerful stories to come out of the Great War. It described the war—not as men experienced it in the trenches—but as women experienced it, dying inwardly of uncertainty and fear in the homeland and powerless to do anything about it. That Christmas—the first without Frede—was the saddest and dreariest Maud had ever experienced.

Stirring within Maud was a new heroine: Emily. She had long yearned to write a book more geared to adults. Actually, Emily was not new, but had been born in her mind years before. With Emily, Maud at last dared to see her own self three-dimensionally. The Story Girl was the middle step between Anne and Emily. As Maud had been rereading her journal, she had begun to see, before her eyes, as with a negative in a developing tray (she loved photography, by the way, and was very good at it), her own development as a *person*. Emily would be Maud, as revealed in fiction. All the frustrations she endured as a sensitive child in love with beauty and ideas at the hands of rigid adult autocrats, she poured out into the imagining that always preceded the actual writing. Feeling energized at the prospect of writing a new book, Maud began working on *Emily of New Moon*. "It ought to be good. 'Emily' is a dear little soul and I have some good experiences waiting for her. And it is such a relief to be done of the 'Anne gang.' I had gone so stale on them" (*Selected Journals III*, 16).

Early in 1922, responding to British critics who sneered at what they called "sentiment" in her books (most recently in her just published book, *Rilla of Ingleside),* Maud lambasted them where it hurt least—*in her journal:* "Can't they see that civilization is founded on and held together by sentiment? Passion is transient and quite as often destructive as not. Sentiment remains and binds. . . . But my books are not sentimental. I have always tried in them to register normal and ordinary emotions—not merely passionate or unique episodes" (*Selected Journals III*, 37).

On February 15, 1922, she finished *Emily of New Moon:* "It is the best book I have ever written—and I have had more intense pleasure in writing it than any of the others—not even excepting *Green Gables*. I have *lived* it, and I hated to pen the last line and write *finis*. Of course, I'll have to write several sequels. . . . They cannot be to me what this book has been" (*Selected Journals III*, 39).

On July 20, Stokes asked her to send him the manuscript of her new book. So she lovingly packed *Emily* up and sent it off: ". . . dear little 'Emily' whom I love far better than I ever loved 'Anne.' I felt as if I were sending part of myself. Will she win a welcome?" (*Selected Journals III*, 61).

By August 19, *Emily of New Moon* was out. Maud thought the cover design to be the prettiest yet; and, miracle of miracles, the little girl actually looked like her inner perception of Emily. But the artist should have gone back to nature school: His moon was an *old* moon—not a new one! (*Selected Journals III*, 147).

Emily's story continued to evolve during 1924. One of Maud's own attributes, she built into the Emily saga: the *flash*. A *flash* is something very like an epiphany—a moment of deep, rare, and even heart-stopping insight into life. But Emily's *flashes* are more limited than that. They have to do with such intense beauty that the heart cannot hold it all. Maud had experienced a flash near Cavendish on August 4, 1923: ". . . rapture so poignant that I wrung my hands with the exquisite pain of it" (*Selected Journals III*, 139). On January 20, 1924, she finished *Emily Climbs*. She acknowledged in her journal that "of course" it wasn't as good as the first one. As for her title—selected almost two months later—she labeled it "a vile title, but the only one I can think of which includes 'Emily's' name" (*Selected Journals III*, 168).

Having watered down Emily enough for the time being, Maud now turned to a project she had always wanted to tackle—an adult novel. This title she *did* know from the first: *The Blue Castle*. As she wrote it, her own health suffered just as is true of her heroine Valancy. Rubio and Waterston note that the novel is significant as well because it launches Montgomery's first "convincing male character, Barney Snaith." The book is her first to be set in Ontario, in the Muskoka district, a beautiful retreat Maud loved to escape to for vacations (*Writing a Life*, 79–80).

Maud finished *The Blue Castle* on February 8, 1925, labeling it "a little comedy for adults" (*Selected Journals III*, 218). Immediately, she began work on her third Emily book. It was tough going, as Ewan was again in one of his hideous bouts of depression. She now called them "the *horrors*." On August 15, *Emily Climbs*, her twelfth book, came out. She also began thinking about a new heroine, Marigold, like the flower she so loved. Two days before Christmas 1925, a call from Norval, Ontario, came through, asking Ewan to become the town's pastor. Ewan accepted the offer.

Oh, how Maud hated to begin 1926 by leaving the manse her family had lived in for fifteen years. January 16 was moving day. As she gazed around the now-empty parlor, Maud cried. In this room she had wrestled into life *The Golden Road, The Watchman, Anne's House of Dreams, Rainbow Valley, Rilla of Ingleside, Emily of New Moon, Emily Climbs,* and *The Blue Castle.* And not far away—and hardest of all to leave—was the grave of little Hugh.

Norval

Norval was a beautiful little town, complete with a lovely church, a double echo, the scenic Credit River, and a bigger, more commodious manse with something that Maud had almost despaired of ever having: a fireplace.

Unlike Leaskdale, Norval came equipped with something else she had desired for many years: a local kindred spirit. Near the manse was the estate of a wealthy factory owner, E. Y. Barraclough. His wife, one of their parishioners, would become one of Maud's dearest friends and would often go on vacations with the Macdonald family.

Other friends began to come back into Maud's life. Forty years from the time a wide-eyed girl boarded a transcontinental train for the Northwest Territory, Maud returned to Prince Albert to visit Laura Pritchard (now Agnew). The meeting was rapturous; the years slipped away, and they picked up where they had left off. Maud was also able to meet her long-time correspondent Ephraim Weber. Then Nora Lefurgey (now Campbell) moved to Toronto, and soon the two were giggling about life on the Island and the people they knew there so many years before.

One summer day in 1927, Maud received a personal invitation to meet H.R.H. The Prince of Wales, as well as Prime Minister Stanley Baldwin, at the Government House on August 6. The sun was broiling that afternoon, and the long line of guests crawled along inches at a time. Finally, an aide-de-camp came up to Maud, asking if she was Mrs. Macdonald; he said that Baldwin wanted to meet her.

Edward, Prince of Wales, looked bored as he greeted his guests, but Prince George was very congenial and likable. (King Edward VIII would go on to abdicate the throne in order to marry Wallis Simpson, and George would become king by default.) Prime Minister Baldwin told Maud that he adored her books and that they brought him much pleasure. Maud was amazed at how impressed everyone was by her receiving such recognition. By that summer, Maud's growing fame was beginning to alter life on the Island, as growing numbers of tourists began searching for their favorite "Avonlea" sites. Already a rivalry was developing between the protective dragons of the two "Lakes of Shining Waters."

Meanwhile, Stokes wrote Maud, telling her that *The Blue Castle* was doing so well that he wondered if she could write another adult novel in the same vein. She had been hoping he would ask because she already had one in mind—it would be titled *The Tangled Web* and would involve a wealthy old woman who would tangle up her entire family by setting forces in motion that would radically change all the familial relationships.

As a result of the reappearance of her old Island friend Nora Lefurgey, and the incidents and people they would remember each time they got together, Maud was able to ignite an otherwise cold plot and complete *Pat of Silverbush.* The heart of the story is none other than the dear old Park Corner house of Uncle John and Aunt Annie, overlooking the Lake of Shining Waters. On January 15, 1934, Maud began on the Pat sequel, *Mistress Pat.* She was also gathering material for yet another Anne book, *Anne of Windy Poplars.* Because Maud had reached back into the past and sandwiched *Anne of Windy Poplars* between *Anne of the Island* and *Anne's House of Dreams,* the story did not have a complex plot. In its place is a device that writers such as Maud and Annie Hamilton Donnell used well: Each chapter served as a short story, complete in itself and loosely connected for overall effect.

By and large, the eight years at Norval were productive ones for Maud. *Emily's Quest,* the last Emily book, was published shortly after the Macdonalds moved there; *Magic for Marigold* was published in 1929 (Maud had hoped to someday write a sequel to it but never did); *A Tangled Web* was published in 1931, and *Pat of Silverbush* shortly after that; and then the Pat sequel, *Mistress Pat,* in 1935.

Journey's End

Thank God, I can keep the shadows of my life out of my work. I would not wish to darken any other life— I want instead to be a messenger of optimism and sunshine.

—L. M. Montgomery, *Selected Journals I,* 339

Like a heart-stopping explosion of fireworks at the end of a holiday evening, so now Maud's swan song filled her inner skies with dramatic color. *Jane of Lantern Hill,* for instance, was a totally new character. Part of its vibrancy had to do with Maud's own last move, made necessary by Ewan's condition and lost pastorate in Norval. She had always loved Toronto, so here is where her search for the house of her dreams centered. The idea was exhilarating: For the first and only time in her life, she could choose her own house: "Within a few days she was peering in through the windows of a dream house—at 210 Riverside Drive. Set right on the Humber River, at the western edge of Toronto, with a pine-graced ravine and a distant view of Lake Ontario, the handsome pseudo-Tudor house appeared as a welcome journey's end" (*Writing a Life*, 102). It was a period of hope, for the 1934 RKO movie *Anne of Green Gables* had resulted in increased interest in all of Maud's books.

Her own joy in the house of her dreams is incorporated into the fabric of *Jane of Lantern Hill*, for Jane glories in just such a house twice: once on the Island, and once near Toronto. But first, as is often true in Maud's books, the heroine must endure extended suffering before being able to enjoy the fruits of the Promised Land (Gillen, 148; *Writing a Life*, 100–103).

But Maud's dream house was doomed. After a brief Indian summer of joy, storm clouds again gathered about her. First, Chester's ever-troubled marriage stumbled toward divorce, a step that Maud had always viewed as a tragedy. She could not understand this new generation that took marriage so lightly, for it flew in the face of everything she had lived and written for. Second, Ewan's oscillation between sanity and insanity had become more than her nervous system could handle. Third, Luck, the one constant presence and source of love for thirteen years, died, leaving her feeling destitute. Fourth, her restored soul mate, Laura Pritchard, died. Fifth, financial pressures, brought about by the huge mortgage payments on the new house, payment of Stuart's and Chester's university fees, as well as failure of friends and family to repay loans, became overwhelming for her. Sixth, and worst of all, the world was slipping into another holocaust, again spawned by Germany, only this time by a twisted Austrian named Hitler.

Maud still went through the motions, however, gathering the last shreds of her energy together in order to write and complete her eighth and last Anne book, *Anne of Ingleside*. As she tried to write, Ewan "talked to himself, couldn't remember how to dress himself, and sat for days with hair bristling, blue underlip hanging down, eyes glaring, face livid" (*Writing a Life*, 110). The book, involving a lost relationship that ends up being restored, is the supreme example of Maud's ability to ignore the tragedy in her own life as she wrote a book portraying joy and happiness 180 degrees away.

Soon it became clear that it was all too much: No longer could Maud's resilient nervous system handle such a circuit overload. Not even her being elected to the Literary and Art Institute of France or being made a Companion of the Order of the British Empire by King George VI could possibly compensate. In 1938, she suffered a severe nervous breakdown but struggled valiantly to the end of *Anne of Ingleside* and the gathering of stories for *The Road to Yesterday*.

In 1941 Maud wrote one final letter to her pen pal MacMillan; to her other pen pal, Weber, she sighed, "I do not think I will ever recover" (Bolger, 218). Then, on April 24, 1942, she sank gradually into that last sleep, wracked with the pain not only of her own suffering but also that of World War II. Ewan would outlive her only until the following year.

On Wednesday, April 28, 1942, Maud was brought home to her beloved Island by Ewan, Chester, and Stuart—and there she lay in state in Green Gables, the house (the David and Margaret Macneill house) she had made famous around the world. After the short funeral service, she was buried on the crest of the hill overlooking Green Gables—the spot she herself had selected nineteen years before.

> I want to be buried in Cavendish graveyard when my time comes. I want to lie among my kindred in the old spot I love so much better than any other spot on earth. . . . Here only can I rest at last—here it is fitting I should be buried. And it is fitting that Ewan should rest here, too. . . .
>
> I selected a plot on the crest of the hill, looking down on the beautiful scene I always loved—the pond, the shore, the sand-dunes, the harbor. . . . There, sometime I shall lie and the wind will creep up from the sea to sing over me and the old gulf will croon me a lullaby. (*Selected Journals III*, 138–39)

— — —

> Then whisper, blossom, in thy sleep
>   How I may upward climb
> The Alpine path, so hard, so steep,
>   That leads to heights sublime;
> How I may reach that far-off goal
>   Of true and honoured fame,
> And write upon its shining scroll
>   A woman's humble name.

— — —

—Joseph Leininger Wheeler, Ph.D.
The Grey House
Conifer, Colorado

The Works of Lucy Maud Montgomery

1908   *Anne of Green Gables* (Page, Boston); Anne #1

1909   *Anne of Avonlea* (Page, Boston); Anne #2

1910   *Kilmeny of the Orchard* (Page, Boston)

1911   *The Story Girl* (Page, Boston); Story Girl #1

1912   *Chronicles of Avonlea* (Page, Boston)

1913   *The Golden Road* (Page, Boston); Story Girl #2

1915   *Anne of the Island* (Page, Boston); Anne #3

1916   *The Watchman and Other Poems* (McClelland and Stewart, Boston)

1917   *Anne's House of Dreams* (Stokes, New York); Anne #4

1919   *Rainbow Valley* (Stokes, New York); Anne #5

1920   *Further Chronicles of Avonlea* (Page, Boston)

1921   *Rilla of Ingleside* (Stokes, New York); Anne #6

1923   *Emily of New Moon* (Stokes, New York); Emily #1

1925   *Emily Climbs* (Stokes, New York); Emily #2

1926   *The Blue Castle* (Stokes, New York); first adult book

1927   *Emily's Quest* (Stokes, New York); Emily #3

1929   *Magic for Marigold* (Stokes, New York); only Marigold book

1931   *A Tangled Web* (Stokes, New York); second adult book

1933   *Pat of Silverbush* (Stokes, New York); Pat #1

1935   *Mistress Pat* (Stokes, New York); Pat #2

1936   *Anne of Windy Poplars* (Stokes, New York); Anne #7

1937   *Jane of Lantern Hill* (Stokes, New York); only Jane book

1939   *Anne of Ingleside* (Stokes, New York); Anne #8

1960   *The Green Gables Letters from L. M. Montgomery to Ephraim Weber* (ed. Wilfred Eggleston; McGraw-Hill Ryerson, Toronto)

1974   *The Road to Yesterday* (McGraw-Hill Ryerson, Toronto)

1975   *The Alpine Path: The Story of My Career* (first published in *Everywoman's World,* June–Nov. 1917; Fitzhenry & Whiteside, Don Mills, Ontario)

1979   *The Doctor's Sweetheart and Other Stories* (ed. Catherine McClay; McGraw-Hill Ryerson, Toronto)

1980   *My Dear Mr. M.: Letters to G. B. MacMillan* (ed. Francis W. P. Bolger and Elizabeth Epperly; McGraw-Hill Ryerson, Toronto)

1985   *Selected Journals of L. M. Montgomery,* Vol. I: *1889–1910* (ed. Mary Rubio and Elizabeth Waterston; Oxford University Press, Toronto)

1987   *Selected Journals of L. M. Montgomery,* Vol. II: *1910–1921* (ed. Mary Rubio and Elizabeth Waterston; Oxford University Press, Toronto)

   Akin to Anne: Tales of Other Orphans (ed. Rea Wilmhurst; McClelland & Stewart, Toronto)

   The Poetry of Lucy Maud Montgomery (ed. John Ferns and Kevin McCabe; Fitzhenry & Whiteside, Don Mills, Ontario)

1989   *Along the Shore: Tales by the Sea* (ed. Rea Wilmhurst; McClelland & Stewart, Toronto)

1990   *Among the Shadows: Tales from the Darker Side* (ed. Rea Wilmhurst; McClelland & Stewart, Toronto)

1991   *After Many Days: Tales of Time Passed* (ed. Rea Wilmhurst; McClelland & Stewart, Toronto)

PROLOGUE

I was born in the little village of Clifton, Prince Edward Island. "Old Prince Edward Island" is a good place in which to be born—a good place in which to spend a childhood. I can think of none better. . . .

Prince Edward Island . . . is really a beautiful Province—the most beautiful place in America, I believe. Elsewhere are more lavish landscapes and grander scenery, but for chaste, restful loveliness it is unsurpassed. "Compassed by the inviolate sea," it floats on the waves of the blue gulf, a green seclusion and "haunt of ancient peace."

Much of the beauty of the Island is due to the vivid colour contrasts— the rich red of the winding roads, the brilliant emerald of the uplands and meadows, the glowing sapphire of the encircling sea. It is the sea which makes Prince Edward Island in more senses than the geographical. You cannot get away from the sea down there. Save for a few places in the interior, it is ever visible somewhere, if only in a tiny blue gap between distant hills, or a turquoise gleam through the dark boughs of spruce fringing an estuary. Great is our love for it; its tang gets into our blood; its siren call rings ever in our ears; no matter where we wander in lands afar, the murmur of its waves ever summons us back in our dreams to the homeland. . . .

And yet we cannot define the charm of Prince Edward Island in terms of land or sea. It is too elusive—too subtle. Sometimes I have thought it was the touch of austerity in an Island landscape that gives it its peculiar charm. And whence comes that austerity? Is it in the dark dappling of spruce and fir? Is it in the glimpses of sea and river? Is it in the bracing tang of the salt air? Or does it go deeper still, down to the very soul of the land? For lands have personality just as well as human beings; and to know that personality you must live in the land and companion it, and draw sustenance of body and spirit from it; so only can you really know a land and be known of it.

—L. M. Montgomery, *The Alpine Path*, 11

Chapter 1
MRS. RACHEL LYNDE
IS SURPRISED

Mrs. Rachel Lynde lived just where the Avonlea main road dipped down into a little hollow, fringed with alders and ladies' eardrops and traversed by a brook that had its source away back in the woods of the old Cuthbert place. It was reputed to be an intricate, headlong brook in its earlier course through those woods, with dark secrets of pool and cascade; but by the time it reached Lynde's Hollow it was a quiet, well-conducted little stream, for not even a brook could run past Mrs. Rachel Lynde's door without due regard for decency and decorum. It probably was conscious that Mrs. Rachel was sitting at her window, keeping a sharp eye on everything that passed, from brooks and children up, and that if she noticed anything odd or out of place she would never rest until she had ferreted out the whys and wherefores thereof.

There are plenty of people, in Avonlea and out of it, who can attend closely to their neighbours' business by dint of neglecting their own; but Mrs. Rachel Lynde was one of those capable creatures who can manage their own concerns and those of other folks into the bargain. She was a notable housewife; her work was always done and well done; she "ran" the Sewing Circle, helped run the Sunday school, and was the strongest prop of the Church Aid Society and Foreign Missions Auxiliary. Yet with all this Mrs. Rachel found abundant time to sit for hours at her kitchen window, knitting "cotton warp" quilts—she had knitted sixteen of them, as Avonlea housekeepers were wont to tell in awed voices—and keeping a sharp eye on the main road that crossed the hollow and wound up the steep red hill beyond. Since Avonlea occupied a little triangular peninsula jutting out into the Gulf of St. Lawrence, with water on two sides of it, anybody who went out of it or into it had to pass over that hill road and so run the unseen gauntlet of Mrs. Rachel's all-seeing eye.

She was sitting there one afternoon in early June. The sun was coming in at the window, warm and bright; the orchard on the slope below the house was in a bridal flush of pinky-white bloom, hummed over by a myriad of bees. Thomas Lynde—a meek little man whom Avonlea people called "Rachel Lynde's husband"—was sowing his late turnip seed on the hill field beyond the barn; and Matthew Cuthbert ought to have been sowing his on the big red brook field away over by Green Gables. Mrs. Rachel knew that he ought because she had heard him tell Peter Morrison the evening before in William J. Blair's store over at Carmody that he meant to sow his turnip seed the next afternoon. Peter had asked him, of course, for Matthew Cuthbert had never been known to volunteer information about anything in his whole life.

And yet here was Matthew Cuthbert, at half-past three on the afternoon of a busy day, placidly driving over the hollow and up the hill; moreover, he wore a white collar and his best suit of clothes, which was plain proof that he was going out of Avonlea; and he had the buggy and the sorrel mare, which betokened that he was going a considerable distance. Now, where was Matthew Cuthbert going, and why was he going there?

Had it been any other man in Avonlea, Mrs. Rachel, deftly putting this and that together, might have given a pretty good guess as to both questions. But Matthew so rarely went from home that it must be something pressing and unusual that was taking him; he was the shyest man alive and hated to have to go among strangers or to any place where he might have to talk. Matthew, dressed up with a white collar and driving in a buggy, was something that didn't happen often. Mrs. Rachel, ponder as she might, could make nothing of it and her afternoon's enjoyment was spoiled.

"I'll just step over to Green Gables after tea and find out from Marilla where he's gone and why," the worthy woman finally concluded. "He doesn't generally go to town this time of year and he *never* visits; if he'd run out of turnip seed, he wouldn't dress up and take the buggy to go for more; he wasn't driving fast enough to be going for the doctor. Yet something must have happened since last night to start him off. I'm clean puzzled, that's what, and I won't know a minute's peace of mind or conscience until I know what has taken Matthew Cuthbert out of Avonlea today."

Accordingly, after tea Mrs. Rachel set out. She had not far to go; the big, rambling, orchard-embowered house where the Cuthberts lived was a scant quarter of a mile up the road from Lynde's Hollow. To be sure, the long lane made it a good deal farther. Matthew Cuthbert's father, as shy and silent as his son after him, had got as far away as he possibly could from his fellowmen without actually retreating into the woods when he founded his homestead. Green Gables was built at the farthest edge of his cleared land and there it was to this day, barely visible from the main road along which all the other Avonlea houses were so sociably situated. Mrs. Rachel Lynde did not call living in such a place *living* at all.

"It's just *staying*, that's what," she said as she stepped along the deep-rutted, grassy lane bordered with wild rose bushes. "It's no wonder Matthew and Marilla are both a little odd, living away back here by themselves. Trees aren't much company, though dear knows if they were there'd be enough of them. I'd rather look at people. To be sure, they seem contented enough; but then, I suppose, they're used to it. A body can get used to anything, even to being hanged, as the Irishman said."

With this Mrs. Rachel stepped out of the lane into the backyard of Green Gables. Very green and neat and precise was that yard, set about on one side with great patriarchal willows and on the other with prim Lombardies. Not a stray stick nor stone was to be seen, for Mrs. Rachel would have seen it if there had been. Privately, she was of the opinion that Marilla Cuthbert swept that yard over as often as she swept her house. One could have eaten a meal off the ground without overbrimming the proverbial peck of dirt.

Mrs. Rachel rapped smartly at the kitchen door and stepped in when bidden to do so. The kitchen at Green Gables was a cheerful apartment—or would have been cheerful if it had not been so painfully clean as to give it something of the appearance of an unused parlour. Its windows looked east and west; through the west one, looking out on the backyard, came a flood of mellow June sunlight; but the east one, whence you got a glimpse of the bloom white cherry trees in the left orchard and nodding, slender birches down in the hollow by the brook, was greened over by a tangle of vines. Here sat Marilla Cuthbert, when she sat at all, always slightly distrustful of sunshine, which seemed to her too dancing and irresponsible a thing for a world that was meant to be taken seriously; and here she sat now, knitting, and the table behind her was laid for supper.

Mrs. Rachel, before she had fairly closed the door, had taken mental note of everything that was on that table. There were three plates laid, so that Marilla must be expecting someone home with Matthew to tea; but the dishes were everyday dishes and there was only crab apple preserves and one kind of cake, so that the expected company could not be any particular company. Yet what of Matthew's white collar and the sorrel mare? Mrs. Rachel was getting fairly dizzy with this unusual mystery about quiet, unmysterious Green Gables.

"Good evening, Rachel," Marilla said briskly. "This is a real fine evening, isn't it? Won't you sit down? How are all your folks?"

Something that for lack of any other name might be called friendship existed and always had existed between Marilla Cuthbert and Mrs. Rachel, in spite of—or perhaps because of—their dissimilarity.

Marilla was a tall, thin woman, with angles and without curves; her dark hair showed some gray streaks and was always twisted up in a hard little knot behind with two wire hairpins stuck aggressively through it. She looked like a woman of narrow experience and rigid conscience, which she was; but there was a saving something about her mouth that, if it had been ever so slightly developed, might have been considered indicative of a sense of humour.

"We're all pretty well," said Mrs. Rachel. "I was kind of afraid *you* weren't, though, when I saw Matthew starting off today. I thought maybe he was going to the doctor's."

Marilla's lips twitched understandingly. She had expected Mrs. Rachel up; she had known that the sight of Matthew jaunting off so unaccountably would be too much for her neighbor's curiosity.

"Oh, no, I'm quite well, although I had a bad headache yesterday," she said. "Matthew went to Bright River. We're getting a little boy from an orphan asylum in Nova Scotia and he's coming on the train tonight."

If Marilla had said that Matthew had gone to Bright River to meet a kangaroo from Australia, Mrs. Rachel could not have been more astonished. She was actually stricken dumb for five seconds. It was unsupposable that Marilla was making fun of her, but Mrs. Rachel was almost forced to suppose it.

"Are you in earnest, Marilla?" she demanded when her voice returned to her.

"Yes, of course," said Marilla, as if getting boys from orphan asylums in Nova Scotia were part of the usual spring work on any well-regulated Avonlea farm instead of being an unheard-of innovation.

Mrs. Rachel felt that she had received a severe mental jolt. She thought in exclamation points. *A boy! Marilla and Matthew Cuthbert of all people adopting a boy! From an orphan asylum! Well, the world is certainly turning upside down! I will be surprised at nothing after this! Nothing!*

"What on earth put such a notion into your head?" she demanded disapprovingly.

This had been done without her advice being asked and must perforce be disapproved.

"Well, we've been thinking about it for some time—all winter in fact," returned Marilla. "Mrs. Alexander Spencer was up here one day before Christmas and she said she was going to get a little girl from the asylum over in Hopetown in the spring. Her cousin lives there, and Mrs. Spencer has visited her and knows all about it. So Matthew and I have talked it over off and on ever since. We thought we'd get a boy. Matthew is getting up in years, you know—he's sixty—and he isn't so spry as he once was. His heart troubles him a good deal. And you know how desperate hard it's got to be to get hired help. There's never anybody to be had but those stupid, half-grown little French boys; and as soon as you do get one broke into your ways and taught something, he's up and off to the lobster canneries or the States. At first Matthew suggested getting a Barnado boy. But I said 'no' flat to that. 'They may be all right—I'm not saying they're not—but no London street Arabs for me,' I said. 'Give me a native born at least. There'll be a risk, no matter who we get. But I'll feel easier in my mind and sleep sounder at nights if we get a born Canadian.' So in the end we decided to ask Mrs. Spencer to pick us out one when she went over to get her little girl. We heard last week she was going, so we sent her word by Richard Spencer's folks at Carmody to bring us a smart, likely boy of about ten or eleven. We decided that would be the best age—old enough to be of some use in doing chores right off and young enough to be trained up proper. We mean to give him a good home and schooling. We had a telegram from Mrs. Alexander Spencer today—the mailman brought it from the station—saying they were coming on the five-thirty train tonight. So Matthew went to Bright River to meet him. Mrs. Spencer will drop him off there. Of course she goes on to White Sands station herself."

Mrs. Rachel prided herself on always speaking her mind; she proceeded to speak it now, having adjusted her mental attitude to this amazing piece of news.

"Well, Marilla, I'll just tell you plain that I think you're doing a mighty foolish thing—a risky thing, that's what. You don't know what you're getting. You're bringing a strange child into your house and home and you don't know a single thing about him nor what his disposition is like nor what sort of parents he had nor how he's likely to turn out. Why, it was only last week I read in the paper how a man and his wife up west of the Island took a boy out of an orphan asylum and he set fire to the house at night—set it *on purpose*, Marilla—and nearly burnt them to a crisp in their beds. And I know another case where an adopted boy used to suck the eggs—they couldn't break him of it. If you had asked my advice in the matter—which you didn't do, Marilla—I'd have said for mercy's sake not to think of such a thing, that's what."

This Job's comforting seemed neither to offend nor alarm Marilla. She knitted steadily on.

"I don't deny there's something in what you say, Rachel. I've had some qualms myself. But Matthew was terrible set on it. I could see that, so I gave in. It's so seldom Matthew sets his mind on anything that when he does I always feel it's my duty to give in. And as for the risk, there's risks in pretty near everything a body does in this world. There's risks in people's having children of their own if it comes to that—they don't always turn out well. And then Nova Scotia is right close to the Island. It isn't as if we were getting him from England or the States. He can't be much different from ourselves."

"Well, I hope it will turn out all right," said Mrs. Rachel in a tone that plainly indicated her painful doubts. "Only don't say I didn't warn you if he burns Green Gables down or puts strychnine in the well—I heard of a case over in New Brunswick where an orphan asylum child did that and the whole family died in fearful agonies. Only, it was a girl in that instance."

"Well, we're not getting a girl," said Marilla, as if poisoning wells were a purely feminine accomplishment and not to be dreaded in the case of a boy. "I'd never dream of taking a girl to bring up. I wonder at Mrs. Alexander Spencer for doing it. But there, *she* wouldn't shrink from adopting a whole orphan asylum if she took it into her head."

Mrs. Rachel would have liked to stay until Matthew came home with his imported orphan. But reflecting that it would be a good two hours at least before his arrival she concluded to go up the road to Robert Bell's and tell them the news. It would certainly make a sensation second to none, and Mrs. Rachel dearly loved to make a sensation. So she took herself away, somewhat to Marilla's relief, for the latter felt her doubts and fears reviving under the influence of Mrs. Rachel's pessimism.

"Well, of all things that ever were or will be!" exclaimed Mrs. Rachel when she was safely out in the lane. "It does really seem as if I must be dreaming. Well, I'm sorry for that poor young one and no mistake. Matthew and Marilla don't know anything about children and they'll expect him to be wiser and steadier than his own grandfather, if so be's he ever had a grandfather, which is doubtful. It seems uncanny to think of a child at Green Gables somehow; there's never been one there, for

Matthew and Marilla were grown up when the new house was built—
if they ever *were* children, which is hard to believe when one looks at
them. I wouldn't be in that orphan's shoes for anything. My, but I pity
him, that's what."

So said Mrs. Rachel to the wild rose bushes out of the fullness of her
heart; but if she could have seen the child who was waiting patiently at
the Bright River station at that very moment, her pity would have been
still deeper and more profound.

Chapter 2

MATTHEW CUTHBERT IS SURPRISED

Matthew Cuthbert and the sorrel mare jogged comfortably over the eight miles to Bright River. It was a pretty road, running along between snug farmsteads, with now and again a bit of balsamy fir wood to drive through or a hollow where wild plums hung out their filmy bloom. The air was sweet with the breath of many apple orchards, and the meadows sloped away in the distance to horizon mists of pearl and purple; while "the little birds sang as if it were / the one day of summer in all the year."

Matthew enjoyed the drive after his own fashion, except during the moments when he met women and had to nod to them—for on Prince Edward Island, you are supposed to nod to all and sundry you meet on the road whether you know them or not.

Matthew dreaded all women except Marilla and Mrs. Rachel; he had an uncomfortable feeling that the mysterious creatures were secretly laughing at him. He may have been quite right in thinking so, for he was an odd-looking personage, with an ungainly figure and long iron-gray hair that touched his stooping shoulders, and a full, soft brown beard that he had worn ever since he was twenty. In fact, he had looked at twenty very much as he looked at sixty, lacking a little of the grayness.

When he reached Bright River, there was no sign of any train. He thought he was too early, so he tied his horse in the yard of the small Bright River hotel and went over to the station house. The long platform was almost deserted; the only living creature in sight being a girl who was sitting on a pile of shingles at the extreme end. Matthew, barely noting that it *was* a girl, sidled past her as quickly as possible without looking at her. Had he looked, he could hardly have failed to notice the tense rigidity and expectation of her attitude and expression. She was sitting there waiting for something or somebody and, since sitting and waiting was the

9

only thing to do just then, she sat and waited with all her might and main.

Matthew encountered the stationmaster locking up the ticket office preparatory to going home for supper, and he asked him if the five-thirty train would soon be along.

"The five-thirty train has been in and gone half an hour ago," answered that brisk official. "But there was a passenger dropped off for you—a little girl. She's sitting out there on the shingles. I asked her to go into the ladies' waiting room, but she informed me gravely that she preferred to stay outside. 'There is more scope for imagination,' she said. She's a case, I should say."

"I'm not expecting a girl," said Matthew blankly. "It's a boy I've come for. He should be here. Mrs. Alexander Spencer was to bring him over from Nova Scotia for me."

The stationmaster whistled.

"Guess there's some mistake," he said. "Mrs. Spencer came off the train with that girl and gave her into my charge. Said you and your sister were adopting her from an orphan asylum and that you would be along for her presently. That's all *I* know about it—and I haven't got any more orphans concealed hereabouts."

"I don't understand," said Matthew helplessly, wishing that Marilla was at hand to cope with the situation.

"Well, you'd better question the girl," said the stationmaster carelessly. "I dare say she'll be able to explain—she's got a tongue of her own, that's certain. Maybe they were out of boys of the brand you wanted."

He walked jauntily away, being hungry, and the unfortunate Matthew was left to do that which was harder for him than bearding a lion in its den: walk up to a girl—a strange girl—an orphan girl—and demand of her why she wasn't a boy. Matthew groaned in spirit as he turned about and shuffled gently down the platform toward her.

She had been watching him ever since he had passed her and she had her eyes on him now. Matthew was not looking at her and would not have seen what she was really like if he had been, but an ordinary observer would have seen this:

A child of about eleven, garbed in a very short, very tight, very ugly dress of yellowish gray wincey.[1] She wore a faded brown sailor hat, and beneath the hat, extending down her back, were two braids of very thick, decidedly red hair. Her face was small, white, and thin, also much freckled; her mouth was large, and so were her eyes, which looked green in some lights and moods and gray in others.

---

[1] Linsey-woolsey.

So far, the ordinary observer; an extraordinary observer might have seen that the chin was very pointed and pronounced; that the big eyes were full of spirit and vivacity; that the mouth was sweet-lipped and expressive; that the forehead was broad and full. In short, our discerning extraordinary observer might have concluded that no commonplace soul inhabited the body of this stray woman-child of whom shy Matthew Cuthbert was so ludicrously afraid.

Matthew, however, was spared the ordeal of speaking first, for as soon as she concluded that he was coming to her, she stood up, grasping with one thin brown hand the handle of a shabby, old-fashioned carpetbag; the other she held out to him.

"I suppose you are Mr. Matthew Cuthbert of Green Gables?" she said in a peculiarly clear, sweet voice. "I'm very glad to see you. I was beginning to be afraid you weren't coming for me, and I was imagining all the things that might have happened to prevent you. I had made up my mind that if you didn't come for me tonight, I'd go down the track to that big wild cherry tree at the bend and climb up into it to stay all night. I wouldn't be a bit afraid, and it would be lovely to sleep in a wild cherry tree all white with bloom in the moonshine, don't you think? You could imagine you were dwelling in marble halls, couldn't you? And I was quite sure you would come for me in the morning, if you didn't tonight."

Matthew had taken the scrawny little hand awkwardly in his; then and there he decided what to do. He could not tell this child with the glowing eyes that there had been a mistake; he would take her home and let Marilla do that. She couldn't be left at Bright River anyhow, no matter what mistake had been made, so all questions and explanations might as well be deferred until he was safely back at Green Gables.

"I'm sorry I was late," he said shyly. "Come along. The horse is over in the yard. Give me your bag."

"Oh, I can carry it," the child responded cheerfully. "It isn't heavy. I've got all my worldly goods in it, but it isn't heavy. And if it isn't carried in just a certain way, the handle pulls out—so I'd better keep it because I know the exact knack of it. It's an extremely old carpetbag. Oh, I'm very glad you've come, even if it would have been nice to sleep in the wild cherry tree. We've got to drive a long piece, haven't we? Mrs. Spencer said it was eight miles. I'm glad because I love driving. Oh, it seems so wonderful that I'm going to live with you and belong to you. I've never belonged to anybody—not really. But the asylum was the worst. I've only been in four months, but that was enough. I don't suppose you ever were an orphan in an asylum, so you can't possibly understand what it is like.

It's worse than anything you could imagine. Mrs. Spencer said it was wicked of me to talk like that, but I didn't mean to be wicked. It's so easy to be wicked without knowing it, isn't it? They were good, you know—the asylum people. But there is so little scope for the imagination in an asylum—only just in the other orphans. It *was* pretty interesting to imagine things about them—to imagine that perhaps the girl who sat next to you was really the daughter of a belted earl, who had been stolen away from her parents in her infancy by a cruel nurse who died before she could confess. I used to lie awake at nights and imagine things like that, because I didn't have time in the day. I guess that's why I'm so thin—I *am* dreadful thin, ain't I? There isn't a pick on my bones. I do love to imagine I'm nice and plump, with dimples in my elbows."

With this, Matthew's companion stopped talking, partly because she was out of breath and partly because they had reached the buggy. Not another word did she say until they had left the village and were driving down a steep little hill, the road part of which had been cut so deeply into the soft soil that the banks, fringed with blooming wild cherry trees and slim white birches, were several feet above their heads.

The child put out her hand and broke off a branch of wild plum that brushed against the side of the buggy.

"Isn't that beautiful? What did that tree, leaning out from the bank, all white and lacy, make you think of?" she asked.

"Well now, I dunno," said Matthew.

"Why, a bride, of course—a bride all in white with a lovely misty veil. I've never seen one, but I can imagine what she would look like. I don't ever expect to be a bride myself. I'm so homely, nobody will ever want to marry me—unless it might be a foreign missionary. I suppose a foreign missionary mightn't be very particular. But I do hope that some day I shall have a white dress. That is my highest ideal of earthly bliss. I just love pretty clothes. And I've never had a pretty dress in my life that I can remember—but of course it's all the more to look forward to, isn't it? And then I can imagine that I'm dressed gorgeously. This morning when I left the asylum I felt so ashamed because I had to wear this horrid old wincey dress. All the orphans had to wear them, you know. A merchant in Hopeton last winter donated 300 yards of wincey to the asylum. Some people said it was because he couldn't sell it, but I'd rather believe that it was out of the kindness of his heart, wouldn't you? When we got on the train, I felt as if everybody must be looking at me and pitying me. But I just went to work and imagined that I had on the most beautiful pale blue silk dress—because when you *are* imagining, you might as well imagine something worthwhile—and a big hat that's all flowers and nodding plumes, and a gold watch, and kid gloves and boots. I felt cheered up right away, and I enjoyed my trip to the Island with all my might. I wasn't a bit sick coming over in the boat. Neither was Mrs. Spencer, although she generally is. She said she hadn't time to get sick, watching to see that I didn't fall overboard. She said she never saw the beat of me for prowling about. But if it kept her from being seasick, it's a mercy I did prowl, isn't it? And I wanted to see everything that was to be seen on that boat, because I didn't know whether I'd ever have another opportunity. Oh, there are a lot more cherry trees all in bloom! This Island is the bloomiest place. I just love it already, and I'm so glad I'm going to live here. I've always heard that Prince Edward Island was the prettiest place in the world, and I used to imagine I was living here, but I never really expected I would. It's delightful when your imaginations come true, isn't it? But those red roads are so funny. When we got into the train at Charlottetown and the red roads began to flash past, I asked Mrs. Spencer what made them red and she said she didn't know and for pity's sake not to ask her any more questions. She said I must have asked her a thousand already. I suppose I had, too, but how are you going to find out about things if you don't ask questions? And what *does* make the road red?"

"Well now, I dunno," said Matthew.

"Well, that is one of the things to find out sometime. Isn't it splendid to think of all the things there are to find out about? It just makes me feel glad to be alive—it's such an interesting world. It wouldn't be half so interesting if we knew all about everything, would it? There'd be no scope for imagination then, would there? But am I talking too much? People are always telling me I do. Would you rather I didn't talk? If you say so, I'll stop. I *can* stop when I make up my mind to it, although it's difficult."

Matthew, much to his own surprise, was enjoying himself. Like most quiet folks, he liked talkative people when they were willing to do the talking themselves and did not expect him to keep up his end of it. But he had never expected to enjoy the society of a little girl. Women were bad enough in all conscience, but little girls were worse. He detested the way they had of sidling past him timidly, with sidewise glances, as if they expected him to gobble them up at a mouthful if they ventured to say a word. This was the Avonlea type of well-bred little girl. But this freckled witch was very different, and although he found it rather difficult for his slower intelligence to keep up with her brisk mental processes, he thought that he "kind of liked her chatter." So he said as shyly as usual: "Oh, you can talk as much as you like. I don't mind."

"Oh, I'm so glad. I know you and I are going to get along together fine. It's such a relief to talk when one wants to and not be told that children should be seen and not heard. I've had that said to me a million times if I have once. And people laugh at me because I use big words. But if you have big ideas, you have to use big words to express them, haven't you?"

"Well now, that seems reasonable," said Matthew.

"Mrs. Spencer said that my tongue must be hung in the middle. But it isn't—it's firmly fastened at one end. Mrs. Spencer said your place was named Green Gables. I asked her all about it. And she said there were trees all around it. I was gladder than ever. I just love trees. And there weren't any at all about the asylum, only a few poor weeny-teeny things out in front with little whitewashed cagey things about them. They just looked like orphans themselves, those trees did. It used to make me want to cry to look at them. I used to say to them, 'Oh, you *poor* little things! If you were out in a great big woods with other trees all around you and little mosses and Junebells growing over your roots and a brook not far away and birds singing in your branches, you could grow, couldn't you? But you can't where you are. I know just exactly how you feel, little trees.' I felt sorry to leave them behind this morning. You do get so attached to things like that, don't you? Is there a brook anywhere near Green Gables? I forgot to ask Mrs. Spencer that."

"Well now, yes, there's one right below the house."

"Fancy! It's always been one of my dreams to live near a brook. I never expected I would, though. Dreams don't often come true, do they? Wouldn't it be nice if they did? But just now I feel pretty nearly perfectly happy. I can't feel exactly perfectly happy because—well, what colour would you call this?"

She twitched one of her long, glossy braids over her thin shoulder and held it up before Matthew's eyes. Matthew was not used to deciding on the tints of ladies' tresses, but in this case there couldn't be much doubt.

"It's red, ain't it?" he said.

The girl let the braid drop back with a sigh that seemed to come from her very toes and to exhale forth all the sorrows of the ages.

"Yes, it's red," she said resignedly. "Now you see why I can't be perfectly happy. Nobody could who had red hair. I don't mind the other things so much—the freckles and the green eyes and my skinniness. I can imagine them away. I can imagine that I have a beautiful rose-leaf complexion and lovely starry violet eyes. But I *cannot* imagine that red hair away. I do my best. I think to myself, *Now my hair is a glorious black, black as the raven's wing.* But all the time I *know* it is just plain red, and it breaks my heart. It will be my lifelong sorrow. I read of a girl once in a novel who had a lifelong sorrow, but it wasn't red hair. Her hair was pure gold rippling back from her alabaster brow. What is an alabaster brow? I never could find out. Can you tell me?"

"Well now, I'm afraid I can't," said Matthew, who was getting a little dizzy. He felt as he had once felt in his rash youth when another boy had enticed him on the merry-go-round at a picnic.

"Well, whatever it was it must have been something nice because she was divinely beautiful. Have you ever imagined what it must feel like to be divinely beautiful?"

"Well now, no, I haven't," confessed Matthew ingenuously.

"I have, often. Which would you rather be if you had the choice— divinely beautiful or dazzlingly clever or angelically good?"

"Well now, I—I don't know exactly."

"Neither do I. I can never decide. But it doesn't make much real difference, for it isn't likely I'll ever be either. It's certain I'll never be angelically good. Mrs. Spencer says—Oh, Mr. Cuthbert! Oh, Mr. Cuthbert! Oh, Mr. Cuthbert!!!"

That was not what Mrs. Spencer had said; neither had the child tumbled out of the buggy nor had Matthew done anything astonishing. They had simply rounded a curve in the road and found themselves in the "Avenue."

The "Avenue," so called by the Newbridge people, was a stretch of road four or five hundred yards long, completely arched over with huge, wide-spreading apple trees, planted years ago by an eccentric old farmer. Overhead was one long canopy of snowy fragrant bloom. Below the boughs, the air was full of a purple twilight, and far ahead a glimpse of painted sunset sky shone like a great rose window at the end of a cathedral aisle.

Its beauty seemed to strike the child dumb. She leaned back in the buggy, her thin hands clasped before her, her face lifted rapturously to the white splendor above. Even when they had passed out and were driving down the long slope to Newbridge, she never moved or spoke. Still with rapt face, she gazed afar into the sunset west, with eyes that saw visions trooping splendidly across that glowing background. Through Newbridge, a bustling little village where dogs barked at them and small boys hooted and curious faces peered from the windows, they drove, still in silence. When three more miles had dropped away behind them, the child had not spoken. She could keep silence, it was evident, as energetically as she could talk.

"I guess you're feeling pretty tired and hungry," Matthew ventured at last, accounting for her long visitation of dumbness with the only reason he could think of. "But we haven't very far to go now—only another mile."

She came out of her reverie with a deep sigh and looked at him with the dreamy gaze of a soul that had been wondering afar, star-led.

"Oh, Mr. Cuthbert," she whispered, "that place we came through— that white place—what was it?"

"Well now, you must mean the Avenue," said Matthew after a few moments' profound reflection. "It is a kind of pretty place."

"Pretty? Oh, *pretty* doesn't seem the right word to use. Nor beautiful, either. They don't go far enough. Oh, it was wonderful—wonderful. It's the first thing I ever saw that couldn't be improved upon by imagination. It just satisfied me here." She put one hand on her breast. "It made a strange, funny ache and yet it was a pleasant ache. Did you ever have an ache like that, Mr. Cuthbert?"

"Well now, I just can't recollect that I ever had."

"I have it lots of times—whenever I see anything royally beautiful. But they shouldn't call that lovely place the Avenue. There is no meaning in a name like that. They should call it—let me see—the White Way of Delight. Isn't that a nice imaginative name? When I don't like the name of a place or a person, I always imagine a new one and always think of them so. There was a girl at the asylum whose name was Hepzibah Jenkins, but I always imagined her as Rosalia DeVere. Other people may call that place the Avenue, but I shall always call it the White Way of Delight. Have we really only another mile to go before we get home? I'm glad and I'm sorry. I'm sorry because this drive has been so pleasant and I'm always sorry when pleasant things end. Something still pleasanter may come after, but you can never be sure. And it's so often the case that it isn't pleasanter. That has been my experience anyhow. But I'm glad to think of getting home. You see, I've never had a real home since I can remember. It gives me that pleasant ache again just to think of coming to a really truly home. Oh, isn't that pretty!"

They had driven over the crest of a hill. Below them was a pond, looking almost like a river, so long and winding was it. A bridge spanned it midway, and from there to its lower end, where an amber-hued belt of sand hills shut it in from the dark blue gulf beyond, the water was a glory of many shifting hues—the most spiritual shadings of crocus and rose and ethereal green, with other elusive tintings for which no name has ever been found. Above the bridge the pond ran up into fringing groves of fir and maple and lay all darkly translucent in their wavering shadows. Here and there a wild plum leaned out from the bank like a white-clad girl tiptoeing to her own reflection. From the marsh at the head of the pond came the clear, mournfully sweet chorus of the frogs. There was a little gray house peering around a white apple orchard on a slope beyond and, although it was not yet quite dark, a light was shining from one of its windows.

"That's Barry's Pond," said Matthew.

"Oh, I don't like that name, either. I shall call it—let me see—the Lake of Shining Waters. Yes, that is the right name for it. I know because of the thrill. When I hit on a name that suits exactly, it gives me a thrill. Do things ever give you a thrill?"

Matthew ruminated.

"Well now, yes. It always kind of gives me a thrill to see them ugly white grubs that spade up in the cucumber beds. I hate the look of them."

"Oh, I don't think that can be exactly the same kind of a thrill. Do you think it can? There doesn't seem to be much connection between grubs and lakes of shining waters, does there? But why do other people call it Barry's Pond?"

"I reckon because Mr. Barry lives up there in that house. Orchard Slope's the name of his place. If it wasn't for that big bush behind, you could see Green Gables from here. But we have to go over the bridge and around by the road, so it's near half a mile farther."

"Has Mr. Barry any little girls? Well, not so very little either—about my size."

"He's got one about eleven. Her name is Diana."

"Oh!" with a long indrawing of breath. "What a perfectly lovely name!"

"Well now, I dunno. There's something dreadful heathenish about it, seems to me. I'd ruther Jane or Mary or some sensible name like that. But when Diana was born, there was a schoolmaster boarding there and they gave him the naming of her and he called her Diana."

"I wish there had been a schoolmaster like that around when *I* was born, then. Oh, here we are at the bridge. I'm going to shut my eyes tight. I'm always afraid going over bridges. I can't help imagining that perhaps, just as we get to the middle, they'll crumple up like a jackknife and nip us. So I shut my eyes. But I always have to open them for all[2] when I think we're getting near the middle. Because, you see, if the bridge *did* crumple up, I'd want to *see* it crumple. What a jolly rumble it makes! I always like the rumble part of it. Isn't it splendid there are so many things to like in this world? There, we're over. Now I'll look back. Good night, dear Lake of Shining Waters. I always say good night to the things I love, just as I would to people. I think they like it. That water looks as if it was smiling at me."

When they had driven up the further hill and around a corner, Matthew said, "We're pretty near home now. That's Green Gables—"

"Oh, don't tell me," she interrupted breathlessly, catching at his partially raised arm and shutting her eyes that she might not see his gesture. "Let me guess. I'm sure I'll guess right."

She opened her eyes and looked about her. They were on the crest of a hill. The sun had set some time since, but the landscape was still clear in the mellow afterlight. To the west, a dark church spire rose up against a marigold sky. Below was a little valley, and beyond, a long, gently rising slope with snug farmsteads scattered along it. From one to another the child's eyes darted, eager and wistful. At last they lingered on one away to the left, far back from the road, dimly white with blossoming trees in the twilight of the surrounding woods. Over it, in the stainless southwest sky, a great crystal-white star was shining like a lamp of guidance and promise.

"That's it, isn't it?" she said, pointing.

Matthew slapped the reins on the sorrel's back delightedly.

"Well now, you've guessed it! But I reckon Mrs. Spencer described it so's you could tell."

"No, she didn't—really she didn't. All she said might just as well have been about most of those other places. I hadn't any real idea what it looked like. But just as soon as I saw it, I felt it was home. Oh, it seems as if I must be in a dream. Do you know, my arm must be black and blue from the elbow up, for I've pinched myself so many times today. Every little while a horrible sickening feeling would come over me and I'd be so afraid it was all a dream. Then I'd pinch myself to see if it was real—until suddenly I remembered that even supposing it was only a dream I'd better go on dreaming as long as I could; so I stopped pinching. But it *is* real and we're nearly home."

With a sigh of rapture, she relapsed into silence. Matthew stirred uneasily. He felt glad that it would be Marilla and not he who would

---

[2] After all.

have to tell this waif of the world that the home she longed for was not to be hers after all. They drove over Lynde's Hollow, where it was already quite dark, but not so dark that Mrs. Rachel could not see them from her window vantage, and up the hill and into the long lane of Green Gables. By the time they arrived at the house, Matthew was shrinking from the approaching revelation with an energy he did not understand. It was not of Marilla or himself he was thinking, or of the trouble this mistake was probably going to make for them, but of the child's disappointment. When he thought of that rapt light being quenched in her eyes, he had an uncomfortable feeling that he was going to assist at murdering something—much the same feeling that came over him when he had to kill a lamb or calf or any other innocent little creature.

The yard was quite dark as they turned into it, and the poplar leaves were rustling silkily all around it.

"Listen to the trees talking in their sleep," she whispered as he lifted her to the ground. "What nice dreams they must have!"

Then, holding tightly to the carpetbag that contained "all her worldly goods," she followed him into the house.

Chapter 3

MARILLA CUTHBERT IS SURPRISED

Marilla came briskly forward as Matthew opened the door. But when her eyes fell on the odd little figure in the stiff, ugly dress, with the long braids of red hair and the eager, luminous eyes, she stopped short in amazement.

"Matthew Cuthbert, who's that?" she ejaculated.[1] "Where is the boy?"

"There wasn't any boy," said Matthew wretchedly. "There was only *her.*"

He nodded at the child, remembering that he had never even asked her name.

"No boy! But there *must* have been a boy," insisted Marilla. "We sent word to Mrs. Spencer to bring a boy."

"Well, she didn't. She brought *her.* I asked the stationmaster. And I had to bring her home. She couldn't be left there, no matter where the mistake had come in."

"Well, this is a pretty piece of business!" cried Marilla.

During this dialogue, the child had remained silent, her eyes roving from one to the other, all the animation fading out of her face. Suddenly, she seemed to grasp the full meaning of what had been said. Dropping her precious carpetbag, she sprang forward a step and clasped her hands.

"You don't want me!" she cried. "You don't want me because I'm not a boy! I might have expected it. Nobody ever did want me. I might have known it was all too beautiful to last. I might have known nobody really did want me. Oh, what shall I do? I'm going to burst into tears!"

Burst into tears she did. Sitting down on a chair by the table, flinging her arms out upon it, and burying her face in them, she proceeded to cry stormily. Marilla and Matthew looked at each other deprecatingly[2] across

---

[1] Demanded.

[2] Helplessly.

20

"Matthew Cuthbert, who's that?"

the stove. Neither of them knew what to say or do. Finally, Marilla stepped lamely into the breach.

"Well, well, there's no need to cry so about it."

"Yes, there *is* need!" The child raised her head quickly, revealing a tear-stained face and trembling lips. "*You* would cry, too, if you were an orphan and had come to a place you thought was going to be home and found that they didn't want you because you weren't a boy. Oh, this is the most *tragical* thing that ever happened to me!"

Something like a reluctant smile, rather rusty from long disuse, mellowed Marilla's grim expression.

"Well, don't cry anymore. We're not going to turn you out-of-doors tonight. You'll have to stay here until we investigate this affair. What's your name?"

The child hesitated for a moment.

"Will you please call me Cordelia?" she said eagerly.

"*Call* you Cordelia! Is that your name?"

"No-o-o, it's not exactly my name, but I would love to be called Cordelia. It's such a perfectly elegant name."

"I don't know what on earth you mean. If Cordelia isn't your name, what is?"

"Anne Shirley," reluctantly faltered forth the owner of that name, "but, oh, please do call me Cordelia. It can't matter much to you what you call me if I'm only going to be here a little while, can it? And Anne is such an unromantic name."

"Unromantic fiddlesticks!" said the unsympathetic Marilla. "Anne is a real good plain, sensible name. You've no need to be ashamed of it."

"Oh, I'm not ashamed of it," explained Anne, "only I like Cordelia better. I've always imagined that my name was Cordelia—at least, I always have of late years. When I was young, I used to imagine it was Geraldine, but I like Cordelia better now. But if you call me Anne, please call me Anne spelled with an *e*."

"What difference does it make how it's spelled?" asked Marilla with another rusty smile as she picked up the teapot.

"Oh, it makes *such* a difference. It *looks* so much nicer. When you hear a name pronounced, can't you always see it in your mind, just as if it was printed out? I can; and A-n-n looks dreadful, but A-n-n-e looks so much more distinguished. If you'll only call me Anne spelled with an *e*, I shall try to reconcile myself to not being called Cordelia."

"Very well, then, Anne spelled with an *e*, can you tell us how this mistake came to be made? We sent word to Mrs. Spencer to bring us a boy. Were there no boys at the asylum?"

"Oh, yes, there was an abundance of them. But Mrs. Spencer said *distinctly* that you wanted a girl about eleven years old. And the matron said she thought I would do. You don't know how delighted I was. I couldn't sleep all last night for joy. Oh," she added reproachfully, turning to Matthew, "why didn't you tell me at the station that you didn't want me and leave me there? If I hadn't seen the White Way of Delight and the Lake of Shining Waters, it wouldn't be so hard."

"What on earth does she mean?" demanded Marilla, staring at Matthew.

"She—she's just referring to some conversation we had on the road," said Matthew hastily. "I'm going out to put the mare in, Marilla. Have tea ready when I come back."

"Did Mrs. Spencer bring anybody over besides you?" continued Marilla when Matthew had gone out.

"She brought Lily Jones for herself. Lily is only five years old and she is very beautiful. She has nut-brown hair. If I was very beautiful and had nut-brown hair, would you keep me?"

"No. We want a boy to help Matthew on the farm. A girl would be of no use to us. Take off your hat. I'll lay it and your bag on the hall table."

Anne took off her hat meekly. Matthew came back presently, and they sat down to supper. But Anne could not eat. In vain she nibbled at the bread and butter and pecked at the crab apple preserve out of the little scalloped glass dish by her plate. She did not really make any headway at all.

"You're not eating anything," said Marilla sharply, eyeing her as if it were a serious shortcoming.

Anne sighed.

"I can't. I'm in the depths of despair. Can you eat when you are in the depths of despair?"

"I've never been in the depths of despair, so I can't say," responded Marilla.

"Weren't you? Well, did you ever try to *imagine* you were in the depths of despair?"

"No, I didn't."

"Then I don't think you can understand what it's like. It's a very uncomfortable feeling indeed. When you try to eat, a lump comes right up in your throat and you can't swallow anything, not even if it was a chocolate caramel. I had one chocolate caramel once two years ago, and it was simply delicious. I've often dreamed since then that I had a lot of chocolate caramels, but I always wake up just when I'm going to eat them. I do hope you won't be offended because I can't eat. Everything is extremely nice, but still I cannot eat."

"I guess she's tired," said Matthew, who hadn't spoken since his return from the barn. "Best put her to bed, Marilla."

Marilla had been wondering where Anne should be put to bed. She had prepared a couch in the kitchen chamber for the desired and expected boy. But, although it was neat and clean, it did not seem quite the thing to put a girl there somehow. But the spare room was out of the question for such a stray waif, so there remained only the east gable room. Marilla lighted a candle and told Anne to follow her, which Anne spiritlessly did, taking her hat and carpetbag from the hall table as she passed. The hall was fearsomely clean; the little gable chamber in which she presently found herself seemed still cleaner.

Marilla set the candle on a three-legged, three-cornered table and turned down the bedclothes.

"I suppose you have a nightgown?" she questioned.

Anne nodded.

"Yes, I have two. The matron of the asylum made them for me. They're fearfully skimpy. There is never enough to go around in an asylum, so things are always skimpy—at least in a poor asylum like ours. I hate skimpy nightdresses. But one can dream just as well in them as in lovely trailing ones with frills around the neck, that's one consolation."

"Well, undress as quick as you can and go to bed. I'll come back in a few minutes for the candle. I daren't trust you to put it out yourself. You'd likely set the place on fire."

When Marilla had gone, Anne looked around wistfully. The white-washed walls were so painfully bare and staring that she thought they must ache over their own bareness. The floor was bare, too, except for a round, braided mat in the middle such as Anne had never seen before. In one corner was the bed, a high, old-fashioned one, with four dark, low-turned posts. In the other corner was the aforesaid three-cornered table adorned with a fat red-velvet pincushion hard enough to turn the point of the most adventurous pin. Above it hung a little six by eight mirror. Midway between table and bed was the window, with an icy white muslin frill over it, and opposite it was the washstand. The whole apartment was of a rigidity not to be described in words, but which sent a shiver to the very marrow of Anne's bones. With a sob, she hastily discarded her garments, put on the skimpy nightgown, and sprang into bed, where she burrowed face downward into the pillow and pulled the clothes over her head. When Marilla came up for the light, various skimpy articles of raiment scattered most untidily over the floor and a certain tempestuous appearance of the bed were the only indications of any presence save her own.

She deliberately picked up Anne's clothes, placed them neatly on a prim yellow chair, and then, taking up the candle, went over to the bed.

"Good night," she said, a little awkwardly but not unkindly.

Anne's white face and big eyes appeared over the bedclothes with a startling suddenness.

"How can you call it a *good* night when you know it must be the very worst night I've ever had?" she said reproachfully.

Then she dived down into invisibility again.

Marilla went slowly down to the kitchen and proceeded to wash the supper dishes. Matthew was smoking—a sure sign of perturbation of mind. He seldom smoked, for Marilla set her face against it as a filthy habit; but at certain times and seasons he felt driven to it and then Marilla winked at the practice, realizing that a mere man must have some vent for his emotions.

"Well, this is a pretty kettle of fish," she said wrathfully. "This is what comes of sending word instead of going ourselves. Robert Spencer's folks have twisted that message somehow. One of us will have to drive over and see Mrs. Spencer tomorrow, that's certain. This girl will have to be sent back to the asylum."

"Yes, I suppose so," said Matthew reluctantly.

"You *suppose* so! Don't you know it?"

"Well now, she's a real nice little thing, Marilla. It's kind of a pity to send her back when she's so set on staying here."

"Matthew Cuthbert, you don't mean to say you think we ought to keep her!"

Marilla's astonishment could not have been greater if Matthew had expressed a predilection for standing on his head.

"Well now, no, I suppose not—not exactly," stammered Matthew, uncomfortably driven into a corner for his precise meaning. "I suppose—we could hardly be expected to keep her."

"I should say not. What good would she be to us?"

"We might be some good to her," said Matthew suddenly and unexpectedly.

"Matthew Cuthbert, I believe that child has bewitched you! I can see as plain as plain that you want to keep her."

"Well now, she's a real interesting little thing," persisted Matthew. "You should have heard her talk coming from the station."

"Oh, she can talk fast enough. I saw that at once. It's nothing in her favor, either. I don't like children who have so much to say. I don't want an orphan girl, and if I did, she isn't the style I'd pick out. There's something

I don't understand about her. No, she's got to be dispatched straightway back to where she came from."

"I could hire a French boy to help me," said Matthew, "and she'd be company for you."

"I'm not suffering for company," said Marilla shortly. "And I'm not going to keep her."

"Well now, it's just as you say, of course, Marilla," said Matthew, rising and putting his pipe away. "I'm going to bed."

To bed went Matthew. And to bed, when she had put her dishes away, went Marilla, frowning most resolutely. And upstairs, in the east gable, a lonely, heart-hungry, friendless child cried herself to sleep.

Chapter 4

MORNING AT GREEN GABLES

It was broad daylight when Anne awoke and sat up in bed, staring confusedly at the window through which a flood of cheery sunshine was pouring and outside of which something white and feathery waved across glimpses of blue sky.

For a moment she could not remember where she was. First came a delightful thrill, as of something very pleasant; then a horrible remembrance. This was Green Gables, and they didn't want her because she wasn't a boy!

But it was morning and, yes, it was a cherry tree in full bloom outside of her window. With a bound she was out of bed and across the floor. She pushed up the sash—it went up stiffly and creakily, as if it hadn't been opened for a long time, which was the case; and it stuck so tight that nothing was needed to hold it up.

Anne dropped on her knees and gazed out into the June morning, her eyes glistening with delight. Oh, wasn't it beautiful? Wasn't it a lovely place? Suppose she wasn't really going to stay here! She would imagine she was. There was scope for imagination here.

A huge cherry tree grew outside, so close that its boughs tapped against the house, and it was so thickset with blossoms that hardly a leaf was to be seen. On both sides of the house was a big orchard, one of apple trees and one of cherry trees, also showered over with blossoms; and their grass was all sprinkled with dandelions. In the garden below were lilac trees purple with flowers, and their dizzily sweet fragrance drifted up to the window on the morning wind.

Below the garden, a green field lush with clover sloped down to the hollow where the brook ran and where scores of white birches grew, upspringing airily out of an undergrowth suggestive of delightful possibilities in ferns and mosses and woodsy things generally. Beyond it was a

27

hill, green and feathery with spruce and fir; there was a gap in it where the gray gable end of the little house she had seen from the other side of the Lake of Shining Waters was visible.

Off to the left were the big barns and beyond them, away down over green, low-sloping fields, was a sparkling blue glimpse of sea.

Anne's beauty-loving eyes lingered on it all, taking everything greedily in. She had looked on so many unlovely places in her life, poor child, but this was as lovely as anything she had ever dreamed.

She knelt there, lost to everything but the loveliness around her, until she was startled by a hand on her shoulder. Marilla had come in unheard by the small dreamer.

"It's time you were dressed," she said curtly.

Marilla really did not know how to talk to the child, and her uncomfortable ignorance made her crisp and curt when she did not mean to be.

Anne stood up and drew a long breath.

"Oh, isn't it wonderful!" she said, waving her hand comprehensively at the good world outside.

"It's a big tree," said Marilla, "and it blooms great, but the fruit don't amount to much never—small and wormy."

"Oh, I don't mean just the tree; of course it's lovely—yes, it's *radiantly* lovely—it blooms as if it meant it—but I meant everything, the garden and the orchard and the brook and the woods, the whole big, dear world. Don't you feel as if you just loved the world on a morning like this? And I can hear the brook laughing all the way up here. Have you ever noticed what cheerful things brooks are? They're always laughing. Even in wintertime I've heard them under the ice. I'm so glad there's a brook near Green Gables. Perhaps you think it doesn't make any difference to me when you're not going to keep me, but it does. I shall always like to remember that there is a brook at Green Gables even if I never see it again. If there wasn't a brook, I'd be *haunted* by the uncomfortable feeling that there ought to be one. I'm not in the depths of despair this morning. I never can be in the morning. Isn't it a splendid thing that there are mornings? But I feel very sad. I've just been imagining that it was really me you wanted after all and that I was to stay here for ever and ever. It was a great comfort while it lasted. But the worst of imagining things is that the time comes when you have to stop, and that hurts."

"You'd better get dressed and come downstairs and never mind your imaginings," said Marilla as soon as she could get a word in edgewise. "Breakfast is waiting. Wash your face and comb your hair. Leave the window up and turn your bedclothes back over the foot of the bed. Be as smart as you can."

Anne could evidently be smart to some purpose for she was downstairs in ten minutes' time, with her clothes neatly on, her hair brushed and braided, her face washed, and a comfortable consciousness pervading her soul that she had fulfilled all Marilla's requirements. As a matter of fact, however, she had forgotten to turn back the bedclothes.

"I'm pretty hungry this morning," she announced as she slipped into the chair Marilla placed for her. "The world doesn't seem such a howling wilderness as it did last night. I'm so glad it's a sunshiny morning. But I like rainy mornings real well, too. All sorts of mornings are interesting, don't you think? You don't know what's going to happen through the day, and there's so much scope for imagination. But I'm glad it's not rainy today because it's easier to be cheerful and bear up under affliction on a sunshiny day. I feel that I have a good deal to bear up under. It's all very well to read about sorrows and imagine yourself living through them heroically, but it's not so nice when you really come to have them, is it?"

"For pity's sake, hold your tongue," said Marilla. "You talk entirely too much for a little girl."

Thereupon Anne held her tongue so obediently and thoroughly that her continued silence made Marilla rather nervous, as if in the presence of something not exactly natural. Matthew also held his tongue—but this at least was natural—so that the meal was a very silent one.

As it progressed Anne became more and more abstracted, eating mechanically, with her big eyes fixed unswervingly and unseeingly on the sky outside the window. This made Marilla more nervous than ever; she had an uncomfortable feeling that while this odd child's body might be there at the table, her spirit was far away in some remote airy cloudland, borne aloft on the wings of imagination. Who would want such a child about the place?

Yet Matthew wished to keep her, of all unaccountable things! Marilla felt that he wanted it just as much this morning as he had the night before, and that he would go on wanting it. That was Matthew's way—take a whim into his head and cling to it with the most amazing silent persistency—a persistency ten times more potent and effectual in its very silence than if he had talked it out.

When the meal was ended, Anne came out of her reverie and offered to wash the dishes.

"Can you wash dishes right?" asked Marilla distrustfully.

"Pretty well. I'm better at looking after children, though. I've had so much experience at that. It's such a pity you haven't any here for me to look after."

"I don't feel as if I wanted any more children to look after than I've got at present. *You're* problem enough, in all conscience. What's to be done with you I don't know. Matthew is a most ridiculous man."

"I think he's lovely," said Anne reproachfully. "He is so very sympathetic. He didn't mind how much I talked—he seemed to like it. I felt that he was a kindred spirit as soon as ever I saw him."

"You're both strange enough, if that's what you mean by kindred spirits," said Marilla with a sniff. "Yes, you may wash the dishes. Take plenty of hot water, and be sure you dry them well. I've got enough to attend to this morning, for I'll have to drive over to White Sands in the afternoon and see Mrs. Spencer. You'll come with me and we'll settle what's to be done with you. After you've finished the dishes, go upstairs and make your bed."

Anne washed the dishes deftly enough, as Marilla, who kept a sharp eye on the process, discerned. Later on, she made her bed less successfully, for she had never learned the art of wrestling with a feather tick. But it was done somehow and smoothed down; and then Marilla, to get rid of her, told her she might go out-of-doors and amuse herself until dinnertime.

Anne flew to the door, face alight, eyes glowing. On the very threshold she stopped short, wheeled about, came back and sat down by the table, light and glow as effectually blotted out as if someone had clapped an extinguisher on her.

"What's the matter now?" demanded Marilla.

"I don't dare go out," said Anne in the tone of a martyr relinquishing all earthly joys. "If I can't stay here, there is no use in my loving Green Gables. And if I go out there and get acquainted with all those trees and flowers and the orchard and the brook, I'll not be able to help loving it. It's hard enough now, so I won't make it any harder. I want to go out so much—everything seems to be calling to me, 'Anne, Anne, come out to us. Anne, Anne, we want a playmate'—but it's better not. There is no use in loving things if you have to be torn from them, is there? And it's *so* hard to keep from loving things, isn't it? That was why I was so glad when I thought I was going to live here. I thought I'd have so many things to love and nothing to hinder me. But that brief dream is over. I am resigned to my fate now, so I don't think I'll go out for fear I'll get unresigned again. What is the name of that geranium on the windowsill, please?"

"That's the apple-scented geranium."

"Oh, I don't mean that sort of a name. I mean just a name you gave it yourself. Didn't you give it a name? May I give it one then? May I call it—let me see—Bonny would do—may I call it Bonny while I'm here? Oh, do let me!"

"Goodness, I don't care. But where on earth is the sense of naming a geranium?"

"Oh, I like things to have handles even if they are only geraniums. It makes them seem more like people. How do you know but that it hurts a geranium's feelings just to be called a geranium and nothing else? You wouldn't like to be called nothing but a woman all the time. Yes, I shall call it Bonny. I named that cherry tree outside my bedroom window this morning. I called it Snow Queen because it was so white. Of course, it won't always be in blossom, but one can imagine that it is, can't one?"

"I never in all my life saw or heard anything to equal her," muttered Marilla, beating a retreat down to the cellar after potatoes. "She *is* kind of interesting, as Matthew says. I can feel already that I'm wondering what on earth she'll say next. She'll be casting a spell over me, too. She's cast it over Matthew. That look he gave me when he went out said everything he said or hinted last night over again. I wish he was like other men and would talk things out. A body could answer back then and argue him into reason. But what's to be done with a man who just *looks?*"

Anne had relapsed into reverie, with her chin in her hands and her eyes on the sky, when Marilla returned from her cellar pilgrimage. There Marilla left her until the early dinner was on the table.

"I suppose I can have the mare and buggy this afternoon, Matthew?" said Marilla.

Matthew nodded and looked wistfully at Anne.

Marilla intercepted the look and said grimly, "I'm going to drive over to White Sands and settle this thing. I'll take Anne with me, and Mrs. Spencer will probably make arrangements to send her back to Nova Scotia at once. I'll set your tea out for you, and I'll be home in time to milk the cows."

Still Matthew said nothing, and Marilla had a sense of having wasted words and breath. There is nothing more aggravating than a man who won't talk back—unless it is a woman who won't.

Matthew hitched the sorrel into the buggy in due time, and Marilla and Anne set off. Matthew opened the yard gate for them, and as they drove slowly through, he said, to nobody in particular it seemed:

"Little Jerry Buote from the Creek was here this morning, and I told him I guessed I'd hire him for the summer."

Marilla made no reply, but she hit the unlucky sorrel such a vicious clip with the whip that the fat mare, unused to such treatment, whizzed indignantly down the lane at an alarming pace. Marilla looked back once as the buggy bounced along and saw that aggravating Matthew leaning over the gate, looking wistfully after them.

Chapter 5
ANNE'S HISTORY

"Do you know," said Anne confidentially, "I've made up my mind to enjoy this drive. It's been my experience that you can nearly always enjoy things if you make up your mind firmly that you will. Of course, you must make it up *firmly*. I am not going to think about going back to the asylum while we're having our drive. I'm just going to think about the drive. Oh, look, there's one little early wild rose out! Isn't it lovely? Don't you think it must be glad to be a rose? Wouldn't it be nice if roses could talk? I'm sure they could tell us such lovely things. And isn't pink the most bewitching color in the world? I love it, but I can't wear it. Redheaded people can't wear pink, not even in imagination. Did you ever know of anybody whose hair was red when she was young but got to be another color when she grew up?"

"No, I don't know as I ever did," said Marilla mercilessly, "and I shouldn't think it likely to happen in your case, either."

Anne sighed.

"Well, that is another hope gone. My life is a perfect graveyard of buried hopes. That's a sentence I read in a book once, and I say it over to comfort myself whenever I'm disappointed in anything."

"I don't see where the comforting comes in myself," said Marilla.

"Why, because it sounds so nice and romantic, just as if I were a heroine in a book, you know. I am so fond of romantic things, and a graveyard full of buried hopes is about as romantic a thing as one can imagine, isn't it? I'm rather glad I have one. Are we going across the Lake of Shining Waters today?"

"We're not going over Barry's Pond, if that's what you mean by your Lake of Shining Waters. We're going by the shore road."

" 'Shore road' sounds nice," said Anne dreamily. "Is it as nice as it sounds? Just when you said 'shore road,' I saw it in a picture in my mind, as quick as that! And White Sands is a pretty name, too; but I don't like it as well as Avonlea. Avonlea is a lovely name. It just sounds like music. How far is it to White Sands?"

"It's five miles; and as you're evidently bent on talking, you might as well talk to some purpose by telling me what you know about yourself."

"Oh, what I *know* about myself isn't really worth telling," said Anne eagerly. "If you'll only let me tell you what I *imagine* about myself, you'll think it ever so much more interesting."

"No, I don't want any of your imaginings. Just you stick to bald facts. Begin at the beginning. Where were you born and how old are you?"

"I was eleven last March," said Anne, resigning herself to bald facts with a little sigh. "And I was born in Bolingbroke, Nova Scotia. My father's name was Walter Shirley, and he was a teacher at Bolingbroke High School. My mother's name was Bertha Shirley. Aren't Walter and Bertha lovely names? I'm so glad my parents had nice names. It would be a real disgrace to have a father named—well, say Jedediah, wouldn't it?"

"I guess it doesn't matter what a person's name is as long as he behaves himself," said Marilla, feeling herself called upon to inculcate a good and useful moral.

"Well, I don't know." Anne looked thoughtful. "I read in a book once that a rose by any other name would smell as sweet, but I've never been able to believe it. I don't believe a rose *would* be as nice if it was called a thistle or a skunk cabbage. I suppose my father could have been a good man even if he had been called Jedediah; but I'm sure it would have been a cross. Well, my mother was a teacher at the high school, too, but when she married Father, she gave up teaching, of course. A husband was enough responsibility. Mrs. Thomas said that they were a pair of babies and as poor as church mice. They went to live in a weeny-teeny little yellow house in Bolingbroke. I've never seen that house, but I've imagined it thousands of times. I think it must have had honeysuckle over the parlour window and lilacs in the front yard and lilies of the valley just inside the gate. Yes, and muslin curtains in all the windows. Muslin curtains give a house such an air. I was born in that house. Mrs. Thomas said that I was the homeliest baby she ever saw, I was so scrawny and tiny and nothing but eyes, but that Mother thought I was perfectly beautiful. I should think a mother would be a better judge than a poor woman who came in to scrub, wouldn't you? I'm glad she was satisfied with me anyhow; I would feel so bad if I thought I was a disappointment to her— because she didn't live very long after that, you see. She died of fever when I was just three months old. I do wish she'd lived long enough for me to remember calling her Mother. I think it would be so sweet to say 'Mother,' don't you? And Father died four days afterward from fever, too. That left me an orphan, and folks were at their wits' end, so Mrs.

Thomas said, what to do with me. You see, nobody wanted me even then. It seems to be my fate. Father and Mother had both come from places far away and it was well known they hadn't any relatives living. Finally, Mrs. Thomas said she'd take me, though she was poor and had a drunken husband. She brought me up by hand. Do you know if there is anything in being brought up by hand that ought to make people who are brought up that way better than other people? Because whenever I was naughty, Mrs. Thomas would ask me how I could be such a bad girl when she had brought me up by hand—reproachful-like.

"Mr. and Mrs. Thomas moved away from Bolingbroke to Marysville, and I lived with them until I was eight years old. I helped look after the Thomas children—there were four of them younger than me—and I can tell you they took a lot of looking after. Then Mr. Thomas was killed falling under a train, and his mother offered to take Mrs. Thomas and the children, but she didn't want me. Mrs. Thomas was at *her* wits' end, so she said, what to do with me. Then Mrs. Hammond from up the river came down and said she'd take me, seeing I was handy with children, and I went up the river to live with her in a little clearing among the stumps. It was a very lonesome place. I'm sure I could never have lived there if I hadn't had an imagination. Mr. Hammond worked a little sawmill up there, and Mrs. Hammond had eight children. She had twins three times. I like babies in moderation, but twins three times in succession is *too much*. I told Mrs. Hammond so firmly, when the last pair came. I used to get so dreadfully tired carrying them about.

"I lived upriver with Mrs. Hammond for over two years, and then Mr. Hammond died and Mrs. Hammond broke up housekeeping. She divided her children among her relatives and went to the States. I had to go to the asylum at Hopeton, because nobody would take me. They didn't want me at the asylum, either; they said they were overcrowded as it was. But they had to take me, and I was there four months until Mrs. Spencer came."

Anne finished up with another sigh, of relief this time. Evidently, she did not like talking about her experiences in a world that had not wanted her.

"Did you ever go to school?" demanded Marilla, turning the sorrel mare down the shore road.

"Not a great deal. I went a little the last year I stayed with Mrs. Thomas. When I went upriver, we were so far from a school that I couldn't walk it in winter, and there was vacation in summer, so I could only go in the spring and fall. But of course I went while I was at the asylum. I can read pretty well and I know ever so many pieces of poetry by heart—'The Battle of Hohenlinden' and 'Edinburgh After Flodden,' and 'Bingen on the Rhine,' and lots of the 'Lady of the Lake,' and most of 'The Seasons,' by James Thompson. Don't you just love poetry that gives you a crinkly feeling up and down your back? There is a piece in the Fifth Reader— 'The Downfall of Poland'—that is just full of thrills. Of course, I wasn't in the Fifth Reader—I was only in the Fourth—but the big girls used to lend me theirs to read."

"Were those women—Mrs. Thomas and Mrs. Hammond—good to you?" asked Marilla, looking at Anne out of the corner of her eye.

"O-o-o-h," faltered Anne. Her sensitive little face suddenly flushed scarlet, and embarrassment sat on her brow. "Oh, they *meant* to be—I know they meant to be just as good and kind as possible. And when people mean to be good to you, you don't mind very much when they're not quite—always. They had a good deal to worry them, you know. It's very trying to have a drunken husband, you see; and it must be very trying to have twins three times in succession, don't you think? But I feel sure they meant to be good to me."

Marilla asked no more questions. Anne gave herself up to a silent rapture over the shore road, and Marilla guided the sorrel abstractedly while she pondered deeply. Pity was suddenly stirring in her heart for the child. What a starved, unloved life she had had—a life of drudgery and poverty and neglect; for Marilla was shrewd enough to read between the lines of Anne's history and divine the truth. No wonder she had been so delighted at the prospect of a real home. It was a pity she had to be sent back. What if she, Marilla, should indulge Matthew's unaccountable whim and let her stay? He was set on it; and the child seemed a nice, teachable little thing.

She's got too much to say, thought Marilla, *but she might be trained out of that. And there's nothing rude or slangy in what she does say. She's ladylike. It's likely her people were nice folks.*

The shore road was "woodsy and wild and lonesome." On the right hand, scrub firs, their spirits quite unbroken by long years of tussle with the gulf winds, grew thickly. On the left were the steep red sandstone cliffs, so near the track in places that a mare of less steadiness than the sorrel might have tried the nerves of the people behind her. Down at the base of the cliffs were heaps of surf-worn rocks or little sandy coves inlaid with pebbles as with ocean jewels; beyond lay the sea, shimmering and blue, and over it soared the gulls, their pinions flashing silvery in the sunlight.

"Isn't the sea wonderful?" said Anne, rousing from a long, wide-eyed silence. "Once, when I lived in Marysville, Mr. Thomas hired an express wagon and took us all to spend the day at the shore ten miles away. I enjoyed every moment of that day, even if I had to look after the children all the time. I lived it over in happy dreams for years. But this shore is nicer than the Marysville shore. Aren't those gulls splendid? Would you like to be a gull? I think I would—that is, if I couldn't be a human girl. Don't you think it would be nice to wake up at sunrise and swoop down over the water and away out over that lovely blue all day; and then at night to fly back to one's nest? Oh, I can just imagine myself doing it. What big house is that just ahead, please?"

"That's the White Sands Hotel. Mr. Kirke runs it, but the season hasn't begun yet. There are heaps of Americans come there for the summer. They think this shore is just about right."

"I was afraid it might be Mrs. Spencer's place," said Anne mournfully. "I don't want to get there. Somehow, it will seem like the end of everything."

Chapter 6

MARILLA MAKES UP
HER MIND

Get there they did, however, in due season. Mrs. Spencer lived in a big yellow house at White Sands Cove, and she came to the door with surprise and welcome mingled on her benevolent face.

"Dear, dear," she exclaimed, "you're the *last* folks I was looking for today, but I'm real glad to see you. You'll put your horse in? And how are you, Anne?"

"I'm as well as can be expected, thank you," said Anne smilelessly. A blight seemed to have descended on her.

"I suppose we'll stay a little while to rest the mare," said Marilla, "but I promised Matthew I'd be home early. The fact is, Mrs. Spencer, there's been a strange mistake somewhere, and I've come over to see where it is. We sent word, Matthew and I, for you to bring us a boy from the asylum. We told your brother Robert to tell you we wanted a boy ten or eleven years old."

"Marilla Cuthbert, you don't say so!" said Mrs. Spencer in distress. "Why, Robert sent the word down by his daughter Nancy and she said you wanted a girl—didn't she, Flora Jane?" appealing to her daughter who had come out to the steps.

"She certainly did, Miss Cuthbert," corroborated Flora Jane earnestly.

"I'm dreadful sorry," said Mrs. Spencer. "It is too bad; but it certainly wasn't my fault, you see, Miss Cuthbert. I did the best I could and I thought I was following your instructions. Nancy is a terrible flighty thing. I've often had to scold her well for her heedlessness."

"It was our own fault," said Marilla resignedly. "We should have come to you ourselves and not left an important message to be passed along by word of mouth in that fashion. Anyhow, the mistake has been made and the only thing to do now is to set it right. Can we send the child back to the asylum? I suppose they'll take her back, won't they?"

"I suppose so," said Mrs. Spencer thoughtfully, "but I don't think it will be necessary to send her back. Mrs. Peter Blewett was up here yesterday, and she was saying to me how much she wished she'd sent by me for a little girl to help her. Mrs. Peter has a large family, you know, and she finds it hard to get help. Anne will be the very girl for her. I call it positively providential."

Marilla did not look as if she thought Providence had much to do with the matter. Here was an unexpected good chance to get this unwelcome orphan off her hands, and she did not even feel grateful for it.

She knew Mrs. Peter Blewett only by sight as a small, shrewish-faced woman without an ounce of superfluous flesh on her bones. But she had heard of her. "A terrible worker and driver," Mrs. Peter was said to be; and discharged servant girls told fearsome tales of her temper and stinginess and her family of pert, quarrelsome children. Marilla felt a qualm of conscience at the thought of handing Anne over to her tender mercies.

"Well, I'll go in and we'll talk the matter over," she said.

"And if there isn't Mrs. Peter coming up the lane this blessed minute!" exclaimed Mrs. Spencer, bustling her guests through the hall into the parlour, where a deadly chill struck on them as if the air had been strained so long through dark green, closely drawn blinds that it had lost every particle of warmth it had ever possessed. "That is real lucky, for we can settle the matter right away. Take the armchair, Miss Cuthbert. Anne, you sit here on the ottoman and don't wriggle. Let me take your hats. Flora Jane, go out and put the kettle on. Good afternoon, Mrs. Blewett. We were just saying how fortunate it was you happened along. Let me introduce you two ladies. Mrs. Blewett, Miss Cuthbert. Please excuse me for just a moment. I forgot to tell Flora Jane to take the buns out of the oven."

Mrs. Spencer whisked away after pulling up the blinds. Anne, sitting mutely on the ottoman, with her hands clasped tightly in her lap, stared at Mrs. Blewett as one fascinated. Was she to be given into the keeping of this sharp-faced, sharp-eyed woman? She felt a lump coming up in her throat, and her eyes smarted painfully. She was beginning to be afraid she couldn't keep the tears back when Mrs. Spencer returned, flushed and beaming, quite capable of taking any and every difficulty, physical, mental, or spiritual, into consideration and settling it out of hand.

"It seems there's been a mistake about this little girl, Mrs. Blewett," she said. "I was under the impression that Mr. and Miss Cuthbert wanted a little girl to adopt. I was certainly told so. But it seems it was a boy they wanted. So if you're still of the same mind you were yesterday, I think she'll be just the thing for you."

Mrs. Blewett darted her eyes over Anne from head to foot.

"How old are you and what's your name?" she demanded.

"Anne Shirley," faltered the shrinking child, not daring to make any stipulations regarding the spelling thereof, "and I'm eleven years old."

"Humph! You don't look as if there was much to you. But you're wiry. I don't know but the wiry ones are the best after all. Well, if I take you, you'll have to be a good girl, you know—good and smart and respectful. I'll expect you to earn your keep, and no mistake about that. Yes, I suppose I might as well take her off your hands, Miss Cuthbert. The baby's awful fractious, and I'm clean worn out attending to him. If you like, I can take her right home now."

Marilla looked at Anne and softened at sight of the child's pale face with its look of mute misery—the misery of a helpless little creature who finds itself once more caught in the trap from which it had escaped. Marilla felt an uncomfortable conviction that, if she denied the appeal of that look, it would haunt her to her dying day. Moreover, she did not fancy Mrs. Blewett. To hand a sensitive, "high-strung" child over to such a woman! No, she could not take the responsibility of doing that!

"Well, I don't know," she said slowly. "I didn't say that Matthew and I had absolutely decided that we wouldn't keep her. In fact, I may say that Matthew is disposed to keep her. I just came over to find out how the mistake had occurred. I think I'd better take her home again and talk it over with Matthew. I feel that I oughtn't to decide on anything without consulting him. If we make up our mind not to keep her, we'll bring or send her over to you tomorrow night. If we don't, you may know that she is going to stay with us. Will that suit you, Mrs. Blewett?"

"I suppose it'll have to," said Mrs. Blewett ungraciously.

During Marilla's speech, a sunrise had been dawning on Anne's face. First the look of despair faded out; then came a faint flush of hope; her eyes grew deep and bright as morning stars. The child was quite transfigured; and a moment later, when Mrs. Spencer and Mrs. Blewett went out in quest of a recipe the latter had come to borrow, she sprang up and flew across the room to Marilla.

"Oh, Miss Cuthbert, did you really say that perhaps you would let me stay at Green Gables?" she said in a breathless whisper, as if speaking aloud might shatter the glorious possibility. "Did you really say it? Or did I only imagine that you did?"

"I think you'd better learn to control that imagination of yours, Anne, if you can't distinguish between what is real and what isn't," said Marilla crossly. "Yes, you did hear me say just that and no more. It isn't decided yet and perhaps we will conclude to let Mrs. Blewett take you after all. She certainly needs you much more than I do."

"I'd rather go back to the asylum than go to live with her," said Anne passionately. "She looks exactly like a—like a gimlet."

Marilla smothered a smile under the conviction that Anne must be reproved for such a speech.

"A little girl like you should be ashamed of talking so about a lady and a stranger," she said severely. "Go back and sit down quietly and hold your tongue and behave as a good girl should."

"I'll try to do and be anything you want me, if you'll only keep me," said Anne, returning meekly to her ottoman.

When they arrived back at Green Gables that evening, Matthew met them in the lane. Marilla from afar had noted him prowling along it and guessed his motive. She was prepared for the relief she read in his face when he saw that she had at least brought Anne back with her. But she said nothing to him, relative to the affair, until they were both out in the yard behind the barn milking the cows. Then she briefly told him Anne's history and the result of the interview with Mrs. Spencer.

"I wouldn't give a dog I liked to that Blewett woman," said Matthew with unusual vim.

"I don't fancy her style myself," admitted Marilla, "but it's that or keeping her ourselves, Matthew. And since you seem to want her, I suppose I'm willing—or have to be. I've been thinking over the idea until I've got kind of used to it. It seems a sort of duty. I've never brought up a child, especially a girl, and I dare say I'll make a terrible mess of it. But I'll do my best. So far as I'm concerned, Matthew, she may stay."

Matthew's shy face was a glow of delight.

"Well now, I reckoned you'd come to see it in that light, Marilla," he said. "She's such an interesting little thing."

"It'd be more to the point if you could say she was a useful little thing," retorted Marilla, "but I'll make it my business to see she's trained to be that. And mind, Matthew, you're not to go interfering with my methods. Perhaps an old maid doesn't know much about bringing up a child, but I guess she knows more than an old bachelor. So you just leave me to manage her. When I fail, it'll be time enough to put your oar in."

"There, there, Marilla, you can have your own way," said Matthew reassuringly. "Only be as good and kind to her as you can be without spoiling her. I kind of think she's one of the sort you can do anything with if you only get her to love you."

Marilla sniffed, to express her contempt for Matthew's opinions concerning anything feminine, and walked off to the dairy with the pails.

I won't tell her tonight that she can stay, she reflected as she strained the milk into the creamers. *She'd be so excited that she wouldn't sleep a wink. Marilla Cuthbert, you're fairly in for it. Did you ever suppose you'd see the day when you'd be adopting an orphan girl? It's surprising enough; but not so surprising as that Matthew should be at the bottom of it, him that always seemed to have such a mortal dread of little girls. Anyhow, we've decided on the experiment and goodness only knows what will come of it.*

Chapter 7
ANNE SAYS HER PRAYERS

When Marilla took Anne up to bed that night, she said stiffly, "Now, Anne, I noticed last night that you threw your clothes all about the floor when you took them off. That is a very untidy habit, and I can't allow it at all. As soon as you take off any article of clothing, fold it neatly and place it on the chair. I haven't any use at all for little girls who aren't neat."

"I was so harrowed up in my mind last night that I didn't think about my clothes at all," said Anne. "I'll fold them nicely tonight. They always made us do that at the asylum. Half the time, though, I'd forget, I'd be in such a hurry to get into bed nice and quiet and imagine things."

"You'll have to remember a little better if you stay here," admonished Marilla. "There, that looks something like.[1] Say your prayers now and get into bed."

"I never say any prayers," announced Anne.

Marilla looked horrified.

"Why, Anne, what do you mean? Were you never taught to say your prayers? God always wants little girls to say their prayers. Don't you know who God is, Anne?"

" 'God is a Spirit, infinite, eternal, and unchangeable, in His being, wisdom, power, holiness, justice, goodness, and truth,' " responded Anne promptly and glibly.

Marilla looked rather relieved.

"So you do know something then, thank goodness! You're not quite a heathen. Where did you learn that?"

"Oh, at the asylum Sunday school. They made us learn the whole catechism. I liked it pretty well. There's something splendid about some of the words. 'Infinite, eternal, and unchangeable.' Isn't that grand? It has such a roll to it—just like a big organ playing. You couldn't quite call it poetry, I suppose, but it sounds a lot like it, doesn't it?"

---

[1]More like it.

"We're not talking about poetry, Anne—we are talking about saying your prayers. Don't you know it's a terrible wicked thing not to say your prayers every night? I'm afraid you are a very bad little girl."

"You'd find it easier to be bad than good if you had red hair," said Anne reproachfully. "People who haven't red hair don't know what trouble is. Mrs. Thomas told me that God made my hair red *on purpose,* and I've never cared about Him since. And anyhow I'd always be too tired at night to bother saying prayers. People who have to look after twins can't be expected to say their prayers. Now, do you honestly think they can?"

Marilla decided that Anne's religious training must be begun at once. Plainly, there was no time to be lost.

"You must say your prayers while you are under my roof, Anne."

"Why, of course, if you want me to," assented Anne cheerfully. "I'd do anything to oblige you. But you'll have to tell me what to say for this once. After I get into bed, I'll imagine out a real nice prayer to say always. I believe that it will be quite interesting, now that I come to think of it."

"You must kneel down," said Marilla in embarrassment.

Anne knelt at Marilla's knee and looked up gravely.

"Why must people kneel down to pray? If I really wanted to pray, I'll tell you what I'd do. I'd go out into a great big field all alone or into the deep, deep woods, and I'd look up into the sky—up—up—up—into that lovely blue sky that looks as if there was no end to its blueness. And then I'd just *feel* a prayer. Well, I'm ready. What am I to say?"

Marilla felt more embarrassed than ever. She had intended to teach Anne the childish classic "Now I lay me down to sleep." But she had, as I have told you, the glimmerings of a sense of humour—which is simply another name for a sense of the fitness of things; and it suddenly occurred to her that that simple little prayer, sacred to white-robed child-hood lisping at motherly knees, was entirely unsuited to this freckled witch of a girl who knew and cared nothing about God's love, since she had never had it translated to her through the medium of human love.

"You're old enough to pray for yourself, Anne," she said finally. "Just thank God for your blessings and ask Him humbly for the things you want."

"Well, I'll do my best," promised Anne, burying her face in Marilla's lap. "Gracious heavenly Father—that's the way the ministers say it in church, so I suppose it's all right in a private prayer, isn't it?" she interjected, lifting her head for a moment. "Gracious heavenly Father, I thank Thee for the White Way of Delight and the Lake of Shining Waters and Bonny and the Snow Queen. I'm really extremely grateful for them. And that's all the blessings I can think of just now to thank Thee for. As for the things I want, they're so numerous that it would take a great deal of time to name them all, so I will only mention the two most important. Please let me stay at Green Gables, and please let me be good-looking when I grow up. I remain, Yours respectfully, Anne Shirley.

"There, did I do it all right?" she asked eagerly, getting up. "I could have made it much more flowery if I'd had a little more time to think it over."

Poor Marilla was only preserved from complete collapse by remembering that it was not irreverence, but simply spiritual ignorance on the part of Anne that was responsible for this extraordinary petition. She tucked the child up in bed, mentally vowing that she should be taught a prayer the very next day, and was leaving the room with the light when Anne called her back.

"I've just thought of it now. I should have said 'Amen' in place of 'Yours respectfully,' shouldn't I?—the way the ministers do. I'd forgotten it, but I felt a prayer should be finished off in some way, so I put in the other. Do you suppose it will make any difference?"

"I—I don't suppose it will," said Marilla. "Go to sleep now, like a good child. Good night."

"I can say good night tonight with a clear conscience," said Anne, cuddling luxuriously down among her pillows.

Marilla retreated to the kitchen, set the candle firmly on the table, and glared at Matthew.

"Matthew Cuthbert, it's about time somebody adopted that child and taught her something. She's next door to a perfect heathen. Will you believe that she never said a prayer in her life till tonight? I'll send to the manse tomorrow and borrow the Peep of Day series,[2] that's what I'll do. And she shall go to Sunday school just as soon as I can get some suitable clothes made for her. I foresee that I shall have my hands full. Well, well, we can't get through this world without our share of trouble. I've had a pretty easy life of it so far, but my time has come at last, and I suppose I'll just have to make the best of it."

---

[2] Methodist Sunday school tracts by Mrs. Favell Lee.

Chapter 8
ANNE'S BRINGING-UP
IS BEGUN

For reasons best known to herself, Marilla did not tell Anne that she was to stay at Green Gables until the next afternoon. During the forenoon, she kept the child busy with various tasks and watched over her with a keen eye while she did them. By noon she had concluded that Anne was smart and obedient, willing to work and quick to learn; her most serious shortcoming seemed to be a tendency to fall into daydreams in the middle of a task and forget all about it until such time as she was sharply recalled to earth by a reprimand or a catastrophe.

When Anne had finished washing the dinner dishes, she suddenly confronted Marilla with the air and expression of one desperately determined to learn the worst. Her thin little body trembled from head to foot; her face flushed and her eyes dilated until they were almost black. She clasped her hands tightly and said in an imploring voice:

"Oh, please, Miss Cuthbert, won't you tell me if you are going to send me away or not? I've tried to be patient all the morning, but I really feel that I cannot bear not knowing any longer. It's a dreadful feeling. Please tell me."

"You haven't scalded the dishcloth in clean hot water as I told you to do," said Marilla immovably. "Just go and do it before you ask any more questions, Anne."

Anne went and attended to the dishcloth. Then she returned to Marilla and fastened imploring eyes on the latter's face.

"Well," said Marilla, unable to find any excuse for deferring her explanation longer, "I suppose I might as well tell you. Matthew and I have decided to keep you—that is, if you will try to be a good little girl and show yourself grateful. Why, child, whatever is the matter?"

"I'm crying," said Anne in a tone of bewilderment. "I can't think why. I'm glad as glad can be. Oh, *glad* doesn't seem the right word at all. I was glad about the White Way and the cherry blossoms—but this! Oh, it's something more than glad. I'm so happy. I'll try to be so good. It will be uphill work, I expect, for Mrs. Thomas often told me I was desperately wicked. However, I'll do my very best. But can you tell me why I'm crying?"

"I suppose it's because you're all excited and worked up," said Marilla disapprovingly. "Sit down on that chair and try to calm yourself. I'm afraid you both cry and laugh far too easily. Yes, you can stay here and we will try to do right by you. You must go to school; but it's only a fortnight till vacation so it isn't worthwhile for you to start before it opens again in September."

"What am I to call you?" asked Anne. "Shall I always say Miss Cuthbert? Can I call you Aunt Marilla?"

"No, you'll call me just plain Marilla. I'm not used to being called Miss Cuthbert and it would make me nervous."

"It sounds awfully disrespectful to say just Marilla," protested Anne.

"I guess there'll be nothing disrespectful in it if you're careful to speak respectfully. Everybody, young and old, in Avonlea calls me Marilla except the minister. He says Miss Cuthbert—when he thinks of it."

"I'd love to call you Aunt Marilla," said Anne wistfully. "I've never had an aunt or any relation at all—not even a grandmother. It would make me feel as if I really belonged to you. Can't I call you Aunt Marilla?"

"No. I'm not your aunt and I don't believe in calling people names that don't belong to them."

"But we could imagine you were my aunt."

"I couldn't," said Marilla grimly.

"Do you never imagine things different from what they really are?" asked Anne, wide-eyed.

"No."

"Oh!" Anne drew a long breath. "Oh, Miss—Marilla, how much you miss!"

"I don't believe in imagining things different from what they really are," retorted Marilla. "When the Lord puts us in certain circumstances, He doesn't mean for us to imagine them away. And that reminds me. Go into the sitting room, Anne—be sure your feet are clean and don't let any flies in—and bring me out the illustrated card that's on the mantelpiece. The Lord's Prayer is on it, and you'll devote your spare time this afternoon to learning it by heart. There's to be no more of such praying as I heard last night."

"I suppose I was very awkward," said Anne apologetically, "but then, you see, I'd never had any practice. You couldn't really expect a person to pray very well the first time she tried, could you? I thought out a splendid prayer after I went to bed, just as I promised you I would. It was nearly as long as a minister's and so poetical. But would you believe it? I couldn't remember one word when I woke up this morning. And I'm afraid I'll never be able to think out another one as good. Somehow, things never are so good when they're thought out a second time. Have you ever noticed that?"

"Here is something for you to notice, Anne. When I tell you to do a thing, I want you to obey me at once and not stand stock-still and discourse about it. Just you go and do as I bid you."

Anne promptly departed for the sitting room across the hall; she failed to return. After waiting ten minutes, Marilla laid down her knitting and marched after her with a grim expression. She found Anne standing motionless before a picture hanging on the wall between the two windows, with her hands clasped behind her, her face uplifted, and her eyes astar with dreams. The white and green light strained through apple trees and clustering vines outside fell over the rapt little figure with a half-unearthly radiance.

"Anne, whatever are you thinking of?" demanded Marilla sharply.

Anne came back to earth with a start.

"That," she said, pointing to the picture—a rather vivid chromo entitled "Christ Blessing Little Children"—"and I was just imagining I was one of them—that I was the little girl in the blue dress, standing off by herself in the corner as if she didn't belong to anybody, like me. She looks lonely and sad, don't you think? I guess she hadn't any father or mother of her own. But she wanted to be blessed, too, so she just crept shyly up on the outside of the crowd, hoping nobody would notice her—except Him. I'm sure I know just how she felt. Her heart must have beat and her hands must have got cold, like mine did when I asked you if I could stay. She was afraid He mightn't notice her. But it's likely He did, don't you think? I've been trying to imagine it all out—her edging a little nearer all the time until she was quite close to Him; and then He would look at her and put His hand on her hair and, oh, such a thrill of joy as would run over her! But I wish the artist hadn't painted Him so sorrowful-looking. All His pictures are like that, if you've noticed. But I don't believe He could really have looked so sad or the children would have been afraid of Him."

"Anne," said Marilla, wondering why she had not broken into this speech long before, "you shouldn't talk that way. It's irreverent—positively irreverent."

Anne's eyes marveled. "Why, I felt just as reverent as could be. I'm sure I didn't mean to be irreverent."

"Well, I don't suppose you did—but it doesn't sound right to talk so familiarly about such things. And another thing, Anne, when I send you after something, you're to bring it at once and not fall into mooning and imagining before pictures. Remember that. Take that card and come right to the kitchen. Now, sit down in the corner and learn that prayer by heart."

Anne set the card up against the jugful of apple blossoms she had brought in to decorate the dinner table—Marilla had eyed that decoration askance but had said nothing—propped her chin on her hands, and fell to studying it intently for several silent minutes.

"I like this," she announced at length. "It's beautiful. I've heard it before—I heard the superintendent of the asylum Sunday school say it over once. But I didn't like it then. He had such a cracked voice and he prayed it so mournfully. I really felt sure he thought praying was a disagreeable duty. This isn't poetry, but it makes me feel just the same way poetry does. 'Our Father who art in heaven, hallowed be Thy name.' That is just like a line of music. Oh, I'm so glad you thought of making me learn this, Miss—Marilla."

"Well, learn it and hold your tongue," said Marilla shortly.

Anne tipped the vase of apple blossoms near enough to bestow a soft kiss on a pink-cupped bud, then studied diligently for some moments longer.

"Marilla," she demanded presently, "do you think I shall ever have a bosom friend in Avonlea?"

"A—a what kind of friend?"

"A bosom friend—an intimate friend, you know—a really kindred spirit to whom I can confide my inmost soul. I've dreamed of meeting her all my life. I never really supposed I would, but so many of my loveliest dreams have come true all at once that perhaps this one will, too. Do you think it's possible?"

"Diana Barry lives over at Orchard Slope and she's about your age. She's a very nice little girl, and perhaps she will be a playmate for you when she comes home. She's visiting her aunt over at Carmody just now. You'll have to be careful how you behave yourself, though. Mrs. Barry is a very particular woman. She won't let Diana play with any little girl who isn't nice and good."

Anne looked at Marilla through the apple blossoms, her eyes aglow with interest.

"What is Diana like? Her hair isn't red, is it? Oh, I hope not. It's bad enough to have red hair myself, but I positively couldn't endure it in a bosom friend."

"Diana is a very pretty little girl. She has black eyes and hair and rosy cheeks. And she is good and smart, which is better than being pretty."

Marilla was as fond of morals as the Duchess in Wonderland and was firmly convinced that one should be tacked on to every remark made to a child who was being brought up.

But Anne waved the moral inconsequently aside and seized only on the delightful possibilities before it.

"Oh, I'm so glad she's pretty. Next to being beautiful oneself—and that's impossible in my case—it would be best to have a beautiful bosom friend. When I lived with Mrs. Thomas, she had a bookcase in her sitting room with glass doors. There weren't any books in it; Mrs. Thomas kept her best china and her preserves there—when she had any preserves to keep. One of the doors was broken. Mr. Thomas smashed it one night when he was slightly intoxicated. But the other was whole, and I used to pretend that my reflection in it was another little girl who lived in it. I called her Katie Maurice, and we were very intimate. I used to talk to her by the hour, especially on Sunday, and tell her everything. Katie was the comfort and consolation of my life. We used to pretend that the bookcase was enchanted and that if I only knew the spell, I could open the door and step right into the room where Katie Maurice lived, instead of into Mrs. Thomas's shelves of preserves and china. And then Katie Maurice would have taken me by the hand and led me out into a wonderful place, all flowers and sunshine and fairies, and we would have lived there happy forever after. When I went to live with Mrs. Hammond, it just broke my heart to leave Katie Maurice. She felt it dreadfully, too; I know she did, for she was crying when she kissed me good-bye through the bookcase door. There was no bookcase at Mrs. Hammond's. But just up the river a little way from the house there was a long, green little valley, and the loveliest echo lived there. It echoed back every word you said, even if you didn't talk a bit loud. So I imagined that it was a little girl called Violetta and we were great friends and I loved her almost as well as I loved Katie Maurice—not quite, but almost, you know. The night before I went to the asylum, I said good-bye to Violetta, and, oh, her good-bye came back to me in such sad, sad tones. I had become so attached to her that I hadn't the heart to imagine a bosom friend at the asylum, even if there had been any scope for imagination there."

"I think it's just as well there wasn't," said Marilla drily. "I don't approve of such goings-on. You seem to half believe your own imaginations. It will be well for you to have a real live friend to put such nonsense out of your head. But don't let Mrs. Barry hear you talking about your Katie Maurices and your Violettas or she'll think you tell stories."

"Oh, I won't. I couldn't talk of them to everybody—their memories are too sacred for that. But I thought I'd like to have you know about them. Oh, look, here's a big bee just tumbled out of an apple blossom. Just think what a lovely place to live—in an apple blossom! Fancy going to sleep in it when the wind was rocking it. If I wasn't a human girl, I think I'd like to be a bee and live among the flowers."

"Yesterday you wanted to be a seagull," sniffed Marilla. "I think you are very fickle-minded. I told you to learn that prayer and not talk. But it seems impossible for you to stop talking if you've got anybody that will listen to you. So go up to your room and learn it."

"Oh, I know it pretty nearly all now—all but just the last line."

"Well, never mind, do as I tell you. Go to your room and finish learning it well, and stay there until I call you down to help me get tea."

"Can I take the apple blossoms with me for company?" pleaded Anne.

"No. You don't want your room cluttered up with flowers. You should have left them on the tree in the first place."

"I did feel a little that way, too," said Anne. "I kind of felt I shouldn't shorten their lovely lives by picking them—I wouldn't want to be picked if I were an apple blossom. But the temptation was *irresistible*. What do you do when you meet with an irresistible temptation?"

"Anne, did you hear me tell you to go to your room?"

Anne sighed, retreated to the east gable, and sat down in a chair by the window.

"There—I know this prayer. I learned that last sentence coming upstairs. Now I'm going to imagine things into this room so that they'll always stay imagined. The floor is covered with a white velvet carpet with pink roses all over it, and there are pink silk curtains at the windows. The walls are hung with gold and silver brocade tapestry. The furniture is mahogany. I never saw any mahogany, but it does sound *so* luxurious. This is a couch all heaped with gorgeous silken cushions, pink and blue and crimson and gold, and I am reclining gracefully on it. I can see my reflection in that splendid big mirror hanging on the wall. I am tall and regal, clad in a gown of trailing white lace, with a pearl cross on my breast and pearls in my hair. My hair is of midnight darkness, and my skin is a clear ivory pallor. My name is the Lady Cordelia Fitzgerald. No, it isn't—I can't make *that* seem real."

She danced up to the little looking glass and peered into it. Her pointed freckled face and solemn gray eyes peered back at her.

"You're only Anne of Green Gables," she said earnestly, "and I see you, just as you are looking now, whenever I try to imagine I'm the Lady Cordelia. But it's a million times nicer to be Anne of Green Gables than Anne of nowhere in particular, isn't it?"

She bent forward, kissed her reflection affectionately, and betook herself to the open window.

"Dear Snow Queen, good afternoon. And good afternoon, dear birches down in the hollow. And good afternoon, dear gray house up on the hill. I wonder if Diana is to be my bosom friend. I hope she will, and I shall love her very much. But I must never quite forget Katie Maurice and Violetta. They would feel so hurt if I did and I'd hate to hurt anybody's feelings, even a little bookcase girl's or a little echo girl's. I must be careful to remember them and send them a kiss every day."

Anne blew a couple of airy kisses from her fingertips past the cherry blossoms and then, with her chin in her hands, drifted luxuriously out on a sea of daydreams.

Chapter 9

MRS. RACHEL LYNDE IS PROPERLY HORRIFIED

Anne had been a fortnight at Green Gables before Mrs. Lynde arrived to inspect her. Mrs. Rachel, to do her justice, was not to blame for this. A severe and unseasonable attack of grippe had confined that good lady to her house ever since the occasion of her last visit to Green Gables. Mrs. Rachel was not often sick and had a well-defined contempt for people who were; but grippe, she asserted, was like no other illness on earth and could only be interpreted as one of the special visitations of Providence. As soon as her doctor allowed her to put her foot out-of-doors, she hurried up to Green Gables, bursting with curiosity to see Matthew and Marilla's orphan, concerning whom all sorts of stories and suppositions had gone abroad in Avonlea.

Anne had made good use of every waking moment of that fortnight. Already she was acquainted with every tree and shrub about the place. She had discovered that a lane opened out below the apple orchard and ran up through a belt of woodland; and she had explored it to its farthest end in all its delicious vagaries of brook and bridge, fir coppice and wild cherry arch, corners thick with fern, and branching byways of maple and mountain ash.

She had made friends with the spring down in the hollow—that wonderful deep, clear icy-cold spring. It was set about with smooth red sandstones and rimmed in by great palmlike clumps of water fern; and beyond it was a log bridge over the brook.

That bridge led Anne's dancing feet up over a wooded hill beyond, where perpetual twilight reigned under the straight, thick-growing firs and spruces; the only flowers there were a myriad of delicate Junebells, those shyest and sweetest of woodland blooms, and a few pale, aerial starflowers, like the spirits of last year's blossoms. Gossamers glimmered like threads of silver among the trees, and the fir boughs and tassels seemed to utter friendly speech.

All these raptured voyages of exploration were made in the odd half hours that she was allowed for play, and Anne talked Matthew and Marilla half deaf over her discoveries. Not that Matthew complained, to be sure; he listened to it all with a wordless smile of enjoyment on his face. Marilla permitted the "chatter" until she found herself becoming too interested in it, whereupon she always promptly quenched Anne by a curt command to hold her tongue.

Anne was out in the orchard when Mrs. Rachel came, wandering at her own sweet will through the lush, tremulous grasses splashed with ruddy evening sunshine; so that good lady had an excellent chance to talk her illness fully over, describing every ache and pulse beat with such evident enjoyment that Marilla thought even grippe must bring its compensations. When details were exhausted, Mrs. Rachel introduced the real reason for her call.

"I've been hearing some surprising things about you and Matthew."

"I don't suppose you are any more surprised than I am myself," said Marilla. "I'm getting over my surprise now."

"It was too bad there was such a mistake," said Mrs. Rachel sympathetically. "Couldn't you have sent her back?"

"I suppose we could, but we decided not to. Matthew took a fancy to her. And I must say I like her myself—although I admit she has her faults. The house seems a different place already. She's a real bright little thing."

Marilla said more than she had intended to say when she began, for she read disapproval in Mrs. Rachel's expression.

"It's a great responsibility you've taken on yourself," said that lady gloomily, "especially when you've never had any experience with children. You don't know much about her or her real disposition, I suppose, and there's no guessing how a child like that will turn out. But I don't want to discourage you, I'm sure, Marilla."

"I'm not feeling discouraged," was Marilla's dry response. "When I make up my mind to do a thing, it stays made up. I suppose you'd like to see Anne. I'll call her in."

Anne came running in presently, her face sparkling with the delight of her orchard rovings; but abashed at finding herself in the unexpected presence of a stranger, she halted confusedly inside the door. She certainly was an odd-looking little creature in the short, tight wincey dress she had worn from the asylum, below which her thin legs seemed ungracefully long. Her freckles were more numerous and obtrusive than ever; the wind had ruffled her hatless hair into overbrilliant disorder, and it had never looked redder than at that moment.

"Well, they didn't pick you for your looks, that's sure and certain," was Mrs. Rachel Lynde's emphatic comment. Mrs. Rachel was one of those delightful and popular people who pride themselves on speaking their minds without fear or favor. "She's terrible skinny and homely, Marilla. Come here, child, and let me have a look at you. Lawful heart, did anyone ever see such freckles? And hair as red as carrots! Come here, child, I say."

Anne "came there," but not exactly as Mrs. Rachel expected. With one bound, she crossed the kitchen floor and stood before Mrs. Rachel, her face scarlet with anger, her lips quivering, and her whole slender form trembling from head to foot.

"I hate you," she cried in a choked voice, stamping her foot on the floor. "I hate you—I hate you—I hate you—" She gave a louder stamp with each assertion of hatred. "How dare you call me skinny and ugly! How dare you say I'm freckled and redheaded! You are a rude, impolite, unfeeling woman!"

"Anne!" exclaimed Marilla in consternation.

But Anne continued to face Mrs. Rachel undauntedly, head up, eyes blazing, hands clenched, passionate indignation exhaling from her like an atmosphere.

"How dare you say such things about me!" she repeated vehemently. "How would you like to have such things said about you? How would you like to be told that you are fat and clumsy and probably hadn't a spark of imagination in you? I don't care if I do hurt your feelings by saying so! I hope I hurt them. You have hurt mine worse than they were ever hurt before, even by Mrs. Thomas's intoxicated husband. And I'll *never* forgive you for it, never, never!"

Stamp! Stamp!

"Did anybody ever see such a temper!" exclaimed the horrified Mrs. Rachel.

"Anne, go to your room and stay there until I come up," said Marilla, recovering her powers of speech with difficulty.

Anne, bursting into tears, rushed to the hall door, slammed it until the tins on the porch wall outside rattled in sympathy, and fled through the hall and up the stairs like a whirlwind. A subdued slam above told that the door of the east gable had been shut with equal vehemence.

"Well, I don't envy you your job bringing *that* up, Marilla," said Mrs. Rachel with unspeakable solemnity.

"I hate you," she cried in a choked voice.

Marilla opened her lips to say she knew not what of apology or depre-cation. What she did say was a surprise to herself then and ever afterward. "You shouldn't have twitted her about her looks, Rachel."

"Marilla Cuthbert, you don't mean to say that you are upholding her in such a terrible display of temper as we've just seen?" demanded Mrs. Rachel indignantly.

"No," said Marilla slowly, "I'm not trying to excuse her. She's been very naughty, and I'll have to give her a talking to about it. But we must make allowances for her. She's never been taught what is right. And you *were* too hard on her, Rachel."

Marilla could not help tacking on that last sentence, although she was again surprised at herself for doing it. Mrs. Rachel got up with an air of offended dignity.

"Well, I see that I'll have to be very careful what I say after this, Marilla, since the fine feelings of orphans, brought from goodness knows where, have to be considered before anything else. Oh, no, I'm not vexed—don't worry yourself. I'm too sorry for you to leave any room for anger in my mind. You'll have your own troubles with that child. But if you'll take my advice—which I suppose you won't do, although I've brought up ten chil-dren and buried two—you'll do that 'talking to' you mention with a fair-sized birch switch. I should think *that* would be the most effective language for that kind of a child. Her temper matches her hair, I guess. Well, good evening, Marilla. I hope you'll come down to see me often as usual. But you can't expect me to visit here again in a hurry, if I'm liable to be flown at and insulted in such a fashion. It's something new in *my* experience."

Whereat Mrs. Rachel swept out and away—if a fat woman who always waddled *could* be said to sweep away—and Marilla with a very solemn face betook herself to the east gable.

On the way upstairs, she pondered uneasily as to what she ought to do. She felt no little dismay over the scene that had just been enacted. How unfortunate that Anne should have displayed such temper before Mrs. Rachel Lynde, of all people! Then Marilla suddenly became aware of an uncomfortable and rebuking consciousness that she felt more humilia-tion over this than sorrow over the discovery of such a serious defect in Anne's disposition. And how was she to punish her? The amiable sugges-tion of the birch switch—to the efficiency of which all of Mrs. Rachel's own children could have borne smarting testimony—did not appeal to Marilla. She did not believe she could whip a child. No, some other method of punishment must be found to bring Anne to a proper real-ization of the enormity of her offense.

Marilla found Anne face downward on her bed, crying bitterly, quite oblivious of muddy boots on a clean counterpane.

"Anne," she said, not ungently.

No answer.

"Anne," with greater severity, "get off that bed this minute and listen to what I have to say to you."

Anne squirmed off the bed and sat rigidly on a chair beside it, her face swollen and tear-stained and her eyes fixed stubbornly on the floor.

"This is a nice way for you to behave, Anne! Aren't you ashamed of yourself?"

"She hadn't any right to call me ugly and redheaded," retorted Anne, evasive and defiant.

"You hadn't any right to fly into such a fury and talk the way you did to her, Anne. I was ashamed of you—thoroughly ashamed of you. I wanted you to behave nicely to Mrs. Lynde, and instead of that, you have disgraced me. I'm sure I don't know why you should lose your temper like that just because Mrs. Lynde said you were red-haired and homely. You say it yourself often enough."

"Oh, but there's such a difference between saying a thing yourself and hearing other people say it," wailed Anne. "You may know a thing is so, but you can't help hoping other people don't quite think it is. I suppose you think I have an awful temper, but I couldn't help it. When she said those things, something just rose right up in me and choked me. I *had* to fly out at her."

"Well, you made a fine exhibition of yourself, I must say. Mrs. Lynde will have a nice story to tell about you everywhere—and she'll tell it, too. It was a dreadful thing for you to lose your temper like that, Anne."

"Just imagine how you would feel if somebody told you to your face that you were skinny and ugly," pleaded Anne tearfully.

An old remembrance suddenly rose up before Marilla. She had been a very small child when she had heard one aunt say of her to another, "What a pity she is such a dark, homely little thing." Marilla was every day of fifty before the sting had gone out of that memory.

"I don't say that I think Mrs. Lynde was exactly right in saying she did to you, Anne," she admitted in a softer tone. "Rachel is too outspoken. But that is no excuse for such behavior on your part. She was a stranger and an elderly person and my visitor—all three very good reasons why you should have been respectful to her. You were rude and saucy and"—Marilla had a saving inspiration of punishment—"you must go to her and tell her you are very sorry for your bad temper and ask her to forgive you."

"I can never do that," said Anne determinedly and darkly. "You can punish me in any way you like, Marilla. You can shut me up in a dark, damp dungeon inhabited by snakes and toads and feed me only on bread and water, and I shall not complain. But I cannot ask Mrs. Lynde to forgive me."

"We're not in the habit of shutting people up in dark, damp dungeons," said Marilla drily, "especially as they're rather scarce in Avonlea. But apologize to Mrs. Lynde you must and shall, and you'll stay here in your room until you can tell me you're willing to do it."

"I shall have to stay here forever then," said Anne mournfully, "because I can't tell Mrs. Lynde I'm sorry I said those things to her. How can I? I'm *not* sorry. I'm sorry I vexed you; but I'm *glad* I told her just what I did. It was a great satisfaction. I can't say I'm sorry when I'm not, can I? I can't even *imagine* I'm sorry."

"Perhaps your imagination will be in better working order by the morning," said Marilla, rising to depart. "You'll have the night to think over your conduct and come to a better frame of mind. You said you would try to be a very good girl if we kept you at Green Gables, but I must say it hasn't seemed very much like it this evening."

Leaving this Parthian shaft[1] to rankle in Anne's stormy bosom, Marilla descended to the kitchen, grievously troubled in mind and vexed in soul. She was as angry with herself as with Anne, because whenever she recalled Mrs. Rachel's dumbfounded countenance, her lips twitched with amusement and she felt a most reprehensible desire to laugh.

---

[1] Horsemen from the ancient eastern kingdom of Parthia were known for their habit of discharging missiles backward while in actual or pretended flight (*Annotated Anne*, 118).

Chapter 10

ANNE'S APOLOGY

Marilla said nothing to Matthew about the affair that evening, but when Anne proved still refractory the next morning, an explanation had to be made to account for her absence from the breakfast table. Marilla told Matthew the whole story, taking pains to impress him with a due sense of the enormity of Anne's behavior.

"It's a good thing Rachel Lynde got a calling down. She's a meddlesome old gossip," was Matthew's consolatory rejoinder.

"Matthew Cuthbert, I'm astonished at you. You know that Anne's behavior was dreadful, and yet you take her part! I suppose you'll be saying next that she oughtn't to be punished at all."

"Well, now—no—not exactly," said Matthew uneasily. "I reckon she ought to be punished a little. But don't be too hard on her, Marilla. Recollect she hasn't ever had anyone to teach her right. You're—you're going to give her something to eat, aren't you?"

"When did you ever hear of me starving people into good behaviour?" demanded Marilla indignantly. "She'll have her meals regular, and I'll carry them up to her myself. But she'll stay up there until she's willing to apologize to Mrs. Lynde, and that's final, Matthew."

Breakfast, dinner, and supper were very silent meals—for Anne still remained obdurate. After each meal, Marilla carried a well-filled tray to the east gable and brought it down later on, not noticeably depleted. Matthew eyed its last descent with a troubled eye. Had Anne eaten anything at all?

When Marilla went out that evening to bring the cows from the back pasture, Matthew, who had been hanging about the barns and watching, slipped into the house with the air of a burglar and crept upstairs. As a general thing, Matthew gravitated between the kitchen and the little bedroom off the hall where he slept; once in a while he ventured uncomfortably into the parlour or sitting room when the minister came to tea. But he had never been upstairs in his own house since the spring he helped Marilla paper the spare bedroom, and that was four years ago.

He tiptoed along the hall and stood for several minutes outside the door of the east gable before he summoned courage to tap on it with his fingers and then open the door to peep in.

Anne was sitting on the yellow chair by the window, gazing mournfully out into the garden. Very small and unhappy she looked, and Matthew's heart smote him. He softly closed the door and tiptoed over to her.

"Anne," he whispered, as if afraid of being overheard, "how are you making it, Anne?"

Anne smiled wanly.

"Pretty well. I imagine a good deal, and that helps to pass the time. Of course, it's rather lonesome. But then, I may as well get used to that."

Anne smiled again, bravely facing the long years of solitary imprisonment before her.

Matthew recollected that he must say what he had come to say without loss of time, lest Marilla return prematurely.

"Well now, Anne, don't you think you'd better do it and have it over with?" he whispered. "It'll have to be done sooner or later, you know, for Marilla's a dreadful determined woman—dreadful determined, Anne. Do it right off, I say, and have it over."

"Do you mean apologize to Mrs. Lynde?"

"Yes—apologize—that's the very word," said Matthew eagerly. "Just smooth it over, so to speak. That's what I was trying to get at."

"I suppose I could do it to oblige you," said Anne thoughtfully. "It would be true enough to say I am sorry, because I *am* sorry now. I wasn't a bit sorry last night. I was mad clear through, and I stayed mad all night. I know I did because I woke up three times and I was just furious every time. But this morning it was all over. I wasn't in a temper anymore—and it left a dreadful sort of goneness, too. I felt so ashamed of myself. But I just couldn't think of going and telling Mrs. Lynde so. It would be so humiliating. I made up my mind I'd stay shut up here forever rather than do that. But still—I'd do anything for you—if you really want me to—"

"Well now, of course I do. It's terrible lonesome downstairs without you. Just go and smooth it over—that's a good girl."

"Very well," said Anne resignedly. "I'll tell Marilla as soon as she comes in that I've repented."

"That's right—that's right, Anne. But don't tell Marilla I said anything about it. She might think I was putting my oar in, and I promised not to do that."

"Wild horses won't drag the secret from me," promised Anne solemnly. "How would wild horses drag a secret from a person anyhow?"

But Matthew was gone, scared at his own success. He fled hastily to the remotest corner of the horse pasture lest Marilla should suspect what he had been up to. Marilla herself, upon her return to the house, was agreeably surprised to hear a plaintive voice calling, "Marilla," over the banisters.

"Well?" she said, going into the hall.

"I'm sorry I lost my temper and said rude things, and I'm willing to go and tell Mrs. Lynde so."

"Very well." Marilla's crispness gave no sign of her relief. She had been wondering what under the canopy[1] she should do if Anne did not give in. "I'll take you down after milking."

Accordingly, after milking, behold Marilla and Anne walking down the lane, the former erect and triumphant, the latter drooping and dejected. But halfway down, Anne's dejection vanished as if by enchantment. She lifted her head and stepped lightly along, her eyes fixed on the sunset sky and an air of subdued exhilaration about her. Marilla beheld the change disapprovingly. This was no meek penitent such as it behooved her to take into the presence of the offended Mrs. Lynde.

"What are you thinking of, Anne?" she asked sharply.

"I'm imagining out what I must say to Mrs. Lynde," answered Anne dreamily.

This was satisfactory—or should have been so. But Marilla could not rid herself of the notion that something in her scheme of punishment was going askew. Anne had no business to look so rapt and radiant.

Rapt and radiant Anne continued until they were in the very presence of Mrs. Lynde, who was sitting knitting by her kitchen window. Then the radiance vanished. Mournful penitence appeared on every feature. Before a word was spoken, Anne suddenly went down on her knees before the astonished Mrs. Rachel and held out her hands beseechingly.

"Oh, Mrs. Lynde, I am so extremely sorry," she said with a quiver in her voice. "I could never express all my sorrow, no, not if I used up a whole dictionary. You must just imagine it. I behaved terribly to you—and I've disgraced the dear friends, Matthew and Marilla, who have let me stay at Green Gables, although I'm not a boy. I'm a dreadfully wicked and ungrateful girl, and I deserve to be punished and cast out by respectable people forever. It was very wicked of me to fly into a temper because you told me the truth. It *was* the truth; every word you said was true. My hair is red and I'm freckled and skinny and ugly. What I said to

---

[1] What under the sun, moon, and stars.

you was true, too, but I shouldn't have said it. Oh, Mrs. Lynde, please, please, forgive me. If you refuse, it will be a lifelong sorrow to me. You wouldn't like to inflict a lifelong sorrow on a poor little orphan girl, would you, even if she had a dreadful temper? Oh, I am sure you wouldn't. Please say you forgive me, Mrs. Lynde."

Anne clasped her hands together, bowed her head, and waited for the word of judgment.

There was no mistaking her sincerity—it breathed in every tone of her voice. Both Marilla and Mrs. Lynde recognized its unmistakable ring. But the former understood in dismay that Anne was actually enjoying her valley of humiliation—was reveling in the thoroughness of her abasement. Where was the wholesome punishment upon which she, Marilla, had plumed herself? Anne had turned it into a species of positive pleasure.

Good Mrs. Lynde, not being overburdened with perception, did not see this. She only perceived that Anne had made a very thorough apology, and all resentment vanished from her kindly, if somewhat officious, heart.

"There, there, get up, child," she said heartily. "Of course I forgive you. I guess I was a little too hard on you, anyway. But I'm such an outspoken person. You just mustn't mind me, that's what. It can't be denied your hair is terrible red; but I knew a girl once—went to school with her, in fact—whose hair was every mite as red as yours when she was young, but when she grew up, it darkened to a real handsome auburn. I wouldn't be a mite surprised if yours did, too—not a mite."

"Oh, Mrs. Lynde!" Anne drew a long breath as she rose to her feet. "You have given me a hope. I shall always feel that you are a benefactor. Oh, I could endure anything if I only thought my hair would be a handsome auburn when I grew up. It would be so much easier to be good if one's hair was a handsome auburn, don't you think? And now may I go out into your garden and sit on that bench under the apple trees while you and Marilla are talking? There is so much more scope for imagination out there."

"Laws, yes, run along, child. And you can pick a bouquet of them white June lilies over in the corner if you like."

As the door closed behind Anne, Mrs. Lynde got briskly up to light a lamp.

"She's a real odd little thing. Take this chair, Marilla; it's easier than the one you've got; I just keep that for the hired boy to sit on. Yes, she certainly is an odd child, but there is something kind of taking about her after all. I don't feel so surprised at you and Matthew keeping her as I did—nor so sorry for you, either. She may turn out all right. Of course, she has a strange way of expressing herself—a little too—well, too kind of forcible, you know; but she'll likely get over that now that she's come to live among civilized folks. And then, her temper's pretty quick, I guess. But there's one comfort: A child that has a quick temper, just blaze up and cool down, ain't never likely to be sly or deceitful. Preserve me from a sly child, that's what. On the whole, Marilla, I kind of like her."

When Marilla went home, Anne came out of the fragrant twilight of the orchard with a sheaf of white narcissi in her hands.

"I apologized pretty well, didn't I?" she said proudly as they went down the lane. "I thought since I had to do it, I might as well do it thoroughly."

"You did it thoroughly, all right enough," was Marilla's comment. Marilla was dismayed at finding herself inclined to laugh over the recollection. She had also an uneasy feeling that she ought to scold Anne for apologizing so well; but then, that was ridiculous! She compromised with her conscience by saying severely:

"I hope you won't have occasion to make many more such apologies. I hope you'll try to control your temper now, Anne."

"That wouldn't be so hard if people wouldn't twit me about my looks," said Anne with a sigh. "I don't get cross about other things, but I'm *so* tired of being twitted about my hair and it just makes me boil right over. Do you suppose my hair will really be a handsome auburn when I grow up?"

"You shouldn't think so much about your looks, Anne. I'm afraid you are a very vain little girl."

"How can I be vain when I know I'm homely?" protested Anne. "I love pretty things; and I hate to look in the glass and see something that isn't pretty. It makes me feel so sorrowful—just as I feel when I look at any ugly thing. I pity it because it isn't beautiful."

"Handsome is as handsome does," quoted Marilla.

"I've had that said to me before, but I have my doubts about it," remarked skeptical Anne, sniffing at her narcissi. "Oh, aren't these flowers sweet! It was lovely of Mrs. Lynde to give them to me. I have no hard feelings against Mrs. Lynde now. It gives you a lovely, comfortable feeling to apologize and be forgiven, doesn't it? Aren't the stars bright tonight? If you could live in a star, which one would you pick? I'd like that lovely, clear big one away over there above that dark hill."

"Anne, do hold your tongue," said Marilla, thoroughly worn out trying to follow the gyrations of Anne's thoughts.

Anne said no more until they turned into their own lane. A little gypsy wind came down it to meet them, laden with the spicy perfume of young dew-wet ferns. Far up in the shadows, a cheerful light gleamed out through the trees from the kitchen at Green Gables. Anne suddenly came close to Marilla and slipped her hand into the older woman's hard palm.

"It's lovely to be going home and know it's home," she said. "I love Green Gables already, and I never loved any place before. No place ever seemed like home. Oh, Marilla, I'm so happy. I could pray right now and not find it a bit hard."

Something warm and pleasant welled up in Marilla's heart at the touch of that thin little hand in her own—a throb of the maternity she had missed, perhaps. Its very unaccustomedness and sweetness disturbed her. She hastened to restore her sensations to their normal calm by inculcating a moral.

"If you'll be a good girl, you'll always be happy, Anne. And you should never find it hard to say your prayers."

"Saying one's prayers isn't exactly the same thing as praying," said Anne meditatively. "But I'm going to imagine that I'm the wind that is blowing up there in those treetops. When I get tired of the trees, I'll imagine I'm gently waving down here in the ferns—and then I'll fly over to Mrs. Lynde's garden and set the flowers dancing—and then I'll go with one great swoop over the clover field—and then I'll blow over the Lake of Shining Waters and ripple it all up into little sparkling waves. Oh, there's so much scope for imagination in a wind! So I'll not talk anymore just now, Marilla."

"Thanks be to goodness for that," breathed Marilla in devout relief.

Chapter 11
ANNE'S IMPRESSIONS OF SUNDAY SCHOOL

"Well, how do you like them?" said Marilla.

Anne was standing in the gable room, looking solemnly at three new dresses spread out on the bed. One was of snuffy-colored gingham that Marilla had been tempted to buy from a peddler the preceding summer because it looked so serviceable; one was of black-and-white-checked sateen that she had picked up at a bargain counter in the winter; and one was a stiff print of an ugly blue shade that she had purchased that week at a Carmody store.

She had made them up herself, and they were all made alike—plain skirts pulled tightly to plain waists, with sleeves as plain as waist and skirt and as tight as sleeves could be.

"I'll imagine that I like them," said Anne soberly.

"I don't want you to imagine it," said Marilla, offended. "Oh, I can see you don't like the dresses! What is the matter with them? Aren't they neat and clean and new?"

"Yes."

"Then why don't you like them?"

"They're—they're not—pretty," said Anne reluctantly.

"Pretty!" Marilla sniffed. "I didn't trouble my head about getting pretty dresses for you. I don't believe in pampering vanity, Anne, I'll tell you that right off. Those dresses are good, sensible, serviceable dresses, without any frills or furbelows about them, and they're all you'll get this summer. The brown gingham and the blue print will do you for school when you begin to go. The sateen is for church and Sunday school. I'll expect you to keep them neat and clean and not to tear them. I should think you'd be grateful to get most anything after those skimpy wincey things you've been wearing."

"Oh, I *am* grateful," protested Anne. "But I'd be ever so much gratefuller

66

if—if you'd made just one of them with puffed sleeves. Puffed sleeves are so fashionable now. It would give me such a thrill, Marilla, just to wear a dress with puffed sleeves."

"Well, you'll have to do without your thrill. I hadn't any material to waste on puffed sleeves. I think they are ridiculous-looking things anyhow. I prefer the plain, sensible ones."

"But I'd rather look ridiculous when everybody else does than plain and sensible all by myself," persisted Anne mournfully.

"Trust you for that! Well, hang those dresses carefully up in your closet, and then sit down and learn the Sunday school lesson. I got a quarterly from Mr. Bell for you and you'll go to Sunday school tomorrow," said Marilla, disappearing downstairs in high dudgeon.

Anne clasped her hands and looked at the dresses.

"I did hope there would be a white one with puffed sleeves," she whispered disconsolately. "I prayed for one, but I didn't much expect it on that account. I didn't suppose God would have time to bother about a little orphan girl's dress. I knew I'd just have to depend on Marilla for it. Well, fortunately I can imagine that one of them is of snow white muslin with lovely lace frills and three-puffed sleeves."

The next morning, warnings of a sick headache prevented Marilla from going to Sunday school with Anne.

"You'll have to go down and call for Mrs. Lynde, Anne," she said. "She'll see that you get into the right class. Now, mind you behave yourself properly. Stay to preaching afterward and ask Mrs. Lynde to show you our pew. Here's a cent for the collection. Don't stare at people and don't fidget. I shall expect you to tell me the text when you come home."

Anne started off irreproachably, arrayed in the stiff black-and-white sateen, which, while decent as regards length and certainly not open to the charge of skimpiness, contrived to emphasize every corner and angle of her thin figure. Her hat was a little, flat, glossy, new sailor, the extreme plainness of which had likewise much disappointed Anne, who had permitted herself secret visions of a ribbon and flowers. The latter, however, were supplied before Anne reached the main road, for being confronted halfway down the lane with a golden frenzy of wind-stirred buttercups and a glory of wild roses, Anne promptly and liberally garlanded her hat with a heavy wreath of them. Whatever other people might have thought of the result it satisfied Anne, and she tripped gaily down the road, holding her ruddy head with its decoration of pink and yellow very proudly.

When she reached Mrs. Lynde's house, she found that lady gone.

Undaunted, Anne proceeded onward to the church alone. In the porch, she found a crowd of little girls, all more or less gaily attired in whites and blues and pinks, and all staring with curious eyes at this stranger in their midst, with her extraordinary head adornment. Avonlea little girls had already heard strange stories about Anne: Mrs. Lynde said she had an awful temper; Jerry Buote, the hired boy at Green Gables, said she talked all the time to herself or to the trees and flowers like a crazy girl. They looked at her and whispered to each other behind their quarterlies. Nobody made any friendly advances, then or later on when the opening exercises were over and Anne found herself in Miss Rogerson's class.

Miss Rogerson was a middle-aged lady who had taught a Sunday school class for twenty years. Her method of teaching was to ask the printed questions from the quarterly and look sternly over its edge at the particular little girl she thought ought to answer the question. She looked very often at Anne, and Anne, thanks to Marilla's drilling, answered promptly; but it may be questioned if she understood very much about either question or answer.

She did not think she liked Miss Rogerson, and she felt very miserable; every other little girl in the class had puffed sleeves. Anne felt that life was really not worth living without puffed sleeves.

"Well, how did you like Sunday school?" Marilla wanted to know when Anne came home. Her wreath having faded, Anne had discarded it in the lane, so Marilla was spared the knowledge of that for a time.

"I didn't like it a bit. It was horrid."

"Anne Shirley!" said Marilla rebukingly.

Anne sat down on the rocker with a long sigh, kissed one of Bonny's leaves, and waved her hand to a blossoming fuchsia.

"They might have been lonesome while I was away," she explained. "And now about the Sunday school. I behaved well, just as you told me. Mrs. Lynde was gone, but I went right on myself. I went into the church, with a lot of other little girls, and I sat in the corner of a pew by the window while the opening exercises went on. Mr. Bell made an awfully long prayer. I would have been dreadfully tired before he got through if I hadn't been sitting by that window. But it looked right out on the Lake of Shining Waters, so I just gazed at that and imagined all sorts of splendid things."

"You shouldn't have done anything of the sort. You should have listened to Mr. Bell."

"But he wasn't talking to me," protested Anne. "He was talking to God, and he didn't seem to be very much interested in it, either. I think

They looked at her and whispered to each other.

he thought God was too far off to make it worthwhile. I said a little prayer myself, though. There was a long row of white birches hanging over the lake and the sunshine fell down through them, way, way down, deep into the water. Oh, Marilla, it was like a beautiful dream! It gave me a thrill and I just said, 'Thank You for it, God,' two or three times."

"Not out loud, I hope," said Marilla anxiously.

"Oh, no, just under my breath. Well, Mr. Bell did get through at last and they told me to go into the classroom with Miss Rogerson's class. There were nine other girls in it. They all had puffed sleeves. I tried to imagine mine were puffed, too, but I couldn't. Why couldn't I? It was as easy as could be to imagine they were puffed when I was alone in the east gable, but it was awfully hard there among the others who had really truly puffs."

"You shouldn't have been thinking about your sleeves in Sunday school. You should have been attending to the lesson. I hope you knew it."

"Oh, yes; and I answered a lot of questions. Miss Rogerson asked ever so many. I don't think it was fair for her to do all the asking. There were lots I wanted to ask her, but I didn't like to because I didn't think she was a kindred spirit. Then all the other little girls recited a paraphrase. She asked me if I knew any. I told her I didn't, but I could recite, 'The Dog at His Master's Grave' if she liked. That's in the Third Royal Reader. It isn't a really truly religious piece of poetry, but it's so sad and melancholy that it might as well be. She said it wouldn't do, and she told me to learn the nineteenth paraphrase for next Sunday. I read it over in church afterward and it's splendid. There are two lines in particular that just thrill me: 'Quick as the slaughtered squadrons fell / In Midian's evil day.' I don't know what 'squadrons' means, nor 'Midian' either, but it sounds *so* tragical. I can hardly wait until next Sunday to recite it. I'll practice it all week. After Sunday school, I asked Miss Rogerson—because Mrs. Lynde was too far away—to show me your pew. I sat just as still as I could, and the text was Revelation, third chapter, second and third verses. It was a very long text. If I was a minister, I'd pick the short, snappy ones. The sermon was awfully long, too. I suppose the minister had to match it to the text. I didn't think he was a bit interesting. The trouble with him seems to be that he hasn't enough imagination. I didn't listen to him very much. I just let my thoughts run, and I thought of the most surprising things."

Marilla felt helplessly that all this should be sternly reproved, but she was hampered by the undeniable fact that some of the things Anne had said, especially about the minister's sermons and Mr. Bell's prayers, were what she herself had really thought deep down in her heart for years but had never given expression to. It almost seemed to her that those secret, unuttered, critical thoughts had suddenly taken visible and accusing shape and form in the person of this outspoken morsel of neglected humanity.

Chapter 12

A SOLEMN VOW AND PROMISE

It was not until the next Friday that Marilla heard the story of the flower-wreathed hat. She came home from Mrs. Lynde's and called Anne to account.

"Anne, Mrs. Rachel says you went to church last Sunday with your hat rigged out ridiculous with roses and buttercups. What on earth put you up to such a caper? A pretty-looking object you must have been!"

"Oh. I know pink and yellow aren't becoming to me," began Anne.

"Becoming fiddlesticks! It was putting flowers on your hat at all, no matter what color they were, that was ridiculous. You are the most aggravating child!"

"I don't see why it's any more ridiculous to wear flowers on your hat than on your dress," protested Anne. "Lots of little girls there had bouquets pinned on their dresses. What was the difference?"

Marilla was not to be drawn from the safe concrete into dubious paths of the abstract.

"Don't answer me back like that, Anne. It was very silly of you to do such a thing. Never let me catch you at such a trick again. Mrs. Rachel says she thought she would sink through the floor when she saw you come in all rigged out like that. She couldn't get near enough to tell you to take them off till it was too late. She says people talked about it something dreadful. Of course they would think I had no better sense than to let you go decked out like that."

"Oh, I'm so sorry," said Anne, tears welling into her eyes. "I never thought you'd mind. The roses and buttercups were so sweet and pretty that I thought they'd look lovely on my hat. Lots of the little girls had artificial flowers on their hats. I'm afraid I'm going to be a dreadful trial to you. Maybe you'd better send me back to the asylum. That would be terrible; I don't think I could endure it. Most likely I would go into consumption; I'm so thin as it is, you see. But that would be better than being a trial to you."

"Nonsense," said Marilla, vexed at herself for having made the child cry. "I don't want to send you back to the asylum, I'm sure. All I want is that you should behave like other little girls and not make yourself ridiculous. Don't cry anymore. I've got some news for you. Diana Barry came home this afternoon. I'm going up to see if I can borrow a skirt pattern from Mrs. Barry, and if you like, you can come with me and get acquainted with Diana."

Anne rose to her feet with clasped hands, the tears still glistening on her cheeks; the dish towel she had been hemming slipped unheeded to the floor.

"Oh, Marilla, I'm frightened—now that it has come, I'm actually frightened. What if she shouldn't like me! It would be the most tragical disappointment of my life."

"Now, don't get into a fluster. And I do wish you wouldn't use such long words. It sounds so funny in a little girl. I guess Diana'll like you well enough. It's her mother you've got to reckon with. If she doesn't like you, it won't matter how much Diana does. If she has heard about your outburst to Mrs. Lynde and going to church with buttercups around your hat, I don't know what she'll think of you. You must be polite and well-behaved, and don't make any of your startling speeches. For pity's sake, if the child isn't actually trembling!"

Anne *was* trembling. Her face was pale and tense.

"Oh, Marilla, you'd be excited, too, if you were going to meet a little girl you hoped to be your bosom friend and whose mother mightn't like you," she said as she hastened to get her hat.

They went over to Orchard Slope by the shortcut across the brook and up the firry hill grove. Mrs. Barry came to the kitchen door in answer to Marilla's knock. She was a tall, black-eyed, black-haired woman, with a very resolute mouth. She had the reputation of being very strict with her children.

"How do you do, Marilla?" she said cordially. "Come in. And this is the little girl you have adopted, I suppose?"

"Yes, this is Anne Shirley," said Marilla.

"Spelled with an *e,*" gasped Anne, who, tremulous and excited as she was, was determined there should be no misunderstanding on that important point.

Mrs. Barry, not hearing or comprehending, merely shook hands and said kindly, "How are you?"

"I am well in body, although considerably rumpled up in spirit, thank you, ma'am," said Anne gravely. Then aside to Marilla in an audible whisper, "There wasn't anything startling in that, was there, Marilla?"

Diana was sitting on the sofa, reading a book, which she dropped when the callers entered. She was a very pretty little girl, with her mother's black eyes and hair, rosy cheeks, and the merry expression that was her inheritance from her father.

"This is my little girl Diana," said Mrs. Barry. "Diana, you might take Anne out into the garden and show her your flowers. It will be better for you than straining your eyes over that book. She reads entirely too much"—this to Marilla as the little girls went out—"and I can't prevent her, for her father aids and abets her. She's always poring over a book. I'm glad she has the prospect of a playmate—perhaps it will take her more out-of-doors."

Outside in the garden, which was full of mellow sunset light streaming through the dark old firs to the west of it, stood Anne and Diana, gazing bashfully at one another over a clump of gorgeous tiger lilies.

The Barry garden was a bowery wilderness of flowers that would have delighted Anne's heart at any time less fraught with destiny. It was encircled by huge old willows and tall firs, beneath which flourished flowers that loved the shade. Prim, right-angled paths, neatly bordered with clamshells, intersected it like moist red ribbons, and in the beds between, old-fashioned flowers ran riot. There were rosy bleeding hearts and great, splendid crimson peonies; white, fragrant narcissi and thorny, sweet Scotch roses; pink and blue and white columbines and lilac-tinted Bouncing Bets; clumps of southernwood and ribbon grass and mint; purple Adam-and-Eve, daffodils, and masses of sweet clover, white with its delicate, fragrant, feathery sprays; scarlet lightning that shot its fiery lances over prim, white musk flowers—a garden it was where sunshine lingered, and bees hummed, and winds, beguiled into loitering, purred and rustled.

"Oh, Diana," said Anne at last, clasping her hands and speaking almost in a whisper, "do you think—oh, do you think you can like me a little— enough to be my bosom friend?"

Diana laughed. Diana always laughed before she spoke.

"Why, I guess so," she said frankly. "I'm awfully glad you've come to live at Green Gables. It will be jolly to have somebody to play with. There isn't any other girl who lives near enough to play with, and I've no sisters big enough."

"Will you swear to be my friend for ever and ever?" demanded Anne eagerly.

Diana looked shocked.

"Why, it's dreadfully wicked to swear," she said rebukingly.

"Oh no, not my kind of swearing. There are two kinds, you know."

"I never heard of but one kind," said Diana doubtfully.

"There really is another. Oh, it isn't wicked at all. It just means vowing and promising solemnly."

"Well, I don't mind doing that," agreed Diana, relieved. "How do you do it?"

"We must join hands—so," said Anne gravely. "It ought to be over running water. We'll just imagine this path is running water. I'll repeat the oath first. I solemnly swear to be faithful to my bosom friend, Diana Barry, as long as the sun and moon shall endure. Now you say it and put my name in."

Diana repeated the "oath" with a laugh fore and aft. Then she said, "You're a strange girl, Anne. I heard before that you were strange. But I believe I'm going to like you real well."

When Marilla and Anne went home, Diana went with them as far as the log bridge. The two little girls walked with their arms about each other. At the brook, they parted with many promises to spend the next afternoon together.

"Well, did you find Diana a kindred spirit?" asked Marilla as they went up through the garden of Green Gables.

"Oh, yes," sighed Anne, blissfully unconscious of any sarcasm on Marilla's part. "Oh, Marilla, I'm the happiest girl on Prince Edward Island this very moment. I assure you I'll say my prayers with a right good will tonight. Diana and I are going to build a playhouse in Mr. William Bell's birch grove tomorrow. Can I have those broken pieces of china that are out in the woodshed? Diana's birthday is in February and mine is in March. Don't you think that is a very strange coincidence? Diana is going to lend me a book to read. She says it's perfectly splendid and tremendously exciting. She's going to show me a place back in the woods where rice lilies grow. Don't you think Diana has got very soulful eyes? I wish I had soulful eyes. Diana is going to teach me to sing a song called 'Nelly in the Hazel Dell.' She's going to give me a picture to put up in my room; it's a perfectly beautiful picture, she says—a lovely lady in a pale blue silk dress. A sewing machine agent gave it to her. I wish I had something to give Diana. I'm an inch taller than Diana, but she is ever so much fatter; she says she'd like to be thin because it's so much more graceful, but I'm afraid she only said it to soothe my feelings. We're going to the shore some day to gather shells. We have agreed to call the spring down by the log bridge the Dryad's Bubble. Isn't that a perfectly elegant name? I read a story once about a spring called that. A dryad is a sort of grown-up fairy, I think."

"Well, all I hope is you won't talk Diana to death," said Marilla. "But remember this in all your planning, Anne. You're not going to play all the time nor most of it. You'll have your work to do and it'll have to be done first."

Anne's cup of happiness was full, and Matthew caused it to overflow. He had just got home from a trip to the store at Carmody, and he sheepishly produced a small parcel from his pocket and handed it to Anne, with a deprecatory look at Marilla.

"I heard you say you liked chocolate sweeties, so I got you some," he said.

"Humph," sniffed Marilla. "It'll ruin her teeth and stomach. There, there, child, don't look so dismal. You can eat those, since Matthew has gone and got them. He'd better have brought you peppermints. They're wholesomer. Don't sicken yourself eating them all at once now."

"Oh, no, indeed, I won't," said Anne eagerly. "I'll just eat one tonight, Marilla. And I can give Diana half of them, can't I? The other half will taste twice as sweet to me if I give some to her. It's delightful to think I have something to give her."

"I will say it[1] for the child," said Marilla when Anne had gone to her gable, "she isn't stingy. I'm glad, for of all faults, I detest stinginess in a child. Dear me, it's only three weeks since she came, and it seems as if she'd been here always. I can't imagine the place without her. Now, don't be looking I-told-you-so, Matthew. That's bad enough in a woman, but it isn't to be endured in a man. I'm perfectly willing to own up that I'm glad I consented to keep the child and that I'm getting fond of her, but don't you rub it in, Matthew Cuthbert."

---

[1] This.

Chapter 13

THE DELIGHTS OF ANTICIPATION

"It's time Anne was in to do her sewing," said Marilla, glancing at the clock and then out into the yellow August afternoon where everything drowsed in the heat. "She stayed playing with Diana more than half an hour more'n I gave her leave to; and now she's perched out there on the woodpile talking to Matthew, nineteen to the dozen,[1] when she knows perfectly well that she ought to be at her work. And of course he's listening to her like a perfect ninny. I never saw such an infatuated man. The more she talks and the odder the things she says, the more he's delighted, evidently. Anne Shirley, you come right in here this minute, do you hear me!"

A series of staccato taps on the west window brought Anne flying in from the yard, eyes shining, cheeks faintly flushed with pink, unbraided hair streaming behind her in a torrent of brightness.

"Oh, Marilla," she exclaimed breathlessly, "there's going to be a Sunday school picnic next week—in Mr. Harmon Andrews's field, right near the Lake of Shining Waters. And Mrs. Superintendent Bell and Mrs. Rachel Lynde are going to make ice cream—think of it, Marilla—*ice cream!* And, oh, Marilla, can I go to it?"

"Just look at the clock, if you please, Anne. What time did I tell you to come in?"

"Two o'clock—but isn't it splendid about the picnic, Marilla? Please can I go? Oh, I've never been to a picnic—I've dreamed of picnics, but I've never—"

"Yes, I told you to come at two o'clock. And it's a quarter to three. I'd like to know why you didn't obey me, Anne."

"Why, I meant to, Marilla, as much as could be. But you have no idea

---

[1] For every twelve words a normal person can speak, Anne can cram in nineteen (*Annotated Anne*, 143).

how fascinating Idlewild is. And then, of course, I had to tell Matthew about the picnic. Matthew is such a sympathetic listener. Please can I go?"

"You'll have to learn to resist the fascination of Idle-whatever-you-call-it. When I tell you to come in at a certain time I mean that time and not half an hour later. And you needn't stop to discourse with sympathetic listeners on your way, either. As for the picnic, of course you can go. You're a Sunday school scholar, and it's not likely I'd refuse to let you go when all the other little girls are going."

"But—but," faltered Anne, "Diana says that everybody must take a basket of things to eat. I can't cook, as you know, Marilla, and—and—I don't mind going to a picnic without puffed sleeves so much, but I'd feel terribly humiliated if I had to go without a basket. It's been preying on my mind ever since Diana told me."

"Well, it needn't prey any longer. I'll bake you a basket."

"Oh, you dear, good Marilla. Oh, you are so kind to me. Oh, I'm so much obliged to you."

Getting through with her "ohs," Anne cast herself into Marilla's arms and rapturously kissed her sallow cheek. It was the first time in her whole life that childish lips had voluntarily touched Marilla's face. Again that sudden sensation of startling sweetness thrilled her. She was secretly vastly pleased at Anne's impulsive caress, which was probably the reason why she said brusquely:

"There, there, never mind your kissing nonsense. I'd sooner see you doing strictly as you're told. As for cooking, I mean to begin giving you lessons in that some of these days. But you're so featherbrained, Anne, I've been waiting to see if you'd sober down a little and learn to be steady before I begin. You've got to keep your wits about you in cooking and not stop in the middle of things to let your thoughts rove over all creation. Now, get out your patchwork and have your square done before teatime."

"I do *not* like patchwork," said Anne dolefully, hunting out her work-basket and sitting down before a little heap of red and white diamonds with a sigh. "I think some kinds of sewing would be nice; but there's no scope for imagination in patchwork. It's just one little seam after another, and you never seem to be getting anywhere. But of course I'd rather be Anne of Green Gables sewing patchwork than Anne of any other place with nothing to do but play. I wish time went as quick sewing patches as it does when I'm playing with Diana, though. Oh, we do have such elegant times, Marilla. I have to furnish most of the imagination, but I'm well able to do that. Diana is simply perfect in every other way. You know that little piece of land across the brook that runs up between our farm and Mr. Barry's? It belongs to Mr. William Bell, and right in the corner, there is a little ring of white birch trees—the most romantic spot, Marilla. Diana and I have our playhouse there. We call it Idlewild. Isn't that a poetical name? I assure you it took me some time to think it out. I stayed awake nearly a whole night before I invented it. Then, just as I was dropping off to sleep, it came like an inspiration. Diana was *enraptured* when she heard it. We have got our house fixed up elegantly. You must come and see it, Marilla—won't you? We have great big stones, all covered with moss, for seats, and boards from tree to tree for shelves. And we have all our dishes on them. Of course, they're all broken, but it's the easiest thing in the world to imagine that they are whole. There's a piece of a plate with a spray of red and yellow ivy on it that is especially beautiful. We keep it in the parlour, and we have the fairy glass there, too. The fairy glass is as lovely as a dream. Diana found it out in the woods behind their chicken house. It's all full of rainbows—just little young rainbows that haven't grown big yet—and Diana's mother told her it was broken off a hanging lamp they once had. But it's nicer to imagine the fairies lost it one night when they had a ball, so we call it the fairy glass. Matthew is going to make us a table. Oh, we have named that little round pool over in Mr. Barry's field Willowmere. I got that name out of the book Diana lent me. That was a thrilling book, Marilla. The heroine had five lovers.[2] I'd be satisfied with one, wouldn't you? She was very handsome, and she went through great tribulations. She could faint as easy as anything. I'd love to be able to faint, wouldn't you, Marilla? It's so romantic. But I'm really very healthy for all I'm so thin. I believe I'm getting fatter, though. Don't you think I am? I look at my elbows every morning when I get up to see if any dimples are coming. Diana is having a new dress made with elbow sleeves. She is going to wear it to the picnic. Oh, I do hope it will be fine next Wednesday. I don't feel that I could endure the disappointment if anything happened to prevent me from getting to the picnic. I suppose I'd live through it, but I'm certain it would be a lifelong sorrow. It wouldn't matter if I got to a hundred picnics in after-years, they wouldn't make up for missing this one. They're going to have boats on the Lake of Shining Waters—and ice cream, as I told you. I have never tasted ice cream. Diana tried to explain what it was like, but I guess ice cream is one of those things that are beyond imagination."

"Anne, you have talked even on for ten minutes by the clock," said

---

[2] Beaus; suitors.

Marilla. "Now, just for curiosity's sake, see if you can hold your tongue for the same length of time."

Anne held her tongue as desired. But for the rest of the week she talked picnic and thought picnic and dreamed picnic. On Saturday it rained and she worked herself up into such a frantic state lest it should keep on raining, until and over Wednesday, that Marilla made her sew an extra patchwork square by way of steadying her nerves.

On Sunday Anne confided to Marilla on the way home from church that she grew actually cold all over with excitement when the minister announced the picnic from the pulpit.

"Such a thrill as went up and down my back, Marilla! I don't think I'd ever really believed until then that there was honestly going to be a picnic. I couldn't help fearing I'd only imagined it. But when a minister says a thing in the pulpit, you just have to believe it."

"You set your heart too much on things, Anne," said Marilla with a sigh. "I'm afraid there'll be a great many disappointments in store for you through life."

"Oh, Marilla, looking forward to things is half the pleasure of them," exclaimed Anne. "You mayn't get the things themselves, but nothing can prevent you from having the fun of looking forward to them. Mrs. Lynde says, 'Blessed are they who expect nothing, for they shall not be disappointed.' But I think it would be worse to expect nothing than to be disappointed."

Marilla wore her amethyst brooch to church that day as usual. Marilla always wore her amethyst brooch to church. She would have thought it rather sacrilegious to leave it off—as bad as forgetting her Bible or her collection dime. That amethyst brooch was Marilla's most treasured possession. A seafaring uncle had given it to her mother, who in turn had bequeathed it to Marilla. It was an old-fashioned oval, containing a braid of her mother's hair, surrounded by a border of very fine amethysts. Marilla knew too little about precious stones to realize how fine the amethysts actually were; but she thought them very beautiful and was always pleasantly conscious of their violet shimmer at her throat, above her good brown satin dress, even though she could not see it.

Anne had been smitten with delighted admiration when she first saw that brooch.

"Oh, Marilla, it's a perfectly elegant brooch. I don't know how you can pay attention to the sermon or the prayers when you have it on. _I_ couldn't, I know. I think amethysts are just sweet. They are what I used to think diamonds were like. Long ago, before I had ever seen a diamond, I read about them and I tried to imagine what they would be like. I thought they would be lovely glimmering purple stones. When I saw a real diamond in a lady's ring one day, I was so disappointed, I cried. Of course, it was very lovely, but it wasn't my idea of a diamond. Will you let me hold the brooch for one minute, Marilla? Do you think amethysts can be the souls of good violets?"

Chapter 14
ANNE'S CONFESSION

On the Monday evening before the picnic, Marilla came down from her room with a troubled face.

"Anne," she said to that small personage, who was shelling peas by the spotless table and singing "Nelly of the Hazel Dell" with a vigour and expression that did credit to Diana's teaching, "did you see anything of my amethyst brooch? I thought I stuck it in my pincushion when I came home from church yesterday evening, but I can't find it anywhere."

"I—I saw it this afternoon when you were away at the Aid Society," said Anne a little slowly. "I was passing your door when I saw it on the cushion, so I went in to look at it."

"Did you touch it?" said Marilla sternly.

"Y-e-e-s," admitted Anne. "I took it up and I pinned it on my breast just to see how it would look."

"You had no business to do anything of the sort. It's very wrong in a little girl to meddle. You shouldn't have gone into my room in the first place, and you shouldn't have touched a brooch that didn't belong to you in the second. Where did you put it?"

"Oh, I put it back on the bureau. I hadn't it on a minute. Truly, I didn't mean to meddle, Marilla. I didn't think about its being wrong to go in and try on the brooch, but I see now that it was and I'll never do it again. That's one good thing about me. I never do the same naughty thing twice."

"You didn't put it back," said Marilla. "That brooch isn't anywhere on the bureau. You've taken it out or something, Anne."

"I *did* put it back," said Anne quickly—pertly, Marilla thought. "I don't just remember whether I stuck it on the pincushion or laid it in the china tray. But I'm perfectly certain I put it back."

"I'll go and have another look," said Marilla, determining to be just. "If you put that brooch back, it's there still. If it isn't, I'll know you didn't, that's all!"

Marilla went to her room and made a thorough search, not only over the bureau but in every other place she thought the brooch might possibly be. It was not to be found, and she returned to the kitchen.

"Anne, the brooch is gone. By your own admission, you were the last person to handle it. Now, what have you done with it? Tell me the truth at once. Did you take it out and lose it?"

"No, I didn't," said Anne solemnly, meeting Marilla's angry gaze squarely. "I never took the brooch out of your room and that is the truth, if I was to be led to the block for it—although I'm not very certain what a block is. So there, Marilla."

Anne's "so there" was only intended to emphasize her assertion, but Marilla took it as a display of defiance.

"I believe you are telling me a falsehood, Anne," she said sharply. "I know you are. There now, don't say anything more unless you are prepared to tell the whole truth. Go to your room and stay there until you are ready to confess."

"Will I take the peas with me?" said Anne meekly.

"No, I'll finish shelling them myself. Do as I bid you."

When Anne had gone, Marilla went about her evening tasks in a very disturbed state of mind. She was worried about her valuable brooch. What if Anne had lost it? And how wicked of the child to deny having taken it, when anybody could see she must have! With such an innocent face, too!

I don't know what I wouldn't sooner have had happen, thought Marilla as she nervously shelled the peas. *Of course, I don't suppose she meant to steal it or anything like that. She's just taken it to play with or help along that imagination of hers. She must have taken it, that's clear, for there hasn't been a soul in that room since she was in it, by her own story, until I went up tonight. And the brooch is gone, there's nothing surer. I suppose she has lost it and is afraid to own up for fear she'll be punished. It's a dreadful thing to think she tells falsehoods. It's a far worse thing than her fit of temper. It's a fearful responsibility to have a child in your house you can't trust. Slyness and untruthfulness—that's what she has displayed. I declare I feel worse about that than about the brooch. If she'd only have told the truth about it, I wouldn't mind so much.*

Marilla went to her room at intervals all through the evening and searched for the brooch, without finding it. A bedtime visit to the east gable produced no result. Anne persisted in denying that she knew anything about the brooch, but Marilla was only the more firmly convinced that she did.

She told Matthew the story the next morning. Matthew was confounded and puzzled. He could not so quickly lose faith in Anne, but he had to admit that circumstances were against her.

"You're sure it hasn't fell down behind the bureau?" was the only suggestion he could offer.

"I've moved the bureau and I've taken out the drawers and I've looked in every crack and cranny," was Marilla's positive answer. "The brooch is gone and that child has taken it and lied about it. That's the plain, ugly truth, Matthew Cuthbert, and we might as well look it in the face."

"Well now, what are you going to do about it?" Matthew asked forlornly, feeling secretly thankful that Marilla and not he had to deal with the situation. He felt no desire to put his oar in at this time.

"She'll stay in her room until she confesses," said Marilla grimly, remembering the success of this method in the former case. "Then we'll see. Perhaps we'll be able to find the brooch if she'll only tell where she took it; but in any case she'll have to be severely punished, Matthew."

"Well now, you'll have to punish her," said Matthew, reaching for his hat. "I've nothing to do with it, remember. You warned me off yourself."

Marilla felt deserted by everyone. She could not even go to Mrs. Lynde for advice. She went up to the east gable with a very serious face and left it with a face more serious still. Anne steadfastly refused to confess. She persisted in asserting that she had not taken the brooch. The child had evidently been crying, and Marilla felt a pang of pity that she sternly repressed. By night she was, as she expressed it, "beat out."

"You'll stay in this room until you confess, Anne. You can make up your mind to that," she said firmly.

"But the picnic is tomorrow, Marilla," cried Anne. "You won't keep me from going to that, will you? You'll just let me out for the afternoon, won't you? Then I'll stay here as long as you like afterwards *cheerfully*. But I *must* go to the picnic."

"You'll not go to picnics nor anywhere else until you've confessed, Anne."

"Oh, Marilla," gasped Anne.

But Marilla had gone out and shut the door.

Wednesday morning dawned as bright and fair as if expressly made to order for the picnic. Birds sang around Green Gables; the Madonna lilies in the garden sent out whiffs of perfume that entered in on viewless winds at every door and window and wandered through halls and rooms like spirits of benediction. The birches in the hollow waved joyful hands as if watching for Anne's usual morning greeting from the east gable. But

Anne was not at her window. When Marilla took her breakfast up to her, she found the child sitting primly on her bed, pale and resolute, with tight shut lips and gleaming eyes.

"Marilla, I'm ready to confess."

"Ah!" Marilla laid down her tray. Once again her method had succeeded; but her success was very bitter to her. "Let me hear what you have to say then, Anne."

"I took the amethyst brooch," said Anne, as if repeating a lesson she had learned. "I took it just as you said. I didn't mean to take it when I went in. But it did look so beautiful, Marilla, when I pinned it on my breast that I was overcome by an irresistible temptation. I imagined how perfectly thrilling it would be to take it to Idlewild and play I was the Lady Cordelia Fitzgerald. It would be so much easier to imagine I was the Lady Cordelia if I had a real amethyst brooch on. Diana and I made necklaces of roseberries, but what are roseberries compared with amethysts? So I took the brooch. I thought I could put it back before you came home. I went all the way around by the road to lengthen out the time. When I was going over the bridge across the Lake of Shining Waters, I took the brooch off to have another look at it. Oh, how it did shine in the sunlight! And then, when I was leaning over the bridge, it just slipped through my fingers—so—and went down—down—down, all purply-sparkling, and sank forevermore beneath the Lake of Shining Waters. And that's the best I can do at confessing, Marilla."

Marilla felt hot anger surge up into her heart again. This child had taken and lost her treasured amethyst brooch and now sat there calmly reciting the details thereof without the least apparent compunction or repentance.

"Anne, this is terrible," she said, trying to speak calmly. "You are the very wickedest girl I ever heard of."

"Yes, I suppose I am," agreed Anne tranquilly. "And I know I'll have to be punished. It'll be your duty to punish me, Marilla. Won't you please get it over right off because I'd like to go to the picnic with nothing on my mind."

"Picnic indeed! You'll go to no picnic today, Anne Shirley. That shall be your punishment. And it isn't half severe enough either for what you've done!"

"Not go to the picnic!" Anne sprang to her feet and clutched Marilla's hand. "But you *promised* me I might! Oh, Marilla, I must go to the picnic. That was why I confessed. Punish me any way you like but that. Oh, Marilla, please, please, let me go to the picnic. Think of the ice cream! For anything you know I may never have a chance to taste ice cream again."

Marilla disengaged Anne's clinging hand stonily.

"You needn't plead, Anne. You are not going to the picnic and that's final. No, not a word."

Anne realized that Marilla was not to be moved. She clasped her hands together, gave a piercing shriek, and then flung herself face downward on the bed, crying and writhing in an utter abandonment of disappointment and despair.

"For the land's sake!" gasped Marilla, hastening from the room. "I believe the child is crazy. No child in her senses would behave as she does. If she isn't, she's utterly bad. Oh dear, I'm afraid Rachel was right from the first. But I've put my hand to the plough and I won't look back."

That was a dismal morning. Marilla worked fiercely and scrubbed the porch floor and the dairy shelves when she could find nothing else to do. Neither the shelves nor the porch needed it—but Marilla did. Then she went out and raked the yard.

When dinner was ready, she went to the stairs and called Anne. A tear-stained face appeared, looking tragically over the banisters.

"Come down to your dinner, Anne."

"I don't want any dinner, Marilla," said Anne sobbingly. "I couldn't eat anything. My heart is broken. You'll feel remorse of conscience some day, I expect, for breaking it, Marilla, but I forgive you. Remember when the time comes that I forgive you. But please don't ask me to eat anything, especially boiled pork and greens. Boiled pork and greens are so unromantic when one is in affliction."

Exasperated, Marilla returned to the kitchen and poured out her tale of woe to Matthew, who, between his sense of justice and his unlawful sympathy with Anne, was a miserable man.

"Well now, she shouldn't have taken the brooch, Marilla, or told stories about it," he admitted, mournfully surveying his plateful of unromantic pork and greens as if he, like Anne, thought it a food unsuited to crises of feeling, "but she's such a little thing—such an interesting little thing. Don't you think it's pretty rough not to let her go to the picnic when she's so set on it?"

"Matthew Cuthbert, I'm amazed at you. I think I've let her off entirely too easy. And she doesn't appear to realize how wicked she's been at all—that's what worries me most. If she'd really felt sorry, it wouldn't be so bad. And you don't seem to realize it, neither; you're making excuses for her all the time to yourself—I can see that."

"Well now, she's such a little thing," feebly reiterated Matthew. "And there should be allowances made, Marilla. You know she's never had any bringing up."

"Well, she's having it now," retorted Marilla.

The retort silenced Matthew if it did not convince him. That dinner was a very dismal meal. The only cheerful thing about it was Jerry Buote, the hired boy, and Marilla resented his cheerfulness as a personal insult.

When her dishes were washed and her bread sponge set and her hens fed, Marilla remembered that she had noticed a small rent in her best black lace shawl when she had taken it off on Monday afternoon on returning from the Ladies' Aid. She would go and mend it.

The shawl was in a box in her trunk. As Marilla lifted it out, the sunlight, falling through the vines that clustered thickly about the window, struck upon something caught in the shawl—something that glittered and sparkled in facets of violet light. Marilla snatched at it with a gasp. It was the amethyst brooch, hanging to a thread of the lace by its catch!

"Dear life and heart," said Marilla blankly, "what does that mean? Here's my brooch safe and sound that I thought was at the bottom of Barry's Pond. Whatever did that girl mean by saying she took it and lost it? I declare I believe Green Gables is bewitched. I remember now that when I took off my shawl Monday afternoon, I laid it on the bureau for a minute. I suppose the brooch got caught in it somehow. Well!"

Marilla betook herself to the east gable, brooch in hand. Anne had cried herself out and was sitting dejectedly by the window.

"Anne Shirley," said Marilla solemnly, "I've just found my brooch hanging to my black lace shawl. Now I want to know what that rigmarole you told me this morning meant."

"Why, you said you'd keep me here until I confessed," returned Anne wearily, "and so I decided to confess because I was bound[1] to get to the picnic. I thought out a confession last night after I went to bed and made it as interesting as I could. And I said it over and over so that I wouldn't forget it. But you wouldn't let me go to the picnic after all, so all my trouble was wasted."

Marilla had to laugh in spite of herself. But her conscience pricked her.

"Anne, you do beat all! But I was wrong—I see that now. I shouldn't have doubted your word when I'd never known you to tell a story.[2] Of course, it wasn't right for you to confess to a thing you hadn't done—it

---

[1] Determined.

[2] A lie.

was very wrong to do so. But I drove you to it. So if you'll forgive me, Anne, I'll forgive you, and we'll start square again. And now get yourself ready for the picnic."

Anne flew up like a rocket.

"Oh, Marilla, isn't it too late?"

"No, it's only two o'clock. They won't be more than well gathered yet, and it'll be an hour before they have tea. Wash your face and comb your hair and put on your gingham. I'll fill a basket for you. There's plenty of stuff baked in the house. And I'll get Jerry to hitch up the sorrel and drive you down to the picnic ground."

"Oh, Marilla," exclaimed Anne, flying to the washstand. "Five minutes ago, I was so miserable I was wishing I'd never been born, and now I wouldn't change places with an angel!"

That night a thoroughly happy, completely tired-out Anne returned to Green Gables in a state of beatification impossible to describe.

"Oh, Marilla, I've had a perfectly scrumptious time. *Scrumptious* is a new word I learned today. I heard Mary Alice Bell use it. Isn't it very expressive? Everything was lovely. We had a splendid tea, and then Mr. Harmon Andrews took us all for a row on the Lake of Shining Waters—six of us at a time. And Jane Andrews nearly fell overboard. She was leaning out to pick water lilies, and if Mr. Andrews hadn't caught her by her sash just in the nick of time, she'd have fallen in and prob'ly been drowned. I wish it had been me. It would have been such a romantic experience to have been nearly drowned. It would be such a thrilling tale to tell. And we had the ice cream. Words fail me to describe that ice cream. Marilla, I assure you it was sublime."

That evening Marilla told the whole story to Matthew over her stocking basket.

"I'm willing to own up that I made a mistake," she concluded candidly, "but I've learned a lesson. I have to laugh when I think of Anne's 'confession,' although I suppose I shouldn't, for it really was a falsehood. But it doesn't seem as bad as the other would have been, somehow, and anyhow I'm responsible for it. That child is hard to understand in some respects. But I believe she'll turn out all right yet. And there's one thing certain, no house will ever be dull that she's in."

Chapter 15

A Tempest in the School Teapot

"What a splendid day!" said Anne, drawing a long breath. "Isn't it good just to be alive on a day like this? I pity the people who aren't born yet for missing it. They may have good days, of course, but they can never have this one. And it's splendider still to have such a lovely way to go to school by, isn't it?"

"It's a lot nicer than going around by the road; that is so dusty and hot," said Diana practically, peeping into her dinner basket and mentally calculating if the three juicy, toothsome raspberry tarts reposing there were divided among ten girls how many bites each girl would have.

The little girls of Avonlea school always pooled their lunches, and to eat three raspberry tarts all alone, or even to share them only with one's best chum, would have for ever and ever branded as "awful mean" the girl who did it. And yet, when the tarts were divided among ten girls, you just got enough to tantalize you.

The way Anne and Diane went to school *was* a pretty one. Anne thought those walks to and from school with Diana couldn't be improved upon even by imagination. Going around by the main road would have been so unromantic; but to go by Lover's Lane and Willowmere and Violet Vale and the Birch Path was romantic, if ever anything was.

Lover's Lane opened out below the orchard at Green Gables and stretched far up into the woods to the end of the Cuthbert farm. It was the way by which the cows were taken to the back pasture and the wood hauled home in winter. Anne had named it Lover's Lane before she had been a month at Green Gables.

"Not that lovers ever really walk there," she explained to Marilla, "but Diana and I are reading a perfectly magnificent book and there's a Lover's Lane in it. So we want to have one, too. And it's a very pretty name, don't you think? So romantic! We can imagine the lovers into it, you know. I

89

like the lane because you can think out loud there without people calling you crazy."

Anne, starting out alone in the morning, went down Lover's Lane as far as the brook. Here Diana met her, and the two little girls went on up the lane under the leafy arch of maples—"maples are such sociable trees," said Anne; "they're always rustling and whispering to you"—until they came to a rustic bridge. Then they left the lane and walked through Mr. Barry's back field and past Willowmere. Beyond Willowmere came Violet Vale—a little green dimple in the shadow of Mr. Andrew Bell's big woods.

"Of course there are no violets there now," Anne told Marilla, "but Diana says there are millions of them in spring. Oh, Marilla, can't you just imagine you see them? It actually takes away my breath. I named it Violet Vale. Diana says she never saw the beat of me for hitting on fancy names for places. It's nice to be clever at something, isn't it? But Diana named the Birch Path. She wanted to, so I let her; but I'm sure I could have found something more poetical than plain Birch Path. Anybody can think of a name like that. But the Birch Path is one of the prettiest places in the world, Marilla."

It was. Other people besides Anne thought so when they stumbled on it. It was a little narrow, twisting path, winding down over a long hill straight through Mr. Bell's woods, where the light came down sifted through so many emerald screens that it was as flawless as the heart of a diamond. It was fringed in all its length with slim young birches, white-stemmed and lissome-boughed; ferns and starflowers and wild lilies-of-the-valley and scarlet tufts of pigeon berries grew thickly along it; and always there was a delightful spiciness in the air and music of bird calls and the murmur and laugh of wood winds in the trees overhead. Now and then you might see a rabbit skipping across the road if you were quiet—which, with Anne and Diana, happened about once in a blue moon. Down in the valley, the path came out to the main road and then it was just up the spruce hill to the school.

The Avonlea school was a whitewashed building low in the eaves and wide in the windows, furnished inside with comfortable, substantial old-fashioned desks that opened and shut and were carved all over their lids with the initials and hieroglyphics of three generations of schoolchildren. The schoolhouse was set back from the road, and behind it was a dusky fir wood and a brook where all the children put their bottles of milk in the morning to keep cool and sweet until dinner hour.

Marilla had seen Anne start off to school on the first day of September with many secret misgivings. Anne was such an odd girl. How would she get on[1] with the other children? And how on earth would she ever manage to hold her tongue during school hours?

Things went better than Marilla feared, however. Anne came home that evening in high spirits.

"I think I'm going to like school here," she announced. "I don't think much of the master, though. He's all the time curling his moustache and making eyes at Prissy Andrews. Prissy is grown-up, you know. She's sixteen and she's studying for the entrance examination into Queen's Academy at Charlottetown next year. Tillie Boulter says the master is *dead gone* on her. She's got a beautiful complexion and curly brown hair, and she does it up so elegantly. She sits in the long seat at the back, and he sits there, too, most of the time—to explain her lessons, he says. But Ruby Gillis says she saw him writing something on her slate, and when Prissy read it, she blushed as red as a beet and giggled; and Ruby Gillis says she doesn't believe it had anything to do with the lesson."

"Anne Shirley, don't let me hear you talking about your teacher in that way again," said Marilla sharply. "You don't go to school to criticize the master. I guess he can teach *you* something, and it's your business to learn. And I want you to understand right off that you are not to come home telling tales about him. That is something I won't encourage. I hope you were a good girl."

"Indeed I was," said Anne comfortably. "It wasn't so hard as you might imagine, either. I sit with Diana. Our seat is right by the window and we can look down to the Lake of Shining Waters. There are a lot of nice girls in school, and we had scrumptious fun playing at dinnertime. It's so nice to have a lot of little girls to play with. But of course I like Diana best and always will. I *adore* Diana. I'm dreadfully far behind the others. They're all in the fifth book and I'm only in the fourth. I feel that it's kind of a disgrace. But there's not one of them has such an imagination as I have, and I soon found that out. We had reading and geography and Canadian history and dictation today. Mr. Phillips said my spelling was disgraceful, and he held up my slate so that everybody could see it, all marked over. I felt so mortified, Marilla; he might have been politer to a stranger, I think. Ruby Gillis gave me an apple, and Sophia Sloane lent me a lovely pink card with 'May I see you home?' on it. I'm to give it back to her tomorrow. And Tillie Boulter let me wear her bead ring all the afternoon. Can I have some of those pearl beads off the old pincushion in the garret to make myself a ring? And, oh, Marilla, Jane Andrews told me that

---

[1] Get along.

Minnie MacPherson told her that she heard Prissy Andrews tell Sara Gillis that I had a very pretty nose. Marilla, that is the first compliment I have ever had in my life, and you can't imagine what a strange feeling it gave me. Marilla, have I really a pretty nose? I know you'll tell me the truth."

"Your nose is well enough," said Marilla shortly. Secretly, she thought Anne's nose was a remarkably pretty one, but she had no intention of telling her so.

That was three weeks ago, and all had gone smoothly so far. And now, this crisp September morning, Anne and Diana were tripping blithely down the Birch Path, two of the happiest little girls in Avonlea.

"I guess Gilbert Blythe will be in school today," said Diana. "He's been visiting his cousins over in New Brunswick all summer, and he only came home Saturday night. He's *aw'fly* handsome, Anne. And he teases the girls something terrible. He just torments our lives out."

Diana's voice indicated that she rather liked having her life tormented out than not.

"Gilbert Blythe?" said Anne. "Isn't it his name that's written up on the porch wall with Julia Bell's and a big 'Take Notice' over them?"

"Yes," said Diana, tossing her head, "but I'm sure he doesn't like Julia Bell so very much. I've heard him say he studied the multiplication table by her freckles."

"Oh, don't speak about freckles to me," implored Anne. "It isn't delicate when I've got so many. But I do think that writing take-notices up on the wall about the boys and girls is the silliest ever. I should just like to see anybody dare to write my name up with a boy's. Not, of course," she hastened to add, "that anybody would."

Anne sighed. She didn't want her name written up. But it was a little humiliating to know that there was no danger of it.

"Nonsense," said Diana, whose black eyes and glossy tresses had played such havoc with the hearts of Avonlea schoolboys that her name figured on the porch walls in half a dozen take-notices. "It's only meant as a joke. And don't you be too sure your name won't ever be written up. Charlie Sloane is *dead gone* on you. He told his mother—his *mother*, mind you—that you were the smartest girl in school. That's better than being good-looking."

"No, it isn't," said Anne, feminine to the core. "I'd rather be pretty than clever. And I hate Charlie Sloane. I can't bear a boy with goggle eyes. If anyone wrote my name up with his, I'd *never* get over it, Diana Barry. But it *is* nice to keep head[2] of your class."

---

[2] Ahead.

"You'll have Gilbert in your class after this," said Diana, "and he's used to being head of his class, I can tell you. He's only in the fourth book, although he's nearly fourteen. Four years ago, his father was sick and had to go out to Alberta for his health, and Gilbert went with him. They were there three years, and Gil didn't go to school hardly any until they came back. You won't find it so easy to keep head after this, Anne."

"I'm glad," said Anne quickly. "I couldn't really feel proud of keeping head of little boys and girls of just nine or ten. I got up yesterday spelling 'ebullition.' Josie Pye was head and, mind you, she peeped in her book. Mr. Phillips didn't see her—he was looking at Prissy Andrews—but I did. I just swept her a look of freezing scorn, and she got as red as a beet and spelled it wrong after all."

"Those Pye girls are cheats all around," said Diana indignantly as they climbed the fence of the main road. "Gertie Pye actually went and put her milk bottle in my place in the brook yesterday. Did you ever? I don't speak to her now."

When Mr. Phillips was in the back of the room hearing Prissy Andrews's Latin, Diana whispered to Anne, "That's Gilbert Blythe sitting right across the aisle from you, Anne. Just look at him and see if you don't think he's handsome."

Anne looked accordingly. She had a good chance to do so, for the said Gilbert Blythe was absorbed in stealthily pinning the long yellow braid of Ruby Gillis, who sat in front of him, to the back of her seat. He was a tall boy, with curly brown hair, roguish hazel eyes, and a mouth twisted into a teasing smile. Presently, Ruby Gillis started up to take a sum to the master; she fell back into her seat with a little shriek, believing that her hair was pulled out by the roots. Everybody looked at her, and Mr. Phillips glared so sternly that Ruby began to cry. Gilbert had whisked the pin out of sight and was studying his history with the soberest face in the world, but when the commotion subsided he looked at Anne and winked with inexpressible drollery.

"I think your Gilbert Blythe *is* handsome," confided Anne to Diana, "but I think he's very bold. It isn't good manners to wink at a strange girl."

But it was not until the afternoon that things really began to happen.

Mr. Phillips was back in the corner explaining a problem in algebra to Prissy Andrews, and the rest of the scholars were doing pretty much as they pleased, eating green apples, whispering, drawing pictures on their slates, and driving crickets, harnessed to strings, up and down the aisle. Gilbert Blythe was trying to make Anne Shirley look at him and failing utterly, because Anne was at that moment totally oblivious, not only of the very existence of Gilbert Blythe, but of every other scholar in Avonlea school and of Avonlea school itself. With her chin propped on her hands and her eyes fixed on the blue glimpse of the Lake of Shining Waters that the west window afforded, she was far away in a gorgeous dreamland, hearing and seeing nothing save her own wonderful visions.

Gilbert Blythe wasn't used to putting himself out to make a girl look at him and meeting with failure. She *should* look at him, that red-haired Shirley girl with the little pointed chin and the big eyes that weren't like the eyes of any other girl in Avonlea school.

Gilbert reached across the aisle and picked up the end of Anne's long red braid, held it out at arm's length, and said in a piercing whisper, "Carrots! Carrots!"

Then Anne looked at him with a vengeance!

She did more than look. She sprang to her feet, her bright fancies fallen into cureless ruin. She flashed one indignant glance at Gilbert from eyes whose angry sparkle was swiftly quenched in equally angry tears.

"You mean, hateful boy!" she exclaimed passionately. "How dare you!"

And then—Thwack! Anne had brought her slate down on Gilbert's head and cracked it—slate, not head—clear across.

Avonlea school always enjoyed a scene. This was an especially enjoyable one. Everybody said "Oh!" in horrified delight. Diana gasped. Ruby Gillis, who was inclined to be hysterical, began to cry. Tommy Sloane let his team of crickets escape him altogether while he stared openmouthed at the tableau.

Mr. Phillips stalked down the aisle and laid his hand heavily on Anne's shoulder.

"Anne Shirley, what does this mean?" he said angrily.

Anne returned no answer. It was asking too much of flesh and blood to expect her to tell before the whole school that she had been called "Carrots." Gilbert it was who spoke up stoutly.

"It was my fault, Mr. Phillips. I teased her."

Mr. Phillips paid no heed to Gilbert.

"I am sorry to see a pupil of mine displaying such a temper and such a vindictive spirit," he said in a solemn tone, as if the mere fact of being a pupil of his ought to root out all evil passions from the hearts of small imperfect mortals. "Anne, go and stand on the platform in front of the blackboard for the rest of the afternoon."

Anne would have infinitely preferred a whipping to this punishment, under which her sensitive spirit quivered as from a whiplash. With a white,

Thwack! Anne had brought her slate down on Gilbert's head.

set face, she obeyed. Mr. Phillips took a chalk crayon and wrote on the blackboard above her head, "Ann Shirley has a very bad temper. Ann Shirley must learn to control her temper," and then read it out loud so that even the primer class, who couldn't read writing, should understand it.

Anne stood there the rest of the afternoon with that legend[3] above her. She did not cry or hang her head. Anger was still too hot in her heart for that, and it sustained her amid all her agony of humiliation. With resentful eyes and passion-red cheeks, she confronted alike Diana's sympathetic gaze and Charlie Sloane's indignant nods and Josie Pye's malicious smiles. As for Gilbert Blythe, she would not even look at him. She would *never* look at him again! She would never speak to him!

When school was dismissed, Anne marched out with her red head held high. Gilbert Blythe tried to intercept her at the porch door.

"I'm awful sorry I made fun of your hair, Anne," he whispered contritely. "Honest I am. Don't be mad for keeps, now."

Anne swept by disdainfully, without look or sign of hearing.

"Oh, how could you, Anne?" breathed Diana, half reproachfully, half admiringly, as they went down the road. Diana felt that *she* could never have resisted Gilbert's plea.

"I shall never forgive Gilbert Blythe," said Anne firmly. "And Mr. Phillips spelled my name without an *e,* too. The iron has entered into my soul, Diana."

Diana hadn't the least idea what Anne meant, but she understood it was something terrible.

"You mustn't mind Gilbert making fun of your hair," she said soothingly. "Why, he makes fun of all the girls. He laughs at mine because it's so black. He's called me a crow a dozen times; and I never heard him apologize for anything before, either."

"There's a great deal of difference between being called a crow and being called carrots," said Anne with dignity. "Gilbert Blythe has hurt my feelings *excruciatingly,* Diana."

It is possible the matter might have blown over without more excruciation if nothing else had happened. But when things begin to happen, they are apt to keep on.

Avonlea scholars often spent noon hour picking gum in Mr. Bell's spruce grove over the hill and across his big pasture field. From there they could keep an eye on Eben Wright's house, where the master boarded. When they saw Mr. Phillips emerging therefrom, they ran for the schoolhouse; but the distance being about three times longer than Mr. Wright's

---

3 Inscription.

lane, they were very apt to arrive there, breathless and gasping, some three minutes too late.

On the following day, Mr. Phillips was seized with one of his spasmodic fits of reform and announced, before going home to dinner, that he should expect to find all the scholars in their seats when he returned. Anyone who came in late would be punished.

All the boys and some of the girls went to Mr. Bell's spruce grove as usual, fully intending to stay only long enough to "pick a chew." But spruce groves are seductive and yellow nuts of gum beguiling; they picked and loitered and strayed, and as usual the first thing that recalled them to a sense of the flight of time was Jimmy Glover shouting from the top of a patriarchal old spruce, "Master's coming."

The girls, who were on the ground, started first and managed to reach the schoolhouse in time but without a second to spare. The boys, who had to wriggle hastily down from the trees, were later; and Anne, who had not been picking gum at all but was wandering happily in the far end of the grove, waist deep among the bracken, singing softly to herself, with a wreath of rice lilies on her hair as if she were some wild divinity of the shadowy places, was latest of all. Anne could run like a deer, however; run she did, with the impish result that she overtook the boys at the door and was swept into the schoolhouse among them just as Mr. Phillips was in the act of hanging up his hat.

Mr. Phillips' brief reforming energy was over; he didn't want the bother of punishing a dozen pupils; but it was necessary to do something to save his word, so he looked about for a scapegoat and found it in Anne, who had dropped into her seat, gasping for breath, with her forgotten lily wreath hanging askew over one ear and giving her a particularly rakish and dishevelled appearance.

"Anne Shirley, since you seem to be so fond of the boys' company, we shall indulge your taste for it this afternoon," he said sarcastically. "Take those flowers out of your hair and sit with Gilbert Blythe."

The other boys snickered. Diana, turning pale with pity, plucked the wreath from Anne's hair and squeezed her hand. Anne stared at the master as if turned to stone.

"Did you hear what I said, Anne?" queried Mr. Phillips sternly.

"Yes, sir," said Anne slowly, "but I didn't suppose you really meant it."

"I assure you I did"—still the sarcastic inflection that all the children, and Anne especially, hated. It flicked on the raw. "Obey me at once."

For a moment, Anne looked as if she meant to disobey. Then, realizing that there was no help for it, she rose haughtily, stepped across the aisle, sat down beside Gilbert Blythe, and buried her face in her arms on the desk. Ruby Gillis, who got a glimpse of it as it went down, told the others going home from school that she'd "acksually never seen anything like it—it was so white, with awful little red spots in it."

To Anne, this was as the end of all things. It was bad enough to be singled out for punishment from among a dozen equally guilty ones; it was worse still to be sent to sit with a boy; but that that boy should be Gilbert Blythe was heaping insult on injury to a degree utterly unbearable. Anne felt that she could *not* bear it and it would be of no use to try. Her whole being seethed with shame and anger and humiliation.

At first the other scholars looked and whispered and giggled and nudged. But as Anne never lifted her head and as Gilbert worked fractions as if his whole soul was absorbed in them and them only, they soon returned to their own tasks, and Anne was forgotten. When Mr. Phillips called the history class out, Anne should have gone, but Anne did not move, and Mr. Phillips, who had been writing some verses "To Priscilla" before he called the class, was thinking about an obstinate rhyme still and never missed her. Once, when nobody was looking, Gilbert took from his desk a little pink candy heart with a gold motto on it, "You are sweet," and slipped it under the curve of Anne's arm. Whereupon Anne arose, took the pink heart gingerly between the tips of her fingers, dropped it on the floor, ground it to powder beneath her heel, and resumed her position without deigning to bestow a glance on Gilbert.

When school went out, Anne marched to her desk, ostentatiously took out everything therein, books and writing tablet, pen and ink, testament and arithmetic, and piled them neatly on her cracked slate.

"What are you taking all those things home for, Anne?" Diana wanted to know as soon as they were out on the road. She had not dared to ask the question before.

"I am not coming back to school anymore," said Anne.

Diana gasped and stared at Anne to see if she meant it.

"Will Marilla let you stay home?" she asked.

"She'll have to," said Anne. "I'll *never* go to school to that man again."

"Oh, Anne!" Diana looked as if she were ready to cry. "I do think you're mean. What shall I do? Mr. Phillips will make me sit with that horrid Gertie Pye—I know he will, because she is sitting alone. Do come back, Anne."

"I'd do almost anything in the world for you, Diana," said Anne sadly. "I'd let myself be torn limb from limb if it would do you any good. But

I can't do this, so please don't ask it. You harrow up my very soul."

"Just think of all the fun you will miss," mourned Diana. "We are going to build the loveliest new house down by the brook; and we'll be playing ball next week and you've never played ball, Anne. It's tremenjusly exciting. And we're going to learn a new song—Jane Andrews is practicing it up now; and Alice Andrews is going to bring a new Pansy book next week and we're all going to read it out loud, chapter about,[4] down by the brook. And you know you are so fond of reading out loud, Anne."

Nothing moved Anne in the least. Her mind was made up. She would not go to school to Mr. Phillips again; she told Marilla so when she got home.

"Nonsense," said Marilla.

"It isn't nonsense at all," said Anne, gazing at Marilla with solemn, reproachful eyes. "Don't you understand, Marilla? I've been insulted."

"Insulted fiddlesticks! You'll go to school tomorrow as usual."

"Oh, no." Anne shook her head gently. "I'm not going back, Marilla. I'll learn my lessons at home, and I'll be as good as I can be and hold my tongue all the time if it's possible at all. But I will not go back to school, I assure you."

Marilla saw something remarkably like unyielding stubbornness looking out of Anne's small face. She understood that she would have trouble in overcoming it; but she resolved wisely to say nothing more just then.

I'll run down and see Rachel about it this evening, she thought. *There's no use reasoning with Anne now. She's too worked up, and I've an idea she can be awful stubborn if she takes the notion. Far as I can make out from her story, Mr. Phillips has been carrying matters with a rather high hand. But it would never do to say so to her. I'll just talk it over with Rachel. She's sent ten children to school and she ought to know something about it. She'll have heard the whole story, too, by this time.*

Marilla found Mrs. Lynde knitting quilts as industriously and cheerfully as usual.

"I suppose you know what I've come about," she said a little shamefacedly.

Mrs. Rachel nodded.

"About Anne's fuss in school, I reckon," she said. "Tillie Boulter was in on her way home from school and told me about it."

"I don't know what to do with her," said Marilla. "She declares she

---

[4] A chapter at a time.

won't go back to school. I never saw a child so worked up. I've been expecting trouble ever since she started to school. I knew things were going too smooth to last. She's so high-strung. What would you advise, Rachel?"

"Well, since you've asked my advice, Marilla," said Mrs. Lynde amiably—Mrs. Lynde dearly loved to be asked for advice—"I'd just humour her a little at first, that's what I'd do. It's my belief that Mr. Phillips was in the wrong. Of course, it doesn't do to say so to the children, you know. And of course he did right to punish her yesterday for giving way to temper. But today it was different. The others who were late should have been punished as well as Anne, that's what. And I don't believe in making the girls sit with the boys for punishment. It isn't modest. Tillie Boulter was real indignant. She took Anne's part right through and said all the scholars did, too. Anne seems real popular among them, somehow. I never thought she'd take with them so well."

"Then you really think I'd better let her stay home," said Marilla in amazement.

"Yes. That is, I wouldn't say 'school' to her again until she said it herself. Depend upon it, Marilla, she'll cool off in a week or so and be ready enough to go back of her own accord, that's what, while, if you were to make her go back right off, dear knows what freak or tantrum she'd take next and make more trouble than ever. The less fuss made the better, in my opinion. She won't miss much by not going to school, as far as *that* goes. Mr. Phillips isn't any good at all as a teacher. The order he keeps is scandalous, that's what, and he neglects the young fry and puts all his time on those big scholars he's getting ready for Queen's. He'd never have got the school for another year if his uncle hadn't been a trustee—*the* trustee, for he just leads the other two around by the nose, that's what. I declare, I don't know what education on this island is coming to."

Mrs. Rachel shook her head, as much as to say if she were only at the head of the educational system of the province, things would be much better managed.

Marilla took Mrs. Rachel's advice and not another word was said to Anne about going back to school. She learned her lessons at home, did her chores, and played with Diana in the chilly purple autumn twilights; but when she met Gilbert Blythe on the road or encountered him in Sunday school, she passed him by with an icy contempt that was no whit thawed by his evident desire to appease her. Even Diana's efforts as a peacemaker were of no avail. Anne had evidently made up her mind to hate Gilbert Blythe to the end of life.

As much as she hated Gilbert, however, did she love Diana, with all the love of her passionate little heart, equally intense in its likes and dislikes. One evening Marilla, coming in from the orchard with a basket of apples, found Anne sitting alone by the east window in the twilight, crying bitterly.

"Whatever's the matter now, Anne?" she asked.

"It's about Diana," sobbed Anne luxuriously. "I love Diana so, Marilla. I cannot ever live without her. But I know very well when we grow up that Diana will get married and go away and leave me. And oh, what shall I do? I hate her husband—I just hate him furiously. I've been imagining it all out—the wedding and everything—Diana dressed in snowy garments, with a veil, and looking as beautiful and regal as a queen; and me the bridesmaid, with a lovely dress, too, and puffed sleeves, but with a breaking heart hid beneath my smiling face. And then bidding Diana good-bye-e-e—" Here Anne broke down entirely and wept with increasing bitterness.

Marilla turned quickly away to hide her twitching face, but it was no use; she collapsed on the nearest chair and burst into such a hearty and unusual peal of laughter that Matthew, crossing the yard outside, halted in amazement. When had he heard Marilla laugh like that before?

"Well, Anne Shirley," said Marilla as soon as she could speak, "if you must borrow trouble, for pity's sake, borrow it handier home. I should think you had an imagination, sure enough."

Chapter 16

DIANA IS INVITED TO TEA WITH TRAGIC RESULTS

October was a beautiful month at Green Gables, when the birches in the hollow turned as golden as sunshine, and the maples behind the orchard were royal crimson, and the wild cherry trees along the lane put on the loveliest shades of dark red and bronzy green, while the fields sunned themselves in aftermaths.

Anne revelled in the world of colour about her.

"Oh, Marilla," she exclaimed one Saturday morning, coming dancing in with her arms full of gorgeous boughs, "I'm so glad I live in a world where there are Octobers. It would be terrible if we just skipped from September to November, wouldn't it? Look at these maple branches. Don't they give you a thrill—several thrills? I'm going to decorate my room with them."

"Messy things," said Marilla, whose aesthetic sense was not noticeably developed. "You clutter up your room entirely too much with out-of-doors stuff, Anne. Bedrooms were made to sleep in."

"Oh, and dream in, too, Marilla. And you know one can dream so much better in a room where there are pretty things. I'm going to put these boughs in the old blue jug and set them on my table."

"Mind you don't drop leaves all over the stairs, then. I'm going to a meeting of the Aid Society at Carmody this afternoon, Anne, and I won't likely be home before dark. You'll have to get Matthew and Jerry their supper, so mind you don't forget to put the tea to draw until you sit down at the table as you did last time."

"It was dreadful of me to forget," said Anne apologetically, "but that was the afternoon I was trying to think of a name for Violet Vale and it crowded other things out. Matthew was so good. He never scolded a bit. He put the tea down himself and said we could wait awhile as well as not. And I told him a lovely fairy story while we were waiting, so he didn't

102

find the time long at all. It was a beautiful fairy story, Marilla. I forgot the end of it, so I made up an end for it myself, and Matthew said he couldn't tell where the join came in."

"Matthew would think it all right, Anne, if you took a notion to get up and have dinner in the middle of the night. But you keep your wits about you this time. And—I don't really know if I'm doing right—it may make you more addlepated than ever—but you can ask Diana to come over and spend the afternoon with you and have tea here."

"Oh, Marilla!" Anne clasped her hands. "How perfectly lovely! You *are* able to imagine things after all or else you'd never have understood how I've longed for that very thing. It will seem so nice and grown-upish. No fear of my forgetting to put the tea to draw when I have company. Oh, Marilla, can I use the rosebud spray tea set?"

"No indeed! The rosebud tea set! Well, what next? You know I never use that except for the minister or the Aids. You'll put down the old brown tea set. But you can open the little yellow crock of cherry preserves. It's time it was being used anyhow—I believe it's beginning to work.[1] And you can cut some fruitcake and have some of the cookies and snaps."

"I can just imagine myself sitting down at the head of the table and pouring out the tea," said Anne, shutting her eyes ecstatically. "And asking Diana if she takes sugar! I know she doesn't, but of course I'll ask her just as if I didn't know. And then pressing her to take another piece of fruitcake and another helping of preserves. Oh, Marilla, it's a wonderful sensation just to think of it. Can I take her into the spare room to lay off her hat when she comes? And then into the parlour to sit?"

"No. The sitting room will do for you and your company. But there's a bottle half full of raspberry cordial that was left over from the church social the other night. It's on the second shelf of the sitting-room closet, and you and Diana can have it if you like, and a cooky to eat with it along in the afternoon, for I daresay Matthew'll be late coming in to tea since he's hauling potatoes to the vessel."

Anne flew down to the hollow, past the Dryad's Bubble, and up the spruce path to Orchard Slope, to ask Diana to tea. As a result, just after Marilla had driven off to Carmody, Diana came over, dressed in her second best dress and looking exactly as it is proper to look when asked out to tea. At other times she was wont to run into the kitchen without knocking; but now she knocked primly at the front door. And when Anne, dressed in *her* second best, as primly opened it, both little girls

---

[1] Ferment.

shook hands as gravely as if they had never met before. This unnatural solemnity lasted until after Diana had been taken to the east gable to lay off her hat and then had sat for ten minutes in the sitting room, toes in position.

"How is your mother?" inquired Anne politely, just as if she had not seen Mrs. Barry picking apples that morning in excellent health and spirits.

"She is very well, thank you. I suppose Mr. Cuthbert is hauling potatoes to the *Lilly Sands* this afternoon, is he?" said Diana, who had ridden down to Mr. Harmon Andrews's that morning in Matthew's cart.

"Yes. Our potato crop is very good this year. I hope your father's potato crop is good, too."

"It is fairly good, thank you. Have you picked many of your apples yet?"

"Oh, ever so many," said Anne, forgetting to be dignified and jumping up quickly. "Let's go out to the orchard and get some of the Red Sweetings, Diana. Marilla says we can have all that are left on the tree. Marilla is a very generous woman. She said we could have fruitcake and cherry preserves for tea. But it isn't good manners to tell your company what you are going to give them to eat, so I won't tell you what she said we could have to drink. Only it begins with an *r* and a *c* and it's a bright red colour. I love bright red drinks, don't you? They taste twice as good as any other colour."

The orchard, with its great sweeping boughs that bent to the ground with fruit, proved so delightful that the little girls spent most of the afternoon in it, sitting in a grassy corner where the frost had spared the green and the mellow autumn sunshine lingered warmly, eating apples and talking as hard as they could. Diana had much to tell Anne of what went on in school. She had to sit with Gertie Pye and she hated it; Gertie squeaked her pencil all the time and it just made her—Diana's—blood run cold; Ruby Gillis had charmed all her warts away, true's you live, with a magic pebble that Old Mary Joe from the Creek gave her. You had to rub the warts with the pebble and then throw it away over your left shoulder at the time of the new moon and the warts would all go. Charlie Sloane's name was written up with Em White's on the porch wall and Em White was *awful mad* about it; Sam Boulter had "sassed" Mr. Phillips in class and Mr. Phillips whipped him and Sam's father came down to the school and dared Mr. Phillips to lay a hand on one of his children again; and Mattie Andrews had a new red hood and a blue crossover with tassels on it and the airs she put on about it were perfectly sickening; and Lizzie Wright didn't speak to Mamie Wilson because Mamie Wilson's grown-up sister had cut out Lizzie Wright's grown-up sister with her beau; and everybody missed Anne so and wished she'd come to school again; and Gilbert Blythe—

But Anne didn't want to hear about Gilbert Blythe. She jumped up hurriedly and said suppose they go in and have some raspberry cordial.

Anne looked on the second shelf of the sitting-room pantry, but there was no bottle of raspberry cordial there. Search revealed it away back on the top shelf. Anne put it on a tray and set it on the table with a tumbler.

"Now, please help yourself, Diana," she said politely. "I don't believe I'll have any just now. I don't feel as if I wanted any after all those apples."

Diana poured herself out a tumblerful, looked at its bright red hue admiringly, and then sipped it daintily.

"That's awfully nice raspberry cordial, Anne," she said. "I didn't know raspberry cordial was so nice."

"I'm real glad you like it. Take as much as you want. I'm going to run out and stir the fire up. There are so many responsibilities on a person's mind when they're keeping house, isn't there?"

When Anne came back from the kitchen, Diana was drinking her second glassful of cordial; and, being entreated thereto by Anne, she offered no particular objection to the drinking of a third. The tumblerfuls were generous ones and the raspberry cordial was certainly very nice.

"The nicest I ever drank," said Diana. "It's ever so much nicer than Mrs. Lynde's, although she brags of hers so much. It doesn't taste a bit like hers."

"I should think Marilla's raspberry cordial would prob'ly be much nicer than Mrs. Lynde's," said Anne loyally. "Marilla is a famous cook. She is trying to teach me to cook, but I assure you, Diana, it is uphill work. There's so little scope for imagination in cookery. You just have to go by rules. The last time I made a cake, I forgot to put the flour in. I was thinking the loveliest story about you and me, Diana. I thought you were desperately ill with smallpox and everybody deserted you, but I went boldly to your bedside and nursed you back to life; and then I took the smallpox and died and I was buried under those poplar trees in the grave-yard and you planted a rosebush by my grave and watered it with your tears; and you never, never forgot the friend of your youth who sacrificed her life for you. Oh, it was such a pathetic tale, Diana. The tears just rained down over my cheeks while I mixed the cake. But I forgot the flour and the cake was a dismal failure. Flour is so essential to cakes, you know. Marilla was very cross and I don't wonder. I'm a great trial to her.

She was terribly mortified about the pudding sauce last week. We had a plum pudding for dinner on Tuesday, and there was half the pudding and a pitcherful of sauce left over. Marilla said there was enough for another dinner and told me to set it on the pantry shelf and cover it. I meant to cover it just as much as could be, Diana, but when I carried it in, I was imagining I was a nun—of course I'm a Protestant, but I imagined I was a Catholic—taking the veil to bury a broken heart in cloistered seclusion; and I forgot all about covering the pudding sauce. I thought of it next morning and ran to the pantry. Diana, fancy if you can my extreme horror at finding a mouse drowned in that pudding sauce! I lifted the mouse out with a spoon and threw it out in the yard, and then I washed the spoon in three waters. Marilla was out milking, and I fully intended to ask her when she came in if I'd give the sauce to the pigs; but when she did come in, I was imagining that I was a frost fairy going through the woods turning the trees red and yellow, whichever they wanted to be, so I never thought about the pudding sauce again, and Marilla sent me out to pick apples. Well, Mr. and Mrs. Chester Ross from Spencervale came here that morning. You know they are very stylish people, especially Mrs. Chester Ross. When Marilla called me in, dinner was all ready and everybody was at the table. I tried to be as polite and dignified as I could be, for I wanted Mrs. Chester Ross to think I was a ladylike little girl even if I wasn't pretty. Everything went right until I saw Marilla coming with the plum pudding in one hand and the pitcher of pudding sauce, *warmed up,* in the other. Diana, that was a terrible moment. I remembered everything, and I just stood up in my place and shrieked out, 'Marilla, you mustn't use that pudding sauce. There was a mouse drowned in it. I forgot to tell you before.' Oh, Diana, I shall never forget that awful moment if I live to be a hundred. Mrs. Chester Ross just *looked* at me and I thought I would sink through the floor with mortification. She is such a perfect housekeeper and fancy what she must have thought of us. Marilla turned red as fire, but she never said a word—then. She just carried that sauce and pudding out and brought in some strawberry preserves. She even offered me some, but I couldn't swallow a mouthful. It was like heaping coals of fire on my head. After Mrs. Chester Ross went away, Marilla gave me a dreadful scolding. Why, Diana, what is the matter?"

Diana had stood up very unsteadily; then she sat down again, putting her hands to her head.

"I'm—I'm awful sick," she said a little thickly. "I—I—must go right home."

"Oh, you mustn't dream of going home without your tea," cried Anne in distress. "I'll get it right off[2] —I'll go and put the tea down this very minute."

"I must go home," repeated Diana stupidly but determinedly.

"Let me get you a lunch anyhow," implored Anne. "Let me give you a bit of fruitcake and some of the cherry preserves. Lie down on the sofa for a little while, and you'll be better. Where do you feel bad?"

"I must go home," said Diana, and that was all she would say.

In vain Anne pleaded.

"I never heard of company going home without tea," she mourned. "Oh, Diana, do you suppose that it's possible you're really taking the smallpox? If you are, I'll go and nurse you, you can depend on that. I'll never forsake you. But I do wish you'd stay till after tea. Where do you feel bad?"

"I'm awful dizzy," said Diana.

And indeed, she walked very dizzily. Anne, with tears of disappointment in her eyes, got Diana's hat and went with her as far as the Barry yard fence. Then she wept all the way back to Green Gables, where she sorrowfully put the remainder of the raspberry cordial back into the pantry and got tea ready for Matthew and Jerry, with all the zest gone out of the performance.

The next day was Sunday, and as the rain poured down in torrents from dawn till dusk, Anne did not stir abroad from Green Gables. Monday afternoon Marilla sent her down to Mrs. Lynde's on an errand. In a very short space of time, Anne came flying back up the lane, with tears rolling down her cheeks. Into the kitchen she dashed and flung herself face downward on the sofa in an agony.

"Whatever has gone wrong now, Anne?" queried Marilla in doubt and dismay. "I do hope you haven't gone and been saucy to Mrs. Lynde again."

No answer from Anne save more tears and stormier sobs!

"Anne Shirley, when I ask you a question, I want to be answered. Sit right up this very minute and tell me what you are crying about."

Anne sat up, tragedy personified.

"Mrs. Lynde was up to see Mrs. Barry today and Mrs. Barry was in an awful state," she wailed. "She says that I set[3] Diana *drunk* Saturday and sent her home in a disgraceful condition. And she says I must be a thoroughly bad, wicked little girl and she's never, never going to let Diana play with me again. Oh, Marilla, I'm just overcome with woe."

---

2 Away.

3 Got.

Marilla stared in blank amazement.

"Set Diana drunk!" she said when she found her voice. "Anne, are you or Mrs. Barry crazy? What on earth did you give her?"

"Not a thing but raspberry cordial," sobbed Anne. "I never thought raspberry cordial would set people drunk, Marilla—not even if they drank three big tumblerfuls, as Diana did. Oh, it sounds so—so—like Mrs. Thomas's husband! But I didn't mean to set her drunk."

"Drunk fiddlesticks!" said Marilla, marching to the sitting-room pantry. There on the shelf was a bottle that she at once recognized as one containing some of her three-year-old homemade currant wine for which she was celebrated in Avonlea, although certain of the stricter sort, Mrs. Barry among them, disapproved strongly of it. And at the same time Marilla recollected that she had put the bottle of raspberry cordial down in the cellar instead of in the pantry, as she had told Anne.

She went back to the kitchen with the wine bottle in her hand. Her face was twitching in spite of herself.

"Anne, you certainly have a genius for getting into trouble. You went and gave Diana currant wine instead of raspberry cordial. Didn't you know the difference yourself?"

"I never tasted it," said Anne. "I thought it was the cordial. I meant to be so—so—hospitable. Diana got awfully sick and had to go home. Mrs. Barry told Mrs. Lynde she was simply dead drunk. She just laughed sillylike when her mother asked her what was the matter and went to sleep and slept for hours. Her mother smelled her breath and knew she was drunk. She had a fearful headache all day yesterday. Mrs. Barry is so indignant. She will never believe but what I did it on purpose."

"I should think she would better punish Diana for being so greedy as to drink three glassfuls of anything," said Marilla shortly. "Why, three of those big glasses would have made her sick even if it had only been cordial. Well, this story will be a nice handle for those folks who are so down on me for making currant wine, although I haven't made any for three years, ever since I found out that the minister didn't approve. I just kept that bottle for sickness. There, there, child, don't cry. I can't see as you were to blame, although I'm sorry it happened so."

"I must cry," said Anne. "My heart is broken. The stars in their courses fight against me, Marilla. Diana and I are parted forever. Oh, Marilla, I little dreamed of this when first we swore our vows of friendship."

"Don't be foolish, Anne. Mrs. Barry will think better of it when she finds you're not really to blame. I suppose she thinks you've done it for a silly joke or something of that sort. You'd best go up this evening and tell her how it was."

"My courage fails me at the thought of facing Diana's injured mother," sighed Anne. "I wish you'd go, Marilla. You're so much more dignified than I am. Likely she'd listen to you quicker than to me."

"Well, I will," said Marilla, reflecting that it would probably be the wiser course. "Don't cry anymore, Anne. It will be all right."

Marilla had changed her mind about its being all right by the time she got back from Orchard Slope. Anne was watching for her coming and flew to the porch door to meet her.

"Oh, Marilla, I know by your face that it's been no use," she said sorrowfully. "Mrs. Barry won't forgive me?"

"Mrs. Barry indeed!" snapped Marilla. "Of all the unreasonable women I ever saw, she's the worst. I told her it was all a mistake and you weren't to blame, but she just simply didn't believe me. And she rubbed it well in about my currant wine and how I'd always said it couldn't have the least effect on anybody. I just told her plainly that currant wine wasn't meant to be drunk three tumblerfuls at a time and that if a child I had to do with was so greedy, I'd sober her up with a right good spanking."

Marilla whisked into the kitchen, grievously disturbed, leaving a very much distracted little soul in the porch behind her. Presently, Anne stepped out bareheaded into the chill autumn dusk; very determinedly and steadily she took her way down through the sere clover field, over the log bridge, and up through the spruce grove, lighted by a pale little moon hanging low over the western woods. Mrs. Barry, coming to the door in answer to the timid knock, found a white-lipped, eager-eyed suppliant on the doorstep.

Her face hardened. Mrs. Barry was a woman of strong prejudices and dislikes, and her anger was of the cold, sullen sort that is always hardest to overcome. To do her justice, she really believed Anne had made Diana drunk out of sheer malice prepense,[4] and she was honestly anxious to preserve her little daughter from the contamination of further intimacy with such a child.

"What do you want?" she said stiffly.

Anne clasped her hands.

"Oh, Mrs. Barry, please forgive me. I did not mean to—to—intoxicate Diana. How could I? Just imagine if you were a poor little orphan girl that kind people had adopted and you had just one bosom friend in all the world. Do you think you would intoxicate her on purpose? I thought

---

[4] Premeditated malice.

it was only raspberry cordial. I was firmly convinced it was raspberry cordial. Oh, please don't say that you won't let Diana play with me anymore. If you do, you will cover my life with a dark cloud of woe."

This speech, which would have softened good Mrs. Lynde's heart in a twinkling, had no effect on Mrs. Barry except to irritate her still more. She was suspicious of Anne's big words and dramatic gestures and imagined that the child was making fun of her. So she said coldly and cruelly:

"I don't think you are a fit little girl for Diana to associate with. You'd better go home and behave yourself."

Anne's lip quivered.

"Won't you let me see Diana just once to say farewell?" she implored.

"Diana has gone over to Carmody with her father," said Mrs. Barry, going in and shutting the door.

Anne went back to Green Gables calm with despair.

"My last hope is gone," she told Marilla. "I went up and saw Mrs. Barry myself and she treated me very insultingly. Marilla, I do *not* think she is a well-bred woman. There is nothing more to do except to pray and I haven't much hope that that'll do much good because, Marilla, I do not believe that God Himself can do very much with such an obstinate person as Mrs. Barry."

"Anne, you shouldn't say such things," rebuked Marilla, striving to overcome that unholy tendency to laughter that she was dismayed to find growing upon her. And indeed, when she told the whole story to Matthew that night, she did laugh heartily over Anne's tribulations.

But when she slipped into the east gable before going to bed and found that Anne had cried herself to sleep, an unaccustomed softness crept into her face.

"Poor little soul," she murmured, lifting a loose curl of hair from the child's tear-stained face. Then she bent down and kissed the flushed cheek on the pillow.

Chapter 17
A NEW INTEREST IN LIFE

The next afternoon Anne, bending over her patchwork at the kitchen window, happened to glance out and beheld Diana down by the Dryad's Bubble beckoning mysteriously. In a trice Anne was out of the house and flying down to the hollow, astonishment and hope struggling in her expressive eyes. But the hope faded when she saw Diana's dejected countenance.

"Your mother hasn't relented?" she gasped.

Diana shook her head mournfully.

"No, and, oh, Anne, she says I'm never to play with you again. I've cried and cried and I told her it wasn't your fault, but it wasn't any use. I had ever such a time coaxing her to let me come down and say good-bye to you. She said I was only to stay ten minutes and she's timing me by the clock."

"Ten minutes isn't very long to say an eternal farewell in," said Anne tearfully. "Oh, Diana, will you promise faithfully never to forget me, the friend of your youth, no matter what dearer friends may caress thee?"

"Indeed I will," sobbed Diana, "and I'll never have another bosom friend—I don't want to have. I couldn't love anybody as I love you."

"Oh, Diana," cried Anne, clasping her hands, "do you *love* me?"

"Why, of course I do. Didn't you know that?"

"No." Anne drew a long breath. "I thought you *liked* me, of course, but I never hoped you *loved* me. Why, Diana, I didn't think anybody could love me. Nobody ever has loved me since I can remember. Oh, this is wonderful! It's a ray of light that will forever shine on the darkness of a path severed from thee, Diana. Oh, just say it once again."

"I love you devotedly, Anne," said Diana stanchly, "and I always will, you may be sure of that."

"And I will always love thee, Diana," said Anne, solemnly extending her hand. "In the years to come, thy memory will shine like a star over my lonely life, as that last story we read together says. Diana, wilt thou

111

give me a lock of thy jet black tresses in parting to treasure forevermore?"

"Have you got anything to cut it with?" queried Diana, wiping away the tears that Anne's affecting accents had caused to flow afresh and returning to practicalities.

"Yes. I've got my patchwork scissors in my apron pocket, fortunately," said Anne. She solemnly clipped one of Diana's curls. "Fare thee well, my beloved friend. Henceforth we must be as strangers, though living side by side. But my heart will ever be faithful to thee."

Anne stood and watched Diana out of sight, mournfully waving her hand to the latter whenever she turned to look back. Then she returned to the house, not a little consoled for the time being by this romantic parting.

"It is all over," she informed Marilla. "I shall never have another friend. I'm really worse off than ever before, for I haven't Katie Maurice and Violetta now. And even if I had, it wouldn't be the same. Somehow, little dream girls are not satisfying after a real friend. Diana and I had such an affecting farewell down by the spring. It will be sacred in my memory forever. I used the most pathetic language I could think of and said 'thou' and 'thee.' 'Thou' and 'thee' seem so much more romantic than 'you.' Diana gave me a lock of her hair, and I'm going to sew it up in a little bag and wear it around my neck all my life. Please see that it is buried with me, for I don't believe I'll live very long. Perhaps when she sees me lying cold and dead before her, Mrs. Barry may feel remorse for what she has done and will let Diana come to my funeral."

"I don't think there is much fear of your dying of grief as long as you can talk, Anne," said Marilla unsympathetically.

The following Monday Anne surprised Marilla by coming down from her room with her basket of books on her arm and her lips primmed up into a line of determination.

"I'm going back to school," she announced. "That is all there is left in life for me, now that my friend has been ruthlessly torn from me. In school I can look at her and muse over days departed."

"You'd better muse over your lessons and sums," said Marilla, concealing her delight at this development of the situation. "If you're going back to school, I hope we'll hear no more of breaking slates over people's heads and such carryings-on. Behave yourself and do just what your teacher tells you."

"I'll try to be a model pupil," agreed Anne dolefully. "There won't be much fun in it, I expect. Mr. Phillips said Minnie Andrews was a model pupil and there isn't a spark of imagination or life in her. She is just dull and poky and never seems to have a good time. But I feel so depressed that perhaps it will come easy to me now. I'm going round by the road. I couldn't bear to go by the Birch Path all alone. I should weep bitter tears if I did."

Anne was welcomed back to school with open arms. Her imagination had been sorely missed in games, her voice in the singing, and her dramatic ability in the perusal aloud of books at dinner hour. Ruby Gillis smuggled three blue plums over to her during testament reading; Ella May MacPherson gave her an enormous yellow pansy cut from the covers of a floral catalogue—a species of desk decoration much prized in Avonlea school. Sophia Sloane offered to teach her a perfectly elegant new pattern of knit lace, *so* nice for trimming aprons. Katie Boulter gave her a perfume bottle to keep slate water in, and Julia Bell copied carefully on a piece of pale pink paper, scalloped on the edges, the following effusion:

> To Anne
> When twilight drops her curtain down
>   And pins it with a star
> Remember that you have a friend
>   Though she may wander far.

"It's so nice to be appreciated," sighed Anne rapturously to Marilla that night.

The girls were not the only scholars who "appreciated" her. When Anne went to her seat after dinner hour—she had been told by Mr. Phillips to sit with the model Minnie Andrews—she found on her desk a big, luscious "strawberry apple." Anne caught it up all ready to take a bite when she remembered that the only place in Avonlea where strawberry apples grew was in the old Blythe orchard on the other side of the Lake of Shining Waters. Anne dropped the apple as if it were a red-hot coal and ostentatiously wiped her fingers on her handkerchief. The apple lay untouched on her desk until the next morning, when little Timothy Andrews, who swept the school and kindled the fire, annexed it as one of his perquisites. Charlie Sloane's slate pencil, gorgeously bedizened with striped red and yellow paper, costing two cents where ordinary pencils cost only one, which he sent up to her after dinner hour, met with a more favourable reception. Anne was graciously pleased to accept it and rewarded the donor with a smile that exalted that infatuated youth straightway into the seventh heaven of delight and caused him to make such fearful errors in his dictation that Mr. Phillips kept him in after school to rewrite it.

But as "The Caesar's pageant shorn of Brutus's bust / Did but of Rome's best son remind her more," so the marked absence of any tribute or recognition from Diana Barry, who was sitting with Gertie Pye, embittered Anne's little triumph.

"Diana might just have smiled at me once, I think," she mourned to Marilla that night.

But the next morning a note, most fearfully and wonderfully twisted and folded, and a small parcel were passed across to Anne.

> Dear Anne [ran the former],
> Mother says I'm not to play with you or talk to you even in school. It isn't my fault and don't be cross at me, because I love you as much as ever. I miss you awfully to tell all my secrets to, and I don't like Gertie Pye one bit. I made you one of the new bookmarkers out of red tissue paper. They are awfully fashionable now, and only three girls in school know how to make them. When you look at it remember
>
> > Your true friend,
> > Diana Barry

Anne read the note, kissed the bookmark, and dispatched a prompt reply back to the other side of the school.

> My own darling Diana:
> Of course I am not cross at you because you have to obey your mother. Our spirits can commune. I shall keep your lovely present forever. Minnie Andrews is a very nice little girl—although she has no imagination— but after having been Diana's busum friend I cannot be Minnie's. Please excuse mistakes because my spelling isn't very good yet, although much improved.
>
> > Yours until death us do part,
> > Anne or Cordelia Shirley
>
> P.S. I shall sleep with your letter under my pillow tonight.
>
> > A. or C. S.

Marilla pessimistically expected more trouble since Anne had again begun to go to school. But none developed. Perhaps Anne caught something of the "model" spirit from Minnie Andrews; at least she got on very well with Mr. Phillips thenceforth. She flung herself into her studies heart and soul, determined not to be outdone in any class by Gilbert Blythe. The rivalry between them was soon apparent. It was entirely good-natured on Gilbert's side, but it is much to be feared that the same thing cannot be said of Anne, who had certainly an unpraiseworthy tenacity for holding grudges. She was as intense in her hatreds as in her loves. She would not stoop to admit that she meant to rival Gilbert in schoolwork, because that would have been to acknowledge his existence, which Anne persistently ignored; but the rivalry was there and honours fluctuated between them. Now Gilbert was head of the spelling class; now Anne, with a toss of her long red braids, spelled him down. One morning Gilbert had all his sums done correctly and had his name written on the blackboard on the roll of honour; the next morning Anne, having wrestled wildly with decimals the entire evening before, would be first. One awful day they were ties and their names were written up together. It was almost as bad as a "take-notice," and Anne's mortification was as evident as Gilbert's satisfaction. When the written examinations at the end of each month were held, the suspense was terrible. The first month Gilbert came out three marks ahead. The second Anne beat him by five. But her triumph was marred by the fact that Gilbert congratulated her heartily before the whole school. It would have been ever so much sweeter to her if he had felt the sting of his defeat.

Mr. Phillips might not be a very good teacher, but a pupil so inflexibly determined on learning as Anne was could hardly escape making progress under any kind of a teacher. By the end of the term Anne and Gilbert were both promoted into the fifth class and allowed to begin studying the elements of "the branches"—by which Latin, geometry, French, and algebra were meant. In geometry, Anne met her Waterloo.

"It's perfectly awful stuff, Marilla," she groaned. "I'm sure I'll never be able to make head or tail of it. There is no scope for imagination in it at all. Mr. Phillips says I'm the worst dunce he ever saw at it. And Gil—I mean some of the others are so smart at it. It is extremely mortifying, Marilla. Even Diana gets along better than I do. But I don't mind being beaten by Diana. Even although we meet as strangers now, I still love her with an *inextinguishable* love. It makes me very sad at times to think about her. But really, Marilla, one can't stay sad very long in such an interesting world, can one?"

Chapter 18
ANNE TO THE RESCUE

All things great are wound up with all things little. At first glance it might not seem that the decision of a certain Canadian premier to include Prince Edward Island in a political tour could have much or anything to do with the fortunes of little Anne Shirley at Green Gables. But it had.

It was in January that the premier came, to address his loyal supporters and such of his nonsupporters as chose to be present at the monster mass meeting held in Charlottetown. Most of the Avonlea people were on the premier's side of politics; hence, on the night of the meeting nearly all the men and a goodly proportion of the women had gone to town, thirty[1] miles away. Mrs. Rachel Lynde had gone, too. Mrs. Rachel Lynde was a red-hot politician and couldn't have believed that the political rally could be carried through without her, although she was on the opposite side of politics. So she went to town and took her husband—Thomas would be useful in looking after the horse—and Marilla Cuthbert with her. Marilla had a sneaking interest in politics herself, and as she thought it might be her only chance to see a real live premier, she promptly took it, leaving Anne and Matthew to keep house until her return the following day.

Hence, while Marilla and Mrs. Rachel were enjoying themselves hugely at the mass meeting, Anne and Matthew had the cheerful kitchen at Green Gables all to themselves. A bright fire was glowing in the old-fashioned Waterloo stove and blue-white frost crystals were shining on the windowpanes. Matthew nodded over a *Farmers' Advocate* on the sofa, and Anne at the table studied her lessons with grim determination, despite sundry wistful glances at the clock shelf, where lay a new book that Jane Andrews had lent her that day. Jane had assured her that it was warranted to produce any number of thrills, or words to that effect, and Anne's fingers tingled to reach out for it. But that would mean Gilbert

---

[1] Distance on roads of that day.

116

Blythe's triumph on the morrow. Anne turned her back on the clock shelf and tried to imagine it wasn't there.

"Matthew, did you ever study geometry when you went to school?"

"Well now, no, I didn't," said Matthew, coming out of his doze with a start.

"I wish you had," sighed Anne, "because then you'd be able to sympathize with me. You can't sympathize properly if you've never studied it. It is casting a cloud over my whole life. I'm such a dunce at it, Matthew."

"Well now, I dunno," said Matthew soothingly. "I guess you're all right at anything. Mr. Phillips told me last week in Blair's store at Carmody that you was the smartest scholar in school and was making rapid progress. 'Rapid progress' was his very words. There's them as runs down Teddy Phillips and says he ain't much of a teacher, but I guess he's all right."

Matthew would have thought anyone who praised Anne was "all right."

"I'm sure I'd get on better with geometry if only he wouldn't change the letters," complained Anne. "I learn the proposition off by heart, and then he draws it on the blackboard and puts different letters from what are in the book and I get all mixed up. I don't think a teacher should take such a mean advantage, do you? We're studying agriculture now and I've found out at last what makes the roads red. It's a great comfort. I wonder how Marilla and Mrs. Lynde are enjoying themselves. Mrs. Lynde says Canada is going to the dogs the way things are being run at Ottawa and that it's an awful warning to the electors. She says if women were allowed to vote, we would soon see a blessed change. What way do you vote, Matthew?"

"Conservative," said Matthew promptly. To vote Conservative was part of Matthew's religion.

"Then I'm Conservative, too," said Anne decidedly. "I'm glad, because Gil—because some of the boys in school are Grits. I guess Mr. Phillips is a Grit, too, because Prissy Andrews's father is one, and Ruby Gillis says that when a man is courting, he always has to agree with the girl's mother in religion and her father in politics. Is that true, Matthew?"

"Well now, I dunno," said Matthew.

"Did you ever go courting, Matthew?"

"Well now, no, I dunno's I ever did," said Matthew, who had certainly never thought of such a thing in his whole existence.

Anne reflected with her chin in her hands.

"It must be rather interesting, don't you think, Matthew? Ruby Gillis says when she grows up, she's going to have ever so many beaus on the string and have them all crazy about her; but I think that would be too exciting. I'd rather have just one in his right mind. But Ruby Gillis knows a great deal about such matters because she has so many big sisters, and Mrs. Lynde says the Gillis girls have gone off like hotcakes. Mr. Phillips goes up to see Prissy Andrews nearly every evening. He says it is to help her with her lessons, but Miranda Sloane is studying for Queen's, too, and I should think she needed help a lot more than Prissy because she's ever so much stupider, but he never goes to help her in the evenings at all. There are a great many things in this world that I can't understand very well, Matthew."

"Well now, I dunno as I comprehend them all myself," acknowledged Matthew.

"Well, I suppose I must finish up my lessons. I won't allow myself to open that new book Jane lent me until I'm through. But it's a terrible temptation, Matthew. Even when I turn my back on it, I can see it there just as plain. Jane said she cried herself sick over it. I love a book that makes me cry. But I think I'll carry that book into the sitting room and lock it in the jam closet and give you the key. And you must *not* give it to me, Matthew, until my lessons are done, not even if I implore you on my bended knees. It's all very well to say resist temptation, but it's ever so much easier to resist it if you can't get the key. And then shall I run down to the cellar and get some russets, Matthew? Wouldn't you like some russets?"

"Well now, I dunno but what I would," said Matthew, who never ate russets but knew Anne's weakness for them.

Just as Anne emerged triumphantly from the cellar with her plateful of russets came the sound of flying footsteps on the icy boardwalk outside, and the next moment the kitchen door was flung open and in rushed Diana Barry, white-faced and breathless, with a shawl wrapped hastily around her head. Anne promptly let go of her candle and plate in her surprise, and plate, candle, and apples crashed together down the cellar ladder and were found at the bottom embedded in melted grease, the next day, by Marilla, who gathered them up and thanked mercy the house hadn't been set on fire.

"Whatever is the matter, Diana?" cried Anne. "Has your mother relented at last?"

"Oh, Anne, do come quick," implored Diana nervously. "Minnie May is awful sick—she's got croup, Young Mary Joe says—and Father and Mother are away to town and there's nobody to go for the doctor.

Minnie May is awful bad, and Young Mary Joe doesn't know what to do—and, oh, Anne, I'm so scared!"

Matthew, without a word, reached out for cap and coat, slipped past Diana, and away into the darkness of the yard.

"He's gone to harness the sorrel mare to go to Carmody for the doctor," said Anne, who was hurrying on hood and jacket. "I know it as well as if he'd said so. Matthew and I are such kindred spirits I can read his thoughts without words at all."

"I don't believe he'll find the doctor at Carmody," sobbed Diana. "I know that Doctor Blair went to town, and I guess Doctor Spencer would go, too. Young Mary Joe never saw anybody with croup, and Mrs. Lynde is away. Oh, Anne!"

"Don't cry, Di," said Anne cheerily. "I know exactly what to do for croup. You forget that Mrs. Hammond had twins three times. When you look after three pairs of twins, you naturally get a lot of experience. They all had croup regularly. Just wait till I get the ipecac bottle—you mayn't have any at your house. Come on now."

The two little girls hastened out hand in hand and hurried through Lover's Lane and across the crusted field beyond, for the snow was too deep to go by the shorter wood way. Anne, although sincerely sorry for Minnie May, was far from being insensible to the romance of the situation and to the sweetness of once more sharing that romance with a kindred spirit.

The night was clear and frosty, all ebony of shadow and silver of snowy slope; big stars were shining over the silent fields; here and there the dark, pointed firs stood up with snow powdering their branches and the wind whistling through them. Anne thought it was truly delightful to go skimming through all this mystery and loveliness with your bosom friend who had been so long estranged.

Minnie May, aged three, was really very sick. She lay on the kitchen sofa, feverish and restless, while her hoarse breathing could be heard all over the house. Young Mary Joe, a buxom, broad-faced French girl from the Creek, whom Mrs. Barry had engaged to stay with the children during her absence, was helpless and bewildered, quite incapable of thinking what to do, or doing it if she thought of it.

Anne went to work with skill and promptness.

"Minnie May has croup all right; she's pretty bad, but I've seen them worse. First we must have lots of hot water. I declare, Diana, there isn't more than a cupful in the kettle! There, I've filled it up, and Mary Joe, you may put some wood in the stove. I don't want to hurt your feelings, but it seems to me you might have thought of this before if you'd any imagination. Now, I'll undress Minnie May and put her to bed, and you try to find some soft flannel cloths, Diana. I'm going to give her a dose of ipecac first of all."

Minnie May did not take kindly to the ipecac, but Anne had not brought up three pairs of twins for nothing. Down that ipecac went, not only once, but many times during the long, anxious night when the two little girls worked patiently over the suffering Minnie May, and Young Mary Joe, honestly anxious to do all she could, kept on a roaring fire and heated more water than would have been needed for a hospital of croupy babies.

It was three o'clock when Matthew came with the doctor, for he had been obliged to go all the way to Spencervale for one. But the pressing need for assistance was past. Minnie May was much better and was sleeping soundly.

"I was awfully near giving up in despair," explained Anne. "She got worse and worse until she was sicker than ever the Hammond twins were, even the last pair. I actually thought she was going to choke to death. I gave her every drop of ipecac in that bottle, and when the last dose went down, I said to myself—not to Diana or Young Mary Joe, because I didn't want to worry them any more than they were worried, but I had to say it to myself just to relieve my feelings—*This is the last lingering hope and I fear 'tis a vain one.* But in about three minutes, she coughed up the phlegm and began to get better right away. You must just imagine my relief, Doctor, because I can't express it in words. You know there are some things that cannot be expressed in words."

"Yes, I know," nodded the doctor. He looked at Anne as if he were thinking some things about her that couldn't be expressed in words. Later on, however, he expressed them to Mr. and Mrs. Barry.

"That little redheaded girl they have over at Cuthbert's is as smart as they make 'em. I tell you, she saved that baby's life, for it would have been too late by the time I got here. She seems to have a skill and presence of mind perfectly wonderful in a child of her age. I never saw anything like the eyes of her when she was explaining the case out to me."

Anne had gone home in the wonderful, white-frosted winter morning, heavy-eyed from loss of sleep but still talking unweariedly to Matthew as they crossed the long, white field and walked under the glittering fairy arch of the Lover's Lane maples.

"Oh, Matthew, isn't it a wonderful morning? The world looks like something God had just imagined for His own pleasure, doesn't it? Those trees look as if I could blow them away with a breath—Pouf! I'm so glad I live in a world where there are white frosts, aren't you? And I'm so glad Mrs. Hammond had three pairs of twins after all. If she hadn't, I mightn't have known what to do for Minnie May. I'm real sorry I was ever cross with Mrs. Hammond for having twins. But, oh, Matthew, I'm so sleepy. I can't go to school. I just know I couldn't keep my eyes open and I'd be so stupid. But I hate to stay home, for Gil—some of the others will get head of the class, and it's so hard to get up again—although of course the harder it is, the more satisfaction you have when you do get up, haven't you?"

"Well now, I guess you'll manage all right," said Matthew, looking at Anne's white little face and the dark shadows under her eyes. "You just go right to bed and have a good sleep. I'll do all the chores."

Anne accordingly went to bed and slept so long and soundly that it was well on in the white and rosy winter afternoon when she awoke and descended to the kitchen, where Marilla, who had arrived home in the meantime, was sitting knitting.

"Oh, did you see the premier?" exclaimed Anne at once. "What did he look like, Marilla?"

"Well, he never got to be premier on account of his looks," said Marilla. "Such a nose as that man had! But he can speak. I was proud of being a Conservative. Rachel Lynde, of course, being a Liberal, had no use for him. Your dinner is in the oven, Anne; and you can get yourself some blue plum preserve out of the pantry. I guess you're hungry. Matthew has been telling me about last night. I must say, it was fortunate you knew what to do. I wouldn't have had any idea myself, for I never saw a case of croup. There now, never mind talking till you've had your dinner. I can tell by the look of you that you're just full up with speeches, but they'll keep."

Marilla had something to tell Anne, but she did not tell it just then, for she knew if she did, Anne's consequent excitement would lift her clear out of the region of such material matters as appetite or dinner. Not until Anne had finished her saucer of blue plums did Marilla say:

"Mrs. Barry was here this afternoon, Anne. She wanted to see you, but I wouldn't wake you up. She says you saved Minnie May's life, and she is very sorry she acted as she did in that affair of the currant wine. She says she knows now you didn't mean to set Diana drunk, and she hopes you'll forgive her and be good friends with Diana again. You're to go over this evening if you like, for Diana can't stir outside the door on account of a bad cold she caught last night. Now, Anne Shirley, for pity's sake, don't fly clean up into the air."

The warning seemed not unnecessary, so uplifted and aerial was Anne's expression and attitude as she sprang to her feet, her face irradiated with the flame of her spirit.

"Oh, Marilla, can I go right now—without washing my dishes? I'll wash them when I come back, but I cannot tie myself down to anything so unromantic as dishwashing at this thrilling moment."

"Yes, yes, run along," said Marilla indulgently. "Anne Shirley—are you crazy? Come back this instant and put something on you. I might as well call to the wind. She's gone without a cap or wrap. Look at her tearing through the orchard with her hair streaming. It'll be a mercy if she doesn't catch her death of cold."

Anne came dancing home in the purple winter twilight across the snowy places. Afar in the southwest was the great shimmering, pearl-like sparkle of an evening star in a sky that was pale golden and ethereal rose over gleaming white spaces and dark glens of spruce. The tinkles of sleigh bells among the snowy hills came like elfin chimes through the frosty air, but their music was not sweeter than the song in Anne's heart and on her lips.

"You see before you a perfectly happy person, Marilla," she announced. "I'm perfectly happy—yes, in spite of my red hair. Just at present I have a soul above red hair. Mrs. Barry kissed me and cried and said she was so sorry and she could never repay me. I felt fearfully embarrassed, Marilla, but I just said as politely as I could, 'I have no hard feelings for you, Mrs. Barry. I assure you once for all[2] that I did not mean to intoxicate Diana, and henceforth I shall cover the past with the mantle of oblivion.' That was a pretty dignified way of speaking, wasn't it, Marilla? I felt that I was heaping coals of fire on Mrs. Barry's head. And Diana and I had a lovely afternoon. Diana showed me a new fancy crochet stitch her aunt over at Carmody taught her. Not a soul in Avonlea knows it but us, and we pledged a solemn vow never to reveal it to anyone else. Diana gave me a beautiful card with a wreath of roses on it and a verse of poetry:

> If you love me as I love you
> Nothing but death can part us two.

"And that is true, Marilla. We're going to ask Mr. Phillips to let us sit together in school again, and Gertie Pye can go with Minnie Andrews.

---

2 And for all.

We had an elegant tea. Mrs. Barry had the very best china set out, Marilla, just as if I was real company. I can't tell you what a thrill it gave me. Nobody ever used their very best china on my account before. And we had fruitcake and pound cake and doughnuts and two kinds of preserves, Marilla. And Mrs. Barry asked me if I took tea and said, 'Pa, why don't you pass the biscuits to Anne?' It must be lovely to be grown up, Marilla, when just being treated as if you were is so nice."

"I don't know about that," said Marilla with a brief sigh.

"Well, anyway, when I am grown up," said Anne decidedly, "I'm always going to talk to little girls as if they were, too, and I'll never laugh when they use big words. I know from sorrowful experience how that hurts one's feelings. After tea Diana and I made taffy. The taffy wasn't very good, I suppose because neither Diana nor I had ever made any before. Diana left me to stir it while she buttered the plates and I forgot and let it burn; and then when we set it out on the platform to cool, the cat walked over one plate and that had to be thrown away. But the making of it was splendid fun. Then when I came home, Mrs. Barry asked me to come over as often as I could, and Diana stood at the window and threw kisses to me all the way down to Lover's Lane. I assure you, Marilla, that I feel like praying tonight, and I'm going to think out a special brand-new prayer in honour of the occasion."

Chapter 19

A CONCERT, A CATASTROPHE, AND A CONFESSION

"Marilla, can I go over to see Diana just for a minute?" asked Anne, running breathlessly down from the east gable one February evening.

"I don't see what you want to be traipsing about after dark for," said Marilla shortly. "You and Diana walked home from school together and then stood down there in the snow for half an hour more, your tongues going the whole blessed time, clickety-clack. So I don't think you're very badly off to see her again."

"But she wants to see me," pleaded Anne. "She has something very important to tell me."

"How do you know she has?"

"Because she just signaled to me from her window. We have arranged a way to signal with our candles and cardboard. We set the candle on the windowsill and make flashes by passing the cardboard back and forth. So many flashes mean a certain thing. It was my idea, Marilla."

"I'll warrant you it was," said Marilla emphatically. "And the next thing you'll be setting fire to the curtains with your signaling nonsense."

"Oh, we're very careful, Marilla. And it's so interesting. Two flashes mean 'Are you there?' Three mean 'Yes' and four 'No.' Five mean 'Come over as soon as possible, because I have something important to reveal.' Diana has just signaled five flashes, and I'm really suffering to know what it is."

"Well, you needn't suffer any longer," said Marilla sarcastically. "You can go, but you're to be back here in just ten minutes, remember that."

Anne did remember it and was back in the stipulated time, although probably no mortal will ever know just what it cost her to confine the

124

discussion of Diana's important communication within the limits of ten minutes. But at least she had made good use of them.

"Oh, Marilla, what do you think? You know tomorrow is Diana's birthday. Well, her mother told her she could ask me to go home with her from school and stay all night with her. And her cousins are coming over from Newbridge in the big pung sleigh to go to the Debating Club concert at the hall tomorrow night. And they are going to take Diana and me to the concert—if you'll let me go, that is. You will, won't you, Marilla? Oh, I feel so excited!"

"You can calm down then, because you're not going. You're better[1] at home in your own bed, and as for that Club concert, it's all nonsense, and little girls should not be allowed to go out to such places at all."

"I'm sure the Debating Club is a most respectable affair," pleaded Anne.

"I'm not saying it isn't. But you're not going to begin gadding about to concerts and staying out all hours of the night. Pretty doings for children! I'm surprised at Mrs. Barry's letting Diana go."

"But it's such a very special occasion," mourned Anne, on the verge of tears. "Diana has only one birthday in a year. It isn't as if birthdays were common things, Marilla. Prissy Andrews is going to recite 'Curfew Must Not Ring Tonight.' That is such a good moral piece, Marilla, I'm sure it would do me lots of good to hear it. And the choir are going to sing four lovely, pathetic songs that are pretty near as good as hymns. And, oh, Marilla, the minister is going to take part; yes indeed he is; he's going to give an address. That will be just about the same thing as a sermon. Please, mayn't I go, Marilla?"

"You heard what I said, Anne, didn't you? Take off your boots now and go to bed. It's past eight."

"There's just one more thing, Marilla," said Anne with an air of producing the last shot in her locker. "Mrs. Barry told Diana that we might sleep in the spare room bed. Think of the honour of your little Anne being put in the spare room bed."

"It's an honour you'll have to get along without. Go to bed, Anne, and don't let me hear another word out of you."

When Anne, with tears rolling over[2] her cheeks, had gone sorrowfully upstairs, Matthew, who had been apparently sound asleep on the lounge during the whole dialogue, opened his eyes and said decidedly:

"Well now, Marilla, I think you ought to let Anne go."

---

[1] Better off.

[2] Rolling down.

"I don't then," retorted Marilla. "Who's bringing this child up, Matthew, you or me?"

"Well now, you," admitted Matthew.

"Don't interfere then."

"Well now, I ain't interfering. It ain't interfering to have your own opinion. And my opinion is that you ought to let Anne go."

"You'd think I ought to let Anne go to the moon if she took the notion, I've no doubt," was Marilla's amiable rejoinder. "I might have let her spend the night with Diana, if that was all. But I don't approve of this concert plan. She'd go there and catch cold like as not, and have her head filled up with nonsense and excitement. It would unsettle her for a week. I understand that child's disposition and what's good for it better than you, Matthew."

"I think you ought to let Anne go," repeated Matthew firmly.

Argument was not his strong point, but holding fast to his opinion certainly was. Marilla gave a gasp of helplessness and took refuge in silence.

The next morning, when Anne was washing the breakfast dishes in the pantry, Matthew paused on his way out to the barn to say to Marilla again: "I think you ought to let Anne go, Marilla."

For a moment, Marilla looked things not lawful to be uttered. Then she yielded to the inevitable and said tartly, "Very well, she can go, since nothing else'll please you."

Anne flew out of the pantry, dripping dishcloth in hand.

"Oh, Marilla, Marilla, say those blessed words again."

"I guess once is enough to say them. This is Matthew's doings and I wash my hands of it. If you catch pneumonia sleeping in a strange bed or coming out of that hot hall in the middle of the night, don't blame me, blame Matthew. Anne Shirley, you're dripping greasy water all over the floor. I never saw such a careless child."

"Oh, I know I'm a great trial to you, Marilla," said Anne repentantly. "I make so many mistakes. But then just think of all the mistakes I don't make, although I might. I'll get some sand and scrub up the spots before I go to school. Oh, Marilla, my heart was just set on going to that concert. I never was[3] to a concert in my life, and when the other girls talk about them in school, I feel so out of it. You didn't know just how I felt about it, but you see Matthew did. Matthew understands me, and it's so nice to be understood, Marilla."

Anne was too excited to do herself justice as to lessons that morning in

---

3 Went.

school. Gilbert Blythe spelled her down in class and left her clear out of sight in mental arithmetic. Anne's consequent humiliation was less than it might have been, however, in view of the concert and the spare room bed. She and Diana talked so constantly about it all day that with a stricter teacher than Mr. Phillips, dire disgrace must inevitably have been their portion.

Anne felt that she could not have borne it if she had not been going to the concert, for nothing else was discussed that day in school. The Avonlea Debating Club, which met fortnightly all winter, had had several smaller free entertainments; but this was to be a big affair, admission ten cents, in aid of the library. The Avonlea young people had been practicing for weeks, and all the scholars were especially interested in it by reason of older brothers and sisters who were going to take part. Everybody in school over nine years of age expected to go, except Carrie Sloane, whose father shared Marilla's opinions about small girls going out to night concerts. Carrie Sloane cried into her grammar all the afternoon and felt that life was not worth living.

For Anne the real excitement began with the dismissal of school and increased therefrom in crescendo until it reached to a crash of positive ecstasy in the concert itself. They had a "perfectly elegant tea," and then came the delicious occupation of dressing in Diana's little room upstairs. Diana did Anne's front hair in the new pompadour style, and Anne tied Diana's bows with the especial knack she possessed; and they experimented with at least half a dozen different ways of arranging their back hair. At last they were ready, cheeks scarlet and eyes glowing with excitement.

True, Anne could not help a little pang when she contrasted her plain black tam and shapeless, tight-sleeved, homemade gray cloth coat with Diana's jaunty fur cap and smart little jacket. But she remembered in time that she had an imagination and could use it.

Then Diana's cousins, the Murrays from Newbridge, came; they all crowded into the big pung sleigh, among straw and furry robes. Anne reveled in the drive to the hall, slipping along over the satin-smooth roads with the snow crisping under the runners. There was a magnificent sunset, and the snowy hills and deep blue water of the St. Lawrence Gulf seemed to rim in the splendour like a huge bowl of pearl and sapphire brimmed with wine and fire. Tinkles of sleigh bells and distant laughter that seemed like the mirth of wood elves came from every quarter.

"Oh, Diana," breathed Anne, squeezing Diana's mittened hand under the fur robe, "isn't it all like a beautiful dream? Do I really look the same as usual? I feel so different that it seems to me it must show in my looks."

"You look awfully nice," said Diana, who having just received a compliment from one of her cousins, felt that she ought to pass it on. "You've got the loveliest colour."

The programme that night was a series of "thrills" for at least one listener in the audience, and, as Anne assured Diana, every succeeding thrill was thrillier than the last. When Prissy Andrews, attired in a new pink silk waist with a string of pearls about her smooth white throat and real carnations in her hair—rumor whispered that the master had sent all the way to town for them for her—"climbed the slimy ladder, dark without one ray of light," Anne shivered in luxurious sympathy; when the choir sang "Far Above the Gentle Daisies," Anne gazed at the ceiling as if it were frescoed with angels; when Sam Sloane proceeded to explain and illustrate "How Sockery Set a Hen," Anne laughed until people sitting near her laughed, too, more out of sympathy with her than with amusement at a selection that was rather threadbare even in Avonlea; and when Mr. Phillips gave Mark Antony's oration over the dead body of Caesar in the most heart-stirring tones—looking at Prissy Andrews at the end of every sentence—Anne felt that she could rise and mutiny on the spot if but one Roman citizen led the way.

Only one number on the programme failed to interest her. When Gilbert Blythe recited "Bingen on the Rhine," Anne picked up Rhoda Murray's library book and read it until he had finished, when she sat rigidly stiff and motionless while Diana clapped her hands until they tingled.

It was eleven when they got home, sated with dissipation but with the exceeding sweet pleasure of talking it all over still to come. Everybody seemed asleep, and the house was dark and silent. Anne and Diana tiptoed into the parlour, a long, narrow room out of which the spare room opened. It was pleasantly warm and dimly lighted by the embers of a fire in the grate.

"Let's undress here," said Diana. "It's so nice and warm."

"Hasn't it been a delightful time?" sighed Anne rapturously. "It must be splendid to get up and recite there. Do you suppose we will ever be asked to do it, Diana?"

"Yes, of course, some day. They're always wanting the big scholars to recite. Gilbert Blythe does often, and he's only two years older than us. Oh, Anne, how could you pretend not to listen to him? When he came to the line, 'There's another, not a sister,' he looked right down at you."

"Diana," said Anne with dignity, "you are my bosom friend, but I cannot allow even you to speak to me of that person. Are you ready for bed? Let's run a race and see who'll get to the bed first."

The suggestion appealed to Diana. The two little white-clad figures flew down the long room, through the spare room door, and bounded on the bed at the same moment. And then—something—moved beneath them, there was a gasp and a cry—and somebody said in muffled accents, "Merciful goodness!"

Anne and Diana were never able to tell just how they got off that bed and out of the room. They only knew that after one frantic rush, they found themselves tiptoeing shiveringly upstairs.

"Oh, who was it—*what* was it?" whispered Anne, her teeth chattering with cold and fright.

"It was Aunt Josephine," said Diana, gasping with laughter. "Oh, Anne, it was Aunt Josephine, however she came to be there. Oh, and I know she will be furious. It's dreadful—it's really dreadful—but did you ever know[4] anything so funny, Anne?"

"Who is your aunt Josephine?"

"She's Father's aunt and she lives in Charlottetown. She's awfully old—seventy anyhow—and I don't believe she was *ever* a little girl. We were expecting her out for a visit, but not so soon. She's awfully prim and proper, and she'll scold dreadfully about this, I know. Well, we'll have to sleep with Minnie May—and you can't think[5] how she kicks."

Miss Josephine Barry did not appear at the early breakfast the next morning. Mrs. Barry smiled kindly at the two little girls.

"Did you have a good time last night? I tried to stay awake until you came home, for I wanted to tell you Aunt Josephine had come and that you would have to go upstairs after all, but I was so tired, I fell asleep. I hope you didn't disturb your aunt, Diana."

Diana preserved a discreet silence, but she and Anne exchanged furtive smiles of guilty amusement across the table. Anne hurried home after breakfast and so remained in blissful ignorance of the disturbance that presently resulted in the Barry household until the late afternoon, when she went down to Mrs. Lynde's on an errand for Marilla.

"So you and Diana nearly frightened poor old Miss Barry to death last night?" said Mrs. Lynde severely but with a twinkle in her eye. "Mrs. Barry was here a few minutes ago on her way to Carmody. She's feeling real worried over it. Old Miss Barry was in a terrible temper when she got up this morning—and Josephine Barry's temper is no joke, I can tell you that. She wouldn't speak to Diana at all."

---

[4] See.

[5] Imagine.

"It wasn't Diana's fault," said Anne contritely. "It was mine. I suggested racing to see who would get into bed first."

"I knew it!" said Mrs. Lynde with the exultation of a correct guesser. "I knew that idea came out of your head. Well, it's made a nice lot of trouble, that's what. Old Miss Barry came out to stay for a month, but she declares she won't stay another day and is going right back to town tomorrow, Sunday and all as it is. She'd have gone today if they could have taken her. She had promised to pay for a quarter's music lessons for Diana, but now she is determined to do nothing at all for such a tomboy. Oh, I guess they had a lively time of it there this morning. The Barrys must feel cut up. Old Miss Barry is rich and they'd like to keep on the good side of her. Of course, Mrs. Barry didn't say just that to me, but I'm a pretty good judge of human nature, that's what."

"I'm such an unlucky girl," mourned Anne. "I'm always getting into scrapes myself and getting my best friends—people I'd shed my heart's blood for—into them, too. Can you tell me why it is so, Mrs. Lynde?"

"It's because you're too heedless and impulsive, child, that's what. You never stop to think—whatever comes into your head to say or do, you say or do it without a moment's reflection."

"Oh, but that's the best of it," protested Anne. "Something just flashes into your mind, so exciting, and you must out with it. If you stop to think it over, you spoil it all. Haven't you never[6] felt that yourself, Mrs. Lynde?"

No, Mrs. Lynde had not. She shook her head sagely.

"You must learn to think a little, Anne, that's what. The proverb you need to go by is 'Look before you leap'—especially into spare room beds."

Mrs. Lynde laughed comfortably over her mild joke, but Anne remained pensive. She saw nothing to laugh at in the situation, which to her eyes appeared very serious. When she left Mrs. Lynde's, she took her way across the crusted fields to Orchard Slope. Diana met her at the kitchen door.

"Your aunt Josephine was very cross about it, wasn't she?" whispered Anne.

"Yes," answered Diana, stifling a giggle with an apprehensive glance over her shoulder at the closed sitting-room door. "She was fairly dancing with rage, Anne. Oh, how she scolded! She said I was the worst-behaved girl she ever saw and that my parents ought to be ashamed of the way they had brought me up. She says she won't stay, and I'm sure I don't care. But Father and Mother do."

---

[6] Ever.

"Why didn't you tell them it was my fault?" demanded Anne.

"It's likely I'd do such a thing, isn't it?" said Diana with just scorn. "I'm no telltale, Anne Shirley, and anyhow, I was just as much to blame as you."

"Well, I'm going in to tell her myself," said Anne resolutely.

Diana stared.

"Anne Shirley, you'd never! Why—she'll eat you alive!"

"Don't frighten me any more than I am frightened," implored Anne. "I'd rather walk up to a cannon's mouth. But I've got to do it, Diana. It was my fault and I've got to confess. I've had practice in confessing, fortunately."

"Well, she's in the room," said Diana. "You can go in if you want to. I wouldn't dare. And I don't believe you'll do a bit of good."

With this encouragement, Anne bearded the lion in its den—that is to say, walked resolutely up to the sitting-room door and knocked faintly. A sharp "Come in" followed.

Miss Josephine Barry, thin, prim, and rigid, was knitting fiercely by the fire, her wrath quite unappeased and her eyes snapping through her gold-rimmed glasses. She wheeled around in her chair, expecting to see Diana, and beheld a white-faced girl whose great eyes were brimmed up with a mixture of desperate courage and shrinking terror.

"Who are you?" demanded Miss Josephine Barry without ceremony.

"I'm Anne of Green Gables," said the small visitor tremulously, clasping her hands with her characteristic gesture, "and I've come to confess, if you please."

"Confess what?"

"That it was all my fault about jumping into bed on you last night. I suggested it. Diana would never have thought of such a thing, I am sure. Diana is a very ladylike girl, Miss Barry. So you must see how unjust it is to blame her."

"Oh, I must, hey? I rather think Diana did her share of the jumping at least. Such carryings-on in a respectable house!"

"But we were only in fun," persisted Anne. "I think you ought to forgive us, Miss Barry, now that we've apologized. And anyhow, please forgive Diana and let her have her music lessons. Diana's heart is set on her music lessons, Miss Barry, and I know too well what it is to set your heart on a thing and not get it. If you must be cross with anyone, be cross with me. I've been so used in my early days to having people cross at me that I can endure it much better than Diana can."

Much of the snap had gone out of the old lady's eyes by this time and was replaced by a twinkle of amused interest. But she still said severely:

"I don't think it is any excuse for you that you were only in fun. Little girls never indulged in that kind of fun when I was young. You don't know what it is to be awakened out of a sound sleep, after a long and arduous journey, by two great girls coming bounce down on you."

"I don't *know,* but I can *imagine,*" said Anne eagerly. "I'm sure it must have been very disturbing. But then, there is our side of it, too. Have you any imagination, Miss Barry? If you have, just put yourself in our place. We didn't know there was anybody in that bed, and you nearly scared us to death. It was simply awful the way we felt. And then we couldn't sleep in the spare room after being promised. I suppose you are used to sleeping in spare rooms. But just imagine what you would feel like if you were a little orphan girl who had never had such an honour."

All the snap had gone by this time. Miss Barry actually laughed—a sound that caused Diana, waiting in speechless anxiety in the kitchen outside, to give a great gasp of relief.

"I'm afraid my imagination is a little rusty—it's so long since I used it," she said. "I dare say your claim to sympathy is just as strong as mine. It all depends on the way we look at it. Sit down here and tell me about yourself."

"I am very sorry I can't," said Anne firmly. "I would like to, because you seem like an interesting lady, and you might even be a kindred spirit, although you don't look very much like it. But it is my duty to go home to Miss Marilla Cuthbert. Miss Marilla Cuthbert is a very kind lady who has taken me to bring up properly. She is doing her best, but it is very discouraging work. You must not blame her because I jumped on the bed. But before I go, I do wish you would tell me if you will forgive Diana and stay just as long as you meant to in Avonlea."

"I think perhaps I will if you will come over and talk to me occasionally," said Miss Barry.

That evening Miss Barry gave Diana a silver bangle bracelet and told the senior members of the household that she had unpacked her valise.

"I've made up my mind to stay simply for the sake of getting better acquainted with that Anne-girl," she said frankly. "She amuses me, and at my time of life, an amusing person is a rarity."

Marilla's only comment when she heard the story was, "I told you so." This was for Matthew's benefit.

Miss Barry stayed her month out and over. She was a more agreeable guest than usual, for Anne kept her in good humour. They became firm friends.

When Miss Barry went away, she said, "Remember, you Anne-girl, when you come to town, you're to visit me and I'll put you in my very sparest spare room bed to sleep."

"Miss Barry was a kindred spirit, after all," Anne confided to Marilla. "You wouldn't think so to look at her, but she is. You don't find it right out at first, as in Matthew's case, but after a while you come to see it. Kindred spirits are not so scarce as I used to think. It's splendid to find out there are so many of them in the world."

Chapter 20

A GOOD IMAGINATION GONE WRONG

Spring had come once more to Green Gables—the beautiful, capricious, reluctant Canadian spring, lingering along through April and May in a succession of sweet, fresh, chilly days, with pink sunsets and miracles of resurrection and growth. The maples in Lover's Lane were red-budded, and little curly ferns pushed up around the Dryad's Bubble. Away up in the barrens, behind Mr. Silas Sloane's place, the mayflowers blossomed out, pink and white stars of sweetness under their brown leaves. All the school girls and boys had one golden afternoon gathering them, coming home in the clear, echoing twilight with arms and baskets full of flowery spoil.

"I'm so sorry for people who live in lands where there are no mayflowers," said Anne. "Diana says perhaps they have something better, but there couldn't be anything better than mayflowers, could there, Marilla? And Diana says if they don't know what they are like, they don't miss them. But I think that is the saddest thing of all. I think it would be *tragic*, Marilla, not to know what mayflowers are like and *not* to miss them. Do you know what I think mayflowers are, Marilla? I think they must be the souls of the flowers that died last summer and this is their heaven. But we had a splendid time today, Marilla. We had our lunch down in a big mossy hollow by an old well—such a *romantic* spot. Charlie Sloane dared Arty Gillis to jump over it, and Arty did because he wouldn't take a dare. Nobody would in school. It's very *fashionable* to dare. Mr. Phillips gave all the mayflowers he found to Prissy Andrews, and I heard him say 'Sweets to the sweet.' He got that out of a book, I know; but it shows he has some imagination. I was offered some mayflowers too, but I rejected them with scorn. I can't tell you the person's name because I have vowed never to let it cross my lips. We made wreaths of the mayflowers and put them on our hats; and when the time came to go home, we marched in procession down the road, two by two, with our bouquets and wreaths, singing 'My Home on the Hill.' Oh, it was so thrilling, Marilla. All Mr. Silas Sloane's folks rushed out to see us, and everybody we met on the road stopped and stared after us. We made a real sensation."

"Not much wonder! Such silly doings!" was Marilla's response.

After the mayflowers came the violets, and Violet Vale was empurpled with them. Anne walked through it on her way to school with reverent steps and worshipping eyes, as if she trod on holy ground.

"Somehow," she told Diana, "when I'm going through here, I don't really care whether Gil—whether anybody gets ahead of me in class or not. But when I'm up in school, it's all different and I care as much as ever. There's such a lot of different Annes in me. I sometimes think that is why I'm such a troublesome person. If I was just the one Anne, it would be ever so much more comfortable, but then it wouldn't be half so interesting."

One June evening, when the orchards were pink-blossomed again, when the frogs were singing silvery sweet in the marshes about the head of the Lake of Shining Waters, and the air was full of the savor of clover fields and balsamic fir woods, Anne was sitting by her gable window. She had been studying her lessons, but it had grown too dark to see the book, so she had fallen into wide-eyed reverie, looking out past the boughs of the Snow Queen, once more bestarred with its tufts of blossom.

In all essential respects, the little gable chamber was unchanged. The walls were as white, the pincushion as hard, the chairs as stiffly and yellowly upright as ever. Yet the whole character of the room was altered. It was full of a new vital, pulsing personality that seemed to pervade it and to be quite independent of schoolgirl books and dresses and ribbons, and even of the cracked blue jug full of apple blossoms on the table. It was as if all the dreams, sleeping and waking, of its vivid occupant had taken a visible although immaterial form and had tapestried the bare room with splendid filmy tissues of rainbow and moonshine. Presently, Marilla came briskly in with some of Anne's freshly ironed school aprons. She hung them over a chair and sat down with a short sigh. She had had one of her headaches that afternoon, and although the pain had gone, she felt weak and "tuckered out," as she expressed it. Anne looked at her with eyes limpid with sympathy.

"I do truly wish I could have had the headache in your place, Marilla. I would have endured it joyfully for your sake."

"I guess you did your part in attending to the work and letting me rest," said Marilla. "You seem to have got on fairly well and made fewer mistakes than usual. Of course it wasn't exactly necessary to starch Matthew's handkerchiefs! And most people when they put a pie in the oven to warm up for dinner, take it out and eat it when it gets hot instead of leaving it to be burned to a crisp. But that doesn't seem to be your way, evidently."

Headaches always left Marilla somewhat sarcastic.

"Oh, I'm so sorry," said Anne penitently. "I never thought about that pie from the moment I put it in the oven till now, although I felt *instinctively* that there was something missing on the dinner table. I was firmly resolved, when you left me in charge this morning, not to imagine anything but keep my thoughts on facts. I did pretty well until I put the pie in, and then an irresistible temptation came to me to imagine I was an enchanted princess shut up in a lonely tower with a handsome knight riding to my rescue on a coal black steed. So that is how I came to forget the pie. I didn't know I starched the handkerchiefs. All the time I was ironing, I was trying to think of a name for a new island Diana and I have discovered up the brook. It's the most ravishing spot, Marilla. There are two maple trees on it and the brook flows right around it. At last it struck me that it would be splendid to call it Victoria Island because we found it on the Queen's birthday. Both Diana and I are very loyal. But I'm very sorry about the pie and the handkerchiefs. I wanted to be extra good today because it's an anniversary. Do you remember what happened this day last year, Marilla?"

"No, I can't think of anything special."

"Oh, Marilla, it was the day I came to Green Gables! I shall never forget it. It was the turning point in my life. Of course it wouldn't seem so important to you. I've been here for a year, and I've been so happy. Of course I've had my troubles, but one can live down troubles. Are you sorry you kept me, Marilla?"

"No, I can't say I'm sorry," said Marilla, who sometimes wondered how she could have lived before Anne came to Green Gables, "no, not exactly sorry. If you've finished your lessons, Anne, I want you to run over and ask Mrs. Barry if she'll lend me Diana's apron pattern."

"Oh—it's—it's too dark," cried Anne.

"Too dark? Why, it's only twilight. And goodness knows you've gone over often enough after dark."

"I'll go over early in the morning," said Anne eagerly. "I'll get up at sunrise and go over, Marilla."

"What has got into your head now, Anne Shirley? I want that pattern to cut out your new apron this evening. Go at once and be smart, too."

"I'll have to go around by the road, then," said Anne, taking up her hat reluctantly.

"Go by the road and waste half an hour! I'd like to catch you!"

"I can't go through the Haunted Wood, Marilla," cried Anne desperately.

Marilla stared. "The Haunted Wood! Are you crazy? What under the canopy is the Haunted Wood?"

"The spruce wood over the brook," said Anne in a whisper.

"Fiddlesticks! There is no such thing as a haunted wood anywhere. Who has been telling you such stuff?"

"Nobody," confessed Anne. "Diana and I just imagined the wood was haunted. All the places around here are so—so—*commonplace*. We just got this up for our own amusement. We began it in April. A haunted wood is so very romantic, Marilla. We chose the spruce grove because it's so gloomy. Oh, we have imagined the most harrowing things. There's a white lady who walks along the brook just about this time of the night and wrings her hands and utters wailing cries. She appears when there is to be a death in the family. And the ghost of a little murdered child haunts the corner up by Idlewild; it creeps up behind you and lays its cold fingers on your hand—so. Oh, Marilla, it gives me a shudder to think of it! And there's a headless man stalks up and down the path, and skeletons glower at you between the boughs. Oh, Marilla, I wouldn't go through the Haunted Wood after dark now for anything. I'd be sure that white things would reach out from behind the trees and grab me."

"Did ever anyone hear the like!" ejaculated Marilla, who had listened in dumb amazement. "Anne Shirley, do you mean to tell me you believe all that wicked nonsense of your own imagination?"

"Not believe *exactly*," faltered Anne. "At least, I don't believe it in the daylight. But after dark, Marilla, it's different. That is when ghosts walk."

"There are no such things as ghosts, Anne."

"Oh, but there are, Marilla," cried Anne eagerly. "I know people who have seen them. And they are respectable people. Charlie Sloane says that his grandmother saw his grandfather driving home the cows one night after he'd been buried for a year. You know Charlie Sloane's grandmother wouldn't tell a story for anything. She's a very religious woman. And Mrs. Thomas's father was pursued home one night by a lamb of fire with its head cut off hanging by a strip of skin. He said he knew it was the spirit of his brother and that it was a warning he would die within nine days. He didn't, but he died two years after, so you see it was really true. And Ruby Gillis says—"

"Anne Shirley," interrupted Marilla firmly, "I never want to hear you talking in this fashion again. I've had my doubts about that imagination of yours right along, and if this is going to be the outcome of it, I won't countenance any such things. You'll go right over to the Barrys', and you'll go through that spruce grove, just for a lesson and a warning to you. And never let me hear a word out of your head about haunted woods again."

Anne might plead and cry as she liked—and did, for her terror was very real. Her imagination had run away with her and she held the spruce grove in mortal dread after nightfall. But Marilla was inexorable. She marched the shrinking ghost-seer down to the spring and ordered her to proceed straightway over the bridge and into the dusky retreats of wailing ladies and headless spectres beyond.

"Oh, Marilla, how can you be so cruel?" sobbed Anne. "What would you feel like if a white thing did snatch me up and carry me off?"

"I'll risk it," said Marilla unfeelingly. "You know I always mean what I say. I'll cure you of imagining ghosts into places. March, now."

Anne marched. That is, she stumbled over the bridge and went shuddering up the horrible dim path beyond. Anne never forgot that walk. Bitterly did she repent the license she had given to her imagination. The goblins of her fancy lurked in every shadow about her, reaching out their cold, fleshless hands to grasp the terrified small girl who had called them into being. A white strip of birch bark blowing up from the hollow over the brown floor of the grove made her heart stand still. The long-drawn wail of two old boughs rubbing against each other brought out the perspiration in beads on her forehead. The swoop of bats in the darkness over her was as the wings of unearthly creatures. When she reached Mr. William Bell's field, she fled across it as if pursued by an army of white things and arrived at the Barry kitchen door so out of breath that she could hardly gasp out her request for the apron pattern. Diana was away so that she had no excuse to linger. The dreadful return journey had to be faced. Anne went back over it with shut eyes, preferring to take the risk of dashing her brains out among the boughs to that of seeing a white thing. When she finally stumbled over the log bridge, she drew one long, shivering breath of relief.

"Well, so nothing caught you," said Marilla unsympathetically.

"Oh Mar—Marilla," chattered Anne, "I'll b-b-be con-t-tented with c-c-commonplace places after this."

Chapter 21

A New Departure in Flavourings

"Dear me, there is nothing but meetings and partings in this world, as Mrs. Lynde says," remarked Anne plaintively, putting her slate and books down on the kitchen table on the last day of June and wiping her red eyes with a very damp handkerchief. "Wasn't it fortunate, Marilla, that I took an extra handkerchief to school today? I had a presentiment that it would be needed."

"I never thought you were so fond of Mr. Phillips that you'd require two handkerchiefs to dry your tears just because he was going away," said Marilla.

"I don't think I was crying because I was really so very fond of him," reflected Anne. "I just cried because all the others did. It was Ruby Gillis started it. Ruby Gillis has always declared she hated Mr. Phillips, but just as soon as he got up to make his farewell speech she burst into tears. Then all the girls began to cry, one after the other. I tried to hold out, Marilla. I tried to remember the time Mr. Phillips made me sit with Gil—with a boy; and the time he spelled my name without an *e* on the blackboard; and how he said I was the worst dunce he ever saw at geometry and laughed at my spelling; and all the times he had been so horrid and sarcastic; but somehow I couldn't, Marilla, and I just had to cry, too. Jane Andrews has been talking for a *month* about how glad she'd be when Mr. Phillips went away, and she declared she'd never shed a tear. Well, she was worse than any of us and had to borrow a handkerchief from her brother—of course the boys didn't cry—because she hadn't brought one of her own, not expecting to need it. Oh, Marilla, it was heartrending. Mr. Phillips made such a beautiful farewell speech beginning, 'The time has come for us to part.' It was very affecting. And he had tears in his eyes, too, Marilla. Oh, I felt dreadfully sorry and remorseful for all the times I'd talked in school and drawn pictures of him on my slate and

139

made fun of him and Prissy. I can tell you I wished I'd been a model pupil like Minnie Andrews. *She* hadn't anything on her conscience. The girls cried all the way home from school. Carrie Sloane kept saying every few minutes, 'The time has come for us to part,' and that would start us off again whenever we were in any danger of cheering up. I do feel dreadfully sad, Marilla. But one can't feel quite in the depths of despair with two months of vacation before them, can they, Marilla? And besides, we met the new minister and his wife coming from the station. For all I was feeling so bad about Mr. Phillips going away, I couldn't help taking a little interest in a new minister, could I? His wife is very pretty. Not exactly regally lovely, of course—it wouldn't do, I suppose, for a minister to have a regally lovely wife, because it might set a bad example. Mrs. Lynde says the minister's wife over at Newbridge sets a very bad example because she dresses so fashionably. Our new minister's wife was dressed in blue muslin with lovely puffed sleeves and a hat trimmed with roses. Jane Andrews said she thought puffed sleeves were too worldly for a minister's wife, but I didn't make any such uncharitable remark, Marilla, because I know what it is to long for puffed sleeves. Besides, she's only been a minister's wife for a little while, so one should make allowances, shouldn't they? They are going to board with Mrs. Lynde until the manse is ready."

If Marilla, in going down to Mrs. Lynde's that evening, was actuated by any motive save her avowed one of returning the quilting frames she had borrowed the preceding winter, it was an amiable weakness shared by most of the Avonlea people. Many a thing Mrs. Lynde had lent, sometimes never expecting to see it again, came home that night in charge of the borrowers thereof. A new minister, and moreover a minister with a wife, was a lawful object of curiosity in a quiet little country settlement where sensations were few and far between.

Old Mr. Bentley, the minister whom Anne had found lacking in imagination, had been pastor of Avonlea for eighteen years. He was a widower when he came, and a widower he remained, despite the fact that gossip regularly married him to this, that, or the other one, every year of his sojourn. In the preceding February, he had resigned his charge and departed amid the regrets of his people, most of whom had the affection born of long intercourse[1] for their good old minister in spite of his shortcomings as an orator. Since then the Avonlea church had enjoyed a variety of religious dissipation in listening to the many and various candidates and "supplies" who came Sunday after Sunday to preach on trial. These stood or fell by the judgment of the fathers and mothers in

---

[1] Association.

Israel; but a certain small, red-haired girl who sat meekly in the corner of the old Cuthbert pew also had her opinions about them and discussed the same in full with Matthew, Marilla always declining from principle to criticize ministers in any shape or form.

"I don't think Mr. Smith would have done, Matthew," was Anne's final summing up. "Mrs. Lynde says his delivery was so poor, but I think his worst fault was just like Mr. Bentley's—he had no imagination. And Mr. Terry had too much; he let it run away with him just as I did mine in the matter of the Haunted Wood. Besides, Mrs. Lynde says his theology wasn't sound. Mr. Gresham was a very good man and a very religious man, but he told too many funny stories and made the people laugh in church; he was undignified, and you must have some dignity about a minister, mustn't you, Matthew? I thought Mr. Marshall was decidedly attractive; but Mrs. Lynde says he isn't married, or even engaged, because she made special inquiries about him, and she says it would never do to have a young unmarried minister in Avonlea, because he might marry in the congregation and that would make trouble. Mrs. Lynde is a very farseeing woman, isn't she, Matthew? I'm very glad they've called Mr. Allan. I liked him because his sermon was interesting and he prayed as if he meant it and not just as if he did it because he was in the habit of it. Mrs. Lynde says he isn't perfect, but she says she supposes we couldn't expect a perfect minister for seven hundred and fifty dollars a year, and anyhow his theology is sound because she questioned him thoroughly on all the points of doctrine. And she knows his wife's people and they are most respectable and the women are all good housekeepers. Mrs. Lynde says that sound doctrine in the man and good housekeeping in the woman make an ideal combination for a minister's family."

The new minister and his wife were a young, pleasant-faced couple, still in their honeymoon and full of all good and beautiful enthusiasm for their chosen lifework. Avonlea opened its heart to them from the start. Old and young liked the frank, cheerful young man with his high ideals and the bright, gentle little lady who assumed the mistress-ship of the manse. With Mrs. Allan, Anne fell promptly and wholeheartedly in love. She had discovered another kindred spirit.

"Mrs. Allan is perfectly lovely," she announced one Sunday afternoon. "She's taken our class and she's a splendid teacher. She said right away she didn't think it was fair for the teacher to ask all the questions, and you know, Marilla, that is exactly what I've always thought. She said we could ask her any question we liked, and I asked ever so many. I'm good at asking questions, Marilla."

"I believe you," was Marilla's emphatic comment.

"Nobody else asked any except Ruby Gillis, and she asked if there was to be a Sunday school picnic this summer. I didn't think that was a very proper question to ask because it hadn't any connection with the lesson—the lesson was about Daniel in the lions' den—but Mrs. Allan just smiled and said she thought there would be. Mrs. Allan has a lovely smile; she has such *exquisite* dimples in her cheeks. I wish I had dimples in my cheeks, Marilla. I'm not half so skinny as I was when I came here, but I have no dimples yet. If I had, perhaps I could influence people for good. Mrs. Allan said we ought always to try to influence other people for good. She talked so nice about everything. I never knew before that religion was such a cheerful thing. I always thought it was kind of melancholy, but Mrs. Allan's isn't, and I'd like to be a Christian if I could be one like her. I wouldn't want to be one like Mr. Superintendent Bell."

"It's very naughty of you to speak so about Mr. Bell," said Marilla severely. "Mr. Bell is a real good man."

"Oh, of course he's good," agreed Anne. "But he doesn't seem to get any comfort out of it. If I could be good, I'd dance and sing all day because I was glad of it. I suppose Mrs. Allan is too old to dance and sing, and of course it wouldn't be dignified in a minister's wife. But I can just feel she's glad she's a Christian and that she'd be one even if she could get to heaven without it."

"I suppose we must have Mr. and Mrs. Allan up to tea some day soon," said Marilla reflectively. "They've been most everywhere but here. Let me see. Next Wednesday would be a good time to have them. But don't say a word to Matthew about it, for if he knew they were coming, he'd find some excuse to be away that day. He'd got so used to Mr. Bentley, he didn't mind him, but he's going to find it hard to get acquainted with a new minister, and a new minister's wife will frighten him to death."

"I'll be as secret as the dead," assured Anne. "But, oh, Marilla, will you let me make a cake for the occasion? I'd love to do something for Mrs. Allan, and you know I can make a pretty good cake by this time."

"You can make a layer cake," promised Marilla.

Monday and Tuesday, great preparations went on at Green Gables. Having the minister and his wife to tea was a serious and important undertaking, and Marilla was determined not to be eclipsed by any of the Avonlea housekeepers. Anne was wild with excitement and delight. She talked it all over with Diana Tuesday night in the twilight as they sat on the big red stones by the Dryad's Bubble and made rainbows in the water with little twigs dipped in fir balsam.

"Everything is ready, Diana, except my cake, which I'm to make in the morning, and the baking powder biscuits, which Marilla will make just before teatime. I assure you, Diana, that Marilla and I have had a busy two days of it. It's such a responsibility having a minister's family to tea. I never went through such an experience before. You should just see our pantry. It's a sight to behold. We're going to have jellied chicken and cold tongue. We're to have two kinds of jelly, red and yellow, and whipped cream and lemon pie, and cherry pie, and three kinds of cookies, and fruitcake, and Marilla's famous yellow plum preserves that she keeps especially for ministers, and pound cake and layer cake, and biscuits as aforesaid; and new bread and old both, in case the minister is dyspeptic and can't eat new. Mrs. Lynde says ministers mostly are dyspeptic, but I don't think Mr. Allan has been a minister long enough for it to have had a bad effect on him. I just grow cold when I think of my layer cake. Oh, Diana, what if it shouldn't be good! I dreamed last night that I was chased all around by a fearful goblin with a big layer cake for a head."

"It'll be good, all right," assured Diana, who was a very comfortable sort of friend. "I'm sure that piece of the one you made that we had for lunch in Idlewild two weeks ago was perfectly elegant."

"Yes, but cakes have such a terrible habit of turning out bad just when you especially want them to be good," sighed Anne, setting a particularly well-balsamed twig afloat. "However, I suppose I shall just have to trust to Providence and be careful to put in the flour. Oh, look, Diana, what a lovely rainbow! Do you suppose the dryad will come out after we go away and take it for a scarf?"

"You know there is no such thing as a dryad," said Diana. Diana's mother had found out about the Haunted Wood and had been decidedly angry over it. As a result, Diana had abstained from any further imitative flights of imagination and did not think it prudent to cultivate a spirit of belief even in harmless dryads.

"But it's so easy to imagine there is," said Anne. "Every night, before I go to bed, I look out of my window and wonder if the dryad is really sitting here, combing her locks with the spring for a mirror. Sometimes I look for her footprints in the dew in the morning. Oh, Diana, don't give up your faith in the dryad!"

Wednesday morning came. Anne got up at sunrise because she was too excited to sleep. She had caught a severe cold in the head by reason of her dabbling in the spring on the preceding evening; but nothing short of absolute pneumonia could have quenched her interest in culinary matters that morning. After breakfast she proceeded to make her cake.

When she finally shut the oven door upon it, she drew a long breath.

"I'm sure I haven't forgotten anything this time, Marilla. But do you think it will rise? Just suppose perhaps the baking powder isn't good? I used it out of the new can. And Mrs. Lynde says you can never be sure of getting good baking powder nowadays when everything is so adulterated. Mrs. Lynde says the government ought to take the matter up, but she says we'll never see the day when a Tory government will do it. Marilla, what if the cake doesn't rise?"

"We'll have plenty without it," was Marilla's unimpassioned way of looking at the subject.

The cake did rise, however, and came out of the oven as light and feathery as golden foam. Anne, flushed with delight, clapped it together with layers of ruby jelly and, in imagination, saw Mrs. Allan eating it and possibly asking for another piece!

"You'll be using the best tea set, of course, Marilla," she said. "Can I fix up the table with ferns and wild roses?"

"I think that's all nonsense," sniffed Marilla. "In my opinion, it's the eatables that matter and not flummery decorations."

"Mrs. Barry had *her* table decorated," said Anne, who was not entirely guiltless of the wisdom of the serpent, "and the minister paid her an elegant compliment. He said it was a feast for the eye as well as the palate."

"Well, do as you like," said Marilla, who was quite determined not to be surpassed by Mrs. Barry or anybody else. "Only mind you leave enough room for the dishes and the food."

Anne laid herself out to decorate in a manner and after a fashion that should leave Mrs. Barry's nowhere. Having abundance of roses and ferns and a very artistic taste of her own, she made that tea table such a thing of beauty that when the minister and his wife sat down to it, they exclaimed in chorus over its loveliness.

"It's Anne's doings," said Marilla, grimly just; and Anne felt that Mrs. Allan's approving smile was almost too much happiness for this world.

Matthew was there, having been inveigled into the party only goodness and Anne knew how. He had been in such a state of shyness and nervousness that Marilla had given him up in despair, but Anne took him in hand so successfully that he now sat at the table in his best clothes and white collar and talked to the minister not uninterestingly. He never said a word to Mrs. Allan, but that perhaps was not to be expected.

All went merry as a marriage bell until Anne's layer cake was passed. Mrs. Allan, having already been helped to a bewildering variety, declined it. But Marilla, seeing the disappointment on Anne's face, said smilingly:

"Oh, you must take a piece of this, Mrs. Allan. Anne made it on purpose for you."

"In that case, I must sample it," laughed Mrs. Allan, helping herself to a plump triangle, as did also the minister and Marilla.

Mrs. Allan took a mouthful of hers and a most peculiar expression crossed her face; not a word did she say, however, but steadily ate away at it. Marilla saw the expression and hastened to taste the cake.

"Anne Shirley!" she exclaimed. "What on earth did you put into that cake?"

"Nothing but what the recipe said, Marilla," cried Anne with a look of anguish. "Oh, isn't it all right?"

"All right! It's simply horrible. Mrs. Allan, don't try to eat it. Anne, taste it yourself. What flavouring did you use?"

"Vanilla," said Anne, her face scarlet with mortification after tasting the cake. "Only vanilla. Oh, Marilla, it must have been the baking powder. I had my suspicions of that bak—"

"Baking powder fiddlesticks! Go and bring me the bottle of vanilla you used."

Anne fled to the pantry and returned with a small bottle partially filled with a brown liquid and labeled yellowly "Best Vanilla."

Marilla took it, uncorked it, smelled it.

"Mercy on us, Anne, you've flavoured that cake with *anodyne liniment*. I broke the liniment bottle last week and poured what was left into an old empty vanilla bottle. I suppose it's partly my fault—I should have warned you—but for pity's sake, why couldn't you have smelled it?"

Anne dissolved into tears under this double disgrace.

"I couldn't—I had such a cold!" And with this, she fairly fled to the gable chamber, where she cast herself on the bed and wept as one who refuses to be comforted.

Presently, a light step sounded on the stairs and somebody entered the room.

"Oh, Marilla," sobbed Anne without looking up, "I'm disgraced forever. I shall never be able to live this down. It will get out—things always do get out in Avonlea. Diana will ask me how my cake turned out and I shall have to tell her the truth. I shall always be pointed at as the girl who flavoured a cake with anodyne liniment. Gil—the boys in school will never get over laughing at it. Oh, Marilla, if you have a spark of Christian pity, don't tell me that I must go down and wash the dishes after this. I'll wash them when the minister and his wife are gone, but I cannot ever look Mrs. Allan in the face again. Perhaps she'll think I tried to poison her. Mrs. Lynde says she knows an orphan girl who tried to poison her benefactor. But the liniment isn't poisonous. It's meant to be taken internally—although not in cakes. Won't you tell Mrs. Allan so, Marilla?"

"Suppose you jump up and tell her so yourself," said a merry voice.

Anne flew up, to find Mrs. Allan standing by her bed, surveying her with laughing eyes.

"My dear little girl, you mustn't cry like this," she said, genuinely disturbed by Anne's tragic face. "Why, it's all just a funny mistake that anybody might make."

"Oh, no, it takes me to make such a mistake," said Anne forlornly. "And I wanted to have that cake so nice for you, Mrs. Allan."

"Yes, I know, dear. And I assure you I appreciate your kindness and thoughtfulness just as much as if it had turned out all right. Now, you mustn't cry anymore, but come down with me and show me your flower garden. Miss Cuthbert tells me you have a little plot all your own. I want to see it, for I'm very much interested in flowers."

Anne permitted herself to be led down and comforted, reflecting that it was really providential that Mrs. Allan was a kindred spirit. Nothing more was said about the liniment cake, and when the guests went away, Anne found that she had enjoyed the evening more than could have been expected, considering that terrible incident. Nevertheless, she sighed deeply.

"Marilla, isn't it nice to think that tomorrow is a new day with no mistakes in it yet?"

"I'll warrant you'll make plenty in it," said Marilla. "I never saw your beat[2] for making mistakes, Anne."

"Yes, and well I know it," admitted Anne mournfully. "But have you ever noticed one encouraging thing about me, Marilla? I never make the same mistake twice."

"I don't know as that's much benefit when you're always making new ones."

"Oh, don't you see, Marilla? There *must* be a limit to the mistakes one person can make, and when I get to the end of them, then I'll be through with them. That's a very comforting thought."

"Well, you'd better go and give that cake to the pigs," said Marilla. "It isn't fit for any human to eat, not even Jerry Buote."

---

[2] Equal.

Chapter 22

ANNE IS INVITED OUT TO TEA

"And what are your eyes popping out of your head about now?" asked Marilla when Anne had just come in from a run to the post office. "Have you discovered another kindred spirit?"

Excitement hung around Anne like a garment, shone in her eyes, kindled in every feature. She had come dancing up the lane, like a wind-blown sprite, through the mellow sunshine and lazy shadows of the August evening.

"No, Marilla, but, oh, what do you think? I am invited to tea at the manse tomorrow afternoon! Mrs. Allan left the letter for me at the post office. Just look at it, Marilla. 'Miss Anne Shirley, Green Gables.' That is the first time I was ever called 'Miss.' Such a thrill as it gave me! I shall cherish it forever among my choicest treasures."

"Mrs. Allan told me she meant to have all the members of her Sunday school class to tea in turn," said Marilla, regarding the wonderful event very coolly. "You needn't get in such a fever over it. Do learn to take things calmly, child."

For Anne to take things calmly would have been to change her nature. All "spirit and fire and dew," as she was, the pleasures and pains of life came to her with trebled intensity. Marilla felt this and was vaguely troubled over it, realizing that the ups and downs of existence would probably bear hardly on this impulsive soul and not sufficiently understanding that the equally great capacity for delight might more than compensate. Therefore Marilla conceived it to be her duty to drill Anne into a tranquil uniformity of disposition as impossible and alien to her as to a dancing sunbeam in one of the brook shallows. She did not make much headway, as she sorrowfully admitted to herself. The downfall of some dear hope or plan plunged Anne into "deeps of affliction." The fulfilment thereof exalted her to dizzy realms of delight. Marilla had almost begun

147

to despair of ever fashioning this waif of the world into her model little
girl of demure manners and prim deportment. Neither would she have
believed that she really liked Anne much better as she was.

Anne went to bed that night speechless with misery because Matthew
had said the wind was around northeast and he feared it would be a rainy
day tomorrow. The rustle of the poplar leaves about the house worried
her, it sounded so like pattering raindrops, and the dull, faraway roar of
the gulf, to which she listened delightedly at other times, loving its
strange, sonorous, haunting rhythm, now seemed like a prophecy of
storm and disaster to a small maiden who particularly wanted a fine day.
Anne thought that the morning would never come.

But all things have an end, even nights before the day on which you
are invited to take tea at the manse. The morning, in spite of Matthew's
predictions, was fine, and Anne's spirits soared to their highest.

"Oh, Marilla, there is something in me today that makes me just love
everybody I see," she exclaimed as she washed the breakfast dishes. "You
don't know how good I feel! Wouldn't it be nice if it could last? I believe
I could be a model child if I were just invited out to tea every day. But,
oh, Marilla, it's a solemn occasion, too. I feel so anxious. What if I
shouldn't behave properly? You know I never had tea at a manse before,
and I'm not sure that I know all the rules of etiquette, although I've been
studying the rules given in the Etiquette Department of the *Family
Herald* ever since I came here. I'm so afraid I'll do something silly or
forget to do something I should do. Would it be good manners to take a
second helping of anything if you wanted to *very* much?"

"The trouble with you, Anne, is that you're thinking too much about
yourself. You should just think of Mrs. Allan and what would be nicest
and most agreeable for her," said Marilla, hitting for once in her life on
a very sound and pithy piece of advice. Anne instantly realized this.

"You are right, Marilla. I'll try not to think about myself at all."

Anne evidently got through her visit without any serious breach of
"etiquette," for she came home through the twilight, under a great, high-
sprung sky gloried over with trails of saffron and rosy clouds, in a beati-
fied state of mind and told Marilla all about it happily, sitting on the big
red sandstone slab at the kitchen door with her tired curly head in
Marilla's gingham lap.

A cool wind was blowing down over the long harvest fields from the
rims of firry western hills and whistling through the poplars. One clear
star hung above the orchard, and the fireflies were flitting over in Lover's
Lane, in and out among the ferns and rustling boughs. Anne watched

them as she talked and somehow felt that wind and stars and fireflies were all tangled up together into something unutterably sweet and enchanting.

"Oh, Marilla, I've had a most *fascinating* time. I feel that I have not lived in vain and I shall always feel like that even if I should never be invited to tea at a manse again. When I got there, Mrs. Allan met me at the door. She was dressed in the sweetest dress of pale pink organdy, with dozens of frills and elbow sleeves, and she looked just like a seraph. I really think I'd like to be a minister's wife when I grow up, Marilla. A minister mightn't mind my red hair because he wouldn't be thinking of such worldly things. But then of course one would have to be naturally good and I'll never be that, so I suppose there's no use in thinking about it. Some people are naturally good, you know, and others are not. I'm one of the others. Mrs. Lynde says I'm full of original sin. No matter how hard I try to be good, I can never make such a success of it as those who are naturally good. It's a good deal like geometry, I expect. But don't you think the trying so hard ought to count for something? Mrs. Allan is one of the naturally good people. I love her passionately. You know there are some people, like Matthew and Mrs. Allan, that you can love right off without any trouble. And there are others, like Mrs. Lynde, that you have to try very hard to love. You know you *ought* to love them because they know so much and are such active workers in the church, but you have to keep reminding yourself of it all the time or else you forget. There was another little girl at the manse to tea, from the White Sands Sunday school. Her name was Lauretta Bradley, and she was a very nice little girl. Not exactly a kindred spirit, you know, but still very nice. We had an elegant tea, and I think I kept all the rules of etiquette pretty well. After tea Mrs. Allan played and sang, and she got Lauretta and me to sing, too. Mrs. Allan says I have a good voice and she says I must sing in the Sunday school choir after this. You can't think how I was thrilled at the mere thought. I've longed so to sing in the Sunday school choir, as Diana does, but I feared it was an honour I could never aspire to. Lauretta had to go home early because there is a big concert in the White Sands Hotel tonight and her sister is to recite at it. Lauretta says that the Americans at the hotel give a concert every fortnight in aid of the Charlottetown hospital, and they ask lots of the White Sands people to recite. Lauretta said she expected to be asked herself some day. I just gazed at her in awe. After she had gone, Mrs. Allan and I had a heart-to-heart talk. I told her everything—about Mrs. Thomas and the twins and Katie Maurice and Violetta and coming to Green Gables and my troubles over geometry.

And would you believe it, Marilla? Mrs. Allan told me she was a dunce at geometry, too. You don't know how that encouraged me. Mrs. Lynde came to the manse just before I left, and what do you think, Marilla? The trustees have hired a new teacher and it's a lady. Her name is Miss Muriel Stacy. Isn't that a romantic name? Mrs. Lynde says they've never had a female teacher in Avonlea before and she thinks it is a dangerous innovation. But I think it will be splendid to have a lady teacher, and I really don't see how I'm going to live through the two weeks before school begins, I'm so impatient to see her."

Chapter 23

ANNE COMES TO GRIEF IN AN AFFAIR OF HONOUR

Anne had to live through more than two weeks, as it happened. Almost a month having elapsed since the liniment cake episode, it was high time for her to get into fresh trouble of some sort; little mistakes, such as absentmindedly emptying a pan of skim milk into a basket of yarn balls in the pantry instead of into the pigs' bucket, and walking clean over the edge of the log bridge into the brook while wrapped in imaginative reverie, not really being worth counting.

A week after the tea at the manse, Diana Barry gave a party.

"Small and select," Anne assured Marilla. "Just the girls in our class."

They had a very good time and nothing untoward happened until after tea, when they found themselves in the Barry garden, a little tired of all their games and ripe for any enticing form of mischief that might present itself. This presently took the form of "daring."

Daring was the fashionable amusement among the Avonlea small fry just then. It had begun among the boys, but soon spread to the girls, and all the silly things that were done in Avonlea that summer because the doers thereof were "dared" to do them would fill a book by themselves.

First of all, Carrie Sloane dared Ruby Gillis to climb to a certain point in the huge old willow tree before the front door; which Ruby Gillis, albeit in mortal dread of the fat green caterpillars with which said tree was infested and with the fear of her mother before her eyes if she should tear her new muslin dress, nimbly did, to the discomfiture of the aforesaid Carrie Sloane.

Then Josie Pye dared Jane Andrews to hop on her left leg around the garden without stopping once or putting her right foot to the ground; which Jane Andrews gamely tried to do, but gave out at the third corner and had to confess herself defeated.

151

Josie's triumph being rather more pronounced than good taste permitted, Anne Shirley dared her to walk along the top of the board fence that bounded the garden to the east. Now, to "walk" board fences requires more skill and steadiness of head and heel than one might suppose who has never tried it. But Josie Pye, if deficient in some qualities that make for popularity, had at least a natural and inborn gift, duly cultivated, for walking board fences. Josie walked the Barry fence with an airy unconcern that seemed to imply that a little thing like that wasn't worth a "dare." Reluctant admiration greeted her exploit, for most of the other girls could appreciate it, having suffered many things themselves in their efforts to walk fences. Josie descended from her perch, flushed with victory, and darted a defiant glance at Anne.

Anne tossed her red braids.

"I don't think it's such a very wonderful thing to walk a little low board fence," she said. "I knew a girl in Marysville who could walk the ridge-pole of a roof."

"I don't believe it," said Josie flatly. "I don't believe anybody could walk a ridgepole. *You* couldn't, anyhow."

"Couldn't I?" cried Anne rashly.

"Then I dare you to do it," said Josie defiantly. "I dare you to climb up there and walk the ridgepole of Mr. Barry's kitchen roof."

Anne turned pale, but there was clearly only one thing to be done. She walked toward the house, where a ladder was leaning against the kitchen roof. All the fifth-class girls said, "Oh!" partly in excitement, partly in dismay.

"Don't you do it, Anne," entreated Diana. "You'll fall off and be killed. Never mind Josie Pye. It isn't fair to dare anybody to do anything so dangerous."

"I must do it. My honour is at stake," said Anne solemnly. "I shall walk that ridgepole, Diana, or perish in the attempt. If I am killed, you are to have my pearl bead ring."

Anne climbed the ladder amid breathless silence, gained the ridgepole, balanced herself uprightly on that precarious footing, and started to walk along it, dizzily conscious that she was uncomfortably high up in the world and that walking ridgepoles was not a thing in which your imagination helped you out much. Nevertheless, she managed to take several steps before the catastrophe came. Then she swayed, lost her balance, stumbled, staggered, and fell, sliding down over the sunbaked roof and crashing off it through the tangle of Virginia creeper beneath—all before the dismayed circle below could give a simultaneous, terrified shriek.

Anne balanced herself uprightly on that precarious footing.

If Anne had tumbled off the roof on the side up which she ascended, Diana would probably have fallen heir to the pearl bead ring then and there. Fortunately, she fell on the other side, where the roof extended down over the porch so nearly to the ground that a fall therefrom was a much less serious thing. Nevertheless, when Diana and the other girls had rushed frantically around the house—except Ruby Gillis, who remained as if rooted to the ground and went into hysterics—they found Anne lying all white and limp among the wreck and ruin of the Virginia creeper.

"Anne, are you killed?" shrieked Diana, throwing herself on her knees beside her friend. "Oh, Anne, dear Anne, speak just one word to me and tell me if you're killed."

To the immense relief of all the girls, and especially of Josie Pye, who, in spite of lack of imagination, had been seized with horrible visions of a future branded as the girl who was the cause of Anne Shirley's early and tragic death, Anne sat dizzily up and answered uncertainly:

"No, Diana, I am not killed, but I think I am rendered unconscious."

"Where?" sobbed Carrie Sloane. "Oh, where, Anne?"

Before Anne could answer, Mrs. Barry appeared on the scene. At sight of her, Anne tried to scramble to her feet but sank back again with a sharp little cry of pain.

"What's the matter? Where have you hurt yourself?" demanded Mrs. Barry.

"My ankle," gasped Anne. "Oh, Diana, please find your father and ask him to take me home. I know I can never walk there. And I'm sure I couldn't hop so far on one foot when Jane couldn't even hop around the garden."

Marilla was out in the orchard picking a panful of summer apples when she saw Mr. Barry coming over the log bridge and up the slope, with Mrs. Barry beside him and a whole procession of little girls trailing after him. In his arms he carried Anne, whose head lay limply against his shoulder.

At that moment, Marilla had a revelation. In the sudden stab of fear that pierced to her very heart, she realized what Anne had come to mean to her. She would have admitted that she liked Anne—nay, that she was very fond of Anne. But now she knew as she hurried wildly down the slope that Anne was dearer to her than anything on earth.

"Mr. Barry, what has happened to her?" she gasped, more white and shaken than the self-contained, sensible Marilla had been for many years.

Anne herself answered, lifting her head.

"Don't be very frightened, Marilla. I was walking the ridgepole and I fell off. I expect I have sprained my ankle. But, Marilla, I might have broken my neck. Let us look on the bright side of things."

"I might have known you'd go and do something of the sort when I let you go to that party," said Marilla, sharp and shrewish in her very relief. "Bring her in here, Mr. Barry, and lay her on the sofa. Mercy me, the child has gone and fainted!"

It was quite true. Overcome by the pain of her injury, Anne had one more of her wishes granted to her. She had fainted dead away.

Matthew, hastily summoned from the harvest field, was straightway dispatched for the doctor, who in due time came, to discover that the injury was more serious than they had supposed. Anne's ankle was broken.

That night, when Marilla went up to the east gable, where a white-faced girl was lying, a plaintive voice greeted her from the bed.

"Aren't you very sorry for me, Marilla?"

"It was your own fault," said Marilla, twitching down the blind and lighting a lamp.

"And that is just why you should be sorry for me," said Anne, "because the thought that it *is* all my own fault is what makes it so hard. If I could blame it on anybody, I would feel so much better. But what would you have done, Marilla, if you had been dared to walk a ridgepole?"

"I'd have stayed on good firm ground and let them dare away. Such absurdity!" said Marilla.

Anne sighed. "But you have such strength of mind, Marilla. I haven't. I just felt that I couldn't bear Josie Pye's scorn. She would have crowed over me all my life. And I think I have been punished so much that you needn't be very cross with me, Marilla. It's not a bit nice to faint, after all. And the doctor hurt me dreadfully when he was setting my ankle. I won't be able to go around for six or seven weeks and I'll miss the new lady teacher. She won't be new anymore by the time I'm able to go to school. And Gil—everybody will get ahead of me in class. Oh, I am an afflicted mortal. But I'll try to bear it all bravely if only you won't be cross with me, Marilla."

"There, there, I'm not cross," said Marilla. "You're an unlucky child, there's no doubt about that; but, as you say, you'll have the suffering of it. Here now, try and eat some supper."

"Isn't it fortunate I've got such an imagination?" said Anne. "It will help me through splendidly, I expect. What do people who haven't any imagination do when they break their bones, do you suppose, Marilla?"

Anne had good reason to bless her imagination many a time and oft during the tedious seven weeks that followed. But she was not solely dependent on it. She had many visitors, and not a day passed without one or more of the schoolgirls dropping in to bring her flowers and books and tell her all the happenings in the juvenile world of Avonlea.

"Everybody has been so good and kind, Marilla," sighed Anne happily on the day when she could first limp across the floor. "It isn't very pleasant to be laid up; but there *is* a bright side to it, Marilla. You find out how many friends you have. Why, even Superintendent Bell came to see me, and he's really a very fine man. Not a kindred spirit, of course, but still I like him and I'm awfully sorry I ever criticized his prayers. I believe now he really does mean them, only he has got into the habit of saying them as if he didn't. He could get over that if he'd take a little trouble. I gave him a good broad hint. I told him how hard I tried to make my own little private prayers interesting. He told me all about the time he broke his ankle when he was a boy. It does seem so strange to think of Superintendent Bell ever being a boy. Even my imagination has its limits, for I can't imagine *that*. When I try to imagine him as a boy, I see him with gray whiskers and spectacles, just as he looks in Sunday school, only small. Now, it's so easy to imagine Mrs. Allan as a little girl. Mrs. Allan has been to see me fourteen times. Isn't that something to be proud of, Marilla? When a minister's wife has so many claims on her time! She is such a cheerful person to have visit you, too. She never tells you it's your own fault and she hopes you'll be a better girl on account of it. Mrs. Lynde always told me that when she came to see me; and she said it in a kind of way that made me feel she might hope I'd be a better girl but didn't really believe I would. Even Josie Pye came to see me. I received her as politely as I could, because I think she was sorry she dared me to walk a ridgepole. If I had been killed, she would have to carry a dark burden of remorse all her life. Diana has been a faithful friend. She's been over every day to cheer my lonely pillow. But oh, I shall be so glad when I can go to school, for I've heard such exciting things about the new teacher. The girls all think she is perfectly sweet. Diana says she has the loveliest fair curly hair and such fascinating eyes. She dresses beautifully, and her sleeve puffs are bigger than anybody else's in Avonlea. Every other Friday afternoon she has recitations, and everybody has to say a piece or take part in a dialogue. Oh, it's just glorious to think of it. Josie Pye says she hates it, but that is just because Josie has so little imagination. Diana and Ruby Gillis and Jane Andrews are preparing a dialogue called 'A Morning Visit,' for next Friday. And the Friday afternoons they don't have recitations, Miss Stacy takes them all to the woods for a 'field' day and they study ferns and flowers and birds. And they have physical culture exercises every morning and evening. Mrs. Lynde says she never heard of such goings-on and it all comes of having a lady teacher. But I think it must be splendid, and I believe I shall find that Miss Stacy is a kindred spirit."

"There's one thing plain to be seen, Anne," said Marilla, "and that is that your fall off the Barry roof hasn't injured your tongue at all."

Chapter 24

MISS STACY AND HER PUPILS GET UP A CONCERT

It was October again when Anne was ready to go back to school—a glorious October, all red and gold, with mellow mornings when the valleys were filled with delicate mists as if the spirit of autumn had poured them in for the sun to drain—amethyst, pearl, silver, rose, and smoke blue. The dews were so heavy that the fields glistened like cloth of silver, and there were such heaps of rustling leaves in the hollows of many-stemmed woods to run crisply through. The Birch Path was a canopy of yellow, and the ferns were sere and brown all along it. There was a tang in the very air that inspired the hearts of small maidens tripping, unlike snails, swiftly and willingly to school; and it *was* jolly to be back again at the little brown desk beside Diana, with Ruby Gillis nodding across the aisle and Carrie Sloane sending up notes and Julia Bell passing a "chew" of gum down from the back seat. Anne drew a long breath of happiness as she sharpened her pencil and arranged her picture cards in her desk. Life was certainly very interesting.

In the new teacher, she found another true and helpful friend. Miss Stacy was a bright, sympathetic young woman with the happy gift of winning and holding the affections of her pupils and bringing out the best that was in them mentally and morally. Anne expanded like a flower under this wholesome influence and carried home to the admiring Matthew and the critical Marilla glowing accounts of school work and aims.

"I love Miss Stacy with my whole heart, Marilla. She is so ladylike, and she has such a sweet voice. When she pronounces my name, I feel *instinctively* that she's spelling it with an *e*. We had recitations this afternoon. I just wish you could have been there to hear me recite 'Mary, Queen of Scots.' I just put my whole soul into it. Ruby Gillis told me coming home that the way I said the line, 'Now for my father's arm, she said, my woman's heart farewell,' just made her blood run cold."

"Well now, you might recite it for me some of these days, out in the barn," suggested Matthew.

"Of course I will," said Anne meditatively, "but I won't be able to do it so well, I know. It won't be so exciting as it is when you have a whole schoolful before you hanging breathlessly on your words. I know I won't be able to make your blood run cold."

"Mrs. Lynde says it made *her* blood run cold to see the boys climbing to the very tops of those big trees on Bell's Hill after crows' nests last Friday," said Marilla. "I wonder at Miss Stacy for encouraging it."

"But we wanted a crow's nest for nature study," explained Anne. "That was on our field afternoon. Field afternoons are splendid, Marilla. And Miss Stacy explains everything so beautifully. We have to write compositions on our field afternoons, and I write the best ones."

"It's very vain of you to say so, then. You'd better let your teacher say it."

"But she *did* say it, Marilla. And indeed I'm not vain about it. How can I be, when I'm such a dunce at geometry? Although I'm really beginning to see through it a little, too. Miss Stacy makes it so clear. Still, I'll never be good at it, and I assure you it is a humbling reflection. But I love writing compositions. Mostly, Miss Stacy lets us choose our own subjects; but next week we are to write a composition on some remarkable person. It's hard to choose among so many remarkable people who have lived. Mustn't it be splendid to be remarkable and have compositions written about you after you're dead? Oh, I would dearly love to be remarkable. I think when I grow up, I'll be a trained nurse and go with the Red Crosses to the field of battle as a messenger of mercy. That is, if I don't go out as a foreign missionary. That would be very romantic, but one would have to be very good to be a missionary and that would be a stumbling block. We have physical culture exercises every day, too. They make you graceful and promote digestion."

"Promote fiddlesticks!" said Marilla, who honestly thought it was all nonsense.

But all the field afternoons and recitation Fridays and physical culture contortions paled before a project that Miss Stacy brought forward in November. This was that the scholars of Avonlea school should get up a concert and hold it in the hall on Christmas night for the laudable purpose of helping to pay for a schoolhouse flag. The pupils one and all taking graciously to this plan, the preparations for a programme were begun at once. And of all the excited performers-elect, none was so excited as Anne Shirley, who threw herself into the undertaking heart and soul, hampered as she was by Marilla's disapproval. Marilla thought it all rank foolishness.

"It's just filling your heads up with nonsense and taking time that ought to be put on your lessons," she grumbled. "I don't approve of children's getting up concerts and racing about to practices. It makes them vain and forward and fond of gadding."

"But think of the worthy object," pleaded Anne. "A flag will cultivate a spirit of patriotism, Marilla."

"Fudge! There's precious little patriotism in the thoughts of any of you. All you want is a good time."

"Well, when you can combine patriotism and fun, isn't it all right? Of course it's real nice to be getting up a concert. We're going to have six choruses, and Diana is to sing a solo. I'm in two dialogues—'The Society for the Suppression of Gossip' and 'The Fairy Queen.' The boys are going to have a dialogue, too. And I'm to have two recitations, Marilla. I just tremble when I think of it, but it's a nice thrilly kind of tremble. And we're to have a tableau at the last—'Faith, Hope, and Charity.' Diana and Ruby and I are to be in it, all draped in white with flowing hair. I'm to be Hope, with my hands clasped—so—and my eyes uplifted. I'm going to practice my recitations in the garret. Don't be alarmed if you hear me groaning. I have to groan heartrendingly in one of them, and it's really hard to get up a good artistic groan, Marilla. Josie Pye is sulky because she didn't get the part she wanted in the dialogue. She wanted to be the fairy queen. That would have been ridiculous, for who ever heard of a fairy queen as fat as Josie? Fairy queens must be slender. Jane Andrews is to be the queen, and I am to be one of her maids of honour. Josie says she thinks a red-haired fairy is just as ridiculous as a fat one, but I do not let myself mind what Josie says. I'm to have a wreath of white roses on my hair, and Ruby Gillis is going to lend me her slippers because I haven't any of my own. It's necessary for fairies to have slippers, you know. You couldn't imagine a fairy wearing boots, could you? Especially with copper toes? We are going to decorate the hall with creeping spruce and fir mottoes with pink tissue-paper roses in them. And we are all to march in two by two after the audience is seated, while Emma White plays a march on the organ. Oh, Marilla, I know you are not so enthusiastic about it as I am, but don't you hope your little Anne will distinguish herself?"

"All I hope is that you'll behave yourself. I'll be heartily glad when all this fuss is over and you'll be able to settle down. You are simply good for nothing just now with your head stuffed full of dialogues and groans and tableaus. As for your tongue, it's a marvel it's not clean worn out."

Anne sighed and betook herself to the backyard, over which a young new moon was shining through the leafless poplar boughs from an apple-green western sky, and where Matthew was splitting wood. Anne perched herself on a block and talked the concert over with him, sure of an appreciative and sympathetic listener in this instance at least.

"Well now, I reckon it's going to be a pretty good concert. And I expect you'll do your part fine," he said, smiling down into her eager, vivacious little face.

Anne smiled back at him. Those two were the best of friends, and Matthew thanked his stars many a time and oft that he had nothing to do with bringing her up. That was Marilla's exclusive duty; if it had been his, he would have been worried over frequent conflicts between inclination and said duty. As it was, he was free to "spoil Anne"—Marilla's phrasing—as much as he liked. But it was not such a bad arrangement after all; a little "appreciation" sometimes does quite as much good as all the conscientious "bringing up" in the world.

Chapter 25

MATTHEW INSISTS ON PUFFED SLEEVES

Matthew was having a bad ten minutes of it. He had come into the kitchen, in the twilight of a cold, gray December evening, and had sat down in the wood-box corner to take off his heavy boots, unconscious of the fact that Anne and a bevy of her schoolmates were having a practice of "The Fairy Queen" in the sitting room. Presently, they came trooping through the hall and out into the kitchen, laughing and chattering gaily. They did not see Matthew, who shrank bashfully back into the shadows beyond the wood box with a boot in one hand and a bootjack in the other, and he watched them shyly for the aforesaid ten minutes as they put on caps and jackets and talked about the dialogue and the concert. Anne stood among them, bright-eyed and animated as they; but Matthew suddenly became conscious that there was something about her different from her mates. And what worried Matthew was that the difference impressed him as being something that should not exist. Anne had a brighter face, and bigger, starrier eyes, and more delicate features than the others; even shy, unobservant Matthew had learned to take note of these things; but the difference that disturbed him did not consist in any of these respects. Then in what did it consist?

Matthew was haunted by this question long after the girls had gone, arm in arm, down the long, hard-frozen lane and Anne had betaken herself to her books. He could not refer it to Marilla, who, he felt, would be quite sure to sniff scornfully and remark that the only difference she saw between Anne and the other girls was that they sometimes kept their tongues quiet while Anne never did. This, Matthew felt, would be no great help.

He had recourse to his pipe that evening to help him study it out, much to Marilla's disgust. After two hours of smoking and hard reflection, Matthew arrived at a solution of his problem: Anne was not dressed like the other girls!

The more Matthew thought about the matter, the more he was convinced that Anne never had been dressed like the other girls—never since she had come to Green Gables. Marilla kept her clothed in plain, dark dresses, all made after the same unvarying pattern. If Matthew knew there was such a thing as fashion in dress, it is as much as he did;[1] but he was quite sure that Anne's sleeves did not look at all like the sleeves the other girls wore. He recalled the cluster of little girls he had seen around her that evening—all gay in waists of red and blue and pink and white—and he wondered why Marilla always kept her so plainly and soberly gowned.

Of course, it might be all right. Marilla knew best and Marilla was bringing her up. Probably, some wise, inscrutable motive was to be served thereby. But surely it would do no harm to let the child have one pretty dress—something like Diana Barry always wore. Matthew decided that he would give her one; that surely could not be objected to as an unwarranted putting in of his oar. Christmas was only a fortnight off. A nice new dress would be the very thing for a present. Matthew, with a sigh of satisfaction, put away his pipe and went to bed, while Marilla opened all the doors and aired the house.

The very next evening, Matthew betook himself to Carmody to buy the dress, determined to get the worst over and have done with it. It would be, he felt assured, no trifling ordeal. There were some things Matthew could buy and prove himself no mean bargainer, but he knew he would be at the mercy of shopkeepers when it came to buying a girl's dress.

After much cogitation, Matthew resolved to go to Samuel Lawson's store instead of William Blair's. To be sure, the Cuthberts always had gone to William Blair's; it was almost as much a matter of conscience with them as to attend the Presbyterian church and vote Conservative. But William Blair's two daughters frequently waited on customers there, and Matthew held them in absolute dread. He could contrive to deal with them when he knew exactly what he wanted and could point it out; but in such a matter as this, requiring explanation and consultation, Matthew felt that he must be sure of a man behind the counter. So he would go to Lawson's, where Samuel or his son would wait on him.

Alas! Matthew did not know that Samuel, in the recent expansion of his business, had set up a lady clerk also; she was a niece of his wife's and a very dashing young person indeed, with a huge, drooping pompadour, big, rolling brown eyes, and a most extensive and bewildering smile. She was dressed with exceeding smartness and wore several bangle bracelets

---

[1] That was as far as he went.

that glittered and rattled and tinkled with every movement of her hands. Matthew was covered with confusion at finding her there at all; and those bangles completely wrecked his wits at one fell swoop.

"What can I do for you this evening, Mr. Cuthbert?" Miss Lucilla Harris inquired briskly and ingratiatingly, tapping the counter with both hands.

"Have you any—any—any—well now, say any garden rakes?" stammered Matthew.

Miss Harris looked somewhat surprised, as well she might, to hear a man inquiring for garden rakes in the middle of December.

"I believe we have one or two left over," she said, "but they're upstairs in the lumber room. I'll go and see."

During her absence, Matthew collected his scattered senses for another effort.

When Miss Harris returned with the rake and cheerfully inquired: "Anything else tonight, Mr. Cuthbert?" Matthew took his courage in both hands and replied: "Well now, since you suggest it, I might as well—take—that is—look at—buy some—some hayseed."

Miss Harris had heard Matthew Cuthbert called odd. She now concluded that he was entirely crazy.

"We only keep hayseed in the spring," she explained loftily. "We've none on hand just now."

"Oh, certainly—certainly—just as you say," stammered unhappy Matthew, seizing the rake and making for the door. At the threshold, he recollected that he had not paid for it and he turned miserably back. While Miss Harris was counting out his change, he rallied his powers for a final desperate attempt.

"Well now—if it isn't too much trouble—I might as well—that is— I'd like to look at—at—some sugar."

"White or brown?" queried Miss Harris patiently.

"Oh—well now—brown," said Matthew feebly.

"There's a barrel of it over there," said Miss Harris, shaking her bangles at it. "It's the only kind we have."

"I'll—I'll take twenty pounds of it," said Matthew, with beads of perspiration standing on his forehead.

Matthew had driven halfway home before he was his own man again. It had been a gruesome experience, but it served him right, he thought, for committing the heresy of going to a strange store. When he reached home, he hid the rake in the tool house, but the sugar he carried in to Marilla.

"Brown sugar!" exclaimed Marilla. "Whatever possessed you to get so much? You know I never use it except for the hired man's porridge or black fruitcake. Jerry's gone, and I've made my cake long ago. It's not good sugar, either—it's coarse and dark—William Blair doesn't usually keep sugar like that."

"I—I thought it might come in handy sometime," said Matthew, making good his escape.

When Matthew came to think the matter over, he decided that a woman was required to cope with the situation. Marilla was out of the question. Matthew felt sure she would throw cold water on his project at once. There remained only Mrs. Lynde; for of no other woman in Avonlea would Matthew have dared to ask advice. To Mrs. Lynde he went accordingly, and that good lady promptly took the matter out of the harassed man's hands.

"Pick out a dress for you to give Anne? To be sure I will. I'm going to Carmody tomorrow and I'll attend to it. Have you something particular in mind? No? Well, I'll just go by my own judgment then. I believe a nice rich brown would just suit Anne, and William Blair has some new gloria in that's real pretty. Perhaps you'd like me to make it up for her, too, seeing that if Marilla was to make it, Anne would probably get wind of it before the time and spoil the surprise? Well, I'll do it. No, it isn't a mite of trouble. I like sewing. I'll make it to fit my niece, Jenny Gillis, for she and Anne are as alike as two peas as far as figure goes."

"Well now, I'm much obliged," said Matthew, "and—and—I dunno—but I'd like—I think they make the sleeves different nowadays to what they used to be. If it wouldn't be asking too much, I—I'd like them made in the new way."

"Puffs? Of course. You needn't worry a speck more about it, Matthew. I'll make it up in the very latest fashion," said Mrs. Lynde. To herself, she added when Matthew had gone: *It'll be a real satisfaction to see that poor child wearing something decent for once. The way Marilla dresses her is positively ridiculous, that's what, and I've ached to tell her so plainly a dozen times. I've held my tongue though, for I can see Marilla doesn't want advice and she thinks she knows more about bringing children up than I do, for all she's an old maid. But that's always the way. Folks that has brought up children know that there's no hard and fast method in the world that'll suit every child. But them as never have think it's all as plain and easy as Rule of Three—just set your three terms down so fashion, and the sum'll work out correct. But flesh and blood don't come under the head[2] of arithmetic, and*

---

[2] Heading.

that's where Marilla Cuthbert makes her mistake. I suppose she's trying to cultivate a spirit of humility in Anne by dressing her as she does; but it's more likely to cultivate envy and discontent. I'm sure the child must feel the difference between her clothes and the other girls'. But to think of Matthew taking notice of it! That man is waking up after being asleep for over sixty years.

Marilla knew all the following fortnight that Matthew had something on his mind, but what it was she could not guess, until Christmas Eve, when Mrs. Lynde brought up the new dress. Marilla behaved pretty well on the whole, although it is very likely she distrusted Mrs. Lynde's diplomatic explanation that she had made the dress because Matthew was afraid Anne would find out about it too soon if Marilla made it.

"So this is what Matthew has been looking so mysterious over and grinning about to himself for two weeks, is it?" she said a little stiffly but tolerantly. "I knew he was up to some foolishness. Well, I must say I don't think Anne needed any more dresses. I made her three good, warm, serviceable ones this fall, and anything more is sheer extravagance. There's enough material in those sleeves alone to make a waist, I declare there is. You'll just pamper Anne's vanity, Matthew, and she's as vain as a peacock now. Well, I hope she'll be satisfied at last, for I know she's been hankering after these silly sleeves ever since they came in, although she never said a word after the first. The puffs have been getting bigger and more ridiculous right along; they're as big as balloons now. Next year, anybody who wears them will have to go through a door sideways."

Christmas morning broke on a beautiful white world. It had been a very mild December and people had looked forward to[3] a green Christmas; but just enough snow fell softly in the night to transfigure Avonlea. Anne peeped out from her frosted gable window with delighted eyes. The firs in the Haunted Wood were all feathery and wonderful; the birches and wild cherry trees were outlined in pearl; the ploughed fields were stretches of snowy dimples; and there was a crisp tang in the air that was glorious. Anne ran downstairs singing until her voice reechoed through Green Gables.

"Merry Christmas, Marilla! Merry Christmas, Matthew! Isn't it a lovely Christmas? I'm so glad it's white. Any other kind of Christmas doesn't seem real, does it? I don't like green Christmases. They're *not* green— they're just nasty faded browns and grays. What makes people call them green? Why—why—Matthew, is that for me? Oh, Matthew!"

Matthew had sheepishly unfolded the dress from its paper swathings and held it out with a deprecatory glance at Marilla, who feigned to be

---

3 Anticipated.

contemptuously filling the teapot, but nevertheless watched the scene out of the corner of her eye with a rather interested air.

Anne took the dress and looked at it in reverent silence. Oh, how pretty it was—a lovely soft brown gloria with all the gloss of silk; a skirt with dainty frills and shirrings; a waist elaborately pin-tucked in the most fashionable way, with a little ruffle of filmy lace at the neck. But the sleeves—they were the crowning glory! Long elbow cuffs, and above them two beautiful puffs divided by rows of shirring and bows of brown silk ribbon.

"That's a Christmas present for you, Anne," said Matthew shyly. "Why—why—Anne, don't you like it? Well now—well now."

For Anne's eyes had suddenly filled with tears.

"*Like* it! Oh, Matthew!" Anne laid the dress over a chair and clasped her hands. "Matthew, it's perfectly exquisite. Oh, I can never thank you enough! Look at those sleeves! Oh, it seems to me this must be a happy dream."

"Well, well, let us have breakfast," interrupted Marilla. "I must say, Anne, I don't think you needed the dress; but since Matthew has got it for you, see that you take good care of it. There's a hair ribbon Mrs. Lynde left for you. It's brown, to match the dress. Come now, sit in."[4]

"I don't see how I'm going to eat breakfast," said Anne rapturously. "Breakfast seems so commonplace at such an exciting moment. I'd rather feast my eyes on that dress. I'm so glad that puffed sleeves are still fashionable. It did seem to me that I'd never get over it if they went out before I had a dress with them. I'd never have felt quite satisfied, you see. It was lovely of Mrs. Lynde to give me the ribbon, too. I feel that I ought to be a very good girl indeed. It's at times like this I'm sorry I'm not a model little girl, and I always resolve that I will be in future. But somehow it's hard to carry out your resolutions when irresistible temptations come. Still, I really will make an extra effort after this."

When the commonplace breakfast was over, Diana appeared, crossing the white log bridge in the hollow, a gay little figure in her crimson ulster. Anne flew down the slope to meet her.

"Merry Christmas, Diana! And oh, it's a wonderful Christmas. I've something splendid to show you. Matthew has given me the loveliest dress, with *such* sleeves. I couldn't even imagine any nicer."

"I've got something more for you," said Diana breathlessly. "Here—this box. Aunt Josephine sent us out a big box with ever so many things in it—and this is for you. I'd have brought it over last night, but it didn't

---

[4] Sit down.

come until after dark, and I never feel very comfortable coming through the Haunted Wood in the dark now."

Anne opened the box and peeped in. First a card with "For the Anne-girl and Merry Christmas" written on it; and then, a pair of the daintiest little kid slippers, with beaded toes and satin bows and glistening buckles.

"Oh," said Anne, "Diana, this is too much. I must be dreaming."

"*I* call it providential," said Diana. "You won't have to borrow Ruby's slippers now, and that's a blessing, for they're two sizes too big for you, and it would be awful to hear a fairy shuffling. Josie Pye would be delighted. Mind you, Rob Wright went home with Gertie Pye from the practice night before last. Did you ever hear anything equal to that?"

All the Avonlea scholars were in a fever of excitement that day, for the hall had to be decorated and a last grand rehearsal held.

The concert came off in the evening and was a pronounced success. The little hall was crowded; all the performers did excellently well, but Anne was the bright particular star of the occasion, as even envy, in the shape of Josie Pye, dared not deny.

"Oh, hasn't it been a brilliant evening?" sighed Anne when it was all over and she and Diana were walking home together under a dark, starry sky.

"Everything went off very well," said Diana practically. "I guess we must have made as much as ten dollars. Mind you, Mr. Allan is going to send an account of it to the Charlottetown papers."

"Oh, Diana, will we really see our names in print? It makes me thrill to think of it. Your solo was perfectly elegant, Diana. I felt prouder than you did when it was encored. I just said to myself, *It is my dear bosom friend who is so honoured.*"

"Well, your recitations just brought down the house, Anne. That sad one was simply splendid."

"Oh, I was so nervous, Diana. When Mr. Allan called out my name, I really cannot tell how I ever got up on that platform. I felt as if a million eyes were looking at me and through me, and for one dreadful moment, I was sure I couldn't begin at all. Then I thought of my lovely puffed sleeves and took courage. I knew that I must live up to those sleeves, Diana. So I started in, and my voice seemed to be coming from ever so far away. I just felt like a parrot. It's providential that I practiced those recitations so often up in the garret, or I'd never have been able to get through. Did I groan all right?"

"Yes, indeed, you groaned lovely," assured Diana.

"I saw old Mrs. Sloane wiping away tears when I sat down. It was splendid to think I had touched somebody's heart. It's so romantic to take part in a concert, isn't it? Oh, it's been a very memorable occasion indeed!"

"Wasn't the boys' dialogue fine?" said Diana. "Gilbert Blythe was just splendid. Anne, I do think it's awful mean the way you treat Gil. Wait till I tell you. When you ran off the platform after the fairy dialogue, one of your roses fell out of your hair. I saw Gil pick it up and put it in his breast pocket. There now. You're so romantic that I'm sure you ought to be pleased at that."

"It's nothing to me what that person does," said Anne loftily. "I simply never waste a thought on him, Diana."

That night Marilla and Matthew, who had been out to a concert for the first time in twenty years, sat for a while by the kitchen fire after Anne had gone to bed.

"Well now, I guess our Anne did as well as any of them," said Matthew proudly.

"Yes, she did," admitted Marilla. "She's a bright child, Matthew. And she looked real nice, too. I've been kind of opposed to this concert scheme, but I suppose there's no real harm in it after all. Anyhow, I was proud of Anne tonight, although I'm not going to tell her so."

"Well now, I was proud of her and I did tell her so 'fore she went upstairs," said Matthew. "We must see what we can do for her some of these days, Marilla. I guess she'll need something more than Avonlea school by and by."

"There's time enough to think of that," said Marilla. "She's only thirteen in March. Though tonight it struck me she was growing[5] quite a big girl. Mrs. Lynde made that dress a mite too long, and it makes Anne look so tall. She's quick to learn and I guess the best thing we can do for her will be to send her to Queen's after a spell. But nothing need be said about that for a year or two yet."

"Well now, it'll do no harm to be thinking it over off and on," said Matthew. "Things like that are all the better for lots of thinking over."

---

[5] Growing into.

Chapter 26

THE STORY CLUB
IS FORMED

Junior Avonlea found it hard to settle down to humdrum existence again. To Anne in particular things seemed fearfully flat, stale, and unprofitable after the goblet of excitement she had been sipping for weeks. Could she go back to the former quiet pleasures of those faraway days before the concert? At first, as she told Diana, she did not really think she could.

"I'm positively certain, Diana, that life can never be quite the same again as it was in those olden days," she said mournfully, as if referring to a period of at least fifty years back. "Perhaps after a while I'll get used to it, but I'm afraid concerts spoil people for everyday life. I suppose that is why Marilla disapproves of them. Marilla is such a sensible woman. It must be a great deal better to be sensible; but still, I don't believe I'd really want to be a sensible person, because they are so unromantic. Mrs. Lynde says there is no danger of my ever being one, but you can never tell. I just feel now that I may grow up to be sensible yet. But perhaps that is only because I'm tired. I simply couldn't sleep last night for ever so long. I just lay awake and imagined the concert over and over again. That's one splendid thing about such affairs—it's so lovely to look back at them."

Eventually, however, Avonlea school slipped back into its old groove and took up its old interests. To be sure, the concert left traces. Ruby Gillis and Emma White, who had quarreled over a point of precedence in their platform seats, no longer sat at the same desk and a promising friendship of three years was broken up. Josie Pye and Julia Bell did not "speak" for three months, because Josie Pye had told Bessie Wright that Julia Bell's bow when she got up to recite made her think of a chicken jerking its head, and Bessie told Julia. None of the Sloanes would have any dealings with the Bells, because the Bells had declared that the

170

Sloanes had too much to do in the programme, and the Sloanes had retorted that the Bells were not capable of doing the little they had to do properly. Finally, Charlie Sloane fought Moody Spurgeon MacPherson because Moody Spurgeon had said that Anne Shirley put on airs about her recitations, and Moody Spurgeon was "licked"; consequently, Moody Spurgeon's sister, Ella May, would not "speak" to Anne Shirley all the rest of the winter. With the exception of these trifling frictions, work in Miss Stacy's little kingdom went on with regularity and smoothness.

The winter weeks slipped by. It was an unusually mild winter, with so little snow that Anne and Diana could go to school nearly every day by way of the Birch Path. On Anne's birthday, they were tripping lightly down it, keeping eyes and ears alert amid all their chatter, for Miss Stacy had told them that they must soon write a composition on "A Winter's Walk in the Woods," and it behooved them to be observant.

"Just think, Diana, I'm thirteen years old today," remarked Anne in an awed voice. "I can scarcely realize that I'm in my teens. When I woke this morning, it seemed to me that everything must be different. You've been thirteen for a month, so I suppose it doesn't seem such a novelty to you as it does to me. It makes life seem so much more interesting. In two more years, I'll be really grown up. It's a great comfort to think that I'll be able to use big words then without being laughed at."

"Ruby Gillis says she means to have a beau as soon as she's fifteen," said Diana.

"Ruby Gillis thinks of nothing but beaus," said Anne disdainfully. "She's actually delighted when anyone writes her name up in a take-notice for all she pretends to be so mad. But I'm afraid that is an uncharitable speech. Mrs. Allan says we should never make uncharitable speeches; but they do slip out so often before you think, don't they? I simply can't talk about Josie Pye without making an uncharitable speech, so I never mention her at all. You may have noticed that. I'm trying to be as much like Mrs. Allan as I possibly can, for I think she's perfect. Mr. Allan thinks so, too. Mrs. Lynde says he just worships the ground she treads on, and she doesn't really think it right for a minister to set his affections so much on a mortal being. But then, Diana, even ministers are human and have their besetting sins just like everybody else. I had such an interesting talk with Mrs. Allan about besetting sins last Sunday afternoon. There are just a few things it's proper to talk about on Sundays and that is one of them. My besetting sin is imagining too much and forgetting my duties. I'm striving very hard to overcome it, and now that I'm really thirteen, perhaps I'll get on better."

"In four more years, we'll be able to put our hair up," said Diana. "Alice Bell is only sixteen and she is wearing hers up, but I think that's ridiculous. I shall wait until I'm seventeen."

"If I had Alice Bell's crooked nose," said Anne decidedly, "I wouldn't— but there! I won't say what I was going to because it was extremely uncharitable. Besides, I was comparing it with my own nose and that's vanity. I'm afraid I think[1] too much about my nose ever since I heard that compliment about it long ago. It really is a great comfort to me. Oh, Diana, look, there's a rabbit. That's something to remember for our woods composition. I really think the woods are just as lovely in winter as in summer. They're so white and still, as if they were asleep and dreaming pretty dreams."

"I won't mind writing that composition when its time comes," sighed Diana. "I can manage to write about the woods, but the one we're to hand in Monday is terrible. The idea of Miss Stacy telling us to write a story out of our own heads!"

"Why, it's as easy as a wink," said Anne.

"It's easy for you because you have an imagination," retorted Diana, "but what would you do if you had been born without one? I suppose you have your composition all done?"

Anne nodded, trying hard not to look virtuously complacent and failing miserably.

"I wrote it last Monday evening. It's called 'The Jealous Rival; or, In Death Not Divided.' I read it to Marilla and she said it was stuff and nonsense. Then I read it to Matthew and he said it was fine. That is the kind of critic I like. It's a sad, sweet story. I just cried like a child while I was writing it. It's about two beautiful maidens called Cordelia Montmorency and Geraldine Seymour who lived in the same village and were devotedly attached to each other. Cordelia was a regal brunette with a coronet of midnight hair and duskly flashing eyes. Geraldine was a queenly blonde with hair like spun gold and velvety purple eyes."

"I never saw anybody with purple eyes," said Diana dubiously.

"Neither did I. I just imagined them. I wanted something out of the common. Geraldine had an alabaster brow, too. I've found out what an alabaster brow is. That is one of the advantages of being thirteen. You know so much more than you did when you were only twelve."

"Well, what became of Cordelia and Geraldine?" asked Diana, who was beginning to feel rather interested in their fate.

"They grew in beauty side by side until they were sixteen. Then

---

[1] I've thought.

Bertram DeVere came to their native village and fell in love with the fair Geraldine. He saved her life when her horse ran away with her in a carriage, and she fainted in his arms and he carried her home three miles; because, you understand, the carriage was all smashed up. I found it rather hard to imagine the proposal because I had no experience to go by. I asked Ruby Gillis if she knew anything about how men proposed because I thought she'd likely be an authority on the subject, having so many sisters married. Ruby told me she was hid in the hall pantry when Malcolm Andrews proposed to her sister Susan. She said Malcolm told Susan that his dad had given him the farm in his own name and then said, 'What do you say, darling pet, if we get hitched this fall?' And Susan said, 'Yes—no—I don't know—let me see'—and there they were, engaged as quick as that. But I didn't think that sort of a proposal was a very romantic one, so in the end I had to imagine it out as well as I could. I made it very flowery and poetical, and Bertram went on his knees, although Ruby Gillis says it isn't done nowadays. Geraldine accepted him in a speech a page long. I can tell you I took a lot of trouble with that speech. I rewrote it five times and I look upon it as my masterpiece. Bertram gave her a diamond ring and a ruby necklace and told her they would go to Europe for a wedding tour, for he was immensely wealthy. But then, alas, shadows began to darken over their path. Cordelia was secretly in love with Bertram herself, and when Geraldine told her about the engagement, she was simply furious, especially when she saw the necklace and the diamond ring. All her affection for Geraldine turned to bitter hate and she vowed that she should never marry Bertram. But she pretended to be Geraldine's friend the same as ever. One evening they were standing on the bridge over a rushing turbulent stream, and Cordelia, thinking they were alone, pushed Geraldine over the brink with a wild, mocking 'Ha, ha, ha.' But Bertram saw it all and he at once plunged into the current, exclaiming, 'I will save thee, my peerless Geraldine.' But, alas, he had forgotten he couldn't swim, and they were both drowned, clasped in each other's arms. Their bodies were washed ashore soon afterwards. They were buried in the one grave and their funeral was most imposing, Diana. It's so much more romantic to end a story up with a funeral than a wedding. As for Cordelia, she went insane with remorse and was shut up in a lunatic asylum. I thought that was a poetical retribution for her crime."

"How perfectly lovely!" sighed Diana, who belonged to Matthew's school of critics. "I don't see how you can make up such thrilling things out of your own head, Anne. I wish my imagination was as good as yours."

"It would be if you'd only cultivate it," said Anne cheeringly. "I've just thought of a plan, Diana. Let you and I have a story club all our own and write stories for practice. I'll help you along until you can do them by yourself. You ought to cultivate your imagination, you know. Miss Stacy says so. Only we must take the right way. I told her about the Haunted Wood, but she said we went the wrong way about it in that."

This was how the Story Club came into existence. It was limited to Diana and Anne at first, but soon it was extended to include Jane Andrews and Ruby Gillis and one or two others who felt that their imaginations needed cultivating. No boys were allowed in it—although Ruby Gillis opined that their admission would make it more exciting—and each member had to produce one story a week.

"It's extremely interesting," Anne told Marilla. "Each girl has to read her story out loud and then we talk it over. We are going to keep them all sacredly and have them to read to our descendants. We each write under a nom de plume. Mine is Rosamond Montmorency. All the girls do pretty well. Ruby Gillis is rather sentimental. She puts too much love-making into her stories, and you know too much is worse than too little. Jane never puts any because she says it makes her feel so silly when she has to read it out loud. Jane's stories are extremely sensible. Then Diana puts too many murders into hers. She says most of the time she doesn't know what to do with the people, so she kills them off to get rid of them. I mostly always have to tell them what to write about, but that isn't hard, for I've millions of ideas."

"I think this story writing business is the foolishest yet," scoffed Marilla. "You'll get a pack of nonsense into your heads and waste time that should be put on your lessons. Reading stories is bad enough, but writing them is worse."

"But we're so careful to put a moral into them all, Marilla," explained Anne. "I insist upon that. All the good people are rewarded and all the bad ones are suitably punished. I'm sure that must have a wholesome effect. The moral is the great thing. Mr. Allan says so. I read one of my stories to him and Mrs. Allan, and they both agreed that the moral was excellent. Only they laughed in the wrong places. I like it better when people cry. Jane and Ruby almost always cry when I come to the pathetic parts. Diana wrote her aunt Josephine about our club, and her aunt Josephine wrote back that we were to send her some of our stories. So we copied out four of our very best and sent them. Miss Josephine Barry wrote back that she had never read anything so amusing in her life. That kind of puzzled us because the stories were all very pathetic and almost everybody died. But I'm glad Miss Barry liked them. It shows our club is doing some good in the world. Mrs. Allan says that ought to be our object in everything. I do really try to make it my object, but I forget so often when I'm having fun. I hope I shall be a little like Mrs. Allan when I grow up. Do you think there is any prospect of it, Marilla?"

"I shouldn't say there was a great deal," was Marilla's encouraging answer. "I'm sure Mrs. Allan was never such a silly, forgetful little girl as you are."

"No, but she wasn't always so good as she is now, either," said Anne seriously. "She told me so herself—that is, she said she was a dreadful mischief when she was a girl and was always getting into scrapes. I felt so encouraged when I heard that. Is it very wicked of me, Marilla, to feel encouraged when I hear that other people have been bad and mischievous? Mrs. Lynde says it is. Mrs. Lynde says she always feels shocked when she hears of anyone ever having been naughty, no matter how small they were. Mrs. Lynde says she once heard a minister confess that when he was a boy, he stole a strawberry tart out of his aunt's pantry and she never had any respect for that minister again. Now, I wouldn't have felt that way. I'd have thought that it was real noble of him to confess it, and I'd have thought what an encouraging thing it would be for small boys nowadays who do naughty things and are sorry for them to know that perhaps they may grow up to be ministers in spite of it. That's how I'd feel, Marilla."

"The way I feel at present, Anne," said Marilla, "is that it's high time you had those dishes washed. You've taken half an hour longer than you should with all your chattering. Learn to work first and talk afterwards."

Chapter 27

VANITY AND VEXATION OF SPIRIT

Marilla, walking home one late April evening from an Aid meeting, realized that the winter was over and gone with the thrill of delight that spring never fails to bring to the oldest and saddest as well as to the youngest and merriest. Marilla was not given to subjective analysis of her thoughts and feelings. She probably imagined that she was thinking about the Aids and their missionary box and the new carpet for the vestry room, but under these reflections was a harmonious consciousness of red fields smoking into pale purply mists in the declining sun, of long, sharp-pointed fir shadows falling over the meadow beyond the brook, of still, crimson-budded maples around a mirrorlike wood pool, of a wakening in the world and a stir of hidden pulses under the gray sod. The spring was abroad in the land, and Marilla's sober, middle-aged step was lighter and swifter because of its deep, primal gladness.

Her eyes dwelt affectionately on Green Gables, peering through its network of trees and reflecting the sunlight back from its windows in several little coruscations of glory. Marilla, as she picked her steps along the damp lane, thought that it was really a satisfaction to know that she was going home to a briskly snapping wood fire and a table nicely spread for tea, instead of to the cold comfort of old Aid meeting evenings before Anne had come to Green Gables.

Consequently, when Marilla entered her kitchen and found the fire black out, with no sign of Anne anywhere, she felt justly disappointed and irritated. She had told Anne to be sure and have tea ready at five o'clock, but now she must hurry to take off her second-best dress and prepare the meal herself against[1] Matthew's return from ploughing.

"I'll settle Miss Anne when she comes home," said Marilla grimly as she shaved up kindlings with a carving knife and more vim than was

---

[1] Before.

strictly necessary. Matthew had come in and was waiting patiently for his tea in his corner. "She's gadding off somewhere with Diana, writing stories or practicing dialogues or some such tomfoolery, and never thinking once about the time or her duties. She's just got to be pulled up short and sudden on this sort of thing. I don't care if Mrs. Allan does say she's the brightest and sweetest child she ever knew. She may be bright and sweet enough, but her head is full of nonsense and there's never any knowing what shape it'll break out in next. Just as soon as she grows out of one freak, she takes up with another. But there! Here I am saying the very thing I was so riled with Rachel Lynde for saying at the Aid today. I was real glad when Mrs. Allan spoke up for Anne, for if she hadn't, I know I'd have said something too sharp to Rachel before everybody. Anne's got plenty of faults, goodness knows, and far be it from me to deny it. But I'm bringing her up and not Rachel Lynde, who'd pick faults in the angel Gabriel himself if he lived in Avonlea. Just the same, Anne has no business to leave the house like this when I told her she was to stay home this afternoon and look after things. I must say, with all her faults, I never found her disobedient or untrustworthy before, and I'm real sorry to find her so now."

"Well now, I dunno," said Matthew, who, being patient and wise and, above all, hungry, had deemed it best to let Marilla talk her wrath out unhindered, having learned by experience that she got through with whatever work was on hand much quicker if not delayed by untimely argument. "Perhaps you're judging her too hasty, Marilla. Don't call her untrustworthy until you're sure she has disobeyed you. Mebbe it can all be explained—Anne's a great hand at explaining."

"She's not here when I told her to stay," retorted Marilla. "I reckon she'll find it hard to explain *that* to my satisfaction. Of course I knew you'd take her part, Matthew. But I'm bringing her up, not you."

It was dark when supper was ready, and still no sign of Anne coming hurriedly over the log bridge or up Lover's Lane, breathless and repentant with a sense of neglected duties. Marilla washed and put away the dishes grimly. Then, wanting a candle to light her way down to the cellar, she went up to the east gable for the one that generally stood on Anne's table. Lighting it, she turned around to see Anne herself lying on the bed, face downward among the pillows.

"Mercy on us," said astonished Marilla, "have you been asleep, Anne?"

"No," was the muffled reply.

"Are you sick, then?" demanded Marilla anxiously, going over to the bed.

Anne cowered deeper into her pillows as if desirous of hiding herself forever from mortal eyes.

"No. But please, Marilla, go away and don't look at me. I'm in the depths of despair and I don't care who gets head in class or writes the best composition or sings in the Sunday school choir anymore. Little things like that are of no importance now because I don't suppose I'll ever be able to go anywhere again. My career is closed. Please, Marilla, go away and don't look at me."

"Did anyone ever hear the like?" the mystified Marilla wanted to know. "Anne Shirley, whatever is the matter with you? What have you done? Get right up this minute and tell me. This minute, I say. There now, what is it?"

Anne had slid to the floor in despairing obedience.

"Look at my hair, Marilla," she whispered.

Accordingly, Marilla lifted her candle and looked scrutinizingly at Anne's hair, flowing in heavy masses down her back. It certainly had a very strange appearance.

"Anne Shirley, what have you done to your hair? Why, it's *green!*"

Green it might be called, if it were any earthly colour—a strange, dull, bronzy green, with streaks here and there of the original red to heighten the ghastly effect. Never in all her life had Marilla seen anything so grotesque as Anne's hair at that moment.

"Yes, it's green," moaned Anne. "I thought nothing could be as bad as red hair. But now I know it's ten times worse to have green hair. Oh, Marilla, you little know how utterly wretched I am."

"I little know how you got into this fix, but I mean to find out," said Marilla. "Come right down to the kitchen—it's too cold up here—and tell me just what you've done. I've been expecting something strange for some time. You haven't got into any scrape for over two months, and I was sure another one was due. Now, then, what did you do to your hair?"

"I dyed it."

"Dyed it! Dyed your hair! Anne Shirley, didn't you know it was a wicked thing to do?"

"Yes, I knew it was a little wicked," admitted Anne. "But I thought it was worthwhile to be a little wicked to get rid of red hair. I counted the cost, Marilla. Besides, I meant to be extra good in other ways to make up for it."

"Well," said Marilla sarcastically, "if I'd decided it was worthwhile to dye my hair, I'd have dyed it a decent colour at least. I wouldn't have dyed it green."

"But I didn't mean to dye it green, Marilla," protested Anne dejectedly. "If I was wicked, I meant to be wicked to some purpose. He said it would turn my hair a beautiful raven black—he positively assured me that it would. How could I doubt his word, Marilla? I know what it feels to have your word doubted. And Mrs. Allan says we should never suspect anyone of not telling us the truth unless we have proof that they're not. I have proof now—green hair is proof enough for anybody. But I hadn't then, and I believed every word he said *implicitly.*"

"Who said? Who are you talking about?"

"The peddler that was here this afternoon. I bought the dye from him."

"Anne Shirley, how often have I told you never to let one of those Italians in the house! I don't believe in encouraging them to come around at all."

"Oh, I didn't let him in the house. I remembered what you told me, and I went out, carefully shut the door, and looked at his things on the step. Besides, he wasn't an Italian—he was a German Jew. He had a big box full of very interesting things, and he told me he was working hard to make enough money to bring his wife and children out of Germany. He spoke so feelingly about them that it touched my heart. I wanted to buy something from him to help him in such a worthy object. Then all at once I saw the bottle of hair dye. The peddler said it was warranted to dye any hair a beautiful raven black and wouldn't wash off. In a trice I saw myself with beautiful raven black hair and the temptation was irresistible. But the price of the bottle was seventy-five cents and I had only fifty cents left out of my chicken money. I think the peddler had a very kind heart, for he said that seeing it was me, he'd sell it for fifty cents and that was just giving it away. So I bought it, and as soon as he had gone, I came up here and applied it with an old hairbrush as the directions said. I used up the whole bottle, and oh, Marilla, when I saw the dreadful colour it turned my hair, I repented of being wicked, I can tell you. And I've been repenting ever since."

"Well, I hope you'll repent to good purpose," said Marilla severely, "and that you've got your eyes opened to where your vanity has led you, Anne. Goodness knows what's to be done. I suppose the first thing is to give your hair a good washing and see if that will do any good."

Accordingly, Anne washed her hair, scrubbing it vigorously with soap and water, but for all the difference it made, she might as well have been scouring its original red. The peddler had certainly spoken the truth when he declared that the dye wouldn't wash off, however his veracity might be impeached in other respects.

"Oh, Marilla, what shall I do?" questioned Anne in tears. "I can never live this down. People have pretty well forgotten my other mistakes—the liniment cake and setting Diana drunk and flying into a temper with Mrs. Lynde. But they'll never forget this. They will think I am not respectable. Oh, Marilla, 'what a tangled web we weave when first we practice to deceive.' That is poetry, but it is true. And, oh, how Josie Pye will laugh! Marilla, I *cannot* face Josie Pye. I am the unhappiest girl in Prince Edward Island."

Anne's unhappiness continued for a week. During that time, she went nowhere and shampooed her hair every day. Diana alone of outsiders knew the fatal secret, but she promised solemnly never to tell, and it may be stated here and now that she kept her word.

At the end of the week, Marilla said decidedly, "It's no use, Anne. That is fast dye if ever there was any. Your hair must be cut off; there is no other way. You can't go out with it looking like that."

Anne's lips quivered, but she realized the bitter truth of Marilla's remarks. With a dismal sigh, she went for the scissors.

"Please cut it off at once, Marilla, and have it over. Oh, I feel that my heart is broken. This is such an unromantic affliction. The girls in books lose their hair in fevers or sell it to get money for some good deed, and I'm sure I wouldn't mind losing my hair in some such fashion half so much. But there is nothing comforting in having your hair cut off because you've dyed it a dreadful colour, is there? I'm going to weep all the time you're cutting it off, if it won't interfere. It seems such a tragic thing."

Anne wept then, but later on, when she went upstairs and looked in the glass, she was calm with despair. Marilla had done her work thoroughly and it had been necessary to shingle the hair as closely as possible. The result was not becoming, to state the case as mildly as may be. Anne promptly turned her glass to the wall.

"I'll never, never look at myself again until my hair grows," she exclaimed passionately.

Then she suddenly righted the glass.

"Yes, I will, too. I'll do penance for being wicked that way. I'll look at myself every time I come to my room and see how ugly I am. And I won't try to imagine it away, either. I never thought I was vain about my hair, of all things, but now I know I was, in spite of its being red, because it was so long and thick and curly. I expect something will happen to my nose next."

Anne's clipped head made a sensation in school on the following Monday, but to her relief nobody guessed the real reason for it, not even

Josie Pye, who, however, did not fail to inform Anne that she looked like a perfect scarecrow.

"I didn't say anything when Josie said that to me," Anne confided that evening to Marilla, who was lying on the sofa after one of her headaches, "because I thought it was part of my punishment and I ought to bear it patiently. It's hard to be told you look like a scarecrow, and I wanted to say something back. But I didn't. I just swept her one scornful look and then I forgave her. It makes you feel very virtuous when you forgive people, doesn't it? I mean to devote all my energies to being good after this, and I shall never try to be beautiful again. Of course it's better to be good. I know it is, but it's sometimes so hard to believe a thing even when you know it. I do really want to be good, Marilla, like you and Mrs. Allan and Miss Stacy, and grow up to be a credit to you. Diana says when my hair begins to grow to tie a black velvet ribbon around my head with a bow at one side. She says she thinks it will be very becoming. I will call it a snood—that sounds so romantic. But am I talking too much, Marilla? Does it hurt your head?"

"My head is better now. It was terrible bad this afternoon, though. These headaches of mine are getting worse and worse. I'll have to see a doctor about them. As for your chatter, I don't know that I mind it—I've got so used to it."

Which was Marilla's way of saying that she liked to hear it.

Chapter 28

AN UNFORTUNATE LILY MAID

"Of course you must be Elaine, Anne," said Diana. "I could never have . . . the courage to float down there."

"Nor I," said Ruby Gillis with a shiver. "I don't mind floating down when there's two or three of us in the flat and we can sit up. It's fun then. But to lie down and pretend I was dead—I just couldn't. I'd die really of fright."

"Of course it would be romantic," conceded Jane Andrews. "But I know I couldn't keep still. I'd be popping up every minute or so to see where I was and if I wasn't drifting too far out. And you know, Anne, that would spoil the effect."

"But it's so ridiculous to have a redheaded Elaine," mourned Anne. "I'm not afraid to float down and I'd *love* to be Elaine. But it's ridiculous just the same. Ruby ought to be Elaine because she is so fair and has such lovely long golden hair—Elaine had 'all her bright hair streaming down,' you know. And Elaine was the lily maid. Now, a red-haired person cannot be a lily maid."

"Your complexion is just as fair as Ruby's," said Diana earnestly, "and your hair is ever so much darker than it used to be before you cut it."

"Oh, do you really think so?" exclaimed Anne, flushing sensitively with delight. "I've sometimes thought it was myself—but I never dared to ask anyone for fear she would tell me it wasn't. Do you think it could be called auburn now, Diana?"

"Yes, and I think it is real pretty," said Diana, looking admiringly at the short, silky curls that clustered over Anne's head and were held in place by a very jaunty black velvet ribbon and bow.

They were standing on the bank of the pond, below Orchard Slope, where a little headland fringed with birches ran out from the bank; at its tip was a small wooden platform built out into the water for the convenience of fishermen and duck hunters. Ruby and Jane were spending the midsummer afternoon with Diana, and Anne had come over to play with them.

Anne and Diana had spent most of their playtime that summer on and about the pond. Idlewild was a thing of the past, Mr. Bell having ruthlessly cut down the little circle of trees in his back pasture in the spring. Anne had sat among the stumps and wept, not without an eye to the romance of it; but she was speedily consoled, for, after all, as she and Diana said, big girls of thirteen, going on fourteen, were too old for such childish amusements as playhouses, and there were more fascinating sports to be found about the pond. It was splendid to fish for trout over the bridge, and the two girls learned to row themselves about in the little flat-bottomed dory Mr. Barry kept for duck shooting.

It was Anne's idea that they dramatize Elaine. They had studied Tennyson's poem in school the preceding winter, the superintendent of education having prescribed it in English course for the Prince Edward Island schools. They had analyzed and parsed it and torn it to pieces in general until it was a wonder there was any meaning at all left in it for them, but at least the fair lily maid and Lancelot and Guinevere and King Arthur had become very real people to them, and Anne was devoured by secret regret that she had not been born in Camelot. Those days, she said, were so much more romantic than the present.

Anne's plan was hailed with enthusiasm. The girls had discovered that if the flat were pushed off from the landing place, it would drift down with the current under the bridge and finally strand itself on another headland lower down that ran out at a curve in the pond. They had often gone down like this and nothing could be more convenient for playing Elaine.

"Well, I'll be Elaine," said Anne, yielding reluctantly, for, although she would have been delighted to play the principal character, yet her artistic sense demanded fitness for it, and this, she felt, her limitations made impossible. "Ruby, you must be King Arthur, and Jane will be Guinevere, and Diana must be Lancelot. But first you must be the brothers and the father. We can't have the old, dumb servitor because there isn't room for two in the flat when one is lying down. We must pall the barge all its length in blackest samite. That old black shawl of your mother's will be just the thing, Diana."

The black shawl having been procured, Anne spread it over the flat and then lay down on the bottom, with closed eyes and hands folded over her breast.

"Oh, she does look really dead," whispered Ruby Gillis nervously, watching the still, white little face under the flickering shadows of the birches. "It makes me feel frightened, girls. Do you suppose it's really right to act like this? Mrs. Lynde says that all play-acting is abominably wicked."

"Ruby, you shouldn't talk about Mrs. Lynde," said Anne severely. "It spoils the effect because this is hundreds of years before Mrs. Lynde was born. Jane, you arrange this. It's silly for Elaine to be talking when she's dead."

Jane rose to the occasion. Cloth of gold for coverlet there was none, but an old piano scarf of yellow Japanese crêpe was an excellent substitute. A white lily was not obtainable just then, but the effect of a tall blue iris placed in one of Anne's folded hands was all that could be desired.

"Now she's all ready," said Jane. "We must kiss her quiet brows and, Diana, you say, 'Sister, farewell forever,' and Ruby, you say, 'Farewell, sweet sister,' both of you as sorrowfully as you possibly can. Anne, for goodness' sake, smile a little. You know Elaine 'lay as though she smiled.' That's better. Now push the flat off."

The flat was accordingly pushed off, scraping roughly over an old embedded stake in the process. Diana, Jane, and Ruby only waited long enough to see it caught in the current and headed for the bridge before scampering up through the woods, across the road, and down to the lower headland where, as Lancelot and Guinevere and the king, they were to be in readiness to receive the lily maid.

For a few minutes, Anne, drifting slowly down, enjoyed the romance of her situation to the full. Then something happened not at all romantic. The flat began to leak. In a very few moments, it was necessary for Elaine to scramble to her feet, pick up her cloth of gold coverlet and pall of blackest samite and gaze blankly at a big crack in the bottom of her barge through which the water was literally pouring. That sharp stake at the landing had torn off the strip of batting nailed on the flat. Anne did not know this, but it did not take her long to realize that she was in a dangerous plight. At this rate, the flat would fill and sink long before it could drift to the lower headland. Where were the oars? Left behind at the landing!

Anne gave one gasping little scream that nobody ever heard; she was white to the lips, but she did not lose her self-possession. There was one chance—just one.

"I was horribly frightened," she told Mrs. Allan the next day, "and it seemed like years while the flat was drifting down to the bridge and the water rising in it every moment. I prayed, Mrs. Allan, most earnestly, but I didn't shut my eyes to pray, for I knew the only way God could save me was to let the flat float close enough to one of the bridge piles for me to climb up on it. You know the piles are just old tree trunks and there are lots of knots and old branch stubs on them. It was proper to pray, but I had to do my part by watching out, and right well I knew it. I just said, 'Dear God, please take the flat close to a pile and I'll do the rest,' over and over again. Under such circumstances, you don't think much about making a flowery prayer. But mine was answered, for the flat bumped right into a pile for a minute and I flung the scarf and the shawl over my shoulder and scrambled up on a big providential stub. And there I was, Mrs. Allan, clinging to that slippery old pile with no way of getting up or down. It was a very unromantic position, but I didn't think about that at the time. You don't think much about romance when you have just escaped from a watery grave. I said a grateful prayer at once, and then I gave all my attention to holding on tight, for I knew I should probably have to depend on human aid to get back to dry land."

The flat drifted under the bridge and then promptly sank in midstream. Ruby, Jane, and Diana, already awaiting it on the lower headland, saw it disappear before their very eyes and had not a doubt but that Anne had gone down with it. For a moment, they stood still, white as sheets, frozen with horror at the tragedy; then, shrieking at the tops of their voices, they started on a frantic run up through the woods, never pausing as they crossed the main road to glance the way of the bridge. Anne, clinging desperately to her precarious foothold, saw their flying forms and heard their shrieks. Help would soon come, but meanwhile her position was a very uncomfortable one.

The minutes passed by, each seeming an hour to the unfortunate lily maid. Why didn't somebody come? Where had the girls gone? Suppose they had fainted, one and all! Suppose nobody ever came! Suppose she grew so tired and cramped that she could hold on no longer! Anne looked at the wicked green depths below her, wavering with long, oily shadows, and shivered. Her imagination began to suggest all manner of gruesome possibilities to her.

Then, just as she thought she really could not endure the ache in her arms and wrists another moment, Gilbert Blythe came rowing under the bridge in Harmon Andrews's dory!

Gilbert glanced up and, much to his amazement, beheld a little white, scornful face looking down upon him with big, frightened but also scornful gray eyes.

"Anne Shirley! How on earth did you get there?" he exclaimed.

Without waiting for an answer, he pulled close to the pile and extended his hand. There was no help for it; Anne, clinging to Gilbert Blythe's hand, scrambled down into the dory, where she sat, drabbled and furious, in the stern with her arms full of dripping shawl and wet crêpe. It was certainly extremely difficult to be dignified under the circumstances!

"What has happened, Anne?" asked Gilbert, taking up his oars.

"We were playing Elaine," explained Anne frigidly, without even looking at her rescuer, "and I had to drift down to Camelot in the barge—I mean the flat. The flat began to leak and I climbed out on the pile. The girls went for help. Will you be kind enough to row me to the landing?"

Gilbert obligingly rowed to the landing, and Anne, disdaining assistance, sprang nimbly onto shore.

"I'm very much obliged to you," she said haughtily as she turned away.

But Gilbert had also sprung from the boat and now laid a detaining hand on her arm.

"Anne," he said hurriedly, "look here. Can't we be good friends? I'm awfully sorry I made fun of your hair that time. I didn't mean to vex you and I only meant it for a joke. Besides, it's so long ago. I think your hair is awfully pretty now—honest I do. Let's be friends."

For a moment, Anne hesitated. She had an odd, newly awakened consciousness under all her outraged dignity that the half-shy, half-eager expression in Gilbert's hazel eyes was something that was very good to see. Her heart gave a quick, strange little beat. But the bitterness of her old grievance promptly stiffened up her wavering determination. That scene of two years before flashed back into her recollection as vividly as if it had taken place yesterday. Gilbert had called her "Carrots" and had brought about her disgrace before the whole school. Her resentment, which to other and older people might be as laughable as its cause, was in no whit allayed and softened by time, seemingly. She hated Gilbert Blythe! She would never forgive him!

"No," she said coldly, "I shall never be friends with you, Gilbert Blythe; and I don't want to be!"

"All right!" Gilbert sprang into his skiff with an angry colour in his cheeks. "I'll never ask you to be friends again, Anne Shirley. And I don't care either!"

He pulled away with swift, defiant strokes, and Anne went up the steep, ferny little path under the maples. She held her head very high, but she was conscious of an odd feeling of regret. She almost wished she had

He pulled close to the pile and extended his hand.

answered Gilbert differently. Of course, he had insulted her terribly, but still—! Altogether, Anne rather thought it would be a relief to sit down and have a good cry. She was really quite unstrung, for the reaction from her fright and cramped clinging was making itself felt.

Halfway up the path, she met Jane and Diana rushing back to the pond in a state narrowly removed from positive frenzy. They had found nobody at Orchard Slope, both Mr. and Mrs. Barry being away. Here Ruby Gillis had succumbed to hysterics and was left to recover from them as best she might, while Jane and Diana flew through the Haunted Wood and across the brook to Green Gables. There they had found nobody either, for Marilla had gone to Carmody and Matthew was making hay in the back field.

"Oh, Anne," gasped Diana, fairly falling on the former's neck and weeping with relief and delight, "oh, Anne—we thought—you were—drowned—and we felt like murderers—because we had made—you be—Elaine. And Ruby is in hysterics—oh, Anne, how did you escape?"

"I climbed up on one of the piles," explained Anne wearily, "and Gilbert Blythe came along in Mr. Andrews's dory and brought me to land."

"Oh, Anne, how splendid of him! Why, it's so romantic!" said Jane, finding breath enough for utterance at last. "Of course you'll speak to him after this."

"Of course I won't," flashed Anne with a momentary return of her old spirit. "And I don't want ever to hear the word romantic again, Jane Andrews. I'm awfully sorry you were so frightened, girls. It is all my fault. I feel sure I was born under an unlucky star. Everything I do gets me or my dearest friends into a scrape. We've gone and lost your father's flat, Diana, and I have a presentiment that we'll not be allowed to row on the pond anymore."

Anne's presentiment proved more trustworthy than presentiments are apt to be. Great was the consternation in the Barry and Cuthbert households when the events of the afternoon became known.

"Will you *ever* have any sense, Anne?" groaned Marilla.

"Oh, yes, I think I will, Marilla," returned Anne optimistically. A good cry, indulged in the grateful solitude of the east gable, had soothed her nerves and restored her to her wonted cheerfulness. "I think my prospects of becoming sensible are brighter now than ever."

"I don't see how," said Marilla.

"Well," explained Anne, "I've learned a new and valuable lesson today. Ever since I came to Green Gables, I've been making mistakes, and each mistake has helped to cure me of some great shortcoming. The affair of the amethyst brooch cured me of meddling with things that didn't belong to me. The Haunted Wood mistake cured me of letting my imagination run away with me. The liniment cake mistake cured me of carelessness in cooking. Dyeing my hair cured me of vanity. I never think about my hair and nose now—at least, very seldom. And today's mistake is going to cure me of being too romantic. I have come to the conclusion that it is no use trying to be romantic in Avonlea. It was probably easy enough in towered Camelot hundreds of years ago, but romance is not appreciated now. I feel quite sure that you will soon see a great improvement in me in this respect, Marilla."

"I'm sure I hope so," said Marilla skeptically.

But Matthew, who had been sitting mutely in his corner, laid a hand on Anne's shoulder when Marilla had gone out.

"Don't give up all your romance, Anne," he whispered shyly. "A little of it is a good thing—not too much, of course—but keep a little of it, Anne, keep a little of it."

Chapter 29

AN EPOCH IN ANNE'S LIFE

Anne was bringing the cows home from the back pasture by way of Lover's Lane. It was a September evening, and all the gaps and clearings in the woods were brimmed up with ruby sunset light. Here and there the lane was splashed with it, but for the most part it was already quite shadowy beneath the maples, and the spaces under the firs were filled with a clear violet dusk like airy wine. The winds were out in their tops, and there is no sweeter music on earth than that which the wind makes in the fir trees at evening.

The cows swung placidly down the lane, and Anne followed them dreamily, repeating aloud the battle canto from "Marmion"—which had also been part of their English course the preceding winter and which Miss Stacy had made them learn off by heart—and exulting in its rushing lines and the clash of spears in its imagery. When she came to the lines

The stubborn spearsmen still made good
Their dark impenetrable wood,

she stopped in ecstasy to shut her eyes that she might the better fancy herself one of that heroic ring. When she opened them again, it was to behold Diana coming through the gate that led into the Barry field and looking so important that Anne instantly divined there was news to be told. But betray too eager curiosity she would not.

"Isn't this evening just like a purple dream, Diana? It makes me so glad to be alive. In the mornings, I always think the mornings are best; but when evening comes, I think it's lovelier still."

"It's a very fine evening," said Diana, "but, oh, I have such news, Anne. Guess. You can have three guesses."

"Charlotte Gillis is going to be married in the church after all, and Mrs. Allan wants us to decorate it," cried Anne.

"No. Charlotte's beau won't agree to that, because nobody ever has been married in the church yet, and he thinks it would seem too much like a funeral. It's too mean, because it would be such fun. Guess again."

"Jane's mother is going to let her have a birthday party?"

Diana shook her head, her black eyes dancing with merriment.

"I can't think what it can be," said Anne in despair, "unless it's that Moody Spurgeon MacPherson saw you home from prayer meeting last night. Did he?"

"I should think not," exclaimed Diana indignantly. "I wouldn't be likely to boast of it if he did, the horrid creature! I knew you couldn't guess it. Mother had a letter from Aunt Josephine today, and Aunt Josephine wants you and me to go to town next Tuesday and stop[1] with her for the Exhibition. There!"

"Oh, Diana," whispered Anne, finding it necessary to lean up against a maple tree for support, "do you really mean it? But I'm afraid Marilla won't let me go. She will say that she can't encourage gadding about. That was what she said last week when Jane invited me to go with them in their double-seated buggy to the American concert at the White Sands Hotel. I wanted to go, but Marilla said I'd be better at home learning my lessons, and so would Jane. I was bitterly disappointed, Diana. I felt so heartbroken that I wouldn't say my prayers when I went to bed. But I repented of that and got up in the middle of the night and said them."

"I'll tell you," said Diana, "we'll get Mother to ask Marilla. She'll be more likely to let you go then; and if she does, we'll have the time of our lives, Anne. I've never been to an Exhibition, and it's so aggravating to hear the other girls talking about their trips. Jane and Ruby have been twice, and they're going this year again."

"I'm not going to think about it at all until I know whether I can go or not," said Anne resolutely. "If I did and then was disappointed, it would be more than I could bear. But in case I do go, I'm very glad my new coat will be ready by that time. Marilla didn't think I needed a new coat. She said my old one would do very well for another winter and that I ought to be satisfied with having a new dress. The dress is very pretty, Diana—navy blue and made so fashionably. Marilla always makes my dresses fashionably now, because she says she doesn't intend to have Matthew going to Mrs. Lynde to make them. I'm so glad. It is ever so much easier to be good if your clothes are fashionable. At least, it is easy for me. I suppose it doesn't make such a difference to naturally good people. But Matthew said I must have a new coat, so Marilla bought a

---

[1] Stay.

lovely piece of blue broadcloth, and it's being made by a real dressmaker over at Carmody. It's to be done Saturday night, and I'm trying not to imagine myself walking up the church aisle on Sunday in my new suit and cap, because I'm afraid it isn't right to imagine such things. But it just slips into my mind in spite of me. My cap is so pretty. Matthew bought it for me the day we were over at Carmody. It is one of those little blue velvet ones that are all the rage, with gold cord and tassels. Your new hat is elegant, Diana, and so becoming. When I saw you come into church last Sunday, my heart swelled with pride to think you were my dearest friend. Do you suppose it's wrong for us to think so much about our clothes? Marilla says it is very sinful. But it *is* such an interesting subject, isn't it?"

Marilla agreed to let Anne go to town, and it was arranged that Mr. Barry should take the girls in on the following Tuesday. As Charlottetown was thirty miles away and Mr. Barry wished to go and return the same day, it was necessary to make a very early start. But Anne counted it all joy and was up before sunrise on Tuesday morning. A glance from her window assured her that the day would be fine, for the eastern sky behind the firs of the Haunted Wood was all silvery and cloudless. Through the gap in the trees, a light was shining in the western gable of Orchard Slope, a token that Diana was also up.

Anne was dressed by the time Matthew had the fire on, and she had the breakfast ready when Marilla came down, but for her own part was much too excited to eat. After breakfast the jaunty new cap and jacket were donned, and Anne hastened over the brook and up through the firs to Orchard Slope. Mr. Barry and Diana were waiting for her, and they were soon on the road.

It was a long drive, but Anne and Diana enjoyed every minute of it. It was delightful to rattle along over the moist roads in the early red sunlight that was creeping across the shorn harvest fields. The air was fresh and crisp, and little smoke-blue mists curled through the valleys and floated off from the hills. Sometimes the road went through woods where maples were beginning to hang out scarlet banners; sometimes it crossed rivers on bridges that made Anne's flesh cringe with the old, half-delightful fear; sometimes it wound along a harbor shore and passed by a little cluster of weather-gray fishing huts; again it mounted to hills whence a far sweep of curving upland or misty blue sky could be seen; but wherever it went, there was much of interest to discuss. It was almost noon when they reached town and found their way to "Beechwood." It was quite a fine old mansion, set back from the street in a seclusion of green elms and branching beeches. Miss Barry met them at the door with a twinkle in her sharp black eyes.

"So you've come to see me at last, you Anne-girl," she said. "Mercy, child, how you have grown! You're taller than I am, I declare. And you're ever so much better-looking than you used to be, too. But I dare say you know that without being told."

"Indeed I didn't," said Anne radiantly. "I know I'm not so freckled as I used to be, so I've much to be thankful for, but I really hadn't dared to hope there was any other improvement. I'm so glad you think there is, Miss Barry."

Miss Barry's house was furnished with "great magnificence," as Anne told Marilla afterwards. The two little country girls were rather abashed by the splendour of the parlour where Miss Barry left them when she went to see about dinner.

"Isn't it just like a palace?" whispered Diana. "I never was in Aunt Josephine's house before, and I'd no idea it was so grand. I just wish Julia Bell could see this—she puts on such airs about her mother's parlour."

"Velvet carpet," sighed Anne luxuriously, "*and* silk curtains! I've dreamed of such things, Diana. But do you know I don't believe I feel very comfortable with them after all. There are so many things in this room and all so splendid that there is no scope for imagination. That is one consolation when you are poor—there are so many more things you can imagine about."

Their sojourn in town was something that Anne and Diana dated from for years.[2] From first to last, it was crowded with delights.

On Wednesday, Miss Barry took them to the Exhibition grounds and kept them there all day.

"It was splendid," Anne related to Marilla later on. "I never imagined anything so interesting. I don't really know which department was the most interesting. I think I liked the horses and the flowers and the fancy work best. Josie Pye took first prize for knitted lace. I was real glad she did. And I was glad that I felt glad, for it shows I'm improving, don't you think, Marilla, when I can rejoice in Josie's success? Mr. Harmon Andrews took second prize for Gravenstein apples, and Mr. Bell took first prize for a pig. Diana said she thought it was ridiculous for a Sunday school superintendent to take a prize in pigs, but I don't see why. Do you? She said she would always think of it after this when he was praying so solemnly. Clara Louise MacPherson took a prize for painting, and Mrs. Lynde got first prize for homemade butter and cheese. So Avonlea

---

2 Never forgot.

was pretty well represented, wasn't it? Mrs. Lynde was there that day, and I never knew how much I really liked her until I saw her familiar face among all those strangers. There were thousands of people there, Marilla. It made me feel dreadfully insignificant. And Miss Barry took us up to the grandstand to see the horse races. Mrs. Lynde wouldn't go; she said horse racing was an abomination, and she being a church member thought it her bounden duty to set a good example by staying away. But there were so many there I don't believe Mrs. Lynde's absence would ever be noticed. I don't think, though, that I ought to go very often to horse races, because they *are* awfully fascinating. Diana got so excited that she offered to bet me ten cents that the red horse would win. I didn't believe he would, but I refused to bet, because I wanted to tell Mrs. Allan all about everything, and I felt sure it wouldn't do to tell her that. It's always wrong to do anything you can't tell the minister's wife. It's as good as an extra conscience to have a minister's wife for your friend. And I was very glad I didn't bet, because the red horse *did* win, and I would have lost ten cents. So you see that virtue was its own reward. We saw a man go up in a balloon. I'd love to go up in a balloon, Marilla; it would be simply thrilling. And we saw a man selling fortunes. You paid him ten cents and a little bird picked out your fortune for you. Miss Barry gave Diana and me ten cents each to have our fortunes told. Mine was that I would marry a dark-complected man who was very wealthy, and I would go across water to live. I looked carefully at all the dark men I saw after that, but I didn't care much for any of them, and anyhow I suppose it's too early to be looking out for him yet. Oh, it was a never-to-be-forgotten day, Marilla. I was so tired I couldn't sleep at night. Miss Barry put us in the spare room, according to promise. It was an elegant room, Marilla, but somehow sleeping in a spare room isn't what I used to think it was. That's the worst of growing up, and I'm beginning to realize it. The things you wanted so much when you were a child don't seem half so wonderful to you when you get them."

Thursday the girls had a drive in the park, and in the evening Miss Barry took them to a concert in the Academy of Music, where a noted prima donna was to sing. To Anne the evening was a glittering vision of delight.

"Oh, Marilla, it was beyond description. I was so excited I couldn't even talk, so you may know what it was like. I just sat in enraptured silence. Madame Selitsky was perfectly beautiful and wore white satin and diamonds. But when she began to sing, I never thought about anything else. Oh, I can't tell you how I felt. But it seemed to me that it could never be hard to be good anymore. I felt like I do when I look up to the stars. Tears came into my eyes, but, oh, they were such happy tears. I was so sorry when it was all over, and I told Miss Barry I didn't see how I was ever to return to common life again. She said she thought if we went over to the restaurant across the street and had an ice cream it might help me. That sounded so prosaic, but to my surprise, I found it true. The ice cream was delicious, Marilla, and it was so lovely and dissipated to be sitting there eating it at eleven o'clock at night. Diana said she believed she was born for city life. Miss Barry asked me what my opinion was, but I said I would have to think it over very seriously before I could tell her what I really thought. So I thought it over after I went to bed. That is the best time to think things out. And I came to the conclusion, Marilla, that I wasn't born for city life and that I was glad of it. It's nice to be eating ice cream at brilliant restaurants at eleven o'clock at night once in a while; but as a regular thing I'd rather be in the east gable at eleven, sound asleep, but kind of knowing even in my sleep that the stars were shining outside and that the wind was blowing in the firs across the brook. I told Miss Barry so at breakfast the next morning and she laughed. Miss Barry generally laughed at anything I said, even when I said the most solemn things. I don't think I liked it, Marilla, because I wasn't trying to be funny. But she is a most hospitable lady and treated us royally."

Friday brought going-home time, and Mr. Barry drove in for the girls.

"Well, I hope you've enjoyed yourselves," said Miss Barry as she bade them good-bye.

"Indeed we have," said Diana.

"And you, Anne-girl?"

"I've enjoyed every minute of the time," said Anne, throwing her arms impulsively about the old woman's neck and kissing her wrinkled cheek.

Diana would never have dared to do such a thing and felt rather aghast at Anne's freedom. But Miss Barry was pleased, and she stood on her veranda and watched the buggy out of sight. Then she went back into her big house with a sigh. It seemed very lonely, lacking those fresh young lives. Miss Barry was a rather selfish old lady, if the truth must be told, and had never cared much for anybody but herself. She valued people only as they were of service to her or amused her. Anne had amused her and consequently stood high in the old lady's good graces. But Miss Barry found herself thinking less about Anne's quaint speeches than of her fresh enthusiasms, her transparent emotions, her little winning ways, and the sweetness of her eyes and lips.

I thought Marilla Cuthbert was an old fool when I heard she'd adopted a girl out of an orphan asylum, she said to herself, *but I guess she didn't make much of a mistake after all. If I'd a child like Anne in the house all the time, I'd be a better and happier woman.*

Anne and Diana found the drive home as pleasant as the drive in—pleasanter, indeed, since there was the delightful consciousness of home waiting at the end of it. It was sunset when they passed through White Sands and turned into the shore road. Beyond, the Avonlea hills came out darkly against the saffron sky. Behind them the moon was rising out of the sea that grew all radiant and transfigured in its light. Every little cove along the curving road was a marvel of dancing ripples. The waves broke with a soft swish on the rocks below them, and the tang of the sea was in the strong, fresh air.

"Oh, but it's good to be alive and to be going home," breathed Anne.

When she crossed the log bridge over the brook, the kitchen light of Green Gables winked her a friendly welcome back, and through the open door shone the hearth fire, sending out its warm red glow athwart the chilly autumn night. Anne ran blithely up the hill and into the kitchen, where a hot supper was waiting on the table.

"So you've got back?" said Marilla, folding up her knitting.

"Yes, and, oh, it's so good to be back," said Anne joyously. "I could kiss everything, even to the clock. Marilla, a broiled chicken! You don't mean to say you cooked that for me!"

"Yes, I did," said Marilla. "I thought you'd be hungry after such a drive and need something real appetizing. Hurry and take off your things, and we'll have supper as soon as Matthew comes in. I'm glad you've got back, I must say. It's been fearful lonesome here without you, and I never put in four longer days."

After supper Anne sat before the fire between Matthew and Marilla and gave them a full account of her visit.

"I've had a splendid time," she concluded happily, "and I feel that it marks an epoch in my life. But the best of it all was the coming home."

Chapter 30

THE QUEEN'S CLASS IS ORGANIZED

Marilla laid her knitting on her lap and leaned back in her chair. Her eyes were tired, and she thought vaguely that she must see about having her glasses changed the next time she went to town, for her eyes had grown tired very often of late.

It was nearly dark, for the dull November twilight had fallen around Green Gables, and the only light in the kitchen came from the dancing red flames in the stove.

Anne was curled up Turk-fashion on the hearth rug, gazing into that joyous glow where the sunshine of a hundred summers was being distilled from the maple cordwood. She had been reading, but her book had slipped to the floor, and now she was dreaming, with a smile on her parted lips. Glittering castles in Spain were shaping themselves out of the mists and rainbows of her lively fancy; adventures wonderful and enthralling were happening to her in cloudland—adventures that always turned out triumphantly and never involved her in scrapes like those of actual life.

Marilla looked at her with tenderness that would never have been suffered to reveal itself in any clearer light than that soft mingling of fireshine and shadow. The lesson of a love that should display itself easily in spoken word and open look was one Marilla could never learn. But she had learned to love this slim, gray-eyed girl with an affection all the deeper and stronger from its very undemonstrativeness. Her love made her afraid of being unduly indulgent, indeed. She had an uneasy feeling that it was rather sinful to set one's heart so intensely on any human creature as she had set hers on Anne, and perhaps she performed a sort of unconscious penance for this by being stricter and more critical than if the girl had been less dear to her. Certainly, Anne herself had no idea how Marilla loved her. She sometimes thought wistfully that Marilla was very hard to please and distinctly lacking in sympathy and understanding. But she always checked the thought reproachfully, remembering what she owed to Marilla.

"Anne," said Marilla abruptly, "Miss Stacy was here this afternoon when you were with Diana."

Anne came back from her other world with a start and a sigh.

"Was she? Oh, I'm so sorry I wasn't in. Why didn't you call me, Marilla? Diana and I were only over in the Haunted Wood. It's lovely in the woods now. All the little wood things—the ferns and the satin leaves and the crackerberries—have gone to sleep, just as if somebody had tucked them away until spring under a blanket of leaves. I think it was a little gray fairy with a rainbow scarf that came tiptoeing along the last moonlight night and did it. Diana wouldn't say much about that, though. Diana has never forgotten the scolding her mother gave her about imagining ghosts in the Haunted Wood. It had a very bad effect on Diana's imagination. It blighted it. Mrs. Lynde says Myrtle Bell is a blighted being. I asked Ruby Gillis why Myrtle was blighted, and Ruby said she guessed it was because her young man had gone back on her. Ruby Gillis thinks of nothing but young men, and the older she gets, the worse she is. Young men are all very well in their place, but it doesn't do to drag them into everything, does it? Diana and I are thinking seriously of promising each other that we will never marry but be nice old maids and live together forever. Diana hasn't quite made up her mind though, because she thinks perhaps it would be nobler to marry some wild, dashing, wicked young man and reform him. Diana and I talk a great deal about serious subjects now, you know. We feel that we are so much older than we used to be that it isn't becoming to talk of childish matters. It's such a solemn thing to be almost fourteen, Marilla. Miss Stacy took all us girls who are in our teens down to the brook last Wednesday and talked to us about it. She said we couldn't be too careful what habits we formed and what ideals we acquired in our teens, because by the time we were twenty, our characters would be developed and the foundation laid for our whole future lives. And she said if the foundation was shaky we could never build anything really worthwhile on it. Diana and I talked the matter over coming home from school. We felt extremely solemn, Marilla. And we decided that we would try to be very careful indeed and form respectable habits and learn all we could and be as sensible as possible, so that by the time we were twenty, our characters would be properly developed. It's perfectly appalling to think of being twenty, Marilla. It sounds so fearfully old and grown up. But why was Miss Stacy here this afternoon?"

"That is what I want to tell you, Anne, if you'll ever give me a chance to get a word in edgewise. She was talking about you."

"About me?" Anne looked rather scared. Then she flushed and exclaimed, "Oh, I know what she was saying. I meant to tell you, Marilla, honestly I did, but I forgot. Miss Stacy caught me reading *Ben-Hur* in school yesterday afternoon when I should have been studying my Canadian history. Jane Andrews lent it to me. I was reading it at dinner hour, and I had just got to the chariot race when school went in. I was simply wild to know how it turned out—although I felt sure Ben-Hur must win, because it wouldn't be poetical justice if he didn't—so I spread the history open on my desk lid and then tucked *Ben-Hur* between the desk and my knee. It just looked as if I were studying Canadian history, you know, while all the while I was reveling in *Ben-Hur.* I was so interested in it that I never noticed Miss Stacy coming down the aisle until all at once I just looked up and there she was looking down at me, so reproachful-like. I can't tell you how ashamed I felt, Marilla, especially when I heard Josie Pye giggling. Miss Stacy took *Ben-Hur* away, but she never said a word then. She kept me in at recess and talked to me. She said I had done very wrong in two respects. First, I was wasting the time I ought to have put on my studies; and second, I was deceiving my teacher in trying to make it appear I was reading a history when it was a storybook instead. I had never realized until that moment, Marilla, that what I was doing was deceitful. I was shocked. I cried bitterly and asked Miss Stacy to forgive me and I'd never do such a thing again; and I offered to do penance by never so much as looking at *Ben-Hur* for a whole week, not even to see how the chariot race turned out. But Miss Stacy said she wouldn't require that, and she forgave me freely. So I think it wasn't very kind of her to come up here to you about it after all."

"Miss Stacy never mentioned such a thing to me, Anne, and it's only your guilty conscience that's the matter with you. You have no business to be taking storybooks to school. You read too many novels anyhow. When I was a girl, I wasn't so much as allowed to look at a novel."

"Oh, how can you call *Ben-Hur* a novel when it's really such a religious book?" protested Anne. "Of course it's a little too exciting to be proper reading for Sunday, and I only read it on weekdays. And I never read *any* book now unless either Miss Stacy or Mrs. Allan thinks it is a proper book for a girl thirteen and three-quarters to read. Miss Stacy made me promise that. She found me reading a book one day called *The Lurid Mystery of the Haunted Hall.* It was one Ruby Gillis had lent me, and, oh, Marilla, it was so fascinating and creepy. It just curdled the blood in my veins. But Miss Stacy said it was a very silly, unwholesome book, and she asked me not to read any more of it or any like it. I didn't mind promising not to read any more like it, but it was *agonizing* to give back that book without knowing how it turned out. But my love for Miss Stacy stood the test and I did. It's really wonderful, Marilla, what you can do when you're truly anxious to please a certain person."

"Well, I guess I'll light the lamp and get to work," said Marilla. "I see plainly that you don't want to hear what Miss Stacy had to say. You're more interested in the sound of your own tongue than in anything else."

"Oh, indeed, Marilla, I do want to hear it," cried Anne contritely. "I won't say another word—not one. I know I talk too much, but I am really trying to overcome it, and although I say far too much, yet if you only knew how many things I want to say and don't, you'd give me some credit for it. Please tell me, Marilla."

"Well, Miss Stacy wants to organize a class among her advanced students who mean to study for the Entrance examination into Queen's. She intends to give them extra lessons for an hour after school. And she came to ask Matthew and me if we would like to have you join it. What do you think about it yourself, Anne? Would you like to go to Queen's and pass for a teacher?"

"Oh, Marilla!" Anne straightened to her knees and clasped her hands. "It's been the dream of my life—that is, for the last six months, ever since Ruby and Jane began to talk of studying for the Entrance.[1] But I didn't say anything about it, because I supposed it would be perfectly useless. I'd love to be a teacher. But won't it be dreadfully expensive? Mr. Andrews says it cost him one hundred and fifty dollars to put Prissy through, and Prissy wasn't a dunce in geometry."

"I guess you needn't worry about that part of it. When Matthew and I took you to bring up, we resolved we would do the best we could for you and give you a good education. I believe in a girl being fitted to earn her own living whether she ever has to or not. You'll always have a home at Green Gables as long as Matthew and I are here, but nobody knows what is going to happen in this uncertain world, and it's just as well to be prepared. So you can join the Queen's class if you like, Anne."

"Oh, Marilla, thank you." Anne flung her arms about Marilla's waist and looked up earnestly into her face. "I'm extremely grateful to you and Matthew. And I'll study as hard as I can and do my very best to be a credit to you. I warn you not to expect much in geometry, but I think I can hold my own in anything else if I work hard."

---

[1] Entrance examination.

"I dare say you'll get along well enough. Miss Stacy says you are bright and diligent." Not for worlds would Marilla have told Anne just what Miss Stacy had said about her; that would have been to pamper vanity. "You needn't rush to any extreme of killing yourself over your books. There is no hurry. You won't be ready to try the Entrance for a year and a half yet. But it's well to begin in time and be thoroughly grounded, Miss Stacy says."

"I shall take more interest than ever in my studies now," said Anne blissfully, "because I have a purpose in life. Mr. Allan says everybody should have a purpose in life and pursue it faithfully. Only he says we must first make sure that it is a worthy purpose. I would call it a worthy purpose to want to be a teacher like Miss Stacy, wouldn't you, Marilla? I think it's a very noble profession."

The Queen's class was organized in due time. Gilbert Blythe, Anne Shirley, Ruby Gillis, Jane Andrews, Josie Pye, Charlie Sloane, and Moody Spurgeon MacPherson joined it. Diana Barry did not, as her parents did not intend to send her to Queen's. This seemed nothing short of a calamity to Anne. Never, since the night on which Minnie May had had the croup, had she and Diana been separated in anything. On the evening when the Queen's class first remained in school for the extra lessons and Anne saw Diana go slowly out with the others, to walk home alone through the Birch Path and Violet Vale, it was all the former could do to keep her seat and refrain from rushing impulsively after her chum. A lump came into her throat, and she hastily retired behind the pages of her uplifted Latin grammar to hide the tears in her eyes. Not for the world would Anne have had Gilbert Blythe or Josie Pye see those tears.

"But, oh, Marilla, I really felt that I had tasted the bitterness of death, as Mr. Allan said in his sermon last Sunday, when I saw Diana go out alone," she said mournfully that night. "I thought how splendid it would have been if Diana had only been going to study for the Entrance, too. But we can't have things perfect in this imperfect world, as Mrs. Lynde says. Mrs. Lynde isn't exactly a comforting person sometimes, but there's no doubt she says a great many very true things. And I think the Queen's class is going to be extremely interesting. Jane and Ruby are just going to study to be teachers. That is the height of their ambition. Ruby says she will only teach for two years after she gets through, and then she intends to be married. Jane says she will devote her whole life to teaching and never, never marry, because you are paid a salary for teaching, but a husband won't pay you anything and growls if you ask for a share in the egg and butter money. I expect Jane speaks from mournful experience, for

Mrs. Lynde says that her father is a perfect old crank and meaner than second skimmings.[2] Josie Pye says she is just going to college for education's sake, because she won't have to earn her own living; she says of course it is different with orphans who are living on charity—*they* have to hustle. Moody Spurgeon is going to be a minister. Mrs. Lynde says he couldn't be anything else with a name like that to live up to. I hope it isn't wicked of me, Marilla, but really the thought of Moody Spurgeon being a minister makes me laugh. He's such a funny-looking boy with that big, fat face, his little blue eyes, and his ears sticking out like flaps. But perhaps he will be more intellectual-looking when he grows up. Charlie Sloane says he's going to go into politics and be a member of Parliament, but Mrs. Lynde says he'll never succeed at that, because the Sloanes are all honest people, and it's only rascals that get on in politics nowadays."

"What is Gilbert Blythe going to be?" queried Marilla, seeing that Anne was opening her Caesar.

"I don't happen to know what Gilbert Blythe's ambition in life is—if he has any," said Anne scornfully.

There was open rivalry between Gilbert and Anne now. Previously, the rivalry had been rather one-sided, but there was no longer any doubt that Gilbert was as determined to be first in class as Anne was. He was a foeman worthy of her steel. The other members of the class tacitly acknowledged their superiority and never dreamed of trying to compete with them.

Since the day by the pond when she had refused to listen to his plea for forgiveness, Gilbert, save for the aforesaid determined rivalry, had evinced no recognition whatever of the existence of Anne Shirley. He talked and jested with the other girls, exchanged books and puzzles with them, discussed lessons and plans, sometimes walked home with one or the other of them from prayer meeting or Debating Club. But Anne Shirley he simply ignored. It was in vain that she told herself with a toss of her head that she did not care. Deep down in her wayward, feminine little heart, she knew that she did care and that if she had that chance of the Lake of Shining Waters again she would answer very differently. All at once, as it seemed, and to her secret dismay, she found that the old resentment she had cherished against him was gone—gone just when she most needed its sustaining power. It was in vain that she recalled every incident and emotion of that memorable occasion and tried to feel the old satisfying anger. That day by the pond had witnessed its last

---

[2] So stingy, he'd skim milk twice.

spasmodic flicker. Anne realized that she had forgiven and forgotten without knowing it. But it was too late.

And at least neither Gilbert nor anybody else, not even Diana, should ever suspect how sorry she was and how much she wished she hadn't been so proud and horrid! She determined to "shroud her feelings in deepest oblivion," and it may be stated here and now that she did it so successfully that Gilbert, who possibly was not quite so indifferent as he seemed, could not console himself with any belief that Anne felt his retaliatory scorn. The only poor comfort he had was that she also snubbed Charlie Sloane, unmercifully, continually, and undeservedly.

Otherwise the winter passed away in a round of pleasant duties and studies. For Anne the days slipped by like golden beads on the necklace of the year. She was happy, eager, interested; there were lessons to be learned and honours to be won; delightful books to read; new pieces to be practiced for the Sunday school choir; pleasant Saturday afternoons at the manse with Mrs. Allan. Then, almost before Anne realized it, spring had come again to Green Gables and all the world was abloom once more.

Studies palled just a wee bit then; the Queen's class, left behind in school while the others scattered to green lanes and leafy wood cuts and meadow byways, looked wistfully out of the windows and discovered that Latin verbs and French exercises had somehow lost the tang and zest they had possessed in the crisp winter months. Even Anne and Gilbert lagged and grew indifferent. Teacher and taught were alike glad when the term was ended and the glad vacation days stretched rosily before them.

"But you've done good work this past year," Miss Stacy told them on the last evening, "and you deserve a good, jolly vacation. Have the best time you can in the out-of-doors world and lay in a good stock of health and vitality and ambition to carry you through next year. It will be the tug of war, you know—the last year before the Entrance."

"Are you going to be back next year, Miss Stacy?" asked Josie Pye.

Josie Pye never scrupled to ask questions; in this instance, the rest of the class felt grateful to her; none of them would have dared to ask it of Miss Stacy, but all wanted to, for there had been alarming rumours running at large through the school for some time that Miss Stacy was not coming back the next year—that she had been offered a position in the graded school of her own home district and meant to accept. The Queen's class listened in breathless suspense for her answer.

"Yes, I think I will," said Miss Stacy. "I thought of taking another school, but I have decided to come back to Avonlea. To tell the truth, I've grown so interested in my pupils here that I found I couldn't leave them. So I'll stay and see you through."

"Hurrah!" said Moody Spurgeon. Moody Spurgeon had never been so carried away by his feelings before, and he blushed uncomfortably every time he thought about it for a week.

"Oh, I'm so glad," said Anne with shining eyes. "Dear Miss Stacy, it would be perfectly dreadful if you didn't come back. I don't believe I could have the heart to go on with my studies at all if another teacher came here."

When Anne got home that night, she stacked all her textbooks away in an old trunk in the attic, locked it, and threw the key into the blanket box.

"I'm not even going to look at a schoolbook on vacation," she told Marilla. "I've studied as hard all the term as I possibly could, and I've pored over that geometry until I know every proposition in the first book off by heart, even when the letters *are* changed. I just feel tired of everything sensible, and I'm going to let my imagination run riot for the summer. Oh, you needn't be alarmed, Marilla. I'll only let it run riot within reasonable limits. But I want to have a real good, jolly time this summer, for maybe it's the last summer I'll be a little girl. Mrs. Lynde says that if I keep stretching out next year as I've done this, I'll have to put on longer skirts. She says I'm all running to legs and eyes. And when I put on longer skirts, I shall feel that I have to live up to them and be very dignified. It won't even do to believe in fairies then, I'm afraid; so I'm going to believe in them with all my whole heart this summer. I think we're going to have a very good vacation. Ruby Gillis is going to have a birthday party soon, and there's the Sunday school picnic and the missionary concert next month. And Mr. Barry says that some evening he'll take Diana and me over to the White Sands Hotel and have dinner there. They have dinner there in the evening, you know. Jane Andrews was over once last summer and she says it was a dazzling sight to see the electric lights and the flowers and all the lady guests in such beautiful dresses. Jane says it was her first glimpse into high life and she'll never forget it to her dying day."

Mrs. Lynde came up the next afternoon to find out why Marilla had not been at the Aid meeting on Thursday. When Marilla was not at the Aid meeting, people knew there was something wrong at Green Gables.

"Matthew had a bad spell with his heart Thursday," Marilla explained, "and I didn't feel like leaving him. Oh, yes, he's all right again now, but he takes them spells oftener than he used to and I'm anxious about him.

The doctor says he must be careful to avoid excitement. That's easy enough, for Matthew doesn't go about looking for excitement by any means and never did, but he's not to do any very heavy work either and you might as well tell Matthew not to breathe as not to work. Come and lay off your things, Rachel. You'll stay to tea?"

"Well, seeing you're so pressing, perhaps I might as well stay," said Mrs. Rachel, who had not the slightest intention of doing anything else.

Mrs. Rachel and Marilla sat comfortably in the parlour while Anne got the tea and made hot biscuits that were light and white enough to defy even Mrs. Rachel's criticism.

"I must say Anne has turned out a real smart girl," admitted Mrs. Rachel as Marilla accompanied her to the end of the lane at sunset. "She must be a great help to you."

"She is," said Marilla, "and she's real steady and reliable now. I used to be afraid she'd never get over her featherbrained ways, but she has and I wouldn't be afraid to trust her in anything now."

"I never would have thought she'd have turned out so well that first day I was here three years ago," said Mrs. Rachel. "Lawful heart, shall I ever forget that tantrum of hers! When I went home that night, I says to Thomas, says I, 'Mark my words, Thomas, Marilla Cuthbert'll live to rue the step she's took.' But I was mistaken and I'm real glad of it. I ain't one of those kind of people, Marilla, as can never be brought to own up that they've made a mistake. No, that never was my way, thank goodness. I did make a mistake in judging Anne, but it weren't no wonder, for an odder, unexpecteder witch of a child there never was in this world, that's what. There was no ciphering her out by the rules that worked with other children. It's nothing short of wonderful how she's improved these three years, but especially in looks. She's a real pretty girl got to be, though I can't say I'm overly partial to that pale, big-eyed style myself. I like more snap and colour, like Diana Barry has or Ruby Gillis. Ruby Gillis's looks are real showy. But somehow—I don't know how it is but when Anne and them are together, though she ain't half as handsome, she makes them look kind of common and overdone—something like them white June lilies she calls narcissus alongside of the big red peonies, that's what."

Chapter 31

WHERE THE BROOK AND RIVER MEET

Anne had her "good" summer and enjoyed it wholeheartedly. She and Diana fairly lived outdoors, reveling in all the delights that Lover's Lane and the Dryad's Bubble and Willowmere and Victoria Island afforded. Marilla offered no objections to Anne's gypsyings. The Spencervale doctor who had come the night Minnie May had the croup met Anne at the house of a patient one afternoon early in vacation, looked her over sharply, screwed up his mouth, shook his head, and sent a message to Marilla Cuthbert by another person. It was:

"Keep that redheaded girl of yours in the open air all summer and don't let her read books until she gets more spring into her step."

This message frighted Marilla wholesomely. She read Anne's death warrant by consumption in it unless it was scrupulously obeyed. As a result, Anne had the golden summer of her life as far as freedom and frolic went. She walked, rowed, berried, and dreamed to her heart's content; and when September came, she was bright-eyed and alert, with a step that would have satisfied the Spencervale doctor and a heart full of ambition and zest once more.

"I feel just like studying with might and main," she declared as she brought her books down from the attic. "Oh, you good old friends, I'm glad to see your honest faces once more—yes, even you, geometry. I've had a perfectly beautiful summer, Marilla, and now I'm rejoicing as a strong man to run a race, as Mr. Allan said last Sunday. Doesn't Mr. Allan preach magnificent sermons? Mrs. Lynde says he is improving every day, and the first thing we know some city church will gobble him up and then we'll be left and have to turn to and break in another green preacher. But I don't see the use of meeting trouble halfway, do you, Marilla? I think it would be better just to enjoy Mr. Allan while we have him. If I were a man, I think I'd be a minister. They can have such an influence for good, if their theology is sound; and it must be thrilling to preach splendid sermons and stir your hearers' hearts. Why can't women be ministers, Marilla? I asked Mrs. Lynde that and she was shocked and said it would be a scandalous thing. She said there might be female ministers in the States and she believed there was, but thank goodness we hadn't got to that stage in Canada yet and she hoped we never would. But I don't see why. I think women would make splendid ministers. When there is a social to be got up or a church tea or anything else to raise money, the women have to turn to and do the work. I'm sure Mrs. Lynde can pray every bit as well as Superintendent Bell, and I've no doubt she could preach, too, with a little practice."

"Yes, I believe she could," said Marilla drily. "She does plenty of unofficial preaching as it is. Nobody has much of a chance to go wrong in Avonlea with Rachel to oversee them."

"Marilla," said Anne in a burst of confidence, "I want to tell you something and ask you what you think about it. It has worried me terribly— on Sunday afternoons, that is, when I think specially about such matters. I do really want to be good; and when I'm with you or Mrs. Allan or Miss Stacy, I want it more than ever and I want to do just what would please you and what you would approve of. But mostly when I'm with Mrs. Lynde, I feel desperately wicked and as if I wanted to go and do the very thing she tells me I oughtn't to do. I feel irresistibly tempted to do it. Now, what do you think is the reason I feel like that? Do you think it's because I'm really bad and unregenerate?"

Marilla looked dubious for a moment. Then she laughed.

"If you are, I guess I am, too, Anne, for Rachel often has that very effect on me. I sometimes think she'd have more of an influence for good, as you say yourself, if she didn't keep nagging people to do right. There should have been a special commandment against nagging. But there, I shouldn't talk so. Rachel is a good Christian woman and she means well. There isn't a kinder soul in Avonlea, and she never shirks her share of work."

"I'm very glad you feel the same," said Anne decidedly. "It's so encouraging. I shan't worry so much over that after this. But I dare say there'll be other things to worry me. They keep coming up new all the time— things to perplex you, you know. You settle one question and there's another right after. There are so many things to be thought over and decided when you're beginning to grow up. It keeps me busy all the time thinking them over and deciding what is right. It's a serious thing to grow up, isn't it, Marilla? But when I have such good friends as you and

Matthew and Mrs. Allan and Miss Stacy, I ought to grow up successfully, and I'm sure it will be my own fault if I don't. I feel it's a great responsibility because I have only the one chance. If I don't grow up right, I can't go back and begin over again. I've grown two inches this summer, Marilla. Mr. Gillis measured me at Ruby's party. I'm so glad you made my new dresses longer. That dark green one is so pretty, and it was sweet of you to put on the flounce. Of course I know it wasn't really necessary, but flounces are so stylish this fall and Josie Pye has flounces on all her dresses. I know I'll be able to study better because of mine. I shall have such a comfortable feeling deep down in my mind about that flounce."

"It's worth something to have that," admitted Marilla.

Miss Stacy came back to Avonlea school and found all her pupils eager for work once more. Especially did the Queen's class gird up their loins for the fray, for at the end of the coming year, dimly shadowing their pathway already, loomed up that fateful thing known as "the Entrance," at the thought of which one and all felt their hearts sink into their very shoes. Suppose they did not pass! That thought was doomed to haunt Anne through the waking hours of that winter, Sunday afternoons inclusive, to the almost entire exclusion of moral and theological problems. When Anne had bad dreams, she found herself staring miserably at pass lists of the Entrance exams, where Gilbert Blythe's name was blazoned at the top and in which hers did not appear at all.

But it was a jolly, busy, happy, swift-flying winter. Schoolwork was as interesting, class rivalry as absorbing, as of yore. New worlds of thought, feeling, and ambition and fresh, fascinating fields of unexplored knowledge seemed to be opening out before Anne's eager eyes. "Hills peeped o'er hill and Alps on Alps arose." Much of all this was due to Miss Stacy's tactful, careful, broad-minded guidance. She led her class to think and explore and discover for themselves and encouraged straying from the old beaten paths to a degree that quite shocked Mrs. Lynde and the school trustees, who viewed all innovations on established methods rather dubiously.

Apart from her studies, Anne expanded socially, for Marilla, mindful of the Spencervale doctor's dictum, no longer vetoed occasional outings. The Debating Club flourished and gave several concerts; there were one or two parties almost verging on grown-up affairs; there were sleigh drives and skating frolics galore.

Between times, Anne grew, shooting up so rapidly that Marilla was astonished one day, when they were standing side by side, to find the girl was taller than herself.

"Why, Anne, how you've grown!" she said almost unbelievingly.

A sigh followed on the words. Marilla felt a strange regret over Anne's inches. The child she had learned to love had vanished somehow and here was this tall, serious-eyed girl of fifteen, with the thoughtful brow and the proudly poised little head, in her place. Marilla loved the girl as much as she had loved the child, but she was conscious of a sorrowful sense of loss. And that night when Anne had gone to prayer meeting with Diana, Marilla sat alone in the wintry twilight and indulged in the weakness of a cry. Matthew, coming in with a lantern, caught her at it and gazed at her in such consternation that Marilla had to laugh through her tears.

"I was thinking about Anne," she explained. "She's got to be such a big girl—and she'll probably be away from us next winter. I'll miss her terrible."

"She'll be able to come home often," comforted Matthew, to whom Anne was as yet and always would be the little, eager girl he had brought home from Bright River on that June evening four years before. "The branch railroad will be built to Carmody by that time."

"It won't be the same thing as having her here all the time," sighed Marilla gloomily, determined to enjoy her luxury of grief uncomforted. "But there—men can't understand these things!"

There were other changes in Anne no less real than the physical change. For one thing, she became much quieter. Perhaps she thought all the more and dreamed as much as ever, but she certainly talked less. Marilla noticed and commented on this also.

"You don't chatter half as much as you used to, Anne, nor use half as many big words. What has come over you?"

Anne coloured and laughed a little as she dropped her book and looked dreamily out of the window, where big, fat red buds were bursting out on the creeper in response to the lure of the spring sunshine.

"I don't know—I don't want to talk as much," she said, denting her chin thoughtfully with her forefinger. "It's nicer to think dear, pretty thoughts and keep them in one's heart, like treasures. I don't like to have them laughed at or wondered over. And somehow I don't want to use big words anymore. It's almost a pity, isn't it, now that I'm really growing big enough to say them if I did want to. It's fun to be almost grown up in some ways, but it's not the kind of fun I expected, Marilla. There's so much to learn and do and think that there isn't time for big words. Besides, Miss Stacy says the short ones are much stronger and better. She makes us write all our essays as simply as possible. It was hard at first. I was so used to crowding in all the fine big words I could think of—and I thought of any number of them. But I've got used to it now and I see it's so much better."

"What has become of your Story Club? I haven't heard you speak of it for a long time."

"The Story Club isn't in existence any longer. We hadn't time for it—and anyhow I think we had got tired of it. It was silly to be writing about love and murder and elopements and mysteries. Miss Stacy sometimes has us write a story for training in composition, but she won't let us write anything but what might happen in Avonlea in our own lives, and she criticizes it very sharply and makes us criticize our own, too. I never thought my compositions had so many faults until I began to look for them myself. I felt so ashamed that I wanted to give up altogether, but Miss Stacy said I could learn to write well if I only trained myself to be my own severest critic. And so I am trying to."

"You've only two more months before the Entrance," said Marilla. "Do you think you'll be able to get through?"

Anne shivered. "I don't know. Sometimes I think I'll be all right—and then I get horribly afraid. We've studied hard and Miss Stacy has drilled us thoroughly, but we mayn't get through for all that. We've each got a stumbling block. Mine is geometry of course, and Jane's is Latin, and Ruby's and Charlie's is algebra, and Josie's is arithmetic. Moody Spurgeon says he feels it in his bones that he is going to fail in English history. Miss Stacy is going to give us examinations in June just as hard as we'll have at the Entrance and mark us just as strictly, so we'll have some idea. I wish it was all over, Marilla. It haunts me. Sometimes I wake up in the night and wonder what I'll do if I don't pass."

"Why, go to school next year and try again," said Marilla unconcernedly.

"Oh, I don't believe I'd have the heart for it. It would be such a disgrace to fail, especially if Gil—if the others passed. And I get so nervous in an examination that I'm likely to make a mess of it. I wish I had nerves like Jane Andrews. Nothing rattles her."

Anne sighed and, dragging her eyes from the witcheries of the spring world, the beckoning day of breeze and blue, and the green things upspringing in the garden, buried herself resolutely in her book. There would be other springs, but if she did not succeed in passing the Entrance, Anne felt convinced that she would never recover sufficiently to enjoy them.

Chapter 32
THE PASS LIST IS OUT

With the end of June came the close of the term and the close of Miss Stacy's rule in Avonlea school. Anne and Diana walked home that evening feeling very sober indeed. Red eyes and damp handkerchiefs bore convincing testimony to the fact that Miss Stacy's farewell words must have been quite as touching as Mr. Phillips's had been under similar circumstances three years before. Diana looked back at the schoolhouse from the foot of the spruce hill and sighed deeply.

"It does seem as if it was the end of everything, doesn't it?" she said dismally.

"You oughtn't to feel half as bad as I do," said Anne, hunting vainly for a dry spot on her handkerchief. "You'll be back again next winter, but I suppose I've left the dear old school forever—if I have good luck, that is."

"It won't be a bit the same. Miss Stacy won't be there, nor you nor Jane nor Ruby probably. I shall have to sit all alone, for I couldn't bear to have another deskmate after you. Oh, we have had jolly times, haven't we, Anne? It's dreadful to think they're all over."

Two big tears rolled down by Diana's nose.

"If you would stop crying, I could," said Anne imploringly. "Just as soon as I put away my hanky, I see you brimming up and that starts me off again. As Mrs. Lynde says, 'If you can't be cheerful, be as cheerful as you can.' After all, I dare say I'll be back next year. This is one of the times I *know* I'm not going to pass. They're getting alarmingly frequent."

"Why, you came out splendidly in the exams Miss Stacy gave."

"Yes, but those exams didn't make me nervous. When I think of the real thing, you can't imagine what a horrid, cold, fluttery feeling comes around my heart. And then my number is thirteen, and Josie Pye says it's so unlucky. I am *not* superstitious, and I know it can make no difference. But still I wish it wasn't thirteen."

"I do wish I were going in with you," said Diana. "Wouldn't we have a perfectly elegant time? But I suppose you'll have to cram in the evenings."

"No. Miss Stacy has made us promise not to open a book at all. She says it would only tire and confuse us, and we are to go out walking and not think about the exams at all and go to bed early. It's good advice, but I expect it will be hard to follow; good advice is apt to be, I think. Prissy Andrews told me that she sat up half the night every night of her Entrance week and crammed for dear life; and I had determined to sit up *at least* as long as she did. It was so kind of your aunt Josephine to ask me to stay at Beechwood while I'm in town."

"You'll write to me while you're in, won't you?"

"I'll write Tuesday night and tell you how the first day goes," promised Anne.

"I'll be haunting the post office Wednesday," vowed Diana.

Anne went to town the following Monday, and on Wednesday Diana haunted the post office, as agreed, and got her letter.

> Dearest Diana, [wrote Anne]
>
> Here it is Tuesday night and I'm writing this in the library at Beechwood. Last night I was horribly lonesome all alone in my room and wished so much you were with me. I couldn't "cram" because I'd promised Miss Stacy not to, but it was as hard to keep from opening my history as it used to be to keep me from reading a story before my lessons were learned.
>
> This morning Miss Stacy came for me, and we went to the Academy, calling for Jane and Ruby and Josie on our way. Ruby asked me to feel her hands, and they were cold as ice. Josie said I looked as if I hadn't slept a wink, and she didn't believe I was strong enough to stand the grind of the teacher's course even if I did get through. There are times and seasons even yet when I don't feel that I've made any great headway in learning to like Josie Pye!
>
> When we reached the Academy, there were scores of students there from all over the Island. The first person we saw was Moody Spurgeon sitting on the steps and muttering away to himself. Jane asked him what on earth he was doing and he said he was repeating the multiplication table over and over to steady his nerves

and for pity's sake not to interrupt him, because if he stopped for a moment he got frightened and forgot everything he ever knew, but the multiplication table kept all his facts firmly in their proper place!

When we were assigned to our rooms, Miss Stacy had to leave us. Jane and I sat together, and Jane was so composed that I envied her. No need of the multiplication table for good, steady, sensible Jane! I wondered if I looked as I felt and if they could hear my heart thumping clear across the room. Then a man came in and began distributing the English examination sheets. My hands grew cold then, and my head fairly whirled around as I picked it up. Just one awful moment—Diana, I felt exactly as I did four years ago when I asked Marilla if I might stay at Green Gables—and then everything cleared up in my mind and my heart began beating again—I forgot to say that it had stopped altogether!—for I knew I could do something with *that* paper anyhow.

At noon we went home for dinner and then back again for history in the afternoon. The history was a pretty hard paper, and I got dreadfully mixed up in the dates. Still, I think I did fairly well today. But, oh, Diana, tomorrow the geometry exam comes off, and when I think of it, it takes every bit of determination I possess to keep from opening my Euclid. If I thought the multiplication table would help me any, I would recite it from now till tomorrow morning.

I went down to see the other girls this evening. On my way, I met Moody Spurgeon wandering distractedly around. He said he knew he had failed in history and he was born to be a disappointment to his parents and he was going home on the morning train; and it would be easier to be a carpenter than a minister anyhow. I cheered him up and persuaded him to stay to the end because it would be unfair to Miss Stacy if he didn't. Sometimes I have wished I was born a boy, but when I see Moody Spurgeon, I'm always glad I'm a girl and not his sister.

Ruby was in hysterics when I reached their boarding-house; she had just discovered a fearful mistake she had made in her English paper. When she recovered, we went uptown and had an ice cream. How we wished you had been with us!

Oh, Diana, if only the geometry examination were over! But there, as Mrs. Lynde would say, the sun will go on rising and setting whether I fail in geometry or not. That is true but not especially comforting. I think I'd rather it *didn't* go on if I failed!

Yours devotedly,
Anne

The geometry examination and all the others were over in due time, and Anne arrived home on Friday evening, rather tired but with an air of chastened triumph about her. Diana was over at Green Gables when she arrived, and they met as if they had been parted for years.

"You old darling, it's perfectly splendid to see you back again. It seems like an age since you went to town and, oh, Anne, how did you get along?"

"Pretty well, I think, in everything but the geometry. I don't know whether I passed in it or not, and I have a creepy, crawly presentiment that I didn't. Oh, how good it is to be back! Green Gables is the dearest, loveliest spot in the world."

"How did the others do?"

"The girls say they know they didn't pass, but I think they did pretty well. Josie says the geometry was so easy a child of ten could do it! Moody Spurgeon still thinks he failed in history, and Charlie says he failed in algebra. But we don't really know anything about it and won't until the pass list is out. That won't be for a fortnight. Fancy living a fortnight in such suspense! I wish I could go to sleep and never wake up until it is over."

Diana knew it would be useless to ask how Gilbert Blythe had fared, so she merely said, "Oh, you'll pass all right. Don't worry."

"I'd rather not pass at all than not come out pretty well up on the list," flashed Anne, by which she meant—and Diana knew she meant—that success would be incomplete and bitter if she did not come out ahead of Gilbert Blythe.

With this end in view, Anne had strained every nerve during the examinations. So had Gilbert. They had met and passed each other on the street a dozen times without any sign of recognition, and every time Anne had held her head a little higher and wished a little more earnestly that she had made friends with Gilbert when he asked her, and she vowed a little more determinedly to surpass him in the examination. She knew that all Avonlea junior[1] was wondering which would come out first; she even knew that Jimmy Glover and Ned Wright had a bet on the question and that Josie Pye had said there was no doubt in the world that Gilbert would be first; and she felt that her humiliation would be unbearable if she failed.

But she had another and nobler motive for wishing to do well. She wanted to "pass high" for the sake of Matthew and Marilla—especially Matthew. Matthew had declared to her his conviction that she "would beat the whole Island." That, Anne felt, was something it would be foolish to hope for even in the wildest dreams. But she did hope fervently that she would be among the first ten at least, so that she might see Matthew's kindly brown eyes gleam with pride in her achievement. That, she felt, would be a sweet reward indeed for all her hard work and patient grubbing among unimaginative equations and conjugations.

At the end of the fortnight, Anne took to "haunting" the post office also, in the distracted company of Jane, Ruby, and Josie, opening the Charlottetown dailies with shaking hands and cold, sinkaway feelings as bad as any experienced during the Entrance week. Charlie and Gilbert were not above doing this, too, but Moody Spurgeon stayed resolutely away.

"I haven't got the grit to go there and look at a paper in cold blood," he told Anne. "I'm just going to wait until somebody comes and tells me suddenly whether I've passed or not."

When three weeks had gone by without the pass list appearing, Anne began to feel that she really couldn't stand the strain much longer. Her appetite failed and her interest in Avonlea doings languished. Mrs. Lynde wanted to know what else you could expect with a Tory superintendent of education at the head of affairs, and Matthew, noting Anne's paleness and indifference and the lagging steps that bore her home from the post office every afternoon, began seriously to wonder if he hadn't better vote Grit at the next election.

But one evening the news came. Anne was sitting at her open window, for the time forgetful of the woes of examinations and the cares of the world as she drank in the beauty of the summer dusk, sweet-scented with flower breaths from the garden below and sibilant and rustling from the stir of poplars. The eastern sky above the firs was flushed faintly pink from the reflection of the west, and Anne was wondering dreamily if the spirit of colour looked like that, when she saw Diana come flying down

---

[1] Junior Avonlea.

through the firs, over the log bridge, and up the slope, with a fluttering newspaper in her hand.

Anne sprang to her feet, knowing at once what that paper contained. The pass list was out! Her head whirled and her heart beat until it hurt her. She could not move a step. It seemed an hour to her before Diana came rushing along the hall and burst into the room without even knocking, so great was her excitement.

"Anne, you've passed," she cried, "passed the *very first*—you and Gilbert both—you're ties—but your name is first. Oh, I'm so proud!"

Diana flung the paper on the table and herself on Anne's bed, utterly breathless and incapable of further speech. Anne lighted the lamp, oversetting the matchsafe[2] and using up half a dozen matches before her shaking hands could accomplish the task. Then she snatched up the paper. Yes, she had passed—there was her name at the very top of a list of two hundred! That moment was worth living for.

"You did just splendidly, Anne," puffed Diana, recovering sufficiently to sit up and speak, for Anne, starry-eyed and rapt, had not uttered a word. "Father brought the paper home from Bright River not ten minutes ago—it came out on the afternoon train, you know, and won't be here till tomorrow by mail—and when I saw the pass list, I just rushed over like a wild thing. You've all passed, every one of you, Moody Spurgeon and all, although he's conditioned in history. Jane and Ruby did pretty well—they're halfway up—and so did Charlie. Josie just scraped through with three marks to spare, but you'll see she'll put on as many airs as if she'd led. Won't Miss Stacy be delighted? Oh, Anne, what does it feel like to see your name at the head of a pass list like that? If it were me, I know I'd go crazy with joy. I am pretty near crazy as it is, but you're as calm and cool as a spring evening."

"I'm just dazzled inside," said Anne. "I want to say a hundred things, and I can't find words to say them in. I never dreamed of this—yes, I did, too, just once! I let myself think once, *What if I should come out first?* quakingly, you know, for it seemed so vain and presumptuous to think I could lead the Island. Excuse me a minute, Diana. I must run right out to the field to tell Matthew. Then we'll go up the road and tell the good news to the others."

They hurried to the hayfield below the barn where Matthew was coiling hay, and, as luck would have it, Mrs. Lynde was talking to Marilla at the lane fence.

"Oh, Matthew," exclaimed Anne, "I've passed and I'm first—or one of the first! I'm not vain, but I'm thankful."

---

2 Match container.

"Well now, I always said it," said Matthew, gazing at the pass list delightedly. "I knew you could beat them all easy."

"You've done pretty well, I must say, Anne," said Marilla, trying to hide her extreme pride in Anne from Mrs. Rachel's critical eye.

But that good soul said heartily, "I just guess she has done well, and far be it from me to be backwards in saying it. You're a credit to your friends, Anne, that's what, and we're all proud of you."

That night Anne, who had wound up a delightful evening by a serious little talk with Mrs. Allan at the manse, knelt sweetly by her open window in a great sheen of moonshine and murmured a prayer of gratitude and aspiration that came straight from her heart. There was in it thankfulness for the past and reverent petition for the future; and when she slept on her white pillow, her dreams were as fair and bright and beautiful as maidenhood might desire.

Chapter 33

THE HOTEL CONCERT

"Put on your white organdy, by all means, Anne," advised Diana decidedly. They were together in the east gable chamber; outside it was only twilight—a lovely yellowish green twilight with a clear blue, cloudless sky. A big, round moon, slowly deepening from its pallid luster into burnished silver, hung over the Haunted Wood; the air was full of sweet summer sounds—sleepy birds twittering, freakish breezes, faraway voices and laughter. But in Anne's room the blind was drawn and the lamp lighted, for an important toilet[1] was being made.

The east gable was a very different place from what it had been on that night four years before, when Anne had felt its bareness penetrate to the marrow of her spirit with its inhospitable chill. Changes had crept in, Marilla conniving at them resignedly, until it was as sweet and dainty a nest as a young girl could desire.

The velvet carpet with the pink roses and the pink silk curtains of Anne's early visions had certainly never materialized; but her dreams had kept pace with her growth, and it is not probable she lamented them. The floor was covered with a pretty matting, and the curtains that softened the high window and fluttered in the vagrant breezes were of pale green art muslin. The walls, hung not with gold and silver brocade tapestry, but with a dainty apple blossom paper, were adorned with a few good pictures given Anne by Mrs. Allan. Miss Stacy's photograph occupied the place of honour, and Anne made a sentimental point of keeping fresh flowers on the bracket under it. Tonight a spike of white lilies faintly perfumed the room like the dream of a fragrance. There was no "mahogany furniture," but there was a white-painted bookcase filled with books; a cushioned wicker rocker; a toilet table befrilled with white muslin; a quaint, gilt-framed mirror, with chubby pink cupids and purple grapes painted over its arched top, that used to hang in the spare room; and a low white bed.

---

[1] Toilette.

218

Anne was dressing for a concert at the White Sands Hotel. The guests had got it up in aid of the Charlottetown hospital and had hunted out all the available amateur talent in the surrounding districts to help it along. Bertha Sampson and Pearl Clay of the White Sands Baptist Choir had been asked to sing a duet; Milton Clark of Newbridge was to give a violin solo; Winnie Adella Blair of Carmody was to sing a Scotch ballad; and Laura Spencer of Spencervale and Anne Shirley of Avonlea were to recite.

As Anne would have said at one time, it was "an epoch in her life," and she was deliciously athrill with the excitement of it. Matthew was in the seventh heaven of gratified pride over the honour conferred on his Anne, and Marilla was not far behind, although she would have died rather than admit it and said she didn't think it was very proper for a lot of young folks to be gadding over to the hotel without any responsible person with them.

Anne and Diana were to drive over with Jane Andrews and her brother Billy in their double-seated buggy; and several other Avonlea girls and boys were going, too. There was a party of visitors expected out from town, and after the concert, a supper was to be given to the performers.

"Do you really think the organdy will be best?" queried Anne anxiously. "I don't think it's as pretty as my blue-flowered muslin—and it certainly isn't so fashionable."

"But it suits you ever so much better," said Diana. "It's so soft and frilly and clinging. The muslin is stiff and makes you look too dressed up. But the organdy seems as if it grew on you."

Anne sighed and yielded. Diana was beginning to have a reputation for notable taste in dressing, and her advice on such subjects was much sought after. She was looking very pretty herself on this particular night, in a dress of the lovely wild-rose pink from which Anne was forever debarred; but she was not to take any part in the concert, so her appearance was of minor importance. All her pains were bestowed upon Anne, who, she vowed, must, for the credit of Avonlea, be dressed and combed and adorned to the queen's taste.

"Pull out that frill a little more—so; here, let me tie your sash; now for your slippers. I'm going to braid your hair in two thick braids and tie them halfway up with big white bows—no, don't pull out a single curl over your forehead—just have the soft part. There is no way you do your hair that suits you so well, Anne, and Mrs. Allan says you look like a Madonna when you part it so. I shall fasten this little white house rose just behind your ear. There was just one on my bush, and I saved it for you."

"Shall I put my pearl beads on?" asked Anne. "Matthew brought me a string from town last week, and I know he'd like to see them on me."

Diana pursed up her lips, put her black head on one side critically, and finally pronounced in favour of the beads, which were thereupon tied around Anne's slim, milk-white throat.

"There's something so stylish about you, Anne," said Diana with unenvious admiration. "You hold your head with such an air. I suppose it's your figure. I am just a dumpling. I've always been afraid of it, and now I know it is so. Well, I suppose I shall just have to resign myself to it."

"But you have such dimples," said Anne, smiling affectionately into the pretty, vivacious face so near her own. "Lovely dimples, like little dents in cream. I have given up all hope of dimples. My dimple dream will never come true; but so many of my dreams have that I mustn't complain. Am I all ready now?"

"All ready," assured Diana as Marilla appeared in the doorway, a gaunt figure with grayer hair than of yore and no fewer angles, but with a much softer face. "Come right in and look at our elocutionist, Marilla. Doesn't she look lovely?"

Marilla emitted a sound between a sniff and a grunt.

"She looks neat and proper. I like that way of fixing her hair. But I expect she'll ruin that dress driving over there in the dust and dew with it, and it looks most too thin for these damp nights. Organdy's the most unserviceable stuff in the world anyhow, and I told Matthew so when he got it. But there is no use in saying anything to Matthew nowadays. Time was when he would take my advice, but now he just buys things for Anne regardless, and the clerks at Carmody know they can palm anything off on him. Just let them tell him a thing is pretty and fashionable, and Matthew plunks his money down for it. Mind you keep your skirt clear of the wheel, Anne, and put your warm jacket on."

Then Marilla stalked downstairs, thinking proudly how sweet Anne looked, with that "one moonbeam from the forehead to the crown," and regretting that she could not go to the concert herself to hear her girl recite.

"I wonder if it *is* too damp for my dress," said Anne anxiously.

"Not a bit of it," said Diana, pulling up the window blind. "It's a perfect night, and there won't be any dew. Look at the moonlight."

"I'm so glad my window looks east into the sun rising," said Anne, going over to Diana. "It's so splendid to see the morning coming up over those long hills and glowing through those sharp fir tops. It's new every morning, and I feel as if I washed my very soul in that bath of earliest sunshine. Oh, Diana, I love this little room so dearly. I don't know how I'll get along without it when I go to town next month."

"Don't speak of your going away tonight," begged Diana. "I don't want to think of it, it makes me so miserable, and I do want to have a good time this evening. What are you going to recite, Anne? And are you nervous?"

"Not a bit. I've recited so often in public I don't mind at all now. I've decided to give 'The Maiden's Vow.' It's so pathetic. Laura Spencer is going to give a comic recitation, but I'd rather make people cry than laugh."

"What will you recite if they encore you?"

"They won't dream of encoring me," scoffed Anne, who was not without her own secret hopes that they would and already visioned herself telling Matthew all about it at the next morning's breakfast table. "There are Billy and Jane now—I hear the wheels. Come on."

Billy Andrews insisted that Anne should ride on the front seat with him, so she unwillingly climbed up. She would have much preferred to sit back with the girls, where she could have laughed and chattered to her heart's content. There was not much of either laughter or chatter in Billy. He was a big, fat, stolid youth of twenty, with a round, expressionless face and a painful lack of conversational gifts. But he admired Anne immensely and was puffed up with pride over the prospect of driving to White Sands with that slim, upright figure beside him.

Anne, by dint of talking over her shoulder to the girls and occasionally passing a sop of civility to Billy—who grinned and chuckled and never could think of any reply until it was too late—contrived to enjoy the drive in spite of all. It was a night for enjoyment. The road was full of buggies, all bound for the hotel; and laughter, silver-clear, echoed and reechoed along it. When they reached the hotel, it was a blaze of light from top to bottom. They were met by the ladies of the concert committee, one of whom took Anne off to the performers' dressing room, which was filled with the members of a Charlottetown Symphony Club, among whom Anne felt suddenly shy and frightened and countrified. Her dress, which, in the east gable, had seemed so dainty and pretty, now seemed simple and plain—too simple and plain, she thought, among all the silks and laces that glistened and rustled around her. What were her pearl beads compared to the diamonds of the big, handsome lady near her? And how poor her one wee white rose must look beside all the hothouse flowers the others wore! Anne laid her hat and jacket away and shrank miserably into a corner. She wished herself back into the white room at Green Gables.

It was still worse on the platform of the big concert hall of the hotel, where she presently found herself. The electric lights dazzled her eyes, the perfume and hum bewildered her. She wished she were sitting down in the audience with Diana and Jane, who seemed to be having a splendid time away at the back. She was wedged in between a stout lady in pink silk and a tall, scornful-looking girl in a white lace dress. The stout lady occasionally turned her head squarely around and surveyed Anne through her eyeglasses until Anne, acutely sensitive of being so scrutinized, felt that she must scream aloud; and the white lace girl kept talking audibly to her next neighbour about the "country bumpkins" and "rustic belles" in the audience, languidly anticipating "such fun" from the displays of local talent on the programme. Anne believed that she would hate that white lace girl to the end of life.

Unfortunately for Anne, a professional elocutionist was staying at the hotel and had consented to recite. She was a lithe, dark-eyed woman in a wonderful gown of shimmering gray stuff like woven moonbeams, with gems on her neck and in her dark hair. She had a marvelously flexible voice and wonderful power of expression; the audience went wild over her selection. Anne, forgetting all about herself and her troubles for the time, listened with rapt and shining eyes; but when the recitation ended, she suddenly put her hands over her face. She could never get up and recite after that—never. Had she ever thought she could recite? Oh, if she were only back at Green Gables!

At this unpropitious moment, her name was called. Somehow, Anne—who did not notice the rather guilty little start of surprise the white lace girl gave and would not have understood the subtle compliment implied therein if she had—got on her feet and moved dizzily out to the front. She was so pale that Diana and Jane, down in the audience, clasped each other's hands in nervous sympathy.

Anne was the victim of an overwhelming attack of stage fright. Often as she had recited in public, she had never before faced such an audience as this, and the sight of it paralyzed her energies completely. Everything was so strange, so brilliant, so bewildering—the rows of ladies in evening dress, the critical faces, the whole atmosphere of wealth and culture about her. Very different from this the plain benches at the Debating Club, filled with the homely, sympathetic faces of friends and neighbours. These people, she thought, would be merciless critics. Perhaps, like the white lace girl, they anticipated amusement from her "rustic" efforts. She felt hopelessly, helplessly ashamed and miserable. Her knees trembled, her heart fluttered, a horrible faintness came over her; not a word could she utter, and the next moment she would have fled from the platform despite the humiliation that, she felt, must ever after be her portion if she did so.

But suddenly, as her dilated, frightened eyes gazed out over the audience, she saw Gilbert Blythe away at the back of the room, bending forward with a smile on his face—a smile that seemed to Anne at once triumphant and taunting. In reality, it was nothing of the kind. Gilbert was merely smiling with appreciation of the whole affair in general and of the effect produced by Anne's slender white form and spiritual face against a background of palms in particular. Josie Pye, whom he had driven over, sat beside him, and her face certainly was both triumphant and taunting. But Anne did not see Josie and would not have cared if she had. She drew a long breath and flung her head up proudly, courage and determination tingling over her like an electric shock. She *would not* fail before Gilbert Blythe—he should never be able to laugh at her, never, never! Her fright and nervousness vanished, and she began her recitation, her clear, sweet voice reaching to the farthest corner of the room without a tremor or a break. Self-possession was fully restored to her, and in the reaction from that horrible moment of powerlessness, she recited as she had never done before. When she finished, there were bursts of honest applause. Anne, stepping back to her seat, blushing with shyness and delight, found her hand vigorously clasped and shaken by the stout lady in pink silk.

"My dear, you did splendidly," she puffed. "I've been crying like a baby, actually I have. There, they're encoring you—they're bound to have you back!"

"Oh, I can't go," said Anne confusedly. "But yet—I must or Matthew will be disappointed. He said they would encore me."

"Then don't disappoint Matthew," said the pink lady, laughing.

Smiling, blushing, limpid-eyed, Anne tripped back and gave a quaint, funny little selection that captivated her audience still further. The rest of the evening was quite a little triumph for her.

When the concert was over, the stout pink lady—who was the wife of an American millionaire—took her under her wing and introduced her to everybody; and everybody was very nice to her. The professional elocutionist, Mrs. Evans, came and chatted with her, telling her that she had a charming voice and "interpreted" her selections beautifully. Even the white lace girl paid her a languid little compliment. They had supper in the big, beautifully decorated dining room; Diana and Jane were invited to partake of this also, since they had come with Anne, but Billy was nowhere to be found, having decamped in mortal fear of some such invitation. He was in waiting for them, with the team, however, when it was all over, and the three girls came merrily out into the calm, white moonshine radiance. Anne breathed deeply and looked into the clear sky beyond the dark boughs of the firs.

Oh, it was good to be out again in the purity and silence of the night! How great and still and wonderful everything was, with the murmur of the sea sounding through it and the darkling cliffs beyond like grim giants guarding enchanted coasts.

"Hasn't it been a perfectly splendid time?" sighed Jane as they drove away. "I just wish I was a rich American and could spend my summer at a hotel and wear jewels and low-necked dresses and have ice cream and chicken salad every blessed day. I'm sure it would be ever so much more fun than teaching school. Anne, your recitation was simply great, although I thought at first you were never going to begin. I think it was better than Mrs. Evans'."

"Oh, no, don't say things like that, Jane," said Anne quickly, "because it sounds silly. It couldn't be better than Mrs. Evans', you know, for she is a professional, and I'm only a schoolgirl with a little knack of reciting. I'm quite satisfied if the people just liked mine pretty well."

"I've a compliment for you, Anne," said Diana. "At least I think it must be a compliment because of the tone he said it in. Part of it was, anyhow. There was an American sitting behind Jane and me—such a romantic-looking man, with coal black hair and eyes. Josie Pye says he is a distinguished artist and that her mother's cousin in Boston is married to a man that used to go to school with him. Well, we heard him say—didn't we, Jane?—'Who is that girl on the platform with the splendid Titian hair? She has a face I should like to paint.' There now, Anne. But what does 'Titian hair' mean?"

"Being interpreted, it means plain red, I guess," laughed Anne. "Titian was a very famous artist who liked to paint red-haired women."

"*Did* you see all the diamonds those ladies wore?" sighed Jane. "They were simply dazzling. Wouldn't you just love to be rich, girls?"

"We *are* rich," said Anne stanchly. "Why, we have sixteen years to our credit, and we're happy as queens, and we've all got imaginations, more or less. Look at that sea, girls—all silver and shadow and vision of things not seen. We couldn't enjoy its loveliness any more if we had millions of dollars and ropes of diamonds. You wouldn't change into any of those women if you could. Would you want to be that white lace girl and wear a sour look all your life, as if you'd been born turning up your nose at the world? Or the pink lady, kind and nice as she is, so stout and short that you'd really no figure at all? Or even Mrs. Evans, with that sad, sad look in her eyes? She must have been dreadfully unhappy sometime to have such a look. You *know* you wouldn't, Jane Andrews!"

"I *don't* know—exactly," said Jane, unconvinced. "I think diamonds would comfort a person for a good deal."

"Well, I don't want to be anyone but myself, even if I go uncomforted by diamonds all my life," declared Anne. "I'm quite content to be Anne of Green Gables, with my string of pearl beads. I know Matthew gave me as much love with them as ever went with Madame the Pink Lady's jewels."

Chapter 34

A QUEEN'S GIRL

The next three weeks were busy ones at Green Gables, for Anne was getting ready to go to Queen's, and there was much sewing to be done and many things to be talked over and arranged. Anne's outfit was ample and pretty, for Matthew saw to that, and Marilla for once made no objections whatever to anything he purchased or suggested. Moreover, one evening she went up to the east gable with her arms full of a delicate pale green material.

"Anne, here's something for a nice light dress for you. I don't suppose you really need it, you've plenty of pretty waists; but I thought maybe you'd like something real dressy to wear if you were asked out anywhere of an evening in town, to a party or anything like that. I hear that Jane and Ruby and Josie have got 'evening dresses,' as they call them, and I don't mean you shall be behind them. I got Mrs. Allan to help me pick it in town last week, and we'll get Emily Gillis to make it for you. Emily has got taste, and her fits aren't to be equaled."

"Oh, Marilla, it's just lovely," said Anne. "Thank you so much. I don't believe you ought to be so kind to me—it's making it harder every day for me to go away."

The green dress was made up with as many tucks and frills and shirrings as Emily's taste permitted. Anne put it on one evening for Matthew's and Marilla's benefit and recited "The Maiden's Vow" for them in the kitchen. As Marilla watched the bright, animated face and graceful motions, her thoughts went back to the evening Anne had arrived at Green Gables, and memory recalled a vivid picture of the odd, frightened child in her preposterous yellowish brown wincey dress, the heartbreak looking out of her tearful eyes. Something in the memory brought tears to Marilla's own eyes.

"I declare, my recitation has made you cry, Marilla," said Anne gaily, stooping over Marilla's chair to drop a butterfly kiss on that lady's cheek. "Now, I call that a positive triumph."

"No, I wasn't crying over your piece," said Marilla, who would have scorned to be betrayed into such weakness by any "poetry stuff." "I just couldn't help thinking of the little girl you used to be, Anne. And I was wishing you could have stayed a little girl, even with all your strange ways. You've grown up now and you're going away; and you look so tall and stylish and so—so—different altogether in that dress—as if you didn't belong in Avonlea at all—and I just got lonesome thinking it all over."

"Marilla!" Anne sat down on Marilla's gingham lap, took Marilla's lined face between her hands, and looked gravely and tenderly into Marilla's eyes. "I'm not a bit changed—not really. I'm only just pruned down and branched out. The real *me*—back here—is just the same. It won't make a bit of difference where I go or how much I change outwardly; at heart I shall always be your little Anne, who will love you and Matthew and dear Green Gables more and better every day of her life."

Anne laid her fresh young cheek against Marilla's faded one and reached out a hand to pat Matthew's shoulder. Marilla would have given much just then to have possessed Anne's power of putting her feelings into words; but nature and habit had willed it otherwise, and she could only put her arms close about her girl and hold her tenderly to her heart, wishing that she need never let her go.

Matthew, with a suspicious moisture in his eyes, got up and went out-of-doors. Under the stars of the blue summer night, he walked agitatedly across the yard to the gate under the poplars.

"Well now, I guess she ain't been much spoiled," he muttered proudly. "I guess my putting in my oar occasional never did much harm after all. She's smart and pretty and loving, too, which is better than all the rest. She's been a blessing to us, and there never was a luckier mistake than what Mrs. Spencer made—if it *was* luck. I don't believe it was any such thing. It was Providence, because the Almighty saw we needed her, I reckon."

The day finally came when Anne must go to town. She and Matthew drove in one fine September morning, after a tearful parting with Diana and an untearful, practical one—on Marilla's side at least—with Marilla. But when Anne had gone, Diana dried her tears and went to a beach picnic at White Sands with some of her Carmody cousins, where she contrived to enjoy herself tolerably well; while Marilla plunged fiercely into unnecessary work and kept at it all day long with the bitterest kind of a heartache—the ache that burns and gnaws and cannot wash itself away in ready tears. But that night, when Marilla went to bed, acutely and miserably conscious that the little gable room at the end of the hall was untenanted by any vivid young life and unstirred by any soft breathing, she buried her face in her pillow and wept for her girl in a passion of sobs that appalled her when she grew calm enough to reflect how very wicked it must be to take on so about a sinful fellow creature.

Anne and the rest of the Avonlea scholars reached town just in time to hurry off to the Academy. That first day passed pleasantly enough in a whirl of excitement, meeting all the new students, learning to know the professors by sight, and being assorted and organized into classes. Anne intended taking up the Second Year work, being advised to do so by Miss Stacy; Gilbert Blythe elected to do the same. This meant getting a First Class teacher's license in one year instead of two, if they were successful; but it also meant much more and harder work. Jane, Ruby, Josie, Charlie, and Moody Spurgeon, not being troubled with the stirrings of ambition, were content to take up the Second Class work. Anne was conscious of a pang of loneliness when she found herself in a room with fifty other students, not one of whom she knew, except the tall, brown-haired boy across the room; and knowing him in the fashion she did, did not help her much, as she reflected pessimistically. Yet she was undeniably glad that they were in the same class; the old rivalry could still be carried on, and Anne would hardly have known what to do if it had been lacking.

I wouldn't feel comfortable without it, she thought. *Gilbert looks awfully determined. I suppose he's making up his mind, here and now, to win the medal. What a splendid chin he has! I never noticed it before. I do wish Jane and Ruby had gone in for First Class, too. I suppose I won't feel so much like a cat in a strange garret when I get acquainted, though. I wonder which of the girls here are going to be my friends. It's really an interesting speculation. Of course I promised Diana that no Queen's girl, no matter how much I liked her, should ever be as dear to me as she is; but I've lots of second-best affections to bestow. I like the look of that girl with the brown eyes and the crimson waist. She looks vivid and red-rosy; there's that pale, fair one gazing out of the window. She has lovely hair and looks as if she knew a thing or two about dreams. I'd like to know them both—know them well—well enough to walk with my arm about their waists and call them nicknames. But just now I don't know them and they don't know me, and they probably don't want to know me particularly. Oh, it's lonesome!*

It was lonesomer still when Anne found herself alone in her hall bedroom that night at twilight. She was not to board with the other girls, who all had relatives in town to take pity on them. Miss Josephine Barry would have liked to board her, but Beechwood was so far from the

Academy that it was out of the question; so Miss Barry hunted up a boardinghouse, assuring Matthew and Marilla that it was the very place for Anne.

"The lady who keeps it is a reduced gentlewoman," explained Miss Barry. "Her husband was a British officer, and she is very careful what sort of boarders she takes. Anne will not meet with any objectionable persons under her roof. The table is good, and the house is near the Academy, in a quiet neighbourhood."

All this might be quite true, and indeed, proved to be so, but it did not materially help Anne in the first agony of homesickness that seized upon her. She looked dismally about her narrow little room, with its dull-papered, pictureless walls, its small iron bedstead and empty bookcase; and a horrible choke came into her throat as she thought of her own white room at Green Gables, where she would have the pleasant consciousness of a great green, still outdoors, of sweetpeas growing in the garden, and moonlight falling on the orchard; of the brook below the slope and the spruce boughs tossing in the night wind beyond it; of a vast starry sky and the light from Diana's window shining out through the gap in the trees. Here there was nothing of this; Anne knew that outside of her window was a hard street, with a network of telephone wires shutting out the sky, the tramp of alien feet, and a thousand lights gleaming on stranger faces. She knew that she was going to cry and fought against it.

"I *won't* cry. It's silly—and weak—there's the third tear splashing down by my nose. There are more coming! I must think of something funny to stop them. But there's nothing funny except what is connected with Avonlea, and that only makes things worse—four—five—I'm going home next Friday, but that seems a hundred years away. Oh, Matthew is nearly home by now—and Marilla is at the gate, looking down the lane for him—six—seven—eight—oh, there's no use in counting them! They're coming in a flood presently. I can't cheer up—I don't *want* to cheer up. It's nicer to be miserable!"

The flood of tears would have come, no doubt, had not Josie Pye appeared at that moment. In the joy of seeing a familiar face, Anne forgot that there had never been much love lost between her and Josie. As a part of Avonlea life, even a Pye was welcome.

"I'm so glad you came up," Anne said sincerely.

"You've been crying," remarked Josie with aggravating pity. "I suppose you're homesick—some people have so little self-control in that respect. I've no intention of being homesick, I can tell you. Town's too jolly after that poky old Avonlea. I wonder how I ever existed there so long. You shouldn't cry, Anne; it isn't becoming, for your nose and eyes get red, and then you seem *all* red. I'd a perfectly scrumptious time in the Academy today. Our French professor is simply a duck. His moustache would give you kerwollops of the heart. Have you anything eatable around, Anne? I'm literally starving. Ah, I guessed likely Marilla'd load you up with cake. That's why I called around. Otherwise I'd have gone to the park to hear the band play with Frank Stockley. He boards same place as I do, and he's a sport. He noticed you in class today and asked me who the redheaded girl was. I told him you were an orphan that the Cuthberts had adopted and nobody knew very much about what you'd been before that."

Anne was wondering if, after all, solitude and tears were not more satisfactory than Josie Pye's companionship when Jane and Ruby appeared, each with an inch of Queen's colour ribbon—purple and scarlet—pinned proudly to her coat. As Josie was not "speaking" to Jane just then, she had to subside into comparative harmlessness.

"Well," said Jane with a sigh, "I feel as if I'd lived many moons since the morning. I ought to be home studying my Virgil—that horrid old professor gave us twenty lines to start in on tomorrow. But I simply couldn't settle down to study tonight. Anne, methinks I see the traces of tears. If you've been crying, *do* own up. It will restore my self-respect, for I was shedding tears freely before Ruby came along. I don't mind being a goose so much if somebody else is goosey, too. Cake? You'll give me a teeny piece, won't you? Thank you. It has the real Avonlea flavour."

Ruby, perceiving the Queen's calendar lying on the table, wanted to know if Anne meant to try for the gold medal.

Anne blushed and admitted she was thinking of it.

"Oh, that reminds me," said Josie, "Queen's is to get one of the Avery scholarships after all. The word came today. Frank Stockley told me—his uncle is one of the board of governors, you know. It will be announced in the Academy tomorrow."

An Avery scholarship! Anne felt her heart beat more quickly, and the horizons of her ambition shifted and broadened as if by magic. Before Josie had told the news, Anne's highest pinnacle of aspiration had been a teacher's provincial license, Class First, at the end of the year, and perhaps the medal! But now in one moment Anne saw herself winning the Avery scholarship, taking an arts course at Redmond College, and graduating in a gown and mortarboard, all before the echo of Josie's words had died away. For the Avery scholarship was in English, and Anne felt that here her foot was on her native heath.

A wealthy manufacturer of New Brunswick had died and left part of his fortune to endow a large number of scholarships to be distributed among the various high schools and academies of the Maritime Provinces, according to their respective standings. There had been much doubt whether one would be allotted to Queen's, but the matter was settled at last, and at the end of the year the graduate who made the highest mark in English and English literature would win the scholarship—two hundred and fifty dollars a year for four years at Redmond College. No wonder that Anne went to bed that night with tingling cheeks!

"I'll win that scholarship if hard work can do it," she resolved. "Wouldn't Matthew be proud if I got to be a B.A.? Oh, it's delightful to have ambitions. I'm so glad I have such a lot. And there never seems to be any end to them—that's the best of it. Just as soon as you attain to one ambition, you see another one glittering higher up still. It does make life so interesting."

Chapter 35

THE WINTER AT QUEEN'S

Anne's homesickness wore off, greatly helped in the wearing by her weekend visits home. As long as the open weather lasted, the Avonlea students went out to Carmody on the new branch railway every Friday night. Diana and several other Avonlea young folks were generally on hand to meet them, and they all walked over to Avonlea in a merry party. Anne thought those Friday evening gypsyings over the autumnal hills in the crisp golden air, with the home lights of Avonlea twinkling beyond, were the best and dearest hours in the whole week.

Gilbert Blythe nearly always walked with Ruby Gillis and carried her satchel for her. Ruby was a very handsome young lady, now thinking herself quite as grown up as she really was; she wore her skirts as long as her mother would let her and did her hair up in town, though she had to take it down when she went home. She had large, bright-blue eyes, a brilliant complexion, and a plump, showy figure. She laughed a great deal, was cheerful and good-tempered, and enjoyed the pleasant things of life frankly.

"But I shouldn't think she was the sort of girl Gilbert would like," whispered Jane to Anne.

Anne did not think so either, but she would not have said so for[1] the Avery scholarship. She could not help thinking, too, that it would be very pleasant to have such a friend as Gilbert to jest and chatter with and exchange ideas about books and studies and ambitions. Gilbert had ambitions, she knew, and Ruby Gillis did not seem the sort of person with whom such could be profitably discussed.

There was no silly sentiment in Anne's ideas concerning Gilbert. Boys were to her, when she thought about them at all, merely possible good comrades. If she and Gilbert had been friends, she would not have cared how many other friends he had nor with whom he walked. She had a genius for friendship; girlfriends she had in plenty; but she had a vague

---

[1] Even for.

consciousness that masculine friendship might also be a good thing to round out one's conceptions of companionship and furnish broader standpoints of judgement and comparison. Not that Anne could have put her feelings on the matter into just such clear definition. But she thought that if Gilbert had ever walked home with her from the train, over the crisp fields and along the ferny byways, they might have had many merry and interesting conversations about the new world that was opening around them and their hopes and ambitions therein. Gilbert was a clever young fellow, with his own thoughts about things and a determination to get the best out of life and put the best into it. Ruby Gillis told Jane Andrews that she didn't understand half the things Gilbert Blythe said; he talked just like Anne Shirley did when she had a thoughtful fit on, and for her part, she didn't think it any fun to be bothering about books and that sort of thing when you didn't have to. Frank Stockley had lots more dash and go, but then he wasn't half as good-looking as Gilbert, and she really couldn't decide which she liked best!

In the Academy, Anne gradually drew a little circle of friends about her—thoughtful, imaginative, ambitious students like herself. With the "rose-red girl," Stella Maynard, and the "dream girl," Priscilla Grant, she soon became intimate, finding the latter pale, spiritual-looking maiden to be full to the brim of mischief and pranks and fun, while the vivid, black-eyed Stella had a heart full of wistful dreams and fancies as aerial and rainbowlike as Anne's own.

After the Christmas holidays, the Avonlea students gave up going home on Fridays and settled down to hard work. By this time, all the Queen's scholars had gravitated into their own places in the ranks and the various classes had assumed distinct and settled shadings of individuality. Certain facts had become generally accepted. It was admitted that the medal contestants had practically narrowed down to three—Gilbert Blythe, Anne Shirley, and Lewis Wilson; the Avery scholarship was more doubtful, any one of a certain six being a possible winner. The bronze medal for mathematics was considered as good as won by a fat, funny, little upcountry boy with a bumpy forehead and a patched coat.

Ruby Gillis was the handsomest girl of the year at the Academy; in the Second Year classes, Stella Maynard carried off the palm for beauty, with a small but critical minority in favour of Anne Shirley. Ethel Marr was admitted by all competent judges to have the most stylish modes of hairdressing, and Jane Andrews—plain, plodding, conscientious Jane—carried off the honours in the domestic science course. Even Josie Pye attained a certain preeminence as the sharpest-tongued young lady in attendance at Queen's. So it may be fairly stated that Miss Stacy's old pupils held their own in the wider arena of the academical course.

Anne worked hard and steadily. Her rivalry with Gilbert was as intense as it had ever been in Avonlea school, although it was not known in the class at large, but somehow the bitterness had gone out of it. Anne no longer wished to win for the sake of defeating Gilbert; rather, for the proud consciousness of a well-won victory over a worthy foeman. It would be worthwhile to win, but she no longer thought life would be insupportable if she did not.

In spite of lessons, the students found opportunities for pleasant times. Anne spent many of her spare hours at Beechwood and generally ate her Sunday dinners there and went to church with Miss Barry. The latter was, as she admitted, growing old, but her black eyes were not dim nor the vigour of her tongue in the least abated. But she never sharpened the latter on Anne, who continued to be a prime favourite with the critical old lady.

"That Anne-girl improves all the time," she said. "I get tired of other girls—there is such a provoking and eternal sameness about them. Anne has as many shades as a rainbow and every shade is the prettiest while it lasts. I don't know that she is as amusing as she was when she was a child, but she makes me love her and I like people who make me love them. It saves me so much trouble in making myself love them."

Then, almost before anybody realized it, spring had come. Out in Avonlea, the mayflowers were peeping pinkly out on the sere barrens where snow wreaths lingered, and the "mist of green" was on the woods and in the valleys. But in Charlottetown, harassed Queen's students thought and talked only of examinations.

"It doesn't seem possible that the term is nearly over," said Anne. "Why, last fall it seemed so long to look forward to—a whole winter of studies and classes. And here we are, with the exams looming up next week. Girls, sometimes I feel as if those exams meant everything, but when I look at the big buds swelling on those chestnut trees and the misty blue air at the end of the streets, they don't seem half so important."

Jane and Ruby and Josie, who had dropped in, did not take this view of it. To them the coming examinations were constantly very important indeed—far more important than chestnut buds or Maytime hazes. It was all very well for Anne, who was sure of passing at least, to have her moments of belittling them, but when your whole future depended on them—as the girls truly thought theirs did—you could not regard them philosophically.

"I've lost seven pounds in the last two weeks," sighed Jane. "It's no use to say don't worry. I *will* worry. Worrying helps you some—it seems as if you were doing something when you're worrying. It would be dreadful if I failed to get my license after going to Queen's all winter and spending so much money."

"I don't care," said Josie Pye. "If I don't pass this year, I'm coming back next. My father can afford to send me. Anne, Frank Stockley says that Professor Tremaine said Gilbert Blythe was sure to get the medal and that Emily Clay would likely win the Avery scholarship."

"That may make me feel bad tomorrow, Josie," laughed Anne, "but just now I honestly feel that as long as I know the violets are coming out all purple down in the hollow below Green Gables and that little ferns are poking their heads up in Lover's Lane, it's not a great deal of difference whether I win the Avery or not. I've done my best and I begin to understand what is meant by the 'joy of the strife.' Next to trying and winning, the best thing is trying and failing. Girls, don't talk about exams! Look at that arch of pale green sky over those houses and picture to yourselves what it must look like over the purply-dark beech woods back of Avonlea."

"What are you going to wear for commencement, Jane?" asked Ruby practically.

Jane and Josie both answered at once, and the chatter drifted into a side eddy of fashions. But Anne, with her elbows on the windowsill, her soft cheek laid against her clasped hands, and her eyes filled with visions, looked out unheedingly across city roof and spire to that glorious dome of sunset sky and wove her dreams of a possible future from the golden tissue of youth's own optimism. All the Beyond was hers with its possibilities lurking rosily in the oncoming years—each year a rose of promise to be woven into an immortal chaplet.

Chapter 36

THE GLORY AND THE DREAM

On the morning when the final results of all the examinations were to be posted on the bulletin board at Queen's, Anne and Jane walked down the street together. Jane was smiling and happy; examinations were over and she was comfortably sure she had made a pass at least; further considerations troubled Jane not at all; she had no soaring ambitions and consequently was not affected with the unrest attendant thereon. For we pay a price for everything we get or take in this world; and although ambitions are well worth having, they are not to be cheaply won, but exact their dues of work and self-denial, anxiety and discouragement. Anne was pale and quiet; in ten more minutes she would know who had won the medal and who the Avery. Beyond those ten minutes there did not seem, just then, to be anything worth being called Time.

"Of course you'll win one of them anyhow," said Jane, who couldn't understand how the faculty could be so unfair as to order it otherwise.

"I have no hope of the Avery," said Anne. "Everybody says Emily Clay will win it. And I'm not going to march up to that bulletin board and look at it before everybody. I haven't the moral courage. I'm going straight to the girls' dressing room. You must read the announcements and then come and tell me, Jane. And I implore you in the name of our old friendship to do it as quickly as possible. If I have failed just say so, without trying to break it gently; and whatever you do *don't* sympathize with me. Promise me this, Jane."

Jane promised solemnly; but, as it happened, there was no necessity for such a promise. When they went up the entrance steps of Queen's, they found the hall full of boys who were carrying Gilbert Blythe around on their shoulders and yelling at the tops of their voices, "Hurrah for Blythe, Medalist!"

236

For a moment, Anne felt one sickening pang of defeat and disappointment. So she had failed and Gilbert had won! Well, Matthew would be sorry—he had been so sure she would win.

And then somebody called out: "Three cheers for Miss Shirley, winner of the Avery!"

"Oh, Anne," gasped Jane as they fled to the girls' dressing room amid hearty cheers. "Oh, Anne, I'm so proud! Isn't it splendid?"

And then the girls were around them, and Anne was the center of a laughing, congratulating group. Her shoulders were thumped and her hands shaken vigorously. She was pushed and pulled and hugged, and among it all she managed to whisper to Jane: "Oh, won't Matthew and Marilla be pleased! I must write the news home right away."

Commencement was the next important happening. The exercises were held in the big assembly hall of the Academy. Addresses were given, essays read, songs sung, the public award of diplomas, prizes, and medals made.

Matthew and Marilla were there, with eyes and ears only for one student on the platform—a tall girl in pale green, with faintly flushed cheeks and starry eyes, who read the best essay and was pointed out and whispered about as the Avery winner.

"Reckon you're glad we kept her, Marilla?" whispered Matthew, speaking for the first time since he had entered the hall, when Anne had finished her essay.

"It's not the first time I've been glad," retorted Marilla. "You do like to rub things in, Matthew Cuthbert."

Miss Barry, who was sitting behind them, leaned forward and poked Marilla in the back with her parasol.

"Aren't you proud of that Anne-girl? I am," she said.

Anne went home to Avonlea with Matthew and Marilla that evening. She had not been home since April, and she felt that she could not wait another day. The apple blossoms were out and the world was fresh and young. Diana was at Green Gables to meet her. In her own white room, where Marilla had set a flowering house rose on the windowsill, Anne looked about her and drew a long breath of happiness.

"Oh, Diana, it's so good to be back again. It's so good to see those pointed firs coming out against the pink sky—and that white orchard and the old Snow Queen. Isn't the breath of the mint delicious? And that tea rose—why it's a song and a hope and a prayer all in one. And it's *good* to see you again, Diana!"

"I thought you liked that Stella Maynard better than me," said Diana reproachfully. "Josie Pye told me you did. Josie said you were *infatuated* with her."

Anne laughed and pelted Diana with the faded "June lilies" of her bouquet.

"Stella Maynard is the dearest girl in the world except one and you are that one, Diana," she said. "I love you more than ever—and I've so many things to tell you. But just now I feel as if it were joy enough to sit here and look at you. I'm tired, I think—tired of being studious and ambitious. I mean to spend at least two hours tomorrow lying out in the orchard grass, thinking of absolutely nothing."

"You've done splendidly, Anne. I suppose you won't be teaching now that you've won the Avery?"

"No. I'm going to Redmond in September. Doesn't it seem wonderful? I'll have a brand-new stock of ambition laid in by that time after three glorious, golden months of vacation. Jane and Ruby are going to teach. Isn't it splendid to think we all got through, even to Moody Spurgeon and Josie Pye?"

"The Newbridge trustees have offered Jane their school already," said Diana. "Gilbert Blythe is going to teach, too. He has to. His father can't afford to send him to college next year after all, so he means to earn his own way through. I expect he'll get the school here if Miss Ames decides to leave."

Anne felt a strange little sensation of dismayed surprise. She had not known this; she had expected that Gilbert would be going to Redmond also. What would she do without their inspiring rivalry? Would not work, even at a coeducational college with a real degree in prospect, be rather flat without her friend the enemy?

The next morning at breakfast, it suddenly struck Anne that Matthew was not looking well. Surely, he was much grayer than he had been a year before.

"Marilla," she said hesitatingly when he had gone out, "is Matthew quite well?"

"No, he isn't," said Marilla in a troubled tone. "He's had some real bad spells with his heart this spring and he won't spare himself a mite. I've been real worried about him, but he's some better this while back and we've got a good hired man, so I'm hoping he'll kind of rest and pick up. Maybe he will now you're home. You always cheer him up."

Anne leaned across the table and took Marilla's face in her hands.

"You are not looking as well yourself as I'd like to see you, Marilla. You look tired. I'm afraid you've been working too hard. You must take a rest, now that I'm home. I'm just going to take this one day off to visit all the dear old spots and hunt up my old dreams, and then it will be your turn to be lazy while I do the work."

Marilla smiled affectionately at her girl.

"It's not the work—it's my head. I've a pain so often now—behind my eyes. Dr. Spencer's been fussing with glasses, but they don't do me any good. There is a distinguished oculist coming to the Island the last of June and the doctor says I must see him. I guess I'll have to. I can't read or sew with any comfort now. Well, Anne, you've done real well at Queen's, I must say. To take First Class license in one year and win the Avery scholarship—well, well, Mrs. Lynde says pride goes before a fall and she doesn't believe in the higher education of women at all; she says it unfits them for woman's true sphere. I don't believe a word of it. Speaking of Rachel reminds me—did you hear anything about the Abbey Bank lately, Anne?"

"I heard that it was shaky," answered Anne. "Why?"

"That is what Rachel said. She was up here one day last week and said there was some talk about it. Matthew felt real worried. All we have saved is in that bank—every penny. I wanted Matthew to put it in the Savings Bank in the first place, but old Mr. Abbey was a great friend of Father's and he'd always banked with him. Matthew said any bank with him at the head of it was good enough for anybody."

"I think he has only been its nominal head for many years," said Anne. "He is a very old man; his nephews are really at the head of the institution."

"Well, when Rachel told us that, I wanted Matthew to draw our money right out and he said he'd think about it. But Mr. Russell told him yesterday that the bank was all right."

Anne had her good day in the companionship of the outdoor world. She never forgot that day; it was so bright and golden and fair, so free from shadow and so lavish of blossom. Anne spent some of its rich hours in the orchard; she went to the Dryad's Bubble and Willowmere and Violet Vale; she called at the manse and had a satisfying talk with Mrs. Allan; and finally in the evening she went with Matthew for the cows, through Lover's Lane to the back pasture. The woods were all gloried through with sunset, and the warm splendour of it streamed down through the hill gaps in the west. Matthew walked slowly with bent head; Anne, tall and erect, suited her springing step to his.

"You've been working too hard today, Matthew," she said reproachfully. "Why won't you take things easier?"

"Well now, I can't seem to," said Matthew as he opened the yard gate to let the cows through. "It's only that I'm getting old, Anne, and keep forgetting it. Well, well, I've always worked pretty hard and I'd rather drop in harness."

"If I had been the boy you sent for," said Anne wistfully, "I'd be able to help you so much now and spare you in a hundred ways. I could find it in my heart to wish I had been, just for that."

"Well now, I'd rather have you than a dozen boys, Anne," said Matthew, patting her hand. "Just mind you that—rather than a dozen boys. Well now, I guess it wasn't a boy that took the Avery scholarship, was it? It was a girl—my girl—my girl that I'm proud of."

He smiled his shy smile at her as he went into the yard. Anne took the memory of it with her when she went to her room that night and sat for a long while at her open window, thinking of the past and dreaming of the future. Outside, the Snow Queen was mistily white in the moonshine; the frogs were singing in the marsh beyond Orchard Slope. Anne always remembered the silvery, peaceful beauty and fragrant calm of that night. It was the last night before sorrow touched her life; and no life is ever quite the same again when once that cold, sanctifying touch has been laid upon it.

Chapter 37

THE REAPER WHOSE NAME IS DEATH

"Matthew—Matthew—what is the matter? Matthew, are you sick?" It was Marilla who spoke, alarm in every jerky word. Anne came through the hall, her hands full of white narcissi—it was long before Anne could love the sight or odor of white narcissus again—in time to hear her and to see Matthew standing in the porch doorway, a folded paper in his hand and his face strangely drawn and gray. Anne dropped her flowers and sprang across the kitchen to him at the same moment as Marilla. They were both too late; before they could reach him, Matthew had fallen across the threshold.

"He's fainted," gasped Marilla. "Anne, run for Martin—quick, quick! He's at the barn."

Martin, the hired man, who had just driven home from the post office, started at once for the doctor, calling at Orchard Slope on his way to send Mr. and Mrs. Barry over. Mrs. Lynde, who was there on an errand, came too. They found Anne and Marilla distractedly trying to restore Matthew to consciousness.

Mrs. Lynde pushed them gently aside, tried his pulse, and then laid her ear over his heart. She looked at their anxious faces sorrowfully, and the tears came into her eyes.

"Oh, Marilla," she said gravely, "I don't think—we can do anything for him."

"Mrs. Lynde, you don't think—you can't think Matthew is—is—" Anne could not say the dreadful word; she turned sick and pallid.

"Child, yes. I'm afraid of it. Look at his face. When you've seen that look as often as I have, you'll know what it means."

Anne looked at the still face and there beheld the seal of the Great Presence.

When the doctor came, he said that death had been instantaneous and probably painless, caused in all likelihood by some sudden shock. The secret of the shock was discovered to be in the paper Matthew had held and which Martin had brought from the post office that morning. It contained an account of the failure of the Abbey Bank.

The news spread quickly through Avonlea, and all day friends and neighbours thronged Green Gables and came and went on errands of kindness for the dead and living. For the first time, shy, quiet Matthew Cuthbert was a person of central importance; the white majesty of death had fallen upon him and set him apart as one crowned.

When the calm night came softly down over Green Gables, the old house was hushed and tranquil. In the parlour lay Matthew Cuthbert in his coffin, his long gray hair framing his placid face on which there was a little kindly smile as if he but slept, dreaming pleasant dreams. There were flowers about him—sweet, old-fashioned flowers that his mother had planted in the homestead garden in her bridal days and for which Matthew had always had a secret, wordless love. Anne had gathered them and brought them to him, her anguished, tearless eyes burning in her white face. It was the last thing she could do for him.

The Barrys and Mrs. Lynde stayed with them that night.

Diana, going to the east gable, where Anne was standing at her window, said gently, "Anne dear, would you like to have me sleep with you tonight?"

"Thank you, Diana." Anne looked earnestly into her friend's face. "I think you won't misunderstand me when I say that I want to be alone. I'm not afraid. I haven't been alone one minute since it happened—and I want to be. I want to be quite silent and quiet and try to realize it. I *can't* realize it. Half the time it seems to me that Matthew can't be dead, and the other half it seems as if he must have been dead for a long time and I've had this horrible dull ache ever since."

Diana did not quite understand. Marilla's impassioned grief, breaking all the bounds of natural reserve and lifelong habit in its stormy rush, she could comprehend better than Anne's tearless agony. But she went away kindly, leaving Anne alone to keep her first vigil with sorrow.

Anne hoped that tears would come in solitude. It seemed to her a terrible thing that she could not shed a tear for Matthew, whom she had loved so much and who had been so kind to her; Matthew, who had walked with her last evening at sunset and was now lying in the dim room below with that awful peace on his brow. But no tears came at first, even when she knelt by her window in the darkness and prayed, looking up to the stars beyond the hills—no tears, only the same horrible dull ache of misery that kept on aching until she fell asleep, worn out with the day's pain and excitement.

In the night she awakened, with the stillness and the darkness about her, and the recollection of the day came over her like a wave of sorrow. She could see Matthew's face smiling at her as he had smiled when they parted at the gate that last evening—she could hear his voice saying, "My girl—my girl that I'm proud of." Then the tears came and Anne wept her heart out. Marilla heard her and crept in to comfort her.

"There—there—don't cry so, dearie. It can't bring him back. It—it—isn't right to cry so. I knew that today, but I couldn't help it then. He'd always been such a good, kind brother to me—but God knows best."

"Oh, just let me cry, Marilla," sobbed Anne. "The tears don't hurt me like that ache did. Stay here for a little while with me and keep your arm around me—so. I couldn't have Diana stay; she's good and kind and sweet—but it's not her sorrow—she's outside of it and she couldn't come close enough to my heart to help me. It's our sorrow—yours and mine. Oh, Marilla, what will we do without him?"

"We've got each other, Anne. I don't know what I'd do if you weren't here—if you'd never come. Oh, Anne, I know I've been kind of strict and harsh with you maybe—but you mustn't think I didn't love you as well as Matthew did, for all that. I want to tell you now when I can. It's never been easy for me to say things out of my heart, but at times like this it's easier. I love you as dear as if you were my own flesh and blood, and you've been my joy and comfort ever since you came to Green Gables."

Two days afterwards, they carried Matthew Cuthbert over his homestead threshold and away from the fields he had tilled and the orchards he had loved and the trees he had planted; and then Avonlea settled back to its usual placidity; and even at Green Gables affairs slipped into their old groove and work was done and duties fulfilled with regularity as before, although always with the aching sense of "loss in all familiar things." Anne, new to grief, thought it almost sad that it could be so—that they *could* go on in the old way without Matthew. She felt something like shame and remorse when she discovered that the sunrises behind the firs and the pale pink buds opening in the garden gave her the old inrush of gladness when she saw them—that Diana's visits were pleasant to her and that Diana's merry words and ways moved her to laughter and smiles—that, in brief, the beautiful world of blossom and love and friendship had lost none of its power to please her fancy and thrill her heart, that life still called to her with many insistent voices.

"It seems like disloyalty to Matthew, somehow, to find pleasure in these things now that he has gone," she said wistfully to Mrs. Allan one evening when they were together in the manse garden. "I miss him so much—all the time—and yet, Mrs. Allan, the world and life seem very beautiful and interesting to me for all.[1] Today Diana said something funny and I found myself laughing. I thought when it happened I could never laugh again. And it somehow seems as if I oughtn't to."

"When Matthew was here, he liked to hear you laugh and he liked to know that you found pleasure in the pleasant things around you," said Mrs. Allan gently. "He is just away now; and he likes to know it just the same. I am sure we should not shut our hearts against the healing influences that nature offers us. But I understand your feeling. I think we all experience the same thing. We resent the thought that anything can please us when someone we love is no longer here to share the pleasure with us, and we almost feel as if we were unfaithful to our sorrow when we find our interest in life returning to us."

"I was down to the graveyard to plant a rosebush on Matthew's grave this afternoon," said Anne dreamily. "I took a slip of the little white Scotch rosebush his mother brought out from Scotland long ago; Matthew always liked those roses the best—they were so small and sweet on their thorny stems. It made me feel glad that I could plant it by his grave—as if I were doing something that must please him in taking it there to be near him. I hope he has roses like them in heaven. Perhaps the souls of all those little white roses that he has loved so many summers were all there to meet him. I must go home now. Marilla is all alone, and she gets lonely at twilight."

"She will be lonelier still, I fear, when you go away again to college," said Mrs. Allan.

Anne did not reply; she said good night and went slowly back to Green Gables. Marilla was sitting on the front doorsteps, and Anne sat down beside her. The door was open behind them, held back by a big pink conch shell with hints of sea sunsets in its smooth inner convolutions.

Anne gathered some sprays of pale yellow honeysuckle and put them in her hair. She liked the delicate hint of fragrance, as of some aerial benediction, above her every time she moved.

"Doctor Spencer was here while you were away," Marilla said. "He says that the specialist will be in town tomorrow and he insists that I must go in and have my eyes examined. I suppose I'd better go and have it over. I'll be more than thankful if the man can give me the right kind of glasses to suit my eyes. You won't mind staying here alone while I'm away, will

---

[1] All that.

you? Martin will have to drive me in and there's ironing and baking to do."

"I shall be all right. Diana will come over for company for me. I shall attend to the ironing and baking beautifully—you needn't fear that I'll starch the handkerchiefs or flavour the cake with liniment."

Marilla laughed.

"What a girl you were for making mistakes in them days, Anne. You were always getting into scrapes. I did used to think you were possessed. Do you mind[2] the time you dyed your hair?"

"Yes, indeed. I shall never forget it," smiled Anne, touching the heavy braid of hair that was wound about her shapely head. "I laugh a little now sometimes when I think what a worry my hair used to be to me— but I don't laugh *much,* because it was a very real trouble then. I did suffer terribly over my hair and my freckles. My freckles are really gone, and people are nice enough to tell me my hair is auburn now—all but Josie Pye. She informed me yesterday that she really thought it was redder than ever, or at least my black dress made it look redder, and she asked me if people who had red hair ever got used to having it. Marilla, I've almost decided to give up trying to like Josie Pye. I've made what I would once have called a heroic effort to like her, but Josie Pye won't *be* liked."

"Josie is a Pye," said Marilla sharply, "so she can't help being disagreeable. I suppose people of that kind serve some useful purpose in society, but I must say I don't know what it is any more than I know the use of thistles. Is Josie going to teach?"

"No, she is going back to Queen's next year. So are Moody Spurgeon and Charlie Sloane. Jane and Ruby are going to teach, and they have both got schools—Jane at Newbridge and Ruby at some place up west."

"Gilbert Blythe is going to teach, too, isn't he?"

"Yes"—briefly.

"What a nice-looking young fellow he is," said Marilla absently. "I saw him in church last Sunday and he seemed so tall and manly. He looks a lot like his father did at the same age. John Blythe was a nice boy. We used to be real good friends, he and I. People called him my beau."

Anne looked up with swift interest.

"Oh, Marilla—and what happened? Why didn't you—"

"We had a quarrel. I wouldn't forgive him when he asked me to. I meant to, after a while—but I was sulky and angry and I wanted to punish him first. He never came back—the Blythes were all mighty independent. But

---

2 Remember.

I always felt—rather sorry. I've always kind of wished I'd forgiven him when I had the chance."

"So you've had a bit of romance in your life, too," said Anne softly.

"Yes, I suppose you might call it that. You wouldn't think so to look at me, would you? But you never can tell about people from their outsides. Everybody has forgot about me and John. I'd forgotten myself. But it all came back to me when I saw Gilbert last Sunday."

Chapter 38

THE BEND IN THE ROAD

Marilla went to town the next day and returned in the evening. Anne had gone over to Orchard Slope with Diana and came back to find Marilla in the kitchen, sitting by the table with her head leaning on her hand. Something in her dejected attitude struck a chill in Anne's heart. She had never seen Marilla sit limply inert like that.

"Are you very tired, Marilla?"

"Yes—no—I don't know," said Marilla wearily, looking up. "I suppose I am tired, but I haven't thought about it. It's not that."

"Did you see the oculist? What did he say?" asked Anne anxiously.

"Yes, I saw him. He examined my eyes. He says that if I give up all reading and sewing entirely and any kind of work that strains the eyes, and if I'm careful not to cry, and if I wear the glasses he's given me, he thinks my eyes may not get any worse and my headaches will be cured. But if I don't, he says I'll certainly be stone blind in six months. Blind! Anne, just think of it!"

For a minute, Anne, after her first quick exclamation of dismay, was silent. It seemed to her that she could *not* speak. Then she said bravely but with a catch in her voice:

"Marilla, *don't* think of it. You know he has given you hope. If you are careful, you won't lose your sight altogether; and if his glasses cure your headaches, it will be a great thing."

"I don't call it much hope," said Marilla bitterly. "What am I to live for if I can't read or sew or do anything like that? I might as well be blind— or dead. And as for crying, I can't help that when I get lonesome. But there, it's no good talking about it. If you'll get me a cup of tea, I'll be thankful. I'm about done out. Don't say anything about this to anyone for a spell yet, anyway. I can't bear that folks should come here to question and sympathize and talk about it."

When Marilla had eaten her lunch,[1] Anne persuaded her to go to bed.

---

[1] A small meal.

Then Anne went herself to the east gable and sat down by her window in the darkness, alone with her tears and her heaviness of heart. How sadly things had changed since she had sat there the night after coming home! Then she had been full of hope and joy, and the future had looked rosy with promise. Anne felt as if she had lived years since then, but before she went to bed, there was a smile on her lips and peace in her heart. She had looked her duty courageously in the face and found it a friend—as duty ever is when we meet it frankly.

One afternoon a few days later, Marilla came slowly in from the yard where she had been talking to a caller—a man whom Anne knew by sight as John Sadler from Carmody. Anne wondered what he could have been saying to bring that look to Marilla's face.

"What did Mr. Sadler want, Marilla?"

Marilla sat down by the window and looked at Anne. There were tears in her eyes in defiance of the oculist's prohibition and her voice broke as she said:

"He heard that I was going to sell Green Gables and he wants to buy it."

"Buy it! Buy Green Gables?" Anne wondered if she had heard aright. "Oh, Marilla, you don't mean to sell Green Gables!"

"Anne, I don't know what else is to be done. I've thought it all over. If my eyes were strong, I could stay here and make out to look after things and manage, with a good hired man. But as it is, I can't. I may lose my sight altogether; and anyway, I'll not be fit to run things. Oh, I never thought I'd live to see the day when I'd have to sell my home. But things would only go behind worse and worse all the time, till nobody would want to buy it. Every cent of our money went in that bank; and there's some notes Matthew gave last fall to pay. Mrs. Lynde advises me to sell the farm and board somewhere—with her, I suppose. It won't bring much—it's small and the buildings are old. But it'll be enough for me to live on, I reckon. I'm thankful you're provided for with that scholarship, Anne. I'm sorry you won't have a home to come to on your vacations, that's all, but I suppose you'll manage somehow."

Marilla broke down and wept bitterly.

"You mustn't sell Green Gables," said Anne resolutely.

"Oh, Anne, I wish I didn't have to. But you can see for yourself. I can't stay here alone. I'd go crazy with trouble and loneliness. And my sight would go—I know it would."

"You won't have to stay here alone, Marilla. I'll be with you. I'm not going to Redmond."

"Not going to Redmond!" Marilla lifted her worn face from her hands and looked at Anne. "Why, what do you mean?"

"Just what I say. I'm not going to take the scholarship. I decided so the night after you came home from town. You surely don't think I could leave you alone in your trouble, Marilla, after all you've done for me. I've been thinking and planning. Let me tell you my plans. Mr. Barry wants to rent the farm for next year. So you won't have any bother over that. And I'm going to teach. I've applied for the school here—but I don't expect to get it, for I understand the trustees have promised it to Gilbert Blythe. But I can have the Carmody school. Mr. Blair told me so last night at the store. Of course that won't be quite as nice or convenient as if I had the Avonlea school. But I can board home and drive myself over to Carmody and back, in the warm weather at least. And even in winter, I can come home Fridays. We'll keep a horse for that. Oh, I have it all planned out, Marilla. And I'll read to you and keep you cheered up. You shan't be dull or lonesome. And we'll be real cozy and happy here together, you and I."

Marilla had listened like a woman in a dream.

"Oh, Anne, I could get on real well if you were here, I know. But I can't let you sacrifice yourself so for me. It would be terrible."

"Nonsense!" Anne laughed merrily. "There is no sacrifice. Nothing could be worse than giving up Green Gables—nothing could hurt me more. We must keep the dear old place. My mind is quite made up, Marilla. I'm *not* going to Redmond, and I *am* going to stay here and teach. Don't you worry about me a bit."

"But your ambitions—and—"

"I'm just as ambitious as ever. Only, I've changed the object of my ambitions. I'm going to be a good teacher—and I'm going to save your eyesight. Besides, I mean to study at home here and take a little college course all by myself. Oh, I've dozens of plans, Marilla. I've been thinking them out for a week. I shall give life here my best, and I believe it will give its best to me in return. When I left Queen's, my future seemed to stretch out before me like a straight road. I thought I could see along it for many a milestone. Now there is a bend in it. I don't know what lies around the bend, but I'm going to believe that the best does. It has a fascination of its own, that bend, Marilla. I wonder how the road beyond it goes—what there is of green glory and soft, checkered light and shadows—what new land-scapes—what new beauties—what curves and hills and valleys farther on."

"I don't feel as if I ought to let you give it up," said Marilla, referring to the scholarship.

"But you can't prevent me. I'm sixteen and a half, 'obstinate as a mule,' as Mrs. Lynde once told me," laughed Anne. "Oh, Marilla, don't you go pitying me. I don't like to be pitied, and there is no need for it. I'm heart glad over the very thought of staying at dear Green Gables. Nobody could love it as you and I do—so we must keep it."

"You blessed girl!" said Marilla, yielding. "I feel as if you'd given me a new life. I guess I ought to stick out and make you go to college—but I know I can't, so I ain't going to try. I'll make it up to you though, Anne."

When it became noised abroad in Avonlea that Anne Shirley had given up the idea of going to college and intended to stay home and teach, there was a good deal of discussion over it. Most of the good folks, not knowing about Marilla's eyes, thought she was foolish. Mrs. Allan did not. She told Anne so in approving words that brought tears of pleasure to the girl's eyes. Neither did good Mrs. Lynde. She came up one evening and found Anne and Marilla sitting at the front door in the warm, scented summer dusk. They liked to sit there when the twilight came down and the white moths flew about in the garden and the odor of mint filled the dewy air.

Mrs. Rachel deposited her substantial person upon the stone bench by the door, behind which grew a row of tall pink and yellow hollyhocks, with a long breath of mingled weariness and relief.

"I declare I'm glad to sit down. I've been on my feet all day, and two hundred pounds is a good bit for two feet to carry around. It's a great blessing not to be fat, Marilla. I hope you appreciate it. Well, Anne, I hear you've given up your notion of going to college. I was real glad to hear it. You've got as much education now as a woman can be comfortable with. I don't believe in girls going to college with the men and cramming their heads full of Latin and Greek and all that nonsense."

"But I'm going to study Latin and Greek just the same, Mrs. Lynde," said Anne, laughing. "I'm going to take my arts course right here at Green Gables and study everything that I would at college."

Mrs. Lynde lifted her hands in holy horror. "Anne Shirley, you'll kill yourself."

"Not a bit of it. I shall thrive on it. Oh, I'm not going to overdo things. As Josiah Allen's wife says, I shall be 'mejum.' But I'll have lots of spare time in the long winter evenings, and I've no vocation for fancy work. I'm going to teach over at Carmody, you know."

"I don't know it. I guess you're going to teach right here in Avonlea. The trustees have decided to give you the school."

"Mrs. Lynde!" cried Anne, springing to her feet in her surprise. "Why, I thought they had promised it to Gilbert Blythe!"

"So they did. But as soon as Gilbert heard that you had applied for it, he went to them—they had a business meeting at the school last night, you know—and told them that he withdrew his application and suggested that they accept yours. He said he was going to teach at White Sands. Of course he gave up the school just to oblige you, because he knew how much you wanted to stay with Marilla, and I must say I think it was real kind and thoughtful of him, that's what. Real self-sacrificing, too, for he'll have his board to pay at White Sands, and everybody knows he's got to earn his own way through college. So the trustees decided to take you. I was tickled to death when Thomas came home and told me."

"I don't feel that I ought to take it," murmured Anne. "I mean—I don't think I ought to let Gilbert make such a sacrifice for—for me."

"I guess you can't prevent him now. He's signed papers with the White Sands trustees. So it wouldn't do him any good now if you were to refuse. Of course you'll take the school. You'll get along all right, now that there are no Pyes going. Josie was the last of them, and a good thing she was, that's what. There's been some Pye or other going to Avonlea school for the last twenty years, and I guess their mission in life was to keep schoolteachers reminded that earth isn't their home. Bless my heart! What does all that winking and blinking at the Barry gable mean?"

"Diana is signaling for me to go over," laughed Anne. "You know we keep up the old custom. Excuse me while I run over and see what she wants."

Anne ran down the clover slope like a deer and disappeared in the firry shadows of the Haunted Wood.

Mrs. Lynde looked after her indulgently. "There's a good deal of the child about her yet in some ways."

"There's a good deal more of the woman about her in others," retorted Marilla with a momentary return of her old crispness.

But crispness was no longer Marilla's distinguishing characteristic, as Mrs. Lynde told her Thomas that night: "Marilla Cuthbert has got *mellow*. That's what."

Anne went to the little Avonlea graveyard the next evening to put fresh flowers on Matthew's grave and water the Scotch rosebush. She lingered there until dusk, liking the peace and calm of the little place, with its poplars whose rustle was like low, friendly speech, and its whispering grasses growing at will among the graves. When she finally left it and walked down the long hill that sloped to the Lake of Shining Waters, it

was past sunset and all Avonlea lay before her in a dreamlike afterlight—
"a haunt of ancient peace." There was a freshness in the air as of a wind
that had blown over honey-sweet fields of clover. Home lights twinkled
out here and there among the homestead trees. Beyond lay the sea, misty
and purple, with its haunting, unceasing murmur. The west was a glory
of soft mingled hues, and the pond reflected them all in still softer shadings. The beauty of it all thrilled Anne's heart, and she gratefully opened
the gates of her soul to it.

"Dear old world," she murmured, "you are very lovely, and I am glad
to be alive in you."

Halfway down the hill, a tall lad came whistling out of a gate before
the Blythe homestead. It was Gilbert, and the whistle died on his lips as
he recognized Anne. He lifted his cap courteously, but he would have
passed on in silence if Anne had not stopped and held out her hand.

"Gilbert," she said with scarlet cheeks, "I want to thank you for giving
up the school for me. It was very good of you—and I want you to know
that I appreciate it."

Gilbert took the offered hand eagerly.

"It wasn't particularly good of me at all, Anne. I was pleased to be able
to do you some small service. Are we going to be friends after this? Have
you really forgiven me my old fault?"

Anne laughed and tried unsuccessfully to withdraw her hand. "I
forgave you that day by the pond landing, although I didn't know it.
What a stubborn little goose I was. I've been—I may as well make a
complete confession—I've been sorry ever since."

"We are going to be the best of friends," said Gilbert jubilantly. "We were
born to be good friends, Anne. You've thwarted destiny long enough. I
know we can help each other in many ways. You are going to keep up your
studies, aren't you? So am I. Come, I'm going to walk home with you."

Marilla looked curiously at Anne when the latter entered the kitchen.

"Who was that came up the lane with you, Anne?"

"Gilbert Blythe," answered Anne, vexed to find herself blushing. "I met
him on Barry's Hill."

"I didn't think you and Gilbert Blythe were such good friends that
you'd stand for half an hour at the gate talking to him," said Marilla with
a dry smile.

"We haven't been—we've been good enemies. But we have decided
that it will be much more sensible to be good friends in future. Were we
really there half an hour? It seemed just a few minutes. But, you see, we
have five years' lost conversations to catch up with, Marilla."

"Come, I'm going to walk home with you."

Anne sat long at her window that night companioned by a glad content. The wind purred softly in the cherry boughs, and the mint breaths came up to her. The stars twinkled over the pointed firs in the hollow and Diana's light gleamed through the old gap.

Anne's horizons had closed in since the night she had sat there after coming home from Queen's; but if the path set before her feet was to be narrow, she knew that flowers of quiet happiness would bloom along it. The joys of sincere work and worthy aspiration and congenial friendship were to be hers; nothing could rob her of her birthright of fancy or her ideal world of dreams. And there was always the bend in the road!

" 'God's in His heaven, all's right with the world,'[2] " whispered Anne softly.

---

[2] From Robert Browning's drama *Pippa Passes* (1841).

Afterword
DISCUSSION WITH PROFESSOR WHEELER

(For Formal School, Home School, and Book Club Discussions)

First of all, permit me to define my perception of the role of the teacher. I believe that the ideal teaching relationship involves the teacher and the student, both looking in the same direction, and both having a sense of wonder. A teacher is not an important person dishing out rote learning to an unimportant person. I furthermore do not believe that a Ph.D. automatically brings with it omniscience, despite the way some of us act. In discussions, I tell my students beforehand that my opinions and conclusions are no more valid than theirs, for each of us sees reality from a different perspective.

Now that my role is clear, let's continue. The purpose of the discussion sections of the series is to encourage debate, to dig deeper into the books than would be true without these sections, and to spawn other questions that may build on the ones I begin with. If you take advantage of these sections, you will be gaining just as good an understanding of a book as you would were you actually sitting in one of my classroom circles.

Be sure to keep a journal as you read, because if you don't, most of your insights will be lost forever. Whatever you do, don't merely regurgitate the plot; rather, use each sentence, each paragraph, as a springboard to a fuller understanding of what life is all about. For example, if you are reading about a person, who does that character remind you of in real life? In previous readings? On television or cinema? Why? Draw parallels and spell out differences.

Each of us ought to daily hone our writing skills, our ability to express ourselves with clarity, verve, and power. Here are a number of things you can do to accelerate your progress as a writer:

1. Keep a dictionary at your side at all times; the starting minimum would be a full-sized, hardback collegiate. For those who wish to develop into wordsmiths, invest in an Oxford Unabridged and use it whenever more limited dictionaries fail to fully explain, or even list, an older word. Make it a practice to keep 3 x 5 cards at your side at all times. When you come across an unfamiliar word, don't take the easy way out and pass over it, but stop, look it up, copy it down on one side of a card, and on the other side write down the definition(s) and, if possible, use the word in a sentence. Study these cards every day, and only when the definition and sentence use spring immediately to mind should you move the card into your inactive file; periodically, refresh your memory by going through that stack as well. As you consistently try to add new words to your vocabulary every day, you will be amazed at how much richer life will become.

2. At the back of your journal, reserve a section for vivid metaphors and similes. Each time you find one that jumps out at you, write it down, along with the source and page. Over time, you will develop an appreciation for fresh imagery and avoid hackneyed, cliché-saturated speech.

3. Also keep a place in the back of the journal for writing down insightful lines that don't incorporate metaphors—lines that are aphoristic, that successfully express great truths, living embodiments of Pope's "What oft was thought / But ne'er so well expressed" (*An Essay in Criticism*, 1711).

4. Make it a habit to write down memorable first and last lines and paragraphs in books, chapters, stories, articles, and essays. Have a "Best List" and a "Worst List." Which beginning lines pull you into a story? How do they do that? Unfortunately, too many would-be writers don't pay enough attention to make-or-break lines, not realizing that if the first line/paragraph fails to hook the browsing reader, that person will never stay around long enough to read the rest of what they have spent so much time writing.

The concluding line/paragraph is second only in impact to the beginning one, for it represents the adieu, the distillation, the tug-at-the-heart, that builds on all that has gone before. Like the beginning line, finding just the right way of saying it, getting the right ring or the right tone, is likely to take a lot of effort and frequently a lot of time. The definitive starting point for your list ought to be the beginning and ending paragraphs of Dickens's *Tale of Two Cities*.

5. Pay particular attention (in another section of your journal) to character portraits. Why and how are some characters made so real that it seems you have known them always? Bringing a character to life in print is really the ultimate Pygmalion act. It takes some writers a full book to accomplish it; others can pull it off in mere paragraphs or a page or two.

6. Pay particular attention to dialogue, because when it is done well, it carries the story along. The most effective type of writing—and the most difficult to do—is dialogue that reveals character, thus letting the reader arrive at his or her own conclusions rather than having the writer tell the reader what kind of person the character is.

7. Finally, watch for vivid examples of personification (making inanimate things seem human).

As you do all of these things, and continue to write yourself, your own personal style will deepen, broaden, and become more self-assured and professional.

**The Introduction Must Be Read
Before Beginning the Next Section.**

— — —

Questions to Deepen Your Understanding

Chapter 1. Mrs. Rachel Lynde Is Surprised

1. Why do you feel Montgomery begins the book with Mrs. Lynde? Wouldn't Anne, Matthew, or Marilla have been better? Follow Mrs. Lynde throughout the book and conclude at the end what role she plays. How would the book have been different without her? Gradually construct a three-dimensional portrait of her. Is she merely a gossip? Or is her role more complex than that? Explain.

2. Construct character sketches for the other main characters in the book. Pay particular attention to their growth or lack of it. Which are round (multidimensional) characters and which are flat (static, one-dimensional) ones? Explain why. Which grow the most? Explain.

3. What role does the community play in the book? Gradually, over the course of the book, develop a picture of this island community and what makes it do what it does.

4. Pay careful attention to Marilla's role in the book. How would Anne's story be different without her? What is she like at the beginning of the book? What impact does Anne have on her? What is Marilla like at the end of the book? What have been the key reasons for these changes? What earlier factors caused Marilla to grow into the person she became? Follow the same process with Matthew. Do you know any Matthews or Marillas today? Explain.

5. Obviously, there are risks in adopting. How do these compare with the risks one faces with biological children?

Chapter 2. Matthew Cuthbert Is Surprised
6. What impact does weather have on people's moods? On yours? Is Anne typical in terms of how she responds to different types of weather? Why or why not? Arrive at a conclusion by the last chapter in the book.

7. Personality-wise, do opposites attract? Find as many opposites as you can who are attracted to each other; describe how they are different and how they are alike, then arrive at conclusions. Are alikes or opposites more likely to become close? Give reasons and specifics.

8. The opposite of love is not hate, it is indifference. Hate, on the other hand, is such a charged emotion that it often flip-flops into love—indifference rarely does. Monitor such relationships throughout the story. Have you ever known people who veered from hate to love? Indifference to love? Compare their relationships with those of similar characters in this book. Why do *you* think hate so often reverses itself with equal intensity? Answer the same question in relation to love.

9. What do you think the impact of one's looks is on behavior? How do looks affect Anne's behavior? Perhaps it would also be interesting to compare actual looks with perceived looks.

10. The entire Anne saga is a hymn to beauty. What role does beauty—especially in nature—play in the book? How does Anne respond to beauty? How do her attitudes change, in this respect, during the course of the book?

11. Anne has some strong opinions about names for things and people. What are they? Do you agree that "a rose by any other name" would *not* smell as sweet? Explain.

12. What lessons do you learn in the book about how, and how not, to treat people? How are these lessons internalized?

Chapter 3. Marilla Cuthbert Is Surprised

13. What impact do crusty characters have on your enjoyment of reading a given book? Which characters in this book are the crustiest?

14. Clearly define and compare the roles of girls and women in this book with their counterparts today. What have we gained since Anne's time? What have we lost since then?

15. Do you feel Montgomery effectively captures the intensity of childhood feelings? Elaborate, for it is exceedingly difficult for adults to recapture the agony and rapture of childhood.

Chapter 4. Morning at Green Gables

16. Discuss the concept of imagination in the book—especially Anne's. Then chronicle it through the story and compare it at the end with what it was at the beginning. What causes these changes?

17. Are attitudes self-fulfilling prophecies? In other words, can we create our own daily inner weather? What makes weather either good or bad? What is Anne's inner weather like? How does she respond to different types of weather? Compare her responses with yours.

18. How does slow, shy Matthew do battle with Marilla? How does his way of debating an issue differ from hers? How effective is he against Marilla?

Chapter 5. Anne's History

19. Much of this world's sorrow has to do with being lonely and unwanted. How does Anne feel in this respect? How do her feelings change during the course of the book? What should be our response to loneliness and rejection in the lives of people we meet?

20. Poetry and prose—what does each bring to us? Eventually, Anne becomes an accomplished elocutionist. What does that term imply?

21. Some individuals look for the best in people; others see only the

worst. The truth is, we tend to find what we are looking for or expecting. What lessons can we learn from this?

Chapter 6. Marilla Makes Up Her Mind

22. There is an old phrase, "Man's inhumanity to man," that is apropos to the events of this chapter. Montgomery's most powerful manifestation of it is in this poignant passage:

> Marilla looked at Anne and softened at sight of the child's pale face with its look of mute misery—the misery of a helpless little creature who finds itself once more caught in the trap from which it had escaped. Marilla felt an uncomfortable conviction that, if she denied the appeal of that look, it would haunt her to her dying day.

How often, in life, we find ourselves back in the trap we had already escaped from! Sometimes the reentrapment is of our own doing, sometimes it is not—but the agony is the same. One thing we do know: If we deny the appeal in the eyes of someone who is trapped, the God who notes even the sparrow's fall will remember our dereliction. This moment represents the great divide in the book. How different the story would have been had Marilla denied that eye appeal! Have you ever been in a similar situation?

23. There is much about eyes in the book—eyes that are said to be the windows of the soul. The real tragedy of death is to see the light, the radiance, go out in the eyes. Discuss the subject of eyes, drawing from your own experience and from people you have known. What conclusions do you reach?

24. Too often a person you dislike cannot do anything right in your eyes, and a person you adore cannot do anything wrong. Matthew, in this chapter, puts it this way: "I kind of think she's one of the sort you can do anything with if you only get her to love you."

Much is said in the book about the Pye family, each member being possessed with the fatal genius of alienation. Everything they say stings, bites, or rankles. Do your words and acts elicit love and trust? Or are you burdened with the fatal Pye virus? What are your options?

25. There are certain days in our lives, certain hours, certain moments, that later on, looking back, we belatedly realize were crucial in terms

of our development, or lack of it. In literature, Robert Frost's "The Road Not Taken" is perhaps the best articulation of this. Those days are like train-track switches: Either your train clickety-clacks straight down the old predictable track—or a flagman stops your train, the switch is pulled, and your engine noses onto another track, opening up a world of new options and opportunities. Unfortunately, too many of us lose out at these crossroads by ignoring the flagman and thundering on past, down the easy track. It takes real effort and courage to bring our speeding train to a halt in order to listen to what the flagman has to say.

Note what is said and implied in this chapter about such a day, such a moment. Are you willing to listen to the flagman?

Chapter 7. Anne Says Her Prayers

26. Clearly, our God values order, for it is evident everywhere. Along with order comes neatness, a quality many of us do not come by naturally. Slovenliness is antithetical to godliness, and this is reflected by one of our oldest adages: "Cleanliness is next to godliness." One of Marilla's first lessons has to do with Anne's tendency to leave her clothes on the floor rather than hang them up before she goes to bed. What is your position where cleanliness and slovenliness are concerned?

27. Anne's perceptions about prayer are most insightful. All too often, our prayers degenerate into mere mantras, words we repeat mechanically without ever being aware of what we are really saying. How many of us would have the honesty and insight to follow Anne's example and "go out into a great big field all alone or into the deep, deep woods, and . . . look up into the sky—up—up—up—into that lovely blue sky that looks as if there was no end to its blueness . . . and just *feel* a prayer"? What is prayer to you? Compare your attitude toward prayer with Anne's.

28. How could Anne truly love God, never having interacted much with those whose personal love for God was reflected by their daily inter- actions with others? We do not, after all, fall in love with God in the abstract; rather, we first fall in love with human beings whose lives radiate friendship with the divine. It is only then that we seek out God on our own. Discuss.

Chapter 8. Anne's Bringing-Up Is Begun

29. Anne spends a lot of time daydreaming. One of the saddest legacies of our age is that we have permitted media-generated noise to pulverize silence in our lives. Without silence there can be little real daydreaming. One of Montgomery's most significant truths in the book is this: Out of her daydreaming—continually criticized by Marilla—came the adult Anne, intuitively richer than she would have been without the daydreaming!

We tend to forget, as we get older, that it is in our childhood, adolescent, and teen daydreaming that our sails are set for the life journey. Those thoughts, those plans, those dreams, are every bit as significant and life-affecting—if not more so—as any we may have during our adult lives. What role do daydreams have in your life?

30. Each of us continually struggles to preserve that inner Eden where we can retreat for regeneration. Anne's story is a powerful plea for the preservation of childhood wonder. For various reasons (among them, unrelenting media onslaughts), the average American child loses 95 percent of his or her creativity between the ages of two and eighteen (Wheeler, *Remote Controlled* [Hagerstown, Md.: Review and Herald, 1993]). It is long past time for us parents to begin providing our children with silence and serenity, the divinely ordained potting soil in which imagination and dreams may germinate and grow. And realizing that half of what we learn in a lifetime is learned by the age of six, at no time during our lives is such silence needed more than during those very first years.

Pay particular attention to Anne's world, her immersion into the beauty all around her—the flowers, the sea, the trees, the snow, the sky, the houses, the roads, the people—and chronicle the impact of all these on her inner growth. Discuss.

31. All her life, Anne has longed for a friend; not just any friend, but "a bosom friend—an intimate friend, you know—a really kindred spirit to whom I can confide my innermost soul." All of us yearn for such a friend, such a soul mate, someone who will represent completeness to parts of our psyche that will never achieve full growth until a friend pollinates them with love and empathy, thus bringing them into full bloom at last.

I am reminded, in that respect, of C. S. Lewis's marvelous book *The*

Four Loves, in which he observes that each person close to us draws out qualities we would otherwise never reveal. Thus, whenever a close friend, relative, or soul mate dies, there will ever after be parts of us that will, in effect, wither up and die, for no other person will ever be able to unlock the doors that once permitted access.

Do you have a "bosom friend" (as Anne would say) in your life? Compare your bosom friend (or friends) with Anne's counterpart.

Chapter 9. Mrs. Rachel Lynde Is Properly Horrified

32. Whenever we move, our cat, Pandora, explores every inch of our new diggings, not being willing to settle down and relax until she has passed judgment on every last corner. Children do that, too. Notice how Anne, thanks to time, liberty to roam, and a safe rural environment, within the first two weeks of her Green Gables sojourn had already made her own every tree, shrub, lane, brook, spring, flower, and bridge in the vicinity. A world does not have to be large: Every blade and blossom of a small world may be loved, cherished, and adopted as one's own. How well do you know the area where you live?

33. Mrs. Rachel Lynde always says what is on her mind without taking into consideration the impact on her listeners. Many of those who pride themselves on their intellectual honesty—"telling it like it is"—are, in essence, sadists. Wonderfully, in this story, Mrs. Rachel tries such a below-the-belt tactic once too often. Anne's cup chose that ill-fated moment to run over. Have you ever known people such as Mrs. Rachel? What effect did they have on you? Discuss.

Chapter 10. Anne's Apology

34. Few of us handle clichés with any significant degree of awareness. Anne, however, really thinks about what she is saying: " 'Wild horses won't drag the secret from me,' promised Anne solemnly. 'How would wild horses drag a secret from a person anyhow?' " Think about your conversation—especially your use of clichés—and ask yourself this question: "How often do I say things without paying attention to what they really mean?"

35. *Home.* The lack of having one has so much to do with the sad state of contemporary society, especially for children. Recently, I spoke with a friend whose parents had divorced a number of years ago. Her mother was single, embittered, and living in a small apartment. Her

father lived with a woman he didn't care enough about to marry. "There's no home to go to!" my friend cried. The lack of a home is far worse for children, as more and more long-term studies are pointing out. Children who are victimized by divorce may be afflicted by a number of problems: (1) They tend to be rebellious and are more likely to be juvenile delinquents. (2) They are more likely to turn to substance abuse. (3) They are more likely to have children out of wedlock (one-third of all children born in the United States today are welcomed into the world by only one parent). (4) They are less likely to stay in school, attend college, and enroll in graduate programs. (5) They often avoid marriage because they are afraid that it won't last; when they *do* marry, they tend to view it merely as an option rather than as "until death do us part." (6) They are less likely to view church and God as central to their lives. (7) They are likely to either be greedy because the separated parents tried to outbid each other for the children's affection, or be bitter because one parent would have little or nothing to do with them. Rarely in divorce is the child's best interests a high priority.

Anne yearns above all else for a home, a home where she is wanted and loved. Discuss the consequences of divorce, and the sense of homelessness it engenders in children, in regard to your own life choices.

36. Those whose lives are not filled with love, kisses, and hugs tend to have problems with intimacy when they grow up; often they are incapable of being loving mates or parents themselves. The miracle of Anne is that she wasn't withered or destroyed by her early years, loveless as they were. What can we do about this aspect of life and behavior? Keep in mind the reality that each of us supposedly needs eight hugs a day just to remain sane.

Chapter 11. Anne's Impressions of Sunday School

37. Fashion has always been, and will probably always remain, one of our most worshiped gods. Those who refuse to be slaves to the latest fads are more often than not ridiculed and ostracized. Anne's fashion troubles are minor in comparison with those of many children today: All she wants are puffed sleeves. Discuss our slavery to fashion and peer pressure and what, if anything, we can, or are willing to, do about it.

38. Anne discovers a real truth: Education must be a two-way street. If all a teacher does is pontificate (preach) and all the student does is regurgitate facts, then the results are certain: dead-end learning with virtually everything learned held in a sievelike processing chamber just long enough to be remembered upon being examined—then lost.

Only when the student becomes excited about God's great world, and yearns to learn more about every aspect of it, does education become exciting. There is no question which is more important, teacher or student—if the student is not self-involved, the process is a hopeless one. An engaged student can learn even with a lousy teacher. Of course, tie in a self-motivated student with a visionary teacher who views students as equal partners—and the results are likely to be explosive and far-reaching.

What is your attitude toward learning? How could it become more fun, more exciting, and hence more effective?

39. Long prayers—how I used to resent them as a child! It did seem to me as if some of those who prayed so long that our kneecaps begged for mercy were more on an ego trip than they were interested in our welfare. Some seemed determined to update God on all that had happened on earth since their last public prayer. Others appeared to be insisting on equal time with the minister's sermon. I still feel that two minutes ought to be the maximum length for a public prayer. What is your opinion on the length of prayers?

Chapter 12. A Solemn Vow and Promise
40. Anne loves flowers and their multihued colors. Most children do. Sadly, by the time we become adults, many of us lose this love affair with the flamboyant world of flowers. Our God is extravagant with His use of color—there's nothing parsimonious about Him. What a forlorn world this would be without flowers! Wordsworth maintained that flowers held within them the secrets of the universe and the pathway to the Eternal. What is the role of flowers in your life?

41. Intense are the friendships of childhood. To a child there is no such thing as a stranger. Where other children are concerned, all that's needed for a shared experience to begin is "Wanna play?" Anne has this childlike acceptance of people and fills her life with a garden of friends, each bringing enrichment and fulfillment to her life. What kind of a friendship garden have you cultivated?

42. Anne really *listens*. So often we adults only partially listen. If I made the rounds of a typical party and declared, with a warm smile, that my grandmother had just died, a good share of the people would mumble something like, "Why thank you! Hope everything's going well with you, too!"

How few of us *really* listen to those around us. In conversations, instead of listening intently so we might learn something new, we only half listen and wait for the first pause so *we* may break in, start talking, and show how brilliant we are. Since "good conversationalists" are invariably "good listeners," not many of us would get passing grades in Conversation 101. How about you: do you really listen?

43. Diana always laughs before she speaks—no wonder Anne loves her! Happy people always have friends who love being around them. As Christians, it's particularly important for us to be joyful. After all, we're the bearers of God's good news. Discuss the aspect of joyfulness in those you interact with. Which ones do you most like being with? Why?

44. Stream of consciousness writing did not originate with Laurence Stern, Henry James, James Joyce, or Virginia Woolf. It—as Anne's meandering conversation reveals—has always been with us. The mind refuses to be compartmentalized or organized, preferring to flow into any channel that looks interesting. Since the average person talks at only 150 to 200 words a minute, and the mind thinks at 400 to 600 words a minute, there is a lot of room for stream of consciousness thinking. In your journaling, set aside space for copying down interesting passages from *Anne of Green Gables,* wherein the speaker refuses to stick to the initial subject but insists on flitting here and there, wherever the mind takes him or her.

45. We are never poor so long as we have something to give. Without giving, we become dead seas, for there is no energizing current flowing through us. This is a lesson Anne needs no instruction in: "And I can give Diana half of them, can't I? The other half will taste twice as sweet to me if I give some to her. It's delightful to think I have something to give her." What is the role of such selfless giving in your life?

Chapter 13. The Delights of Anticipation

46. Marilla discovers that the perception of time is different for an adult than it is for a child. When you are young, today is all the time there is: neither yesterday nor tomorrow has much relevance. Adults, on the other hand, tend to live either in the future if they are younger or in the past if they are older—both age groups tending to belittle or pay little attention to the only time frame they can do anything with—TODAY. Discuss time and how we ought to relate to it.

47. "Play" means different things to different people, depending upon many factors, including age. Anne loves play, as do most children and teenagers. Marilla has virtually forgotten what play is. Age is truly a state of mind. Some elderly people retain a childlike sense of wonder about life, whereas some children act like senior citizens.

    Most things are good in moderation, even play. Nonstop play quickly becomes boring and unfulfilling. Nonstop work, on the other hand, shrivels up the spirit and narrows the horizons. Only as we take time to play as well as work—at any age—can we retain a joyful attitude toward life and a continued determination to make a day-by-day difference in our service to others. What is your attitude toward play? Is it what it ought to be?

48. In the nineteenth century, fainting was what women did; it was part of the female stereotype. It was not naturally occurring, however, but resulted from the suffocating clothes and tightly laced stays women wore, which made it difficult for them to breathe. Discuss the extremes to which women have gone through the centuries in order to appear fashionable.

49. Anne revels in the beauty of gems, as is revealed by her insightful description of amethysts as having "the souls of violets." Can you think of equally fresh descriptions of other gems?

Chapter 14. Anne's Confession

50. Appearances can indeed be deceiving. All the signs can point toward guilt—even overwhelming guilt—and yet the accused be innocent. Every year we hear of people imprisoned, and even executed, for crimes they did not commit. Taking all this into consideration against the framework of the amethyst story, what lessons should it teach us, and how should we respond the next time we are faced with what appears to be an airtight case against someone?

Chapter 15. A Tempest in the School Teapot

51. Anne experiences joy with each passing day: " 'What a splendid day!' said Anne, drawing a long breath. 'Isn't it good just to be alive on a day like this? I pity the people who aren't born yet for missing it. They may have good days, of course, but they can never have this one.' "

How can we, like Anne, so fall in love with life and beauty that *every* day, sunny or rainy, cool or hot, we're still able to say, "Lord, thank You for this splendid day You have lent to me"?

52. Note that Anne's generation wrote on slates in school instead of paper. In truth, paper was extremely scarce in those days, and when one did write on a piece of paper, virtually every inch was covered with writing. Discuss the difference between that time and ours when it comes to the accessibility of paper and our attitude toward it.

53. When I read of the teacher's public ridicule of Anne and her subsequent embarrassment, I am reminded of how fragile our feelings of self-worth are, and how little it takes to destroy us. When I think about such things, I'm reminded of scenes that I have no desire to revisit, incorporating as they do words or acts of which I'm deeply ashamed. They bring back to me, in living color, the wounded eyes, the tears, the drooping shoulders, of those victimized by me or by a crowd of which I was a part. It was perhaps funny at the time to publicly embarrass and humiliate these individuals, but it is not funny in retrospect! Each time those memories come up, I renew my determination to never again be a part, either actively or passively, of anything that will erode or destroy anyone's sense of self-worth. Have you ever been part of such public ridicule? Discuss.

Chapter 16. Diana Is Invited to Tea with Tragic Results

54. Ah, October! What would life be like without autumn colors! During my lifetime, I can remember long stretches of time when, because of where we were living, October was little more than a fizzle. Especially do I remember living in seasonless Latin America and Southern California. As every October drew near, I always felt cheated. During my years in Maryland, a busload of us would drive up Highway 1 in the fall, staying each night at beachfront hotels, all the way up to Maine—then we'd turn inland and ride the colors down. One cannot get much closer to heaven than autumn in New England.

Anne lives for her Octobers. How about you? What does fall mean to you? What about the other seasons?

55. Anne's bedroom is much more than a place in which to sleep. It is her window to the world. It reflects her personality just as truly as your house reflects the things you consider important in life. What would your ideal home look like? Your ideal room? Give details. Why would you choose such a house or room? Discuss the implications of your choice.

56. Note that the early Anne tends to be overdramatic and intense. Follow her along through the book. Does she remain the same or does she change? For the better or for the worse? Discuss.

57. As for Anne's school relationships, how do they compare with the ones you have known?

Chapter 17. A New Interest in Life
58. Mrs. Lynde is a good psychologist: Anne would have resisted force to the end of the world, but leaving her to the mercy of waves she had set in motion worked, and she voluntarily returned to school. Have you ever had such psychology used on you? What were the results?

59. There is a lot to be said for old-fashioned one-room schoolhouses such as the one Anne attended. A first grader could listen to third-grade, fifth-grade, or eighth-grade instruction as often as material geared toward first grade; as a result, motivated children often advanced more quickly than would be true in lateral-instruction rooms. Have you ever experienced such a school environment? Would you like to? Why or why not?

60. Anne's deplorable tendency to hold grudges instead of forgiving represents a common problem for many of us. Is it difficult for you to forgive? If so, how have you begun to overcome this problem?

61. There is no question that the rivalry with Gilbert Blythe resulted in considerably more growth on Anne's part than would probably have been true otherwise. Competition can be both good and bad. When is competition bad for us? When is it good?

Chapter 18. Anne to the Rescue
62. In Anne's world, the kitchen tended to be the center of family life. That was generally true in North America up to the time when

plumbing, central heating, and central cooling came in. Once that occurred, and electricity brought comfort and light to every part of the house, family life centering around one room gradually ceased to be. Discuss whether or not we were better off then, or are better off now.

63. The close call with Diana's sister highlights another major difference between our time and Anne's; in her world, most any medical problem could escalate quickly and cause death. Croup was the issue in this story, but it might just as easily have been measles, whooping cough, consumption, smallpox, diphtheria, typhus, scarlet fever—all of which tended, in the absence of effective medical practices and antibiotics, to be fatal. Do we tend to take our health for granted today? Discuss.

64. Anne is honest enough to give credit where it is due in her victory over croup. Belatedly, she realizes that had it not been for her tough orphan years—especially the around-the-clock care necessitated by a large family with more sets of twins than flesh and blood could handle without rage and frustration—she would not have been able to save the child's life. Anne thereby learns a great lesson: It is only during difficult times that we really grow. She also learns, in retrospect, to respect and value the ways in which God seasons us.

I have discovered in my own life that all my side trips, fiascoes, broken dreams, and dead-end alleys were used, sooner or later, to help me grow. Truly, God's ways are not ours. Not until we look back do we recognize that all the hardship and heartbreak we endured was for our betterment. Have you discovered this truth in your own experience? Discuss.

65. Is it wise to always save the good china for company? Might it not be a real morale booster to use it for younger members of the family once in a while? Certainly, Anne feels special when it is used in this way. Discuss.

66. Anne is imbued with the divine gift of thankfulness. Christ Himself made a point of speaking about ingratitude, as well as gratitude, in cases where He had helped or healed.

Gratefulness is one trait that can be developed in children by wise parents. Paradoxically, the more you do for someone, the less likely it is that that person will feel grateful. Parents who do everything for their children, and require little or nothing from them, usually discover that they have raised monsters: people who demand everything and are grateful for nothing.

Discuss this paradox. Have you noticed this truth in your own life, or in the lives of friends or loved ones? What have been the results? What about God—are we any more exempt from expressions of daily gratitude to God than were those He served while He was on earth?

Chapter 19. A Concert, a Catastrophe, and a Confession

67. There is much in Anne's world about memorization and recitations. Memorization of favorite poems, readings, and stories was expected of all students; thus habits of effective speaking and clear articulation were more likely to be developed than is true in schools today. Sadly, today reading aloud is almost a lost art. What can we do to remedy that?

68. Debating in schools was more common in the nineteenth century than it is today. It is always good for us to have to defend a point of view, but there is a definite downside: Debating rarely changes much, unless through the wisdom and insights gained by the debater. Furthermore, many debaters—certainly true in much of today's litigation—tend to win by technicality and character assassination rather than on the strength of the evidence itself. How may we use debating effectively?

69. In the end, memories are all we can take with us. As we grow older, we revisit our memories more often and are either blessed or cursed by them. How about your memories—do they curse or bless you? Discuss.

70. Everyone needs at least one rich relative. Of course, it's preferable to have one who uses that wealth wisely, to bless and help others rather than hoarding it. But there are problems with being rich, not the least of which is deciding whether people love you merely for your money—or for your inner qualities. What are your convictions about rich relatives and friends? What role should wealth have in our lives?

71. It was a slow world when a journey of twenty-five to thirty miles

knocked out a day. How things have changed since then! Today, thanks to jets and time zones, we can get to faraway places before we've even left. What are the advantages of living in a world that moves slowly? The disadvantages? Now apply those questions to our own time. Which period do you prefer? Why?

Chapter 20. A Good Imagination Gone Wrong

72. "I dare you!" is one aspect of childhood that apparently is with us always. What is there about us as children that makes us so unwilling to be viewed as other than brave—no matter how ridiculous, foolish, or outright dangerous a challenge may be?

73. I remember well a favorite aunt who regaled me at night with so many spooky stories that for a long time I was afraid of the dark. Marilla poses a significant question: Is an unbridled imagination dangerous? Ought there to be controls? Where does one draw the line in the exercise of one's imagination?

Chapter 21. A New Departure in Flavourings

74. Since I am a preacher's kid, I empathize with ministers' wives. From watching my mother through the years, I am well aware of how constricting such a world may be. Yet, it can also be a position of great power and influence. What kind of influence was the new minister's wife, Mrs. Allan?

75. Marilla has her faults, but gossip does not appear to be one of them. I am reminded of the story of one dear woman who was legendary in a certain town because she never said anything negative or cutting about anyone. One day, a gossiping neighbor, frustrated and a bit irate about the lady's refusal to say anything but good, barked out, "I can't really understand you. Why, I bet you'd have something good to say about the devil himself!" There was an awkward silence as the woman puckered her forehead in thought. Finally, her eyes brightened, and she said, "Well, I guess I would. Don't you wish more of us were *as diligent* as he is?"

    What is your family's attitude toward gossip? What is your attitude? Are you satisfied with your position, or do you think it ought to be changed? If the latter, in what way?

76. Have you noticed that each chapter in this book is a story all by itself? Most could stand alone, with only a little fine-tuning. Should

more of us incorporate such stories in our writing? Why or why not?

77. What do you think of Anne's joy in the fact that "tomorrow" is a tremendous blessing, for each day is a clean slate, with no mistakes yet marring its pristine surface?

Also, though she continually makes embarrassing mistakes, she rarely repeats the same ones; therefore she comforts herself with the thought that sooner or later, by sheer process of elimination, she'll use up most possible mistakes and end up making far fewer ones in the future. Can you identify with her in this respect? Discuss.

78. What would this book be like without humor? How does Montgomery use humor in her writing?

Chapter 22. Anne Is Invited Out to Tea
79. When I was a child, I enjoyed being handed letters that were addressed to me personally. Unfortunately, with the volume of mail I receive today, it's not nearly so exciting. Today we live in a very different world than the one Anne inhabited: Thanks to telephones, faxes, and e-mail, the traditional letter may someday become extinct. How do you respond to letters addressed to you personally?

80. All too often, we adults get so in the habit of pointing out our children's faults that we fail to thank and commend them for the good things they do. And, as Anne points out so poignantly, "Trying hard ought to count." One thing is certain: We will not try nearly as hard to do right when criticized continually as we will when we are praised on a regular basis.

When someone we love believes in us, we hate to disappoint that person; on the other hand, if that person is always criticizing us and telling us how useless and ineffective we are, we perversely try as hard to live down to such low expectations as we do to live up to high ones. What lessons may we learn from this?

81. In Anne's time, female teachers were rare. Older ones were rarer still, because when a teacher married, she was expected to stay home and raise her own children. And if she didn't marry, she was perceived to be a failure: so unattractive that no man wanted her. In this respect at least, today we live in a better world. Do you prefer that societal attitude or today's? Explain.

Chapter 23. Anne Comes to Grief in an Affair of Honour

82. In this chapter, Marilla experiences an epiphany when she realizes how she really feels about Anne. When she thinks that Anne may be lost to her forever, her crusty heart breaks open and the love within comes pouring out. Have you ever experienced such an epiphany? Discuss.

83. Why is it that we have such a difficult time perceiving older people as ever having been young? Somehow we see them as frozen in time, as incapable, in their superannuated state, of ever having had youthful thoughts. Ask a person you consider "old" to tell you stories about when that person was a child or a teenager. You will be amazed at the youthfulness you'll see return as that person wings back through time.

Chapter 24. Miss Stacy and Her Pupils Get Up a Concert

84. The people you meet in school have the potential to become among the dearest and closest friends life can bring you. You will make many new friends as you get older, but they can never take the place of your earliest friends. Have you discovered this to be true? Have you been blessed by finding at least one "kindred spirit"? As Anne found out, a kindred spirit may be of any age—not necessarily the same age as you are. Discuss the extra dimension such a friend brings into your life.

85. Anne discovers a great truth: An audience affects performance. It is one thing to be alone and hear yourself speak; it is quite another to stand before an audience and declaim. Their eyes, their smiles, their chuckles, their laughs, their groans, their reaching for handkerchiefs, their applause—all contribute to a sense of either "getting through" to them or failing to do so. There is an adrenaline rush you get performing before an audience that is absent when you are by yourself. This is one reason that transcripts are such inadequate recreations of public performances, for they fail to capture the electricity of the live occasion.

Have you ever performed, spoken, recited, or declaimed in front of an audience? Did you experience an extra eloquence or power that you didn't know you had? Discuss.

86. Miss Stacy turns out to be another kindred spirit. Compare her teaching style with that of her predecessor. What dimensions did

each teacher bring to Anne's life? Continue chronicling this in your journal, for later chapters will reveal more about this special teacher.

For most of us, special teachers impact our lives more than any other person, other than parents. Discuss the teacher or teachers who have exercised such an impact on your life. How were you affected?

87. Being "remarkable after death" was something Anne covets for herself. All of us want to be remembered and have our lives mean something to those who come after us. Writing is a form of immortality—but few writers "live" beyond the generation they originally wrote for. Even fewer are read by a third generation; fewer still by a fourth.

    Why do most writers sink so quickly out of sight, to be heard from no more? Why do the few continue to be read through the years? Start with the ones we have shared so far in this series: Alcott, Wallace, Defoe, Dickens, and Montgomery. Why are the works of these authors still being read? What did they say that still speaks to us so many years later?

    Draw up two lists: For the first one, name books and authors that either haven't survived or that you feel won't survive beyond the first generation—and give your reasons. For the second, write down the names of those books and authors that have survived or that you feel will survive, giving your reasons. Compare the two lists. You should now have a recipe for literary immortality, as well as a recipe for ephemera. Apply these principles to your own writing.

Chapter 25. Matthew Insists on Puffed Sleeves

88. Truly, there is no one way to raise a child. It is easy to pontificate on the subject if you have no children; harder if you have one of your own, and harder still if you have more than one. Haven't you heard frustrated parents say, "If he had been our first child, he would have been an only child!" What works for one may not necessarily work for another.

    Discuss the subject of child-rearing, comparing your principles with others you have known. Where are they different? Where are they similar? Try to arrive at principles of child-rearing that will work for everyone.

89. Have you ever, like Anne, had a bad case of stage fright? Were you able to pull out of it, as Anne did? Discuss.

90. What do you feel is the relationship of Christmas to snow? Why do so many Christmas stories feature snow?

Chapter 26. The Story Club Is Formed

91. Anne and her classmates find it difficult after the exciting concert to go back to humdrum class work again. What is it about the roller coaster of life that makes it so hard to stay motivated during the dips?

    Have you ever, after one of those highs, spent many days and nights, like Anne, replaying scenes in your mind's theater—sometimes looking at the cinematography from your point of view, sometimes from the audience's point of view, or at least what you imagine their point of view to have been? How long do such replays go on before they cease to dominate your thoughts? How long should they go on?

    Have you ever known someone who spent the rest of his or her life watching reruns rather than going on with life? Athletes especially seem to fall into this category: one blinding moment of glory—then all downhill from there.

    British poet A. E. Houseman (1859–1936) often wrote about disillusionment and how quickly one's loves and friendships are no more. Two of his favorite subjects were inconstant Time and Fame, whose smiles last but a day. His powerful poem "To an Athlete Dying Young" contains this line: "And the name died before the man." What are the dangers involved in living in the past? Why should we go on with our lives rather than wasting them watching reruns?

92. How often we lose dear friends in our insistence that we be first! I remember well instances in which I did just that, and in so doing lost someone who was once among my closest friends. As life has gone on, I have belatedly discovered a great truth: Nothing is as temporary as one's place in a given pecking order.

    We remember and cherish individuals, *not* because of their prestige or fame, but because of their human qualities: their kindness, humility, selfless service to others, empathy for those who suffer and are passed by, and integrity. Discuss in depth the subject of ambition and how we can avoid permitting it to warp or destroy us.

93. Have you ever been a part of a writing club? If not, how about starting one?

Chapter 27. Vanity and Vexation of Spirit

94. Green hair! Something similar happened in my immediate family—
    and the anguish was the same as Anne's: It seemed as if the world
    had come to an end, and life could not possibly go on. Have you
    ever known, or had, such an experience? Discuss.

Chapter 28. An Unfortunate Lily Maid

95. The poem that launched Anne/Elaine's boat is Tennyson's "The Lady
    of Shalott" (1832, 1842). Here is one stanza to give you a sense of
    the poem's rhythm:

> Heard a carol, mournful, holy,
> Chanted loudly, chanted lowly,
> Till her blood was frozen slowly
> And her eyes were darkened wholly,
>   Turned to tower'd Camelot.
> For ere she reach'd upon the tide
> The first house by the water-side,
> Singing in her song she died.

Find an anthology of Tennyson's poems and copy down the rest of
this poem.

I strongly encourage you to put together not only a library of your
favorite books but also a scrapbook of your favorite poems and a
binder of your favorite short stories. They will immeasurably enrich
your life. And as you continue finding new favorites in your reading,
add them to your collection.

What is the role of poetry (writing it, reading it, reciting it, collecting it) in your life? If you have previously had little to do with it,
would you like to change by making it a part of your life? Explain.

96. There are two schools of thought in literary instruction: (1) enjoy
    and appreciate a given work in its totality, as a work of art to hang
    on the walls of your mind; and (2) dissect it, spread its guts out on
    the table, then stitch it back together so you can learn how it works.
    I'm of the former school, for I've discovered that all too often once
    something has been dissected, never again does it regain its former
    shape. Which approach do you prefer? Explain. Neither approach is
    incorrect; it is merely a matter of preference. Might you prefer parts
    of both? Why or why not?

97. I'm a firm believer in the need for romance in life. Life without a dream is just not worth living. Anne would certainly agree. How about you? Discuss.

Chapter 29. An Epoch in Anne's Life

98. The music made by pines and firs is one of the most beautiful sounds on earth, akin to the sound made by a mountain stream, a waterfall, or waves against the shore. Thank God for the sounds that enrich our lives. What are your favorite sounds?

99. Quite a provocative statement by Anne: that Miss Barry's home is so palatial that it leaves no room for the imagination. What do you think Anne really means by this observation?

100. Equally provocative: that it would be wrong for Anne to do anything she couldn't tell the minister's wife. Just last week I heard a different twist: "I wouldn't do anything I'd be ashamed for my guardian angel to see." Discuss.

101. Is it true, as Anne maintains, that the things you long for as a child don't mean as much when they come later in life? Put another way, does reality generally live up to anticipation? Or is the real joy in life in the wait rather than in the act? Might this be the real reason why multimillionaires, when asked when they were happiest, almost invariably point to their years of struggle rather than to the affluent years following the struggle?

    God has programmed us to always be growing, reaching, moving on to the next challenge, rather than squatting like a hen on achievements we have already hatched. Which brings the greatest joy to you: working toward a goal, or actually achieving it? Why?

102. Miss Barry supposedly has everything money can buy. What, then, did she see in Anne? Why is she lonely without her? Why does she prefer Anne to her own niece, Diana?

Chapter 30. The Queen's Class Is Organized

103. Anne takes seriously her growing-up years. Study this chapter carefully and compare her philosophy of growing up with the one we hear about often: that youth is the time to sow one's wild oats, to play the fool; after all, there will be plenty of time for seriousness later. What is the fallacy in that line of reasoning, according to Anne?

104. When my wife and I moved back to Colorado, one nonnegotiable directive to our real estate agent was this: The house must have a traditional wood-burning fireplace. The fireplace, I submit, is the true heart of a home. What is your opinion of fireplaces? What impact do fires on a cold winter night have on you?

Chapter 31. Where the Brook and River Meet

105. Why do we all need time for rest and regeneration? Discuss this as it relates to yourself and other people you know.

106. What do sermons do for us?

107. Miss Stacy encourages her students to explore beyond the "beaten paths." What does she mean by that? What would be the significance of this advice to us in our very different world today?

108. Miss Stacy also encourages her writing students to choose simple words over complex ones. Why do you think she offers such advice? Do you agree with her? Why or why not?

109. Anne, as she grows up, tends to talk less and think more. Pretty thoughts, she maintains, are treasures to be stored in the heart. What *are* pretty thoughts? Do you consider them treasures worth storing in the heart? Why or why not? Discuss.

110. Miss Stacy also encourages her students to write on what they know firsthand rather than what they know secondhand. Have you found this counsel to be valid in your own writing? Explain.

111. In the British system, such as the one Anne knew, there is no room for late bloomers; rather, the system rewards early seriousness of purpose and high performance. Compare this system with the one you grew up with. Which do you prefer, and why?

Chapter 32. The Pass List Is Out

112. Great moments in life often leave us speechless, just as the ultimate accolade is not a storm of applause but absolute silence. Have you experienced such moments in your life? How did they compare with the moments Anne experienced? There are also moments, as Anne notes, that end up being determining ones. In other words, without them our lives would be radically different. Discuss.

Chapter 33. The Hotel Concert

113. In this chapter, we note that Anne's dreams are keeping pace with her growth. Should this be true for us as well? Explain.

114. Might Diana's gift—taste in dressing, clothes, coiffure, and so on—be just as much an art form as great writing or painting? Explain your position, and give reasons.

115. For the first time that I can remember, we now have a bedroom window that opens directly east, toward the sunrise. Thus I can identify with Anne's delight in welcoming each glorious new day. What direction does your bedroom face?

116. Do you feel sorry for Billy Andrews, doomed as he is to always being passed by, by beauty? Do you know what it's like to almost always be on the losing side? On the other hand, what could Billy have done about it?

Chapter 34. A Queen's Girl

117. Sooner or later there comes a time when the vital presence that brings a house to life is ready to leave, to go on, to stretch its wings. Parents face that moment as each child leaves home and begins adult living. What thoughts go through the minds of Marilla and Matthew when the time arrives for Anne to leave?

Sometimes that vital presence may be someone older; when that presence passes on, what happens to those who remain behind?

118. What would life be without ambitions? What role do goals play?

Chapter 35. The Winter at Queen's

119. Interesting how Anne has a mental picture of the kind of life partner a given person would choose. In certain parts of the world, such as India, even today the parents tend to do the choosing of mates for their children. What might be the advantages, as well as disadvantages, to having another person, such as a parent, make such a decision for you?

120. What guidelines does Anne use in terms of choosing her closest friends?

121. Anne is described as "having as many shades as a rainbow . . . and every shade is the prettiest while it lasts." What does that description

mean to you? Would such a person appeal to you? Why or why not?

122. Americans seem to have a fixation on winning at any cost. Anne wanted to win very much, yet she qualified this desire by saying that second to "trying and winning" is "trying and losing." What do you think she meant by that?

Chapter 36. The Glory and the Dream

123. Anne notes a great truth: that we pay a price for everything in the world. In the end, nothing is truly free. Think of the various professions and what it takes to get to the top and stay there. Think of our sports heroes and our media icons—what price do they pay? One of the freedoms they lose is being able to go anywhere at any time without being mobbed. Just marrying someone demands a price, and a steep one if you plan to be there for that person and your children *for life*. Discuss different types of positions and responsibilities and the price that must be paid for each one.

Chapter 37. The Reaper Whose Name Is Death

124. Death touches each of us in different ways, and we respond in different ways. The world can never be the same after the passing of a dear one. What do you learn about death and its aftermath in this section of the book?

125. What is the role of flowers in grief?

126. What does the statement "Life goes on" mean? What does Anne discover it to mean? How does she come to terms with it?

Chapter 38. The Bend in the Road

127. They say that "Troubles come in threes." What are the three that come to Anne now?

128. What causes Anne to dramatically alter her plans for the future? What are the reasons behind her decision? What does Anne have to say about the "bend in the road" as compared with the earlier "straight road"?

129. All this happens when Anne is only sixteen. Is she more, or less, mature than the average girl of that age today? Give reasons.

130. How does the serenity, the tranquility, of Anne's world compare with the world you live in? If the differences are major, what would it take for you to create a world more like hers?

131. Remembering how important it is that a book end well, how do you feel about the ending to this one? How does it engage the emotions? Be specific. If you had written the ending, would you have written it in the same way? Differently? Explain.

CODA

Reactions, responses, and suggestions are very important to us. Also, if a particular book—especially an older one—has been loved by you or your family, and you would like to see us incorporate it into this series, drop us a line, with any details about its earliest publisher, printing date, and so on, and send it to

Joe Wheeler, Ph.D.
c/o Focus on the Family
Colorado Springs, CO 80920

ABOUT THE EDITOR

Joseph Leininger Wheeler's earliest memories have to do with books and stories—more specifically, of listening to his mother read aloud both in public and to him at home. Wheeler recalls that, as soon as he was able to read, he followed his mother around the house, relentlessly reading his storybooks to her.

Shortly after Wheeler turned eight, his parents moved from California to Latin America as missionaries. From the third through the tenth grade, he was home-schooled by his mother. Of those years, he says today, "I was incredibly lucky and blessed. My mother, a trained teacher and elocutionist, was a voracious reader of books worth reading and had memorized thousands of pages of readings, poetry, and stories. All of that she poured into me. Wherever we went, she encouraged me to devour entire libraries."

At 16, Wheeler returned to California to complete his high school years at Monterey Bay Academy near Santa Cruz. Because of his inherited love of the printed word, Wheeler majored in history at Pacific Union College in the Napa Valley, completing both bachelor's and master's degrees there. After completing a master's in English at California State University in Sacramento, Wheeler attended Vanderbilt University, where he obtained a Ph.D. in English.

Today, after 34 years of teaching at the adult education, college, high school, and junior high levels, Wheeler is Professor Emeritus at Columbia Union College in Takoma Park, Maryland. The world's foremost authority on frontier writer Zane Grey, Wheeler is also the founder and executive director of Zane Grey's West Society and Senior Fellow for Cultural Studies at the Center for the New West in Denver, Colorado. He is editor/compiler of the popular *Christmas in My Heart* series (Review & Herald; Tyndale House; Doubleday, Dell, Bantam); editor/compiler of the story anthologies *Dad in My Heart* and *Mom in My Heart* (Tyndale House); and editor/compiler of the *Great Stories Remembered* and Classic Collection series for Focus on the Family (Tyndale House). Along the way, Wheeler has established nine libraries in schools and colleges, as well as building up his own collection (as large as some college libraries).

Joe Wheeler and his wife, Connie, are the parents of two grown children, Greg and Michelle, and now make their home in Conifer, Colorado.

WELCOME TO THE FAMILY!

Whether you received this book as a gift, borrowed it from a friend, or purchased it yourself, we're glad you read it! It's just one of the many helpful, insightful, and encouraging resources produced by Focus on the Family.

In fact, that's what Focus on the Family is all about—providing inspiration, information, and biblically based advice to people in all stages of life.

It began in 1977 with the vision of one man, Dr. James Dobson, a licensed psychologist and author of 16 best-selling books on marriage, parenting, and family. Alarmed by the societal, political, and economic pressures that were threatening the existence of the American family, Dr. Dobson founded Focus on the Family with one employee—an assistant—and a once-a-week radio broadcast, aired on only 36 stations.

Now an international organization, Focus on the Family is dedicated to preserving Judeo-Christian values and strengthening the family through more than 70 different ministries, including eight separate daily radio broadcasts; television public service announcements; 11 publications; and a steady series of books and award-winning films and videos for people of all ages and interests.

Recognizing the needs of, as well as the sacrifices and important contributions made by, such diverse groups as educators, physicians, attorneys, crisis pregnancy center staff, and single parents, Focus on the Family offers specific outreaches to uphold and minister to these individuals, too. And it's all done for one purpose, and one purpose only: to encourage and strengthen individuals and families through the life-changing message of Jesus Christ.

⌇

For more information, or if we can be of help to your family, simply write to Focus on the Family, Colorado Springs, CO 80995 or call 1-800-A-FAMILY (1-800-232-6459). Friends in Canada may write Focus on the Family, P.O. Box 9800, Stn. Terminal, Vancouver, B.C. V6B 4G3 or call 1-800-661-9800. You may also visit our website: www.family.org, to learn more about the ministry or to find out if there is a Focus on the Family office in your country.

We are here for you!